# Overflowing with Hope

a novel of hope & inspiration

# Overflowing with Hope

Mary Jean Bonar

Tate Publishing & *Enterprises*

*Overflowing with Hope*



---

This title is also available as a Tate Out Loud product. Visit www.tatepublishing.com for more information. Visit www.maryjeanbonar.com



---

Published by Tate Publishing & Enterprises, LLC
127 E. Trade Center Terrace | Mustang, Oklahoma 73064 USA
1.888.361.9473 | www.tatepublishing.com

Tate Publishing is committed to excellence in the publishing industry. The company reflects the philosophy established by the founders, based on Psalm 68:11,
*"The Lord gave the word and great was the company of those who published it."*


*Cover design by Lindsay B. Behrens*
*Interior design by Stephanie Woloszyn*

---

Published in the United States of America

ISBN: 978-1-60462-707-7
1. Fiction: Religious: General
2. Christian Living: Practical Life: Aging
08.01.24

*To the Ladies of the Band*

May the God of hope fill you with all joy and peace
as you trust in him,
so that you may overflow with hope
by the power of the Holy Spirit.

Romans 15:13 NIV

# Acknowledgements

With profound gratitude, I sing praises to my Father in Heaven and give Him the glory for the realization and completion of this book. I have been blessed by His touch and His guidance throughout the assignment and pray that others will be blessed by His touch while reading it.

My heartfelt thanks to Jim, my husband, who supported me during the days when all I could think about was writing and encouraged me to persevere when the pressures of the world seemed to be drawing me from completing the book. My appreciation extends to my children, grandchildren, and the other members of my family whose love and helpfulness contributed in many ways to this novel; I thank my extended family—both living and gone—who have led me to the Lord and walked with me along the pathway of truth.

To all of my friends and family: If you hear a bit of your "voice" in the pages of this book, it is because you have been an influence upon my life. I could not have written about personalities without developing them from those I have known. Thank you all for being a part of who I am and for sharing your lives with mine.

# Table of Contents

# Foreword

As I was reading this book, *Overflowing with Hope*, I concluded that it was the first time I ever read a novel that valued and understood the people and churches of rural Western Pennsylvania. Mary Jean Bonar's novel is filled with beloved characters that provide windows into the people next door to us. You feel their problems and their strength in God. It is like Jan Karon writing a "Mitford" book on Western PA, but better than that is Jean Bonar writing about how God guides our path, blesses our relationships and gives us overflowing hope in all things.

In many books the elderly are presented as having nothing more to offer. In this book you sense their quiet strength in the struggles that they face. You sense the author's understanding and love for her characters. You enjoy their families and their communities of support. Tom Brokow wrote *The Greatest Generation*, which focused on World War II heroics. I must confess that in most of the novels I read, someone shoots someone. Conversely and welcomingly, this book shows the simple—yet profound—heroics of growing old, of being there for someone else, and of holding on to God in uncertain times. You will be inspired by their perseverance of faith. While these heroes will not be larger than life, they live lives enlarged by God. You will go for walks with them in the woods or to a softball game and be enriched by the time shared with them.

From time to time, people have told me that we don't need the small church. Yet in this novel, you sense the significance of the small church as a family and of its value to those in and around it. As you enter into the community of the church of West Hope, you will relish the simple joys of being in relationship. You will laugh with them, and feel their overflowing hope that comes from being a part of a community in God. You have the sense that our unseen God is directing the characters' lives and is watching over them.

The writer to the Hebrews (Chapter 11) described faith and hope as being partners as we live our lives in God when he wrote:

> *Now faith is being sure of what we hope for and certain of what we do not see...By faith we understand that the universe was formed at God's command, so that what is seen was not made out of what was visible.*

Janine Stephens—one of the heroines in this novel—displays these truths in the way she lives her life in the simple knowledge that the wind of the Spirit guides her way. You will love the story of "*The Little Wind*" and how it relates to the unseen presence of God that directs Janine's path.

King Solomon wrote in Ecclesiastes that God *"has made everything beautiful in its time."* Jean Bonar has not only the ability to see the beauty that God has made in pink peonies or grey haired ladies, but to help *us* see it as well. When I was talking with Jean about the characters in her novel, I realized she loved these characters more than some individuals love the actual people in their own lives. This book helps us recognize that God gives us a gift in the people that He puts in our lives.

You cannot read this without feeling affection for the people in it. You will find such joy in a Kitchen Band that you will want to form one yourself. By the way, if you want to know what a Kitchen Band is, you will have to buy the book.

After I finished this book, I felt that I appreciated and understood my mother's courage and faith more. To borrow another phrase from King Solomon, I appreciate how she *"was clothed in strength and dignity"* and how she has the faith *"to laugh at the days to come."* Finally, I believe this book will do that for your relationships as well.

Dr. David L. Bleivik,
General Presbyter of Washington Presbytery,
Presbyterian Church (USA)

This is a delightful Christian story that draws the reader into the interesting reality of men and women in a particular faith community, such that one perceives the providential working of God, the Holy Spirit. Perhaps this could become your story. I heartily recommend *Overflowing with Hope* to anyone who desires a practical illustration of how love for God and neighbor grows in the hearts of those who truly live for Jesus Christ.

Rev. William L. Roemer
Minister of Word and Sacrament
Presbyterian Church (USA)

# Prologue

## A Day the Lord Has Made

*Could the sky be bluer?* She wondered as she walked outside after the rain. *And that sweet fragrance–what is it?*

She began to look around. Her red and white petunias were growing nicely where she had planted them at the outer rim of a circular floral garden. It would be at least a month before they would completely fill in the spaces, but they were standing strong, and the reds were vibrant with the color. The grass throughout the yard was Scotland green. Everything appeared fresh and alive in the clearness of the spring morning…*But what is that lovely fragrance?*

Something caught her eye. There at the side of the driveway were the peonies she had planted last summer, and one was finally in full bloom! The flower was a soft pink, just as she had remembered at her home as a child. Her parents had many such bushes; some white, some deep pink, but this soft pink had been her mother's favorite and hers as well.

She had been waiting for the bloom, and there it was, stretching toward her as though to say, "I'm here, because you wanted me to be. I'm here for your pleasure. Come and enjoy." It was beautiful. *How many petals does a peony have?* She wondered.

*There must be hundreds, each embracing the others just as God had planned for them to do.*

Her heart beat faster. She walked gently toward the sacred flower, not wanting to disturb this beautiful gift from God.

Yes, she had planted it, but it was His creation, and the joy of her thankfulness was as exquisite as the morning and the softly pink peony beckoning to her.

Slowly, slowly she walked, and unmistakably the fragrance intensified. She drew near, not yet bending for the fullness of the scent, savoring every second. She bent her knees, leaned forward, and there it was–just as she had known it would be–the sweetest fragrance of her youth. The memory was vivid as she closed her eyes and drank in the aroma. She was back in time–a precious time–when her mother and father would bend with her to smell the peonies. She felt their presence, and it was bliss. She fell to her knees, tears of joy on her cheeks, and with heartfelt gratitude praised God, not only for this day of days, but also because she knew that her memories, her life today, and all she would ever be were because of His love and care for her.

It was a beautiful morning, indeed, after the rain, on a Tuesday in early June as she reluctantly left the peony and began her morning walk. *The climbing roses are beginning to bloom on the fence.* She had to have a talk with herself not to stop again and smell the roses, as she wanted to do. She would take the time later in the day, or tomorrow.

"Father in Heaven, you have given me too much today. I can't assimilate it all." She forced herself to continue her walk, but she would not forget to observe the blessed day, enjoy it, and be thankful.

Julia would be watching for her, so she must hurry to her

shower and move on with the day. She and Julia had something to do together, and she didn't want to be late.

Julia was sitting near the front door with her bag packed and ready to go, even though she didn't expect Janine for another 25 minutes or so. She lived alone in a two-story house, built around the turn of the century, in the very small borough of West Hope, PA, which was nestled in rolling hills between larger communities and has had no need or desire to grow into anything other than what it was. Folks were born here and pretty much stayed…everyone knew everyone else, and that's the way they liked it.

Julia pulled herself to her feet and looked outside. As she expected, Prudence Eldrich was out sweeping the cobblestone sidewalk in front of her house across the street.

*Honestly! She's going to wear out those old stones. How they've lasted this long, I'll never know…especially hers. I'll bet she's swept them ten thousand times! Emily thinks it's her excuse to go outside so she can watch everything that goes on. Maybe so.*

The cobblestone sidewalks that have been in West Hope for two centuries were "quaint" to some and "stumbling stones" to others. The question of what to do about them has come before the borough council many times, but probably won't be resolved. "Change" is not likely to win any vote here.

Julia lived right on the main–and only–road through the town. Friends used to stop by on a warm summer's day to sit awhile, but many of those friends are now gone or are too old to be venturing out much alone.

*Well, that's the price to pay for living so long, I suppose. But things are different from what they were a "year or so ago" when all I had to do was sit home and try to cope with another day.*

*I'm sure I'd still be in that "old lady rut" if I hadn't done the silly thing I did. At least at the time, it sure seemed silly!* She had started taking piano lessons–and she was then 86 years old! *Why did I even think of doing such a thing?* But then she realized that she really didn't think of it at all. Somehow, the thought just popped into her head.

*Whatever...Must've been the Lord deciding I needed a little amusement.*

She continued to recollect. It was a Sunday morning after her birthday. Of course, Julia had attended Sunday school with her dearest friends–what was left of them–as they had done for sixty years now. She and Jenny went into the sanctuary together, spoke to others around and glanced at the bulletin. She confided to Jenny that she had done a crazy thing: she had decided to teach herself how to play the piano and had purchased an electronic keyboard for herself for her 86th birthday.

"Oh, really? Well, that's very interesting," Jenny had responded.

*Jenny probably thinks I've lost my mind...Maybe I have.*

The music began and soon Pastor Daniel was into his message for the day. Julia wasn't paying much attention–still had the foolish thought on her mind about playing the piano. *I shouldn't have told anyone...* Surely people would laugh at her if they knew.

What was Pastor Daniel talking about? *The bulletin says, "Never Too Old." What? Never too old? Well, that's ridiculous! I'm too old for lots of things; maybe too old to play the piano, too.*

He quoted from Genesis about Sarah having a baby. She was 90 years old when Isaac was born. *Good grief!* Then he was on to talking about Noah being an old man when he built the ark.

*Well, I'm not going to build an ark, and I'm not going to have a baby at the age of 90, that's for sure. Not a chance in the world.*

Pastor Daniel had said to *her*—was he looking straight at *her?* "The Bible reveals that age is never a barrier to our being used by God. Is there something that you want to do? Do you feel that God has called you to it for some reason? You have a purpose for this. Pray for God's help, and do it."

She felt her face turn red, and she looked down at her arthritic hands. *"All things are possible with God,"* she thought. *All things? I wonder.*

Everyone was standing. Pastor Daniel was giving the benediction, and people started moving from their seats. Julia couldn't seem to move and was still thinking of how he had been looking straight at her.

"Julia, are you all right?" Jenny asked.

"Of course," she answered, pulling herself together. Just then the new lady who was sitting in the pew in front of her with her husband introduced herself to her and said that she had overheard her conversation that she was going to teach herself to play the piano.

*Oh, no! Even this person I don't even know thinks I'm a crazy old woman.* The lady said she had taught piano for many years and offered to give her lessons. Free.

Julia was oversensitive and uncomfortable as a result of Pastor Dan looking at her and preaching at her, and now here was this complete stranger making her an offer. She doesn't even know her, so how can she possibly trust her anyway? "I'll have to think about it," she said, not wanting to take the time to get in a discussion with her and hurried out of the church. She was glad to get by the pastor without pausing to shake his hand.

"What do you think about that new woman," she asked Jenny when they got in the car.

"I don't know. She seems nice. Why?"

"Well, she said she'd teach me to play the piano. I don't want someone to teach me. I'm sure I can teach myself. Anyway, these old arthritic fingers are going to have a hard enough time at it. I don't need someone hovering over me, trying to get me to do something I don't want to do or can't do."

"Well, that's up to you," Jenny said, "but she seems like a sincere person, and maybe you could just give it a short try and see what happens."

"Harrumph! Are we going to go to lunch today?"

"Fine with me. I have no reason to go on home."

Jenny drove them the half mile out the country road to the Orchard Restaurant, a good place for a home-cooked meal or cup of soup after church or anytime. The widowed ladies gather there often on Sundays, partly to delay going to an empty house for the rest of the week. Iola, Beatrice, and Harriet were already seated in the small separate dining area when Julia and Jenny arrived.

They were all chattering over this and that, and no one said that they noticed the preacher talking about Julia today. *Well, they know he was. But they are not going to say anything so as not to make me uncomfortable.* She ordered a cup of chicken noodle soup and tried to calm herself down.

That was a new beginning for Julia as it turned out, and this morning in June, she was very happy to see the car park in front of her house, and her piano teacher coming to the door.

"Good morning, Julia. What a beautiful day, and you're looking lovely yourself. It looks like you are all ready to get going."

"Good morning. Yes, I'm ready I guess. I gathered up a few things for us to look at. I found some pretty aprons that anybody could use if they wanted to."

"Well, that's great," said Janine as she picked up the bag and escorted Julia to the car.

Julia was neat as a pin, as usual, wearing dark slacks topped by a softly colored blouse with a flowered broach pinned perfectly in place at the neck. She was short and couldn't have weighed more than 100 pounds. She had said that she had lost a "couple" of inches over the years. Her hair was grey, short, and permanent-waved, and she wore lipstick and blush.

They drove out a small country road to pick up Rachael who lived atop one of the many hills of the community. The drive to her home was steep and unpaved, and although Julia still drove, she would not want to "go-it-alone" to Rachael's, especially after a rain. They were having no problems negotiating today. Actually, the road had completely dried since the morning rain. Fields of ripening hay were waving in the breeze, bending gently to and fro on each side of the narrow drive. The car engine stirred up a rabbit, and they noticed a red-winged blackbird sitting on a fence post, obviously keeping watch over its nest of young.

Rachael lived alone as did many others. Fortunately, some of her family members lived down in West Hope and others on the far side of the hill. She had been recuperating from a terrible automobile accident and would not be going out alone anymore; on the other hand, she would not give up her home and was determined as anyone could be to do for herself.

"Good morning!" Rachael beamed as she came out of the door with her walker. She was hardly five-feet tall, but her personality was so delightful and vibrant that she seemed larger, somehow. Today she wore a loose-fitting, bright blue cotton dress, splashed with bright red and yellow flowers. She was beaming from ear to ear and her face seemed to glow beneath her auburn hair.

She had two bags on the porch ready to go with her.

Janine jumped out of the car to help her, put the bags into the opened trunk, and wondered what surprises Rachael might have today. They were talking a mile a minute as they drove down the lane and on toward the church.

When they arrived at the church, Iola was already there standing at the far side of the parking lot and turned when she heard the car pull up and the doors open.

"Hello!" she said.

"Hello to you," said the others.

"Isn't this a beautiful morning? Look down there. The calves are frolicking and enjoying the day as well."

The picturesque farm was a setting in itself. It should have been captured in paint on that day and was known to have been the subject of several paintings. It had two silos, fields of wheat, a lovely and well-kept old house, a great barn and cattle grazing in the meadow. The farm's beauty put off such a spirit that even a blind person could sense the wonderfully picturesque scene. The members of the church there on the hill considered the scenery as the best part of the landscaping.

"I can see the cows sometimes from my property," said Rachael. "This morning I saw eighteen deer on the opposite hill."

"Beatrice and Adele are here," said Julia. The four turned from their viewing and walked over to their cars that were parked under a cherished giant oak tree.

They opened up their automobile trunks and began lifting out their supplies. Everyone had a shopping bag to carry plus some odds and ends.

"Are we late?" asked Adele.

"No, no. Anyway, we were enjoying looking over Kevin's farm," said Iola.

"Let's go on into the church. Anne should be along any moment."

They had been meeting like this for a few months. Only a few people really knew what the ladies were up to, and the ladies were not eager to talk much about it. They walked inside and locked the doors so that no one could unexpectedly come along and see what they were doing.

# *Part One*
## A Year Or So Ago

# 1
# Life in the Fast Lane

Janine's week had been busy from minute to minute as life continued to gather speed. Her position at Center Church as Director of Music had expanded to include monitoring three choirs, directing occasionally, and serving as principal organist. Her head was always filled with planning, and rehearsals were especially intense during the Holy Seasons for the church year.

It might have been easier if she didn't have "flexible" hours. A nine-to-five job was beginning to be a fantasy in her mind; nevertheless, she loved her work at the church, and now that her three children were gone from the nest, her schedule was a little less complicated, at least.

But why did she say "yes" to the presidency of the Women's Association? It was much more demanding of her than she had anticipated; even so, she knew she could do it, and no one else had volunteered. Her deepest frustration came nearly every evening when bedtime rolled around and she had no time or clarity of mind to turn her attention to her writing. The book was unwritten, her research files were incomplete, and she was constantly setting her dream aside.

*Oh, well. Maybe next year,* she thought as she brushed away the flittering moment. *Next year? Haven't I said that many times before?*

She had spent several hours at the church going through the files of music to decide upon worship music for the rapidly approaching holy seasons of Lent and Easter. Tomorrow would be a better time for studying through the new music she had ordered.

The new choir director preferred that Janine continue to choose the music for the adult choir while she was becoming more familiar with the capabilities of the singers. Janine realized and understood the comfort of singing familiar anthems, but she was not one to take the effortless path. She liked to challenge choirs and herself to always be learning, progressing, and giving their best. The choir director was in complete agreement.

Rounding the corner of the hallway, she stopped into the church office and spoke with Connie—a secretary with exceptional abilities. Connie was indispensable for this smooth-running church and could be counted on for accuracy and promptness. Janine appreciated those qualities and especially enjoyed Connie and her loving interest in the entire congregation.

"Good morning, Connie," Janine said.

"Well, good morning to you. I didn't know you were here."

"I've been going through music for a while. I've been here longer than I anticipated, but I love it."

"I know you do," Connie responded.

"Now, tell me. How are you and how are things at home"

"I'm great and things have calmed down at home, somewhat. The Lord has been good to us. Richard is recovering well from the surgery and feeling stronger every day, and he is now able to take care of his personal needs for the most part."

"That's terrific. I know that he does not like to depend upon someone else. That would be hard for me, too, and probably would be for you as well. We'll keep praying for him. He'll be back to work, good as new before we know it."

"He has a doctor's appointment next week. He's determined to convince the doctor that he's ready to return, but I'm not so sure.... We'll see." Connie said.

"Is Pastor Jim in?"

"He was here a few minutes ago, but when he called Mabel Morrison's family this morning, he found that she was not doing very well. You know how he is.... He was out of here in a flash."

"He's a good man and a wonderful pastor," Janine said. "I'll check in with him in the morning. It's nothing important. I need to get moving anyway. See you tomorrow!"

"Ok. Be careful out there. Looks like it might snow. I think it's supposed to today."

"That's what I heard. I hope it holds off. I have errands to run, groceries to buy, and two piano students coming later this afternoon. I'd really better get moving. Take care.... Bye."

As she got into her car, she picked up the note on the seat. *Hmm, let's see. Should I stop over at the coffee shop and get a sandwich or just keep going? I'd better keep going and go to the drive-through for coffee. No time for food right now, and it looks like those clouds are forming into something ominous.*

*I'll go to the post office first, grab a coffee, and then take the overpass around to Gloria's Gift Shop to pick up the vase I ordered for the wedding. I'll have it gift-wrapped. How long will that take...? Gloria can be so slow sometimes, but she does a beautiful job.... Ok. I'll have her do it. It might actually save time in the long run; then I'll go to the supermarket on that side of town... That'll work!*

The coffee was too hot, so she set it in the cup holder and proceeded to the highway around the city. "What's this? Oh, not again!" Traffic was almost at a standstill and there was no turning back from the entrance with cars in front and behind. This was getting to be almost commonplace as scores of business travelers and convoys of trucks were on the roads.

She crept along, drank all of the coffee, and finally was on her way; if one considered moving at 25-mph as "on the way." What was the holdup this time? "Uh, oh!" Flashing lights were all over the road ahead. Her heart skipped as she worried that someone was hurt. An eighteen-wheeler was overturned with traffic limited to one lane and moving very slowly at that. She turned on the radio and flipped from station to station to find some news concerning the accident. All she found was a nationally broadcast talk show. The news would come on at the top of the hour. In the meantime, she was passing the accident. Nothing else was involved, but the truck was on its side. It looked like the driver was standing there, unhurt…thankfully.

She passed the congestion and moved on, this time at a more normal speed and arrived at the exit and to Gloria's much, much later than she had planned.

"Hi, Gloria. My goodness the traffic today was so slow. Once again, an eighteen-wheeler tried to make that turn at Exit 10 too fast. He turned over. Why, oh why can't they follow the caution signs? I don't think he was hurt. At least I hope not. Anyway, I'm here to pick up the vase."

"Oh, Sweetie, you're just going to love it. It's beautiful, and the bride will be thrilled. I'll go get it for you."

Her shop was exquisite. Janine always tried to purchase her special gifts here. She looked around while Gloria was in the back. As always, new items were on display everywhere. Gloria had an eye for beautiful glass, unusual carvings, imported paper products, linens and more. Gloria returned quickly with the vase, which was a good thing because she felt tempted to look at the beautiful table setting on the other side of the room, and who knew where that would lead?

"This is perfect!" she said when Gloria took the vase out of the box. Imported from Italy, it was shaped into an alluring form and painted with deeply colorful flowers. Anyone would be pleased to have it. Janine was delighted that she had ordered it, and asked Gloria to wrap it for her. They decided upon the wrapping, and surprisingly Gloria moved right along.

"How are your handsome husband and Kathy and her family?" Gloria asked.

"John's great. Busy as usual, but aren't we all? Kathy and her husband love their log home in the country. I'm beginning to understand why she moved from the city. The only noise is the song of birds or in the distance, the bawling of a cow. It's quite a different life for them. The girls have adjusted very well, so the move proved to be a good one. I thought we wouldn't see them much, but John and I love going to our daughter's home. It's almost like a retreat in a quiet part of the world, so we do get out often."

"Must be nice," Gloria said. "Well, here you are. How's that?"

"Gloria, you are so talented. Beautifully done! Thank you so much. And thank you for your suggestion about the vase." She paid her, said her goodbye and was out of the door in decent time after all. She was all smiles and very satisfied that the vase was just right.

*Now, I have barely enough time to shop for the groceries, get home, put them away, put the casserole into the oven, freshen up, teach, and have dinner ready on time. I can do it.... She always did...I just have to stay focused.*

❀ ❀ ❀

She was taking the casserole from the oven when John drove up from work. Perfect timing! Janine liked everything nice and tidy, on time, and done right! She was a bride of the fifties; consequently, a "Leave-It-to-Beaver" kind of mom and housewife. Even though Betty Freidan's book and the ultimate change in society led most women away from homemaking aspirations, she still did her best to adhere to the values and standards of a woman's role in the home. It was more difficult now with her position at the church, her volunteer work in the community, and teaching, but she was not going to hire help to do her *real* job—that of maintaining an orderly home. Her daughter, Kathy, reminded her constantly that she was over-the-top in seeing that everything was in its place, the furniture was polished, the windows shining and the dishes matched the occasion, but she turned a deaf ear to all of that. She knew what was right. She could do it, and so she would!

Today she was using her Pfaltzgraff, Orleans pattern that had a casserole to match. The dishes were blue on white with a tiny orange flower scattered along the edging. She used a white cloth tablecloth, napkins of deep blue and a centerpiece of fresh lilies in orange that she had picked up at the supermarket. The flowers would bring a little sunshine into the room on this very gloomy wintry day.

Perfect!

*I'll just put these utensils in the dishwasher and straighten up and all will be on time when John comes in—. Mmm...the casserole looks great, and John will enjoy the Mandarin-orange salad and fresh rolls from the market bakery.*

*There he is. I'll undo the apron and put it in the drawer.*

"Hi, Honey," she said as he came through the door.

"Hi, Babe," he responded. "How was your day?"

"Good. Dinner's ready. I know you have a board meeting at the church tonight, so I thought you'd want to eat early."

"Oh, that's right! Janine, can you hold up on dinner for a while? I want to talk with you about something. How about getting us each a cup of coffee and come and sit down?"

"John, what is it?" He was clearly upset, and she was getting nervous. "Is it one of the children?"

"No, no, nothing like that."

"Did someone die?"

"No. Honey, go ahead and turn down the stove or whatever. Okay?"

"Okay." She moved on into the kitchen. Absolutely everything she could think of was going through her mind. It had to be something traumatic. He was ashen and obviously shaken. She hurried and covered the casserole with foil, put it in a very low oven, rewrapped the rolls and put the salads in the refrigerator. She poured two cups of coffee and took them to the living room where he was sitting in his favorite chair.

"Here you are," she said and sat down in her favorite place on the sofa. "Now—."

"Okay. You remember last week when there were rumbles about a major layoff in the company?" She nodded. "Well, we figured wrong when we guessed it would be the very youngest employees. They have decided to begin the layoffs at the upper level. They believe they can save more money that way, because the senior workers have the highest wages—which of course, they've earned over the years."

Janine decided to say nothing. She knew what was coming, and thought it best to let him tell it as he thought he should.

"Late this afternoon, Jack called me in to his office. It didn't take long for me to figure out what was happening. He said he was sorry, of course, but he had to do what the company told him to do. I am finished there. Gone.... *Capoot!*

"I cleaned out my desk, and that's it. I mean, no warnings, and probably no benefits. Well, that's not exactly the way they said it. They said there would be a benefit meeting for all discharged employees to *explain* the remaining benefits. So maybe we'll have some kind of income and insurance, I don't know."

"John, how many others did they let go?"

"Looks like a lot. Not many were talking, but I saw others carrying out boxes of their personal items just as I was doing. They gave us boxes. Everything is in the box...all that I have meant to the company for 33 years. One box—and no goodbye."

They did a lot of talking about possibilities while they were having dinner, although neither of them managed to eat more than a few bites of food. Janine knew it was going to be a difficult transition for John and for her, but she believed that in time things would be all right. John was well educated, a very good accountant, and had been in a supervisory position for quite a few years. But it must have been a terribly degrading blow to him to be cast aside for younger workers who didn't have enough knowledge of the company to care about its future.

Before they knew it, time ran out and John had to leave for the board meeting. As she turned on the porch light, she saw that the snow was beginning to fall and naturally was worried about him going out. He kissed her and assured her he would be fine with four-wheel drive and said the snow probably wouldn't amount to much.

She watched his taillights disappear in the snow, kept the porch light on for his return, and busied herself cleaning up. She felt rather shaky with all of the events of the day, and couldn't calm herself down. She thought about John. He was always there for her, encouraging her through everything. *What would I do without him?* Why did she think such thoughts? She wasn't losing John. Life would certainly be different, but they would face whatever came to them together.

She began to feel sad and then actually angry with the company for their inconsiderate discharging of loyal employees. She asked herself the eternal question asked by generations before—*What's wrong with the world these days?*

*Whatever happened to trust and reliability in the workplace? How can those people be comfortable with carelessly bruising the lives of those who have been so faithful?*

Anger took over. She wanted to fight back, but knew it would do no good. She now felt frustration along with the anger, and the snow continued to fall! Nothing felt right. She wanted to pray, but rather than seek the comfort and strength that she knew the Lord could provide, she chose to go on worrying instead.

*Look at that snow coming down.* She stood in the window watching for John to return.

*He should have been home by now. Maybe I should call the church and see if he is still there. No, that might disturb the meeting. I'll give it a little more time.*

She walked over to the organ. She had planned to review the wedding music this evening, so maybe if she concentrated on that, it would ease her mind somewhat. A former piano student was getting married. It would be such a pleasure to play for her wedding as she wished her blessings and happiness with her marriage. The rehearsal would be tomorrow. Janine had performed this wedding music many times, and she shouldn't have any problems with any of it. Cindy was not having a soloist, which always made it easier for the organist. So after assembling the music in order, she started with the first, hoping that this exercise would settle her down somewhat.

She began with J. S. Bach's *"Arioso"* and was soon in another world. Music always did that for her. As she enjoyed the 20-minute prelude and was ready for the processional, she looked over at the clock and her heart skipped.

"John is still not home! I'm going to call the church, or the police, or something," she said aloud.

As she reached for the telephone she saw automobile lights turning into the driveway and hoped and prayed with all her might that it was John and not the police.

She ran to the door just as John was opening up the garage.

"Oh, thank you, Lord. Thank you," she said, as she waited in the opened doorway, not noticing the snow swirling in her face at all.

When John came over to her, she embraced him intensely with relief.

"John, I was worried about you. Is everything all right?"

"I'm sorry, Honey. I should have called you. The meeting went well and everyone was eager to get on home so we broke up rather quickly. I felt the need to talk with Pastor Jim, and I'm so glad I did. He's really a wonderful person to share with. He prayed with me and helped me to know that everything is not lost. He pointed clearly to scripture that tells us that God is in control of our lives and that we need not be concerned with what tomorrow brings. You know what? Whatever tomorrow brings, God will be there!"

"Well, that is a very comforting thought, 'God will be there.'"

"I know. That's one thing we can count on, Janine. So what else do we need? We have so much to be thankful for. I suppose we could count for days the many blessings we do have, so we need to focus upon those, put our lives in God's able hands, and trust in Him. How easy is that?" he asked, smiling from ear to ear.

Janine smiled back, overflowing with her gratitude once again for John and the stability he had always brought her. "Everything's going to be fine," she said and wished that she could trust as wholeheartedly as John.

# 2

# Working the Night Shift

A friend once told Janine that she was a "problem solver," and she believed that was correct. Janine thought she could fix anything that needed it if it was within her realm of operation, so turning everything over to God wasn't so easy for her. John seemed to be sleeping "like a baby." Good for him! Well, if he and God needed any help, she'd try to be ready, but she would not interfere unless John asked her for an opinion.

She always had an opinion, that's for sure. That was definitely not a problem with her. She had one, and she would be glad to share it with almost anybody.

She slept fitfully, with too many thoughts racing through her head. They needed to call the children and tell them about the change that had occurred today, and of course, she knew they would be concerned. She and John would do everything they could to assure them that they need not worry. She thought of Kathy in her country home with a beautiful family and how happy and at peace she had been lately, and of their younger daughter, Deborah, settling into a stunningly new development just outside of Pittsburgh—she a teacher and her husband a medical doctor with lives enwrapped in a social whirl. Janine began to drift off as she thought of Harry and his family of boys in Oklahoma. They were rootin,' tootin' little guys enjoying the outdoors and the casual living of the South.

*What time is it? Oh, my gosh! It's two o'clock. I'm never going to get through the day tomorrow!*

"Lord, help me to calm down. My head is buzzing with too many things tonight."

Would He help her? She believed He would if only she could let go of her determination to do it all. The prayer was not answered.

* * *

Janine awakened to a sense that something was changed, but she was not sure just what it was. Noticing that John was not beside her, and looking at the clock, she knew why. It was 8:32 a.m., and she never sleeps beyond six o'clock! But then, she couldn't get to sleep last night, so no wonder she was sleeping late.

She hurried out of bed, freshened up, walked into the kitchen, and faced the "something that was different." There stood John grinning from ear to ear in his "Dad Cooks Best" apron, stirring a delicious-looking omelet.

"Well, this is nice," she said. "Why didn't you wake me?"

"You were sleeping and snoring. I figured you needed more rest, and since I was up with no plans for the day, I decided to fix us a nice breakfast, take it easy, and get acquainted." He laughed.

"You silly goose. That's really sweet, but I have so much to do today. I'd better just shower, grab a bite on the run and get going. I've already missed my morning walk."

She saw his disappointment....She really should stay, but her schedule was packed for the day. And, she hadn't expected to find herself with a husband at home wanting to spend time with her. She was torn trying to decide what to do.

She looked outside and saw that the snowfall from the night before was practically melted, so the roads should be no problem. She had an appointment at 10:00 a.m. with some of the women from the church who were planning an association event. She could call them and push it to 11:00, skip lunch and get on with the music plan.

"John, you're right. We really should get acquainted after sleeping together last night—so let me make a quick phone call. Do you need any help here?"

"Nope." He smiled, and she knew she had made the right decision. "Everything's taken care of. I'll pour the juice and the coffee and set things out while you do the telephoning. Don't be long. Okay?"

"Okay."

She looked up the number and made one call. It would be fine. She felt like she should fix herself up for this man who had suddenly made himself at home in her kitchen. So, she fussed a tiny little bit with her hair, put on some light makeup, a pretty robe and was back in the kitchen in a flash.

John was whistling, and when she came into the kitchen, he pulled out a chair for her and they had the nicest breakfast. How special it was, and when had they ever had this kind of time without being on a vacation or something?

She tried not to look at the clock, but just couldn't resist.... She was still good on time, and knew it meant a lot to John that they sit and talk awhile this morning, so she tried to concentrate on that.

"Looks like the snow's going to melt away," John said. "I didn't know if I'd be shoveling this morning or not. It was still coming down when I went to sleep last night."

"Honey, I was thinking. Do you think we should call the kids, or wait until the weekend?" Janine asked.

"Well, there's really no hurry. We probably should try to get ourselves oriented a little before rushing to the phone. Here's what I think. How about if we call Deborah and Bob and Kathy and Greg and see if we can meet with all of them on Sunday afternoon—maybe at Kathy's? We don't have to say anything about why.…I could call Kathy today and see if it would be okay with them and ask her if she'd like to invite Deb and Bob. How's that sound?"

"'Fine with me. It would be nice to get together anyway, and all we really have to say is that you were laid off and we aren't sure what we'll want to do about it—but not to worry. We are not going to be in any kind of trouble or anything like that… Right?"

"Right. I also will want to go to the benefits meeting before jumping to conclusions about anything at all. We'll do okay, Jan. You know I've been fairly faithful to put aside something for our latter years, so maybe they've popped up a little sooner than we expected."

"I know I've grumbled about you doing that sometimes, John. I'm sorry. You were right all along. And I still have the work at the church, and that little bit will help out, too. We'll want to sit down and look at the entire picture. You are so good at balancing budgets. I know you'll set us on the right track."

John smiled and seemed very confident. She hoped he wasn't trying to conceal his anxieties, but she sincerely believed he was not.

They agreed on John calling Kathy. He said he had some things he could do during the day with his car that would keep him busy and dirty, which he loved.

Janine started to pick up the breakfast dishes.

"Hey! I can do that," he said. "You go ahead and get ready for your meeting."

"Well, that's nice." She gave him a hug and headed for the shower.

She would be a very busy gal all day, and she was realizing that her life might change a lot. Would John want to begin his daily routines with breakfast and morning conversations? That sounds nice, but absolutely would not work on a daily basis. Her usual morning started with coffee, a banana, and a walk. The walk was necessary for her physical and spiritual health, and she needed both to get her day off on the right foot. Then while showering, she would plan through the upcoming day, get dressed, gather up her necessary items and move along.

Things will be different now…They'd have to work it out together.

*I hope he finds something to do to occupy himself. He's too young to just live a retiree's life and have nothing substantial to do.* This new development could really complicate her life, which is controlled by obligations every minute of the day.

*There's no point in thinking this way. John will not be content just sitting around. He will find other interests…I think.*

Since she couldn't know what the future would hold, she decided to put that aside and get on with the business at hand.

# 3

# Wedding I

Saturday turned into quite an adventure with more interruptions than usual. Nothing important, really, but nothing ran smoothly. Janine had to hurry to get to the wedding, and that disturbed her. She always wanted to be at a wedding at least 40 minutes before the ceremony so that she could collect herself and her music and be ready to enjoy playing a twenty-minute prelude segment.

She and John went flying down the road. John parked the car, and Janine went on in without him. Naturally, she ran into someone she hadn't seen in a long time who wanted to talk, talk, talk. She excused herself graciously as soon as she could as John came through the door. He understood her look of frustration as she moved quickly to the organ.

The church was filling up quickly, and she should have been playing. *Calm down, girl,* she told herself. *You still have the twenty minutes you planned for the prelude. Just get on with it!*

She turned on the organ, pushed all the right buttons, and began with the Bach "Arioso" as she had planned. This was one of her all-time favorites, and it sounded so beautiful in the large sanctuary. She knew everything was going to be all right as the music soothed her soul and she was beginning to enjoy herself. The rehearsal had gone like clockwork last night, and she knew what to expect from the minister and the wedding party. It would be fine, and Cindy, the bride, would appreciate her gift to her today.

The couple was being announced as "Mr. and Mrs.," and everyone applauded. She peeked around the music and watched the kiss that really was a kiss, and then began Jean-Joseph Mouret's *"Rondeau"* for the recessional. How exciting. She had one of the best jobs in the world! She loved the music and the organ, and it was such a blessing to be able to assist the sacred ceremony in this beautiful way.

John and Janine went to the reception. They didn't know many of the guests, and that meant that they could be together and not lost in a crowd of conversations. They danced most of the evening and felt so secure in their love, wishing the wedded couple the same loving relationship with one another. After a nice slow dance, they said good night to the bride and groom and Cindy's family, and took their leave.

Weddings...They definitely have a way of bringing longtime couples to a fresh awareness of the joy of marriage and commitment to one another. Janine and John were thankful for their marriage and once again they felt comfort in the assurance of their love.

## 4

# Wedding II

Sunday afternoon as they were driving to Kathy's, John said, "Greg seemed genuinely excited that we could come today. What was it he said he wanted to prepare for us to eat?"

"Wait a minute. You wrote it down, didn't you? It was a new recipe with turkey, wasn't it?"

"Oh, yes. It was sesame-crusted turkey *mignons*. I remember that I couldn't spell *'mignons.'* It will be served with some kind of creamy wine sauce. And there will be Éclairs....I forget the rest."

"He's such a good cook. Anything he prepares is just yummy, but I could have taken something for the meal, or we could have had soup and sandwich. But that's Greg. Gone are the days when 'Mama' does the cooking in this family."

"Well, Honey, you are still a very good cook, and you do a lot of it in our house, so enjoy it when you have the opportunity to sit down to a meal without being in the kitchen all day."

"Thanks. I will, believe me."

The drive over was very pleasant as the roads were completely clear, and the grasses on the country hills were still splashed with the freshness of snow. Everything was quiet and peaceful, and they welcomed it all.

John knew that Janine always enjoyed driving past the old

row houses in West Hope, so he took the longer way that went directly through the borough.

For some strange reason that she couldn't understand, something seemed to be calling her there, and she felt a very close connection with the community even though she had never met anyone who lived there. She had even had dreams of West Hope, of sitting on someone's porch, walking through the back yards, and talking with the people…It was just the strangest thing.

As they rounded the bend past the apple orchard and entered the eastern end of the town, Janine said, "Some day I'd like to park here and walk past all of the houses. Maybe I could find someone to talk with, and then perhaps I could discover what is in this town that draws me to it. There's not much here really except that quaint little grocery store, a beauty shop and a post office.

"Oh, look! The church on the hill there seems to have had a celebration today, and look at the parking lot. It's full to the limit… Yes! See the sign? *'Congratulations Francine and Lawrence.'*"

"They must have gotten married right after church and had a reception there," John said.

"Could be," said Janine as they continued on past the post office, the row houses, and in no time were out of town. They turned onto McDade Road and on through the countryside for a few miles, through a rural settlement of scattered houses and turned right onto Bear Road.

The snow still lingered there in the wooded areas where tire tracks provided easy access on toward Kathy's.

* * *

Meanwhile, back at the church, the members and guests were joyfully celebrating a wedding. Iola, Beatrice, Virginia, Adele and others were busy in the kitchen finishing up the dishes.

"Once again, we have too many leftovers," Adele said.

"Our church has the world's best cooks. Iola, would you look in the corner cupboard and see if the carryout boxes are there?" Virginia asked.

Iola found them, and they began to package up beans, beets, potatoes, salads, ham, and fried chicken for the City Mission, which Pastor Dan had volunteered to deliver.

The "hit" of the meal was the cake donated and decorated by Beatrice Roberts. It was in three tiers with a bride and groom holding hands on the top.

Around the top tier were the words, "Love is Patient." Around the second tier, "Love is Kind." And around the bottom, "Love is God's Gift." It was very beautifully done, and everyone said it was the most perfect cake for this wedding there could ever be.

It was the first marriage for Francine Cook and Lawrence Simmons, and they had waited a long time to find one another. Everyone was so happy they were married. Francine had always trusted that God would send a husband to her, even though God's clock and hers were not always ticking along together. She was in her late fifties, and Lawrence was in his early sixties when they met.

Lawrence had come to the church at the invitation of Paula Kirkland, a relative of the Cook's. Francine Cook was the organist at the church, and one morning Kevin Kirkland was standing behind her after the postlude; when she finished, he said, "Francine, I'd like you to meet Lawrence Simmons."

She had noticed Lawrence sitting with Kevin and Paula for a few weeks and wondered who he was. He was quite good-looking, seemed about her age, and was taller than most of the congregation.

"Your music is very nice," Lawrence said.

"Thank you," she replied, suddenly not knowing what else to say.

Kevin said, "Lawrence is from Emerson Mills and has just retired from Gerald Publishing. I told him that you are a school teacher, so you both obviously have an interest in books."

*Well, that's certainly reaching long and hard for a mutual interest.*

"I see," she said, frustrated with her inability to find words to say. This had never been a problem for her. She began assembling her music and closing up the organ as Lawrence said, "Well, see you next week."

"Yes...'Nice to meet you," she said.

The next day, Monday, Paula called.

"Hi, Cuz," she said. "How's Aunt Alice today?"

"She's very well, thank you."

No one would ever guess that Alice Cook was 87 years old. She still maintained her own home and had a very sharp mind and memory. She was well known around the church to have the answer to any Bible Trivia question.

"That's wonderful," Paula said. "Kevin and I were wondering if you would like to come to dinner on Friday evening—you and Aunt Alice. Lawrence Simmons is coming and we'd like for him to become better acquainted with some of our church members. He seems interested in the church and we want to encourage him to continue."

"Well, that sounds nice. I'll ask Mother, but I think you can count on us. What can I bring?"

"Nothing...Nothing...It will be simple. No problem. Come around six o'clock if you can."

"Well, thank you very much. See you at six."

Francine didn't know it then, but Paula was working as a matchmaker for the Master. For if ever a match were made in Heaven, this would be it!

Francine and Alice drove over the rolling hills on that lovely summer evening with expectations of a pleasant evening. It was that, all right, and much, much more.

Laura and Edward Davidson were there. Both families raised cattle. Anne and Owen Kendrick were there also. The men were sitting on the porch talking about the herds, and they stood when Francine and Alice arrived.

"Good evening, ladies, and welcome! Sit down a spell if you'd like to. It's a perfect evening for rockin' and talkin,'" Kevin said.

"Good evening Miss Alice and Francine," Edward said. "It's nice to see ya! The ladies are inside fixin' up something that smells mighty good."

"Ladies," said Owen, tipping his hat.

"Good evening, gentlemen," the ladies responded.

"I think I'll go on inside and see what they're up to," said Alice.

"I think I will, too." Francine smiled, and said, "Enjoy your rockin' and talkin.'"

"That we will," said Edward. "That we will," he repeated as he and the other two gentlemen sat down.

The ladies had everything in good order, so they sat down in the parlor and talked about such things as women are likely to find interesting.

Anne asked Paula how her latest quilt was coming along. Anne had been Paula's mentor on quilting, and they sometimes quilted together.

"I finally finished it! Would you like to see it?"

They all were quick to respond that they would and soon were climbing up the beautiful curved staircase to the front bedroom.

There on the bed was one of the most beautiful quilts any of them had ever seen! It was a pattern from the 19th Century, with squares no larger than an inch. There were hundreds—perhaps thousands—of them, and the colors were of faded blues, rose, and white in a fascinating pattern. It was delicate and exquisitely finished and must have taken many hours to complete.

Beatrice said, "Paula, you have outdone yourself! You must enter this into the Applewood Fair this year!"

"Not only the Applewood Fair, but any and all that you can. It is magnificent," said Anne as she fingered the stitches and smoothed it over. What a compliment from one of the best.

They all agreed, and Paula said she didn't know, but she'd give it some consideration.

"Well, you'd better! I'm tellin' you," Bea said.

Alice thought that the ladies in that small gathering all had special talents. Paula's fabulous piecing, matching, and sewing; Francine's gift of music; Bea's cake decorating; Anne, who could stitch up just about anything; and Laura's baking and glorious gladiolus that won many a blue ribbon.

They heard a car door and turned immediately to thoughts of the dinner and welcoming the special guest of the evening.

"Come with me and greet Larry and then we'll put dinner on the table," Paula said.

Lawrence shyly walked up the stone sidewalk lined with multi-colored impatiens, and as he approached the porch, the men stood to welcome him.

He smiled and as he was climbing the steps he saw a group of women bursting from the front screen door.

*My goodness!* He thought. Before he could say anything, Paula, stepped over to stand with Kevin, welcomed Lawrence and began with the introductions.

*It's going pretty well, if only I can remember the names.*

"How do you do…How do you do…Nice to meet you… Hello…Nice to meet you."

Then, there was Francine! She looked so very pretty in her pastel-colored dress and heeled sandals.

Paula said, "And you remember Francine, our wonderful organist."

Lawrence took Francine's hand…He blushed…She blushed… Everyone noticed, secretly smiling and enjoying the moment.

*Look-a there!* Bea thought.

*Well, well!* thought Anne.

*Goody, goody!* Paula's heart proudly jumped.

They all stood still. No one moved the least bit or even breathed.

Lawrence, still holding Francine's hand, softly said, "Yes, I remember. Hello, Francine."

The ladies all leaned in toward the couple to glimpse the spark that had just ignited. Francine didn't remove her hand from Lawrence's. She stood very, very still and finally said, "Hello, Lawrence."

It was a breathless moment. Time stood still. It was totally providential…No one could have stopped it!

Everyone remembered that it was a beautiful summer evening, the meal was delicious, the quilt was beautiful, but they will forever tell the story as the evening the Lord chose to give two of His own the gift of love.

And now on this wintry Sunday in February at the Church of Hope, the couple had pledged their wedding vows before God. They had chosen the "love chapter" from II Corinthians of the Holy Bible to be read: "…love is patient, love is kind…" just as Beatrice had predicted, and the congregation of Hope Church and friends witnessed a beautiful beginning to a beautiful and long-awaited marriage.

# 5

# The Family Portrait

When Janine and John arrived at their destination that day, they saw that Deb and Bob were already there. Deborah was the youngest of the three children. She and her husband made a very handsome couple. They were both in great shape and well matched in character and in preferences.

They bounded over to meet John and Janine, but Prince, a Black Lab, beat them to it.

"Mom, Dad, it's just so good to see you. It seems like ages," Deborah said. They all hugged one another, and arm-in-arm they walked into the house where the granddaughters and Kathy and Greg were waiting. Prince was as excited as the rest of the family.

Greg took the coats and hung them on the tree in the entry, and everyone naturally navigated toward the fireplace. They all agreed that nothing was better than the open fireplace on a brisk, wintry day.

Karen and Meghan were happy to see their grandparents, as usual, and began chatting all about school and their activities. They all eventually sat down on the comfortable furniture surrounding the fireplace.

Kathy and Greg had bought their dream home three years ago, and Kathy was quickly hired as a third-grade teacher at the area's public school. Greg had worked for years as a chemical analyst for a dairy nearby, and the move actually positioned him closer to his job.

Kathy's dream was a log home and Greg's was a commercially-equipped kitchen, so after they moved in, they completely renovated the kitchen the way "The Chef" wanted it. It had commercial ovens, a gas cooking stove, a large refrigerator and a large freezer. The entire center of the room was a working countertop with its own sink. The family benefited greatly from Greg's love for cooking, and they affectionately referred to him as "The Chef." He enjoyed nothing more than to have everyone over for dinner, picnics, lunches and even brunches. They were all considerably spoiled not having to think much about cooking any more, but there had been no complaints from anyone in that regard.

The house sat on a slight knoll at the very end of the lane. It had been beautifully landscaped, utilizing many original trees that were in harmony with the natural presentation of the house. There were rhododendron and azalea bushes bordering the driveway, which looked beautiful in whites and pinks in the summertime. There were birdbaths and feeders and they all enjoyed watching the birds in all seasons. The house was certainly their dream come true.

The great room was aptly named, easily containing a huge six-piece curving sofa in front of the fireplace, a loveseat near the high window, various chairs, tables, a piano, and cupboards. The wood floors were splashed with colorful rugs, and Kathy had decorated the walls with pictures of family members, some of her needlepoint, and other collections. All in all, it was warm, cozy and a very special place to be.

Greg said, "Can I get you a cup of coffee?"

Janine and John were quick to respond, "yes" to that!

"How's the practice, Bob?" John asked.

"We're busy, but better organized since Nancy came on with us. She's a gem. The best receptionist I could ever ask for. I didn't realize what a difference someone could make in the flow of the day. Ethel was a dear lady, and I hated to see her go, but I guess she needed to find something else to do that was better suited to her abilities now that she's seventy-two."

"You'd get such a kick out of her now." Deborah said. "I heard she is one of the most active members of the senior citizens group in her neighborhood, planning all sorts of events. She does enjoy life, and it's really great that she has more time to have some fun, I say…And Bob actually gets home in time for dinner now, believe it or not."

"So what does Nancy do that's so different?" asked Janine.

"Oh, my goodness. She doesn't let anyone come in to sell something to me without a prior appointment, for one thing. It used to be that every time I walked down the hall a drug salesman was following me to show me the latest medicines.

"Also, Nancy schedules patients more realistically; giving me the time I need and time the patient needs for a thorough exam or whatever is necessary. She seems to know just about how long a patient will be there for any sort of ailment. It reduces the stress some."

"I know that means a lot to you, Bob. You are very sincere and caring. Patients love that about you," said Janine.

"And, Deb, how is the semester coming along? Have you completed the plans for your trip to France with your students?"

Deborah taught high-school French in Pittsburgh, and had planned a student visit to France each year for the past few years. She and Bob had journeyed back and forth at least twice during the year. They fell in love with the Parisian culture and were fortunate to negotiate a fantastic deal to purchase a small apartment of their own in Paris. They keep it in the hands of a realtor for rental income, which in the long run has helped to make the payments for them.

Two years ago, Deborah and Bob insisted on taking Janine and John over to spend some time traveling and staying in their neat little flat. Janine was not sure about traveling out of the country, but her family knew all the safe places, and it turned out to be a trip of a lifetime for them. Now when they hear of Deborah's experiences with her students, they can follow the scenery, the cities, and the regions in their minds.

"We'll be leaving on Maundy Thursday." She began to sing, *"I love Paris in the springtime,"* and the family smiled at her imitation of a silver screen French woman. Her excitement came through to everybody.

"Mother, Deb and I have some exciting news," said Kathy.

"Ok," said Janine. She had some news, too, but it could wait. She didn't actually consider her news "exciting."

"Do you want to tell them, Deb?"

"No, no, Kathy. You go ahead."

"Well, Debbie has arranged for us to have a foreign exchange student from France for the month of July. She is 15 years old from Orleans. We've wanted to do this, but we thought it would be better all the way around if Karen and Meghan were a little older. Karen's doing well with French at school, and Deb is going to help me with a refresher course. I hope I remember enough from my high school classes to be able to communicate, but Deb assures me that Claire is fluent in English. It should be a great experience for us as well as give her an opportunity to see America."

"I'm sure it will work out just great," said John. "Debbie has told us so many wonderful stories about the relationships and shared knowledge between these students and their home families. Knowledge is a huge step to understanding and cooperation between peoples."

"We're going to write a letter to Claire to tell her all about us and how happy we are that she is coming," Karen said.

"Yes, and I'm going to give her my bedroom, and Karen is going to let me sleep in her room with her. She'll love the loft and Prince, and the 4th of July!" Meghan said.

"She sure will," said Deb. "She'll share in the celebrations of the birth of this nation, and then you all can help her celebrate Bastille Day on the 14th. I think July is a perfect month to have a French student come to America."

Greg brought in the coffee. "We'll see if my French cooking receives a passing grade. But, she'll want some hamburgers, hotdogs, and homemade apple pie, I'm sure."

"What else is going on in the big city of Pittsburgh?" Janine asked.

"Oh, boy! Busy, busy. The symphony is going strong, so I'm involved in that. The Art Association will be welcoming many artists to the annual art show in the spring. I'll be helping to plan as much as I can before leaving for France. Oh, we're going to the formal dance for the hospital fundraiser in late April. I'm trying to talk Bob into a new tux, but he's sure his will fit just fine by then," said Deborah.

"Ha! And it will! Don't worry about me. You have enough to worry about finding that perfect dress, and gloves, and shoes, and jewelry. There's a major venture."

John spoke up, "Greg, is everything under control in the

kitchen? If you can sit down for a few minutes, Janine and I would like to talk with all of you about something."

"Sure." Greg sat down beside the girls. Prince immediately moved over to be close to them. They all had become very attentive.

"Well, last Thursday I and many others at the plant were laid off permanently in a move by the board to save the company money and get it out of the red."

Everyone was waiting for John to say something more. They heard and understood what he said, but were shocked and didn't know how to respond.

Finally, Deborah spoke up. "Daddy, what are you saying? Did you lose your job?"

"Yep. Exactly."

"Oh, my gosh. Did you know this was going to happen, Dad?" asked Kathy.

Everyone in the room was totally focused on John, with an occasional glance at Janine to perceive her feelings if possible. The daughters were obviously shaken, and Greg and Robert seemed quite stunned.

"There had been talk of reducing the workforce, but I never dreamed they would be cutting those who had been there for as many years as I have. One thing I have learned is that seemingly no one is indispensable. It saves more money to boot us older guys out because we naturally have had pay increases over the years to garner more income. But, I'll tell you…the company is going to find itself in a real mess working with less-experienced personnel…Well, they didn't ask me my opinion anyway. All they wanted to do was get it over with."

"Are you saying you left that day never to return?" asked Greg.

"He came home with a box of his personal things. They gave him a box at least," said Janine.

Deborah was getting angry as she stood. "Well, wasn't that big of them? But, Dad, the basic question now is, 'what will you do?' You are not even of retirement age so you can't collect Social Security…and what about your pension? Will you lose that?"

"Actually, I don't have any answers at this time. There is going to be a meeting about the benefits available for all those released. I'm supposed to receive some word about that this week, I guess. Look. Maybe I'll even get another job."

No one seemed enthusiastic about that premise. After all, Dad was not of an age any employer would jump to hire, but they didn't say so.

"Your mother and I can survive on the securities we have, so we don't want any of you to worry one bit about this. We'll be fine. I'm just going to put it all in God's hands."

Janine spoke up. "We really haven't had time to process this new situation yet, but we will keep you informed every step of the way. That's why we came here today. We wanted to be completely honest with you."

Robert said, "Please promise us one thing more. If you need anything—anything at all—you will tell us.…My goodness! Heaven knows how much you have given of yourselves and even of monetary advances to help all of us out over the years. John, you know we will never, ever let you lose your home, or anything else for that matter."

*Oh, dear.* John and Janine were thinking. *Now they think we're going to go under financially.*

"Robert, really, we will be okay. I'll just have to find enough to do to stay out from under Janine's feet. She is one busy gal. Always has been. But, like I said, we have put money away for a rainy day, and so we'll draw into that as we have to. No problems, but thanks. I know you mean it, and we appreciate your love and concern."

"Let's just all stop worrying now, okay?" Janine asked. "We've told you everything, anyway. Greg, do you need some help in the kitchen?"

"Yes, I do. Come on, it's about time to pull everything together, and you are just the one I'd want to do that."

They went on into the kitchen, the children went up to the loft to watch television, and the others sat in the great room watching the fire in the fireplace.

Deborah was remembering the fortune that her parents had spent on her very fancy wedding and reception. They could now have thousands more dollars in the bank. *And what about that trip to France they financed for me upon graduating from college? I was inconsiderate...I was! I should have thought ahead to these days. I was selfish and hadn't thought of my parents at all. Now what?*

Kathy wanted to pray. *What should I pray for? God doesn't want us to pray for someone not to go bankrupt. Isn't that wrong? If Dad is putting this all in God's hands, then I have to pray for God to hold him in his hands. That's better. That's what I'll do. "Father in Heaven, please take care of my Daddy. He's such a good man and has always given much more than was necessary to his family."* She fought back tears, and didn't want her Dad to see her cry. She got up and stirred the fire, and stood there for a moment collecting her emotions.

John watched both of them. He knew they were troubled. He was sorry that they had to feel that way. But he was troubled, too, when it was new to him. It was natural. They will all feel better when they see that he and their mother were getting along as usual, except he was going to be doing something else, that's all.

Robert had picked up a magazine and was pretending to be very interested in some article. He didn't have the slightest idea of what was on that page. He was thinking of John and Janine, and hoped that they understood how sincere he was about his offer to help out in any way. And, he was thinking about how many patients he had seen who had heart attacks following a traumatic event such as the loss of a job. Many had gone into depression. John was such a robust man, in great health. He wanted to say something to him about looking out for his health. He decided, though, that if he did say something, it could work in the reverse of what he had in mind. Consequently, he kept silent.

Dinner was ready, so everyone went into the kitchen and sat down to a delicious meal.

No one spoke of the job loss again that evening, but it was on everyone's mind.

John and Janine left first, and of course, the four others talked for quite some time about how they would see to it that John had things to do, and that he and Janine would live a normal life far into old, old age.

"Well, that was harder than I expected," John said, as they were driving home. "But, you know what? They'll be fine when they have seen the proof that we are getting along well for ourselves."

"I know. They are juggling many responsibilities in the air right now. I think they felt that they were going to have to keep us afloat. And they would do it, too. Hopefully, it will never come to that. And, you're right, they just need a little time to realize that they won't have to include us into their daily concerns," Janine said. "Let's not call Harry tonight. I think we've had enough for one day, don't you?"

"I agree."

# 6

# The Western Front

Harry had been excited for John when he was told the news. His perspective, unlike the girls' was so different. Retirement for him seemed an eternity away and something that would be wonderful in his life. He often said he would have to work to the age of seventy to put his boys through college.

He and the boys did lots of things together which filled his life with great joy, but working long hours, maintaining the house and property, and finding quality time to spend with the family was challenging and frequently exhausting.

"Hey, Dad, maybe you'll come out and spend some time with us and we can clear some more of the land. I've also been thinking about that other building I need to put up for the ever-mounting stockpile of tools I've gathered. Rhonda calls them 'boys' toys,' but I do use them around here."

"Well, now, there's something I definitely will place high on my list, Harry. Fresh air, hard work, and being there with you guys would be the ticket to a great escapade for me—and thanks for your viewpoint. I'll let you know how it might work out."

Janine just smiled when John told her what Harry had said. "That's Harry for you. He doesn't see in black and white. There are beautiful colors in his life, and he'll follow the rainbow to the end. I think you should go whenever he can find the free time to do the things he's talking about. You know how much you love working with Harry, John."

"When could you go, Janine?"

"Oh, Honey, I can't imagine myself going this time. Lord knows when I could get away, and I wouldn't want to hold you up. You should go. Please…It would be good for you and Harry, and I'll make plans to go out with you some other time. Okay?"

She was working just as hard today as she did as a young woman, never thinking of slowing down and smelling the roses. There would be time enough for that later. As for now, she'd dig in, preferring the rut, the tight schedules, and the challenges of getting it all done—on time, and just right.

"You know what they say: 'All work and no play—'"

"I know, John. Things won't always be this way. I need a little time to adjust to a different schedule. I can't suddenly drop everything I'm doing and the plans I have made. Please try to understand. I'll work on it. I promise."

John wished that she had said, "Great, let's do it," but he knew how she was, and he was used to her having to work around a full schedule. If she were going to leave town, she'd have to have time to reschedule everything. Well, it used to be the same with him, after all. He's still not exactly footloose and fancy-free, but he was beginning to feel that he could adjust in a very short time. Harry had it right; *retirement* could be wonderful.

# 7

# Benefits?

The meeting hall was crowded with the recently laid off personnel of the company. Most of the spouses were along to hear what the management had to say also. Janine actually revised her schedule to go along with John, and he was pleased that she could do that.

The meeting was very well organized with tables of information from various insurance companies and other tables with pension and income charts and explanations of benefits. When everyone was seated, statements were made from the executives, followed by a time for questions. All the troublesome questions that most of the parties had were answered—not entirely to their complete satisfaction, but shockingly not as bad as they feared.

The company would compensate the lost earnings comparable with the amount of income expected from Social Security until the discharged person reached the age of sixty-two, at which time the former employee would be responsible to either file for Social Security or seek other means of income.

As for health benefits, each person would be responsible for choosing the plan that would be best suited to the needs of the family. The company would pay a portion of the cost of each plan in line with the best offer the various companies had provided.

John gathered up all of the information, heard the answers to questions he and others had asked, and they headed out through the doors. Outside of the building there were clusters of people standing around discussing the results of the meeting. Some felt abused and degraded, and others accepted their fate. It all came down to the preparations each individual had made for his own future, and consequently how much help each felt he needed.

John talked with a few of his friends. Most of them were able to resign themselves to this new situation, and were discussing what they might be doing in the future. They vowed to stay in touch as people often do when parting company, and the crowd thinned as each went on his way.

John and Janine sat in the car looking over the papers for a little while before driving on home. John said, "Well, it's not too bad. The cost of insurance seems pretty high, but not totally out of reach. I've talked with some people about what they pay for health insurance, and if you aren't in a plan with a company, it can be outrageous. So I'm glad to see that we will still be on the company plan even though they aren't assuming the bulk of the cost anymore. It looks like we'll not have to draw upon our retirement investments as much as we thought. We should be quite thankful that financially we are still going to be okay--not flush, of course--but at the least, it will be manageable."

"You know, when Gerald was handed a forced retirement, the company sold him and the others out. There was no regard for him at all," said Janine. "That company only wanted to move ahead, and they flushed those poor employees down the drain. At least Bilton Company didn't do that. I must say I'm relieved and maybe a bit surprised."

"Me, too, I guess. I hadn't figured on a lot from them, so I'll not be complaining. The Lord is watching over us, and even in this instance we've come through without too much damage.

Let's not forget that He's working *His Plan*. I wonder what's next? I'm looking forward to finding out."

"John, our lives are good, don't you think? I mean, what more can we do?" asked Janine.

"Only God knows. Let's get on home."

# 8

# Easter Preparations

In West Hope, Harriet was teaching the Sunday school class as best she could. More visiting was going on today than usual, but she understood. Most of the members, she included, were alone all week in their various houses, and coming to church on Sunday was the highlight of the week for them. They had some catching up to do. They were talking about Easter coming next week.

"Are you going to your son's for Easter, Bea?" asked Anne Kendrick.

"They were talking about coming for me. I suppose I'll go. I love to be with the family, but Easter is one of my favorite times to be at church here. I'd just love for them to come to my house instead. We'll see," she answered. "How about you?"

"Oh, we'll be here. Owen wouldn't want to miss. Some of the family will be in, and we'll go over to Alexandra's for dinner."

"That'll be nice," Julia said. "Jenny and I were talking about it just the other day. We'll both be here without family this year, so we're going to fix something between us—not that the food matters much."

Laura Davidson said, "Julia and Jenny, you two come to my house for dinner! I won't take 'No' for an answer. My entire family of thirty some are coming for Easter. We'll have more food than we can possibly eat, and it will be really nice to have you with us."

Julia looked at Jenny, and Julia said, "What time?"

Laura said, "We usually eat around four o'clock because the children always hunt for eggs around the farm first. It's such fun to watch them, so I encourage you to come as soon as you feel you want to and be a part of it."

Jenny said, "That would be nice. What do you say, Julia?"

"I think that's a wonderful invitation. Thank you, Laura. We'll come."

Iola asked, "Laura, who does the cooking for that big crowd?"

"Everybody pitches in and brings food. My daughter came up last week from Statesville. She's such a help, and I'll bake the pies on Saturday."

Everyone knew that Laura's pies were the best. Her secret was that she used lard in the crust. Even though most of her friends and neighbors never used lard themselves due to the "fat content," they ate her pies without hesitation.

Laura's husband, Edward, had not been feeling especially well the past week or so. He couldn't keep up with all the work around the farm, and had to have help for the first time in his eighty-plus years. Laura always did help with the work, but she would possibly be doing a lot more for a while. There had been talk of selling the cattle, but so far it is just talk. It would be a sad day if it happened.

"Will you have the family in, Iola?" asked Harriet.

"Oh, yes. They're coming. I'll be cooking it all myself, which is fine with me. They'll not be here before three o'clock as they are staying home to go to their own churches. I get to do Easter. It's the only holiday I have. All the other holiday gatherings are distributed around, so I really enjoy the cooking and the fussing. I always did."

"And you do a fantastic job of it, too. Every time our Women's Association comes for the annual dinner, your table is set so beautifully, and we are treated to an outstanding dinner," said Adele.

Adele's daughter would be home for Easter. She had been excited about that for several weeks. Her daughter, Darlene, lived in the Midwest and didn't often get "home" for holidays. The class knew she was truly looking forward to her visit.

"Well, the church music is going to be special, I'll bet. Francine has been so happy lately, and do you notice how it comes out in her music? She seems to be raising the decibels on the organ, too, as though she just can't hold back," said Anne.

"That's for sure. I can't control my hearing aid sometimes. When she turns the organ up, I have to turn my hearing aid down in a hurry or it seems my brains will be blown out," said Iola.

"I like it," said Julia.

"I do, too," said Anne.

"Alice told me that Francine and Lawrence want to move to Florida, at least during the winter months. I guess Lawrence had already bought a piece of property and a house before he met Fran, and now they both want to go," Bea said.

"Why don't they?" asked Jenny.

"Well, you know how dedicated Francine has been to Hope Church with the music, and she just can't bring herself to leave the church without an organist," Bea responded.

"Can't we just get another organist?" asked Julia.

"I guess you can hardly find an organist these days. Francine says it takes years of lessons and practice, and today's young people want instant gratification, not years of preparations," said Bea.

"Iola, why can't you play the piano for services until we can find someone else? Surely, there's someone out there," said Laura.

"I can't do that anymore. It makes me too nervous. I haven't spent much time at the piano for years, and I could never get back what I've lost now. It would not be possible." It was obvious that no one was going to change her mind on that!

"Well, then, what? Maybe if the Session would advertise in the paper, or something? Some churches do that. Look how long Fran has served in this church. She certainly deserves some happiness with her new husband," said Adele.

"She does, but she'd feel a lot better if she knew it was what the Lord wanted her to do, so she has talked to the Session about it, and I guess she asked them to pray for the Lord to provide a replacement if it is His will. She's not going to go until she knows that. That's what I heard," said Bea.

Harriet said that's the way it should be. "We should all turn to the Lord for the right answers, and do our best to live according to His purpose whatever it is."

They all agreed.

The bell rang to end the class, and they dismissed with prayer and went on into the sanctuary.

# 9

# He Is Risen!

Kathy, Greg, and the girls came back to Center Church for Easter, just as many others did. The church was filled from back to front, which was extraordinary—especially for the pews in the front. The family missed seeing John in church this morning, but were pleased that he went out to visit Harry and the boys. They could only imagine the good times they all were having together. It's hard to be separated by so many miles from those you love, but Harry tried to shorten the vast, empty space with visits and telephone calls as frequently as possible.

Easter was Janine's favorite Sunday of the year—the day the Lord had made for all as the day of salvation. She wanted to praise Him with all that she had, and what she had was music. The compositions for this day were the finest, and she would play them to His glory the best she could.

She usually played a longer prelude on Easter because the congregation was more tolerant and appreciative of the music on this day than on any other. Instead of the usual chatter during the prelude, most of the people actually listened and were glad to be in the house of the Lord.

Pastor Jim was uplifted by the attendance and wished the flock felt the overwhelming desire to praise the Lord every Sunday. He would not complain. Someone out there would receive a message today that God had called him to hear, and Jim would be the one to deliver it. He was happy for the glorious message of the resurrection to expound upon this morning.

Janine played J. S. Bach's *"Jesu, Joy of Man's Desiring"* first of all, and then a resounding composition with trumpets and full organ. If she had turned up the volume any louder, the chandelier would have begun to sway, but the congregation had come to celebrate, and the music was totally appropriate.

Pastor Jim called the congregation to worship: "He is risen!"

The response echoed: "He is risen, indeed!"

The service was as it always had been—joyful and full of praise. Kathy moved into the choir to sing the *"Hallelujah Chorus"* from Handel's *"Messiah."* The choir director had invited her to do so as she knew the alto part as well as anyone in the choir. The congregation stood and all were overjoyed with it.

Janine played a Bach *"Toccata,"* with everything she had left in her. She would be exhausted from this day, but delightfully so. Easter was the objective of a long, long season of practice and preparation for any church musician. It was the highlight of the year.

Janine hurried home to change her clothes. Even though the girls were growing up, they still wanted to have an Easter Egg Hunt. So, needless to say, she wanted to be there to enjoy that event with the family.

She missed John. She felt no guilt for not going with him after being at church today, but she had felt his absence, and it seemed strange without him. They both loved Easter.

Even though she should hurry along, she could not resist driving around through West Hope. As she did, she read the church sign: "He is risen. Hallelujah!"

*That's right,* she thought. *And that's what it's all about!*

*"He Lives, He Lives,"* she sang as she turned onto Bear Lane rejoicing in this most significant day of all days.

Driving along, she saw that there was a "For Sale" sign on one of the houses.

*Isn't that a nice-looking house? And, it's sitting on a lovely piece of property. I wonder why they would want to sell…? Very nice.* She drove on past.

❀ ❀ ❀

The day was warm, and so were the hearts of the family members as they shared in the Easter celebration. The girls clambered for each egg, running back and forth, having a laughingly good time. They all sat down to a delicious dinner of lamb, complained about eating too much, and were filled with satisfaction and familiar conversations.

Janine spent the night as planned as Meghan moved on over to Karen's room. She looked around the room, in soft pinks with white ruffled window curtains, and remembered how she loved fussing with the little-girl rooms in her own family. Meghan's room wasn't really much different—she had a shelf of dolls, lots of stuffed animals, and a bookcase with classic and non-classic literature, as she was an ardent reader.

There was a music system of some sort, and unlike her mother's old room at Janine's home, a computer and printer. Of course, in today's world the computer is as important as the typewriter or a set of encyclopedias would have been to the generation before. Life moves on.

She loved the softness and innocence of the room and felt very comfortable to be staying the night.

Karen and Meghan joined her on the bed for a while. Janine

loved having the girls near to her, and they talked with her about the things that were on their minds.

Karen was bursting with excitement that she had a part in the school's musical production.

"I will be a member of a group of girls who are in almost every scene. I even have two lines to sing all by myself."

"Well, that's terrific. Those voice lessons are paying off, aren't they?"

"I guess so. By the time I'm a senior, I hope I'll have a much bigger part."

"I'm sure you will, Karen. You've worked hard at your music training. Keep at it."

"I will. I know I haven't had much time lately to practice the piano, Grandma, but I want to get back to lessons as soon as school is out. Will that be ok with you?"

"Absolutely! We'll do it. I'm so happy to teach you, Honey. You have been doing a lot on the piano this year at chorus, which has helped you to keep at it. Now back to exercises and scales."

Janine laughed as Karen scowled. She grabbed her and rolled on the bed with her as they had done together since the girls were toddlers. Meghan eagerly joined in with a squeal, and they all loved just touching and being close.

Grandma needed to catch her breath, so they calmed down for a moment.

"And, little Miss Meghan, what are you going to do all summer? Are you ready to try the piano?"

"I don't think so. Mom has taught me a little bit, but I'd rather dance."

"That's good, too, but you should give some instrument a try."

"Oh, I'm going to. I want to play the drums!"

"The drums?"

"Yes. I'm going to learn at school, and also the violin."

"Meghan, you are one big surprise! Go for it, girl!"

They resumed their romp, and Kathy peeked in to see what all the noise was about. Prince had come with her, and before anyone could think, he was in the mix.

The exercise was enough to put Grandma into exhaustion, but she loved every minute of it. What a joy having grandchildren!

Kathy scooted everyone out of Grandma's room, hugged her mother, and soon all was quiet in the house.

Janine slept deeply from exhaustion and also from the comfort of a good day with loved ones.

The next morning, after a small breakfast, Kathy and Janine decided to take a walk. Prince could hardly contain himself. He ran to the left of the road and sniffed into the trees, came back out and walked a bit with the women, moved to the right and sniffed. He was on a discovery mission to find out if any new animals had moved in. Kathy called him back from a rabbit chase and poured some of her bottled water into a scout pan that she carried for him. All three of them were enjoying the exercise.

They passed the neighbors sitting on the porch of the old farmhouse and they waved. Kathy said she hadn't actually met them yet, but they were always friendly. Daffodils were blooming and touches of green grass could be seen in the yard. The couple on the porch was anticipating the arrival of the first robins and the budding of the trees. Winters were long for the farmers, and yearly revival of the land brought movement and hope as the pulse of the earth greatly affected all of God's creatures.

How quiet it was. Janine forgot that Kathy was with her for a moment as she became lost in her own thoughts. In the country one could easily forget how engaged and crazy the world had truly become. Few in the city would be thinking of spring. More likely, attention would be on those maddening end-of-the-year reports, children's programs and recitals, and shopping for a new season's wardrobe.

Here, the new wardrobe would be green grass and flowering meadows. The new fragrance would not come from Estee Lauder or Ralph Lauren, but rather from apple blossoms, honeysuckle and fresh mown hay.

*Why am I thinking this way? I'm certainly not longing for the country life. The city has always been the life for me with symphonies, great stores, international restaurants and such, and I never want to be far removed from all of that. When did I ever even think about honeysuckle and apple blossoms before?*

Their walk continued past the little country church that Kathy had been attending. She said perhaps twenty to twenty-five people belonged there. It felt cozy to her, and she was helping out by playing the hymns on the piano. The church was of painted wood, sitting up on a high foundation and had a small, yet old cemetery behind it. It obviously had been there for the neighborhood a long time.

"What did they do for music here yesterday?" Janine asked.

"A young woman who is a college student was going to be home with her family, and she planned on providing the piano music. She was always dependable in that manner as she was growing up. I'm sure the congregation enjoyed having her back on the bench, so to speak."

Before long they came to the house with the "For Sale" sign in front. It looked as though the owners were not at home. Janine pointed out to Kathy that the house was for sale, and asked if she knew the people who lived there.

"I haven't seen anyone here lately. I think they have already moved. I see that 'Crisscross Realty' is handling it for them. I did hear that the lady of the house became very ill, and the husband couldn't keep up. That's always a shame."

"It's a fine looking home," said Janine. "I wonder if we might walk around the back. I'm sure no one is here."

"Ok. Let's go look."

The ranch style home had a full-sized basement that opened up to the outside from the back to a nice patio. The yard had been neatly kept—perhaps an acre—with an apple tree, several maple trees, a grape arbor, other bushes and shrubs, and a separate garage. The property seemed to end at the wooded area down behind.

"Well, this is really nice," said Kathy.

"It is!" They began to feel like intruders so they went back to the road and turned back to the house.

"Grandma, Grandma," called Karen. "Granddad just called. He said maybe you could call him this morning. They would not be going outside today until later. He and Uncle Harry were drawing up something inside. I don't know what."

Janine smiled. "Thanks, Honey. I'm going to be getting along home very shortly. I'm having a meeting at my house this week and there are things to be done. I'll call Granddad from there."

She wished she hadn't volunteered to be host. She should have known that she'd need a few days to unwind and rest after Easter. Oh, well. She'd do what she must. Maybe she'd take a tiny little nap this afternoon before she thought any more about the meeting.

"Meghan, thank you for sharing your room with me last night. I slept very well. I can't believe how quiet it was—no cars going by and no sirens in the night. I said my prayers, turned out the light and listened. The silence seemed to cover me with peace somehow. It was so very nice."

"You're welcome, Grandma. Anytime you come, you just figure on using my room. Okay?"

"Okay," she said.

# 10

# Picture This!

Janine resisted the temptation to once again take the longer way home through West Hope because she was eager to get home and call John, and also she had a number of things on her list to do today.

She was soon on the highway, and there weren't as many trucks on the road today—the day after Easter. *Many truckers had one extra day off to enjoy with their families,* Janine decided.

She pulled into the garage and gathered her bag and purse. As soon as she made a pot of coffee, she dialed Harry's phone number. Rhonda answered the phone.

"Oh, Janine, it's you. Great! Hey, boys, it's Grandma. We've missed you. Little James can't understand where you are. He expects you and Granddad to be together."

"I'm sure they are having a good time with Granddad, but he's probably having a better time than anyone."

"I don't know about that, but it's been fun. How was Easter at your church?"

"Wonderful! I love Easter, as you know. I confess that I missed John, but with Kathy and her family there, it was good. We all had a fine day. You should have seen the girls rushing to get the largest amount of eggs. It was fun. I hope they never tire of doing it. Did you all get to church?"

"Of course. We dressed up our little cowboys in their best boots and bejeweled shirts. They really looked spiffy. I'll send you pictures. Here's John. I'll get the boys on in a bit."

"Ok. Thanks, Sweetie."

"Hi, Babe," said John. "So, did you have a nice walk this morning?"

"Yes, I did. The daffodils are blooming and the countryside is turning green. It was very peaceful and such a nice place to walk. No trucks and no loud noises—only the soft mooing of the cows and an occasional bark of a dog in the distance... Very nice."

"I'm glad. I'm really enjoying the out-of-doors here, but we've been making some noise of our own with the chain saw while expanding the open areas up a bit. The boys are going to have lots of room to run here in the yard. It's about the size of a soccer field now."

"John, are you drinking lots of water and getting a rest now and then?"

"Now, now, don't you worry about me. Rhonda keeps a check on that. She sends water out to us in thermos jugs. William brings it out with his wagon, sometimes pulling Charles and James, too. They are a big help and such happy little guys. They keep me smiling, for sure."

She smiled also as she envisioned a "Norman Rockwell" type picture of the three boys and the wagon.

"Janine, are you there?" John asked.

"Oh, yes. Sorry. How's Harry? Did he get the time off work, then?"

"Oh, yes. He took some vacation time. The company is good about it all, and told him to use more time this week if he wants to. We've called a friend of his who does excavation to come over and dig us out a section for the tool shed. Well, Harry calls it a tool shed. I'd call it a big old storage garage. After it gets dug out, we'll start laying the blocks together. He wants to help me set those, as he knows he's better at that than I am. That'll take the biggest part of this week, we figure. Next week I can measure and cut boards for the building while he's at work, and we can put them up together in the evenings. Rhonda said she'd help, and I believe she can. She's quite the partner for Harry."

"Well, sounds like you have some more work to do. Don't rush yourself. I can manage, and you know I'll keep myself busy. I'm happy for Harry and the boys that you are there. Just take care of yourself. Okay?"

"I will. Well, the boys are all lined up to talk with you, so I'll say goodbye. I love you."

"I love you, too," she said with a tinge of sadness and longing to have him home, but she would not say anything about that.

Janine talked to each one of the boys. They went on and on about Granddad and Daddy cutting down trees and how they were helping carry branches into the woods and stacking up wood for the winter. She wished she could see that! They were so sweet and dear to her and were going to grow up without her seeing it happen.

She told them all she loved them. They all told her that they loved her, too. She hung up the phone, and stared into space for a long time.

"'Time waits for no one,'" the old saying goes. It surely doesn't. It really rushes past sometimes. Harry was a little boy a few years ago, wasn't he? Now he has three boys of his own. She sat there thinking of Harry as a youngster, and what a joy he always was to his parents. Everyone loved Harry.

*"I'm just wild about Harry, and Harry's wild about me."* She started to sing the song in her head. She had a song for everything.

Not everyone in the family appreciated her breaking into song all of the time. They would never know how many times she kept the songs to herself so as not to see their raised eyebrows, but she would always have the music and songs—at least for herself.

Her thoughts continued on and on until suddenly she realized that she had been thinking there for a half hour. *Time is rushing by right now!* She hurried into her office to gather up some devotional books from one of the shelves.

# 11

# Out of Focus

*The meeting will be Thursday, and I said I'd give the devotions for Arlene. I think I'd better try to get that settled.*

*I can't even think of what kind of devotion to do. I'm still tired from Sunday. I know I slept well last night, but I think I'm totally exhausted; nevertheless, I'd better get started on this. First, I need to calm down. I need to focus on a prayer and a scripture, or something.*

She couldn't do it. Her mind was whirling. She felt left out by not going to Oklahoma, but how could she go? Well, she could have. John was perfectly willing to go after Easter, but with Harry requesting last week off, it seemed better that John go ahead when he did.

She mustn't forget to call the church tomorrow to reserve the chapel for the piano recital of her two students. They were the only two left to her teaching, except for Karen, who wouldn't be in the recital. Janine had not taken on any new students for a few years, anticipating retirement.

*Retirement? Ha! That's a laugh. I'll never retire. I don't have enough sense to retire. Could I be happy traveling without any responsibilities like some of my friends are doing? I know that I'd never, ever be satisfied doing that.*

She started going from room to room—meandering, eventually turning on the television. She didn't normally enjoy it, but occasionally found it entertaining. She turned the dials to get some news. Nothing seemed to be happening of interest. At least there were no bombings, or anything like that. She turned it off. She had things she should be doing, anyway.

Her thoughts went to the nice house for sale on Bear Road. *I could enjoy living there, she thought.*

*What? I'm losing my mind. Why did I even think of that? I have a very, very full life right here! I am never moving! My goodness!*

She went back to look through the books of devotions, and while she was leafing through, the telephone rang.

*"Allô, mere! Comment allez-vous?"*

"Deborah! I'm fine. How are you? Is everything all right?"

"Absolutely. The students are getting settled into their rooms. Our luggage arrived with us, thank heavens, and the trip over went well. You should have seen everyone as they came into Paris International. It's always the same, and yet ever exciting to be with them and share their new experiences. I just wanted you to know we're here and give you a telephone number in case you need to call. I know you won't, but just in case."

"Well, fine. That's great. Did you call Robert?"

"Yes, I did."

"Ok. So you'll be two weeks, right?"

"Right. That's not much time, really, as you know, but we will take in the main tourist attractions. The group can't wait to get started, and I know they will go from morning to night. We'll be dragging into Pittsburgh when we come back, but it'll be worth it. Did you have a nice Easter?"

"Oh, my, yes, and I enjoyed the day with Kathy's family. We missed you and seeing you dive for the Easter eggs. But the girls had a great time. I talked with your Dad just a while ago, and he's fine, enjoying the out of doors, and being with Harry and the boys."

"That's good. I knew he would. Well, Mom, take care of yourself. Try not to work every minute of every day. There's more to life than constant work, you know? Oh, dear, here I am preaching at you all the way from across the ocean. I'm sorry. You know I love you and mean well. Right?"

"Of course.…I love you, too. Have a great time, dear. Take the students to see the French dancers. But control yourself when you do!"

They both laughed. When she hung up, she was smiling and picturing Deborah truly in her element. She hadn't any children of her own yet, which has turned out to be a blessing for many young people as she has the time and the pleasurable energy to give so much to them. *Her students are incredibly lucky to have her for a teacher, mentor and example.*

# 12

# Blowing in the Wind

She eventually managed to read some devotions, all the while telling herself that she didn't have all day to find the right one. The pressure was on! She went through a devotional book for women. It was fine, but not exactly right.

*Come on, Janine, you don't have all day. Stop being so fussy.*

She always thought those little books were particularly helpful, so what was wrong with her today? If she didn't find something soon, she'd have to resort to writing her own. She had done that for the devotions for an entire year awhile back. It was a rewarding exercise as it brought her closer to the Lord. She remembered how much she loved writing about the scriptures.

That was when she was not so busy! She couldn't possibly settle down enough to do that today. She began to regret that she was in such a predicament now. Where was she going with her life? She felt under great stress and began to think she wasn't going to be able to find a devotion that would satisfy her.

*I'll use one of my old ones.* She stood to go to her files. *I can't do that! The women have heard all of them before.*

*Lord, when did I get myself into such a tizzy? And, why am I noticing this so much now when I thought I was perfectly satisfied with everything as it is? I am satisfied! I'm doing good work. I'm doing all that I can for the church—maybe too much. Can we do too much? We can't. We have to do everything we possibly can. Well, I'm trying.*

She picked up the Bible. Starting with Genesis she read the Creation Story. What a marvelous, marvelous beginning. God created everything. Of course, she knew that. He created the stars, the earth, the waters and the mountains, the animals, and finally Adam and Eve. Then, He rested...He rested.

*Does this mean that God didn't work all of the time? In any case, he doesn't have to work all of the time. He has it all worked out.*

*I remember in the New Testament where Jesus left the crowd and disciples and rested at times. Jesus lived as an example to all of us and he rested. So is it all right for us to take time off? No one had a more important job on this earth than Jesus, and he rested and retreated from it at times.*

Feeling confused and very uncomfortable with her thoughts, Janine thought of one of her favorite hymns, "*What a Friend We Have in Jesus,*" and went over it in her mind. She would take it to the Lord as the hymn said.

She prayed, asking the Lord for help in understanding the scriptures she had just read. Admitting to herself and aloud to God that she was under stress, she prayed for God to calm her, and lead her in the right direction.

She was drawn to the blue book in the stack, picked it up, ruffled through some pages, and came upon a title that intrigued her.

## The Little Wind

(Read Psalm 63)

Over the waters of the South Pacific a little breeze was born. He was gentle and mild and moved very softly.

As he grew a little, he began to truly enjoy being a breeze. He would lift and swoosh, and move very lightly over the ocean. He particularly enjoyed riding on the backs of the dolphins and whales, and they seemed to enjoy having him around. They would frolic and play all day. They all began to move a little faster, turning northward, being drawn to the cooler waters.

The little breeze began to grow and grow. He grew very strong, and as he moved over the waters, he caused the waves to rise and increase and toss about.

He just couldn't control himself. He became stronger and stronger, and could move faster and faster. He turned completely away from the course he was meant to follow. When he blew across dry land, he noticed that everything under him became terribly stirred up, and sometimes torn apart. He wanted to say he was sorry, but he couldn't stop long enough to do that.

He was moving along at a pace now that he did not like. It was a pace he could not manage. He was moving, but accomplishing nothing worthwhile. He longed for the days when he was young, when everything seemed simple, and he could rest once in a while and enjoy his life.

He tried and tried to make himself stop. He made wishes. He made promises. He squeezed everything within himself to find the control he so desperately wanted. The effort was all to no avail.

One day he came to a sea. It was a beautiful sea—very blue and peaceful—and he wanted to stop there and rest; however, all he did was stir the waters. Great waves formed, clouds joined him in his journey, and a terrible storm erupted. It was his fault. If only he knew how to calm himself. The stress was too much. What could he do?

He came upon a boat full of men. He could see that the boat was going to sink because of the strain he was putting upon it. He felt absolutely dreadful. A man in the boat stood. The man looked straight at him, lifted his hand, and said, "Peace. Be still." And because the man spoke with all authority of heaven and earth, the wind listened to him and stopped what he was doing and became calm.

The wind was amazed that he no longer was in a torrent of constant movement and stress. He rejoiced that he could again be the happy little breeze he once was, and realized that all of his own efforts to accomplish this were impossible without the help of the one sent by God who brought peace to him.

He would remember Him. He would turn to Him for help the next time he got himself into an uncontrollable situation. He blew gently on, came once again to the waters, and lived a peaceful and productive life doing what he was born to do.

Janine had read the scripture and the story and associated it with herself immediately. The devotion ended with a suggested discussion or a prayer. The discussion leader could ask the following questions:

- Have you ever felt that your life was out of control? If so, what did you do?
- Do you always feel it is your total responsibility to be in control of your life? If so, why?

- Do we become overwhelmed sometimes because we are following our own course instead of God's?
- Are you willing to let go of your own plans and desires to follow the path God is choosing for you?

❀ ❀ ❀

Janine pondered the questions and knew that she was mainly moving along on her own, and was exhausted trying to figure everything out for herself.

She read the prayer:

> "Father in Heaven, be with us and help us to call upon You at all times for directions in our lives, so that all we do will be for Your Glory. We ask this, Father, not for our own benefit, but so that we will be used to do Your will as You have planned.
>
> We pray, Father, in the name of Your Son, Jesus, who has the authority to calm the storms and set us on the course we should follow. Amen."

❀ ❀ ❀

During the following day, Janine realized even further how important this little story was to her. It could certainly change the way she had been thinking, and it might even change the future. Was she willing to accept that? She wasn't sure, but she knew she had discovered something significant, and she would not set it aside and forget it. She decided to use the story of the little wind as her devotion for Thursday evening.

# 13

# Is Anybody Listening?

Eighteen ladies came to the meeting, all happy to be there and talking over many things. Janine had planned well and had provided seating for everybody. After some cool drinks, they were seated for the meeting.

Janine called the meeting to order as president and then moved on to the devotions. She was especially eager to read *"The Little Wind,"* and had practiced reading it with much emphasis. The ladies were smiling as they listened.

When she finished, someone responded, "That was sweet."

Another asked, "Was that in one of the children's books?"

"No. It really isn't a child's story. It is meant for adults...For us."

"Oh. Well, it was very nice," another responded.

Janine realized that no one caught the meaning. If anyone did, she certainly couldn't sense it. She said, "There are some questions for us to consider which should help us understand the real meaning of this story. Let's go over them."

*These questions will lead everyone to the right way of thinking, I hope.*

The questions were hardly answered at all.

Responses such as "Oh, maybe, a little," to the first question was about all she heard. The rest of the questions prompted shrugs and not much more.

She couldn't believe it! She was totally flabbergasted that no one caught on. How could this be? It was as clear as clear could be. Were they listening, or not? Well, she couldn't keep on the subject forever. She asked them to bow for the prayer. They did, of course, but even then she didn't think they were with her at all.

The meeting continued with the business. They heard reports, planned an upcoming event for the spring, voted to give a small check to a needy student, and discussed other important issues.

As they were preparing to conclude the business, Libby asked if she could read a nice poem by Helen Steiner Rice. Permission was granted, and she said she had found this nice poem when going through cards at the store and wanted to share it.

It was sweet and lovely, and everyone praised her for her selection and caring enough to share it with the group.

They closed with the benediction, Janine served her dessert that she had baked herself (of course), and they sat around for a while longer. She heard nothing about the devotion she had offered, but many went on and on about the poem!

When they left, she plopped down on the sofa and wanted to cry. What was wrong? She believed the devotion was pertinent and helpful, and she felt absolutely frustrated that no one else had a clue as to what the purpose of it was.

She cleaned everything up, vacuumed, put the dishes in the dishwasher, turned off the lights and momentarily forgot the message of the little wind. She was not calm, nor was she happy—but rather in a torrent of emotions.

*Lord, why did I not reach them? I really wanted to.*

She went to bed and decided to go see Pastor Jim in the morning. There were too many things she absolutely did not understand.

## 14

# The Ladies of West Hope

"Good morning, Adele," said Beatrice. "I just got back from Ron's. What's been going on around here?"

"Good morning to you," said Adele. "I'm glad you called. You must have ESP. Darlene left for home this morning, and I'm feeling a little sad. But we had a wonderful visit, so I can't complain."

"Did you and Darlene have a good visit with Candice?"

"Yes, we did. We went over to the house on Saturday. Samantha had fixed a really nice lunch for us. Billie sure married a gem. She had Candice all dressed up in a spring robe, and there was a beautiful bouquet of Easter flowers on the night stand."

Bea said, "Samantha is truly a Godsend to your family, isn't she?"

"She certainly is, and she never complains about taking full care of her mother-in-law. Bea, that's a very big job, you know."

"Yes, I do know. I remember very clearly your eighteen-hour days for years after Candice had that terrible accident. That was just about the worst thing that ever happened. Not only did Candice lose her husband, and pretty much her own life, but she had little Billie who couldn't take care of himself. I'll tell you, Adele, you were a saint to take them in and care for them all those years."

"Now, Bea. You would have done the same thing. We were family."

"I know, but with Candice totally unable to do for herself, you had to use every ounce of energy you had caring for her and your small grandson."

"Well, I had my husband then, and Darlene was actually quite helpful. I think it was harder on her in her teen years than on any of us. But let's get back to your visit with Ron. Did you have a nice Easter with the family?"

"Oh, I did. You know I really wanted to stay home, but he wouldn't let me do that. He believed that I'd be better off with the family on the holiday, and as it turned out, he sure was right. I'll tell you, those great grandbabies of mine are growin' like weeds. We had a fun time together. I showed them how to play ball. They learned a little about swingin' a bat as I pitched."

"My goodness! You pitched? I'd throw my back out doing something like that," said Adele. "I never really learned much about any kind of sport anyway."

"Well, that's because you were brought up like a little lady. Me? I was just one of the boys being raised with all brothers. I didn't want to be left out, so I learned how to compete with them and even their friends. I'll tell you, I was pretty good at baseball. I'd sometimes get picked on a team real early.

"I was wondering how everything went on Easter?" Bea asked. "Was the service nice?"

"It was at that. We had the early service with near to 100 people there."

"Really?"

"Yes. Then we all stayed for a breakfast fit for a farmer. Lucy and Raymond once again cooked eggs, ham, sausage, and biscuits.

Others brought in donuts of every kind, fresh fruit—you name it! It was delicious."

Bea asked, "Did you stay for the regular service, then?"

"Of course! We all did, and there were about 100 more people came in. You should've seen the memorial flowers. They were all over the floor in front of the pulpit and in every window, and there were more on some flower stands in the entry. As usual, the fragrance was powerful and almost overwhelming, but I took care of my sinuses this time. I took an allergy pill early that morning. I brought your lily home to give to you,"

"Oh, thanks for taking care of that. I'll tell you, I did miss coming to my church. Easter is so special. But Ron said he'd come here next year, God willing. This year I'll be eighty-two years old, so I'm not expecting anything from one year to another any more."

"Oh, go on. You know you'll live to be 100. You are the youngest 82-year-old I know of. Oh, before I forget, I wanted to tell you, the church is planning a softball game for the congregation later in the year—with hotdogs and hamburgers—out at the ballpark right after church. I can't remember if I heard of a date, but it should be something to do, don't you think?"

"Something to do? I'd love it. I'm gon'na sign up to pitch."

"Beatrice! You'd better leave that up to the younger folks. We can sit and cheer."

"Not me! I'm gon'na play ball. I get tired of sittin' around. A day of fun in the sun—that's for me."

"I don't see you sitting much when the weather is nice. You work your flowers and cut your grass and such."

"Harrumph! That's work. I do it to keep fit, and it's cheap! It's not what you'd call fun, is it?"

"You seem to enjoy it. I think you should get Silas to cut your grass like I do."

"I don't want to spend my little bit of Social Security paying somebody to do what I can do myself."

"Well, would you like to come over for lunch today? I have ham left over from Easter Sunday and I could use a little friendly visit."

"'Sounds good to me. I'll be over in a while. Thanks. By the way, how's Edward Davidson? Have you heard anything?"

"Oh, yes. Jenny called me yesterday to tell me that he had to go to the doctor on Tuesday. He was fine for the family get-together on Easter, and then on Monday he had a spell of some kind. His daughter, Hannah, was still there and she took him. The doctor ran a few tests and wants him to get an EKG and blood test."

"Oh, dear," said Bea. "Ed is getting up there. He's older than I am—I know that. Laura has always been the healthy one in the family. She's gon'na have to be strong now, that's for sure. Our old friends are old, you know? It's something we're just going to have to face."

"I guess you're right. Well, come on over when you get yourself ready. I'll be here."

"Alrighty. See you soon."

Adele and Beatrice lived near one another in West Hope. They were of entirely different personalities but participated in church life together, which was about all they had left at this stage of their lives.

They were friends, and they knew that friendships were as precious as anything they could claim. The others in their Sunday school class were dear to them as well, but Bea and Adele living close had established a bond together that meant a lot to them.

Iola telephoned Julia later that day.

"Hello," said Julia.

"It's Iola. Are you going to get your hair done Friday as usual?"

"Well, I guess so. I always do. Why do you ask?"

"I had my appointment moved to the morning. Actually, it is right after your appointment, which you always have. But my problem is that my car is in the garage, and won't be done until Friday afternoon. I was thinking that if you could pick me up we could go together. That is if you wouldn't mind sitting and waiting for me to be finished."

"Well, that's fine. I'll come by for you. That won't be any problem. What's new?"

"What could be new around here? Nobody died. That's always good news. Harriet got herself a puppy."

"Oh, my! I can't believe it. She travels so much. What is she going to do when she goes away?"

"Exactly! I said the same thing. She said she'd worry about it later. But for now, she is enjoying the company of the little thing. I wouldn't have one. Too much trouble, if you ask me. A puppy has to be followed around all of the time if you want to protect your carpet and what have you. And you have to take it outside. She can't keep up with that. I told her so. She said her son lives close enough, and he said he'd take care of it when she's gone away."

"Well, that sounds like a pretty good arrangement. She's younger than we are, so I suppose she can handle it."

"It's not that I can't handle it. I could if I wanted to. I just don't want to. Did you talk with that realtor?"

"I did. He wants to buy my house and let me live in it until I die. What do you think of that?"

"You'd better get some advice on that, and watch out for someone raking you across the coals."

"I know. I don't want to sell my house, anyway. I have no intentions of it. Did he stop up there?"

"No. And he might as well not. I'm not going to talk with him about such a thing."

"I wish it would warm up some. Seems kind of cold today, don't you think?"

"Oh, not too bad. Of course it's April. We could get any kind of weather between now and the middle of May…I'd better go. Thanks for agreeing on tomorrow. Will you be coming by around ten o'clock?"

"Yes. That's about right. See you then. Goodbye."

"Goodbye."

The ladies of West Hope lived in separate houses, mostly alone. Iola, Adele, Julia, Beatrice, and Rachael all came to the community because they had married men from the immediate area, and now all five were widows. It always happened that a widow in West Hope, who moved in from another place stayed put when her husband died. There were a large number of those, and many belonged to The Church of Hope.

They came there during the 1930s. Life became very hard during the depression, and they survived because they had one another. Friendships had developed, children played together, and they came to depend upon one another in the borough.

Some women lost husbands during World War II. The community of West Hope actually lost a very large percentage of men during the war. Life had been hard then, also. The friendships deepened, as they will during times of uncertainty, pain and grief. West Hope was a community of the "best hope" in many ways.

Jenny always lived there, and Anne came to the outer community some years back. Harriet actually lived outside of the borough, also, but the church in West Hope was always the church of her husband's family. In the beginning she had no other choice, and today she would say, "Choice or no choice, this will always be the church for me."

Harriet had been the class teacher ever since the original teacher became too ill to continue. She always could be counted upon to help out in various other ways as well. Her husband died suddenly some years back, which automatically enrolled her into the old widow's group, although she was somewhat younger than the rest. Not that anyone *wanted* to get into that group. It has no name, isn't active in any groupie way, and doesn't meet together except on Sunday mornings. They basically have a history that ties them together and gives them a sense of security somehow.

❧ ❧ ❧

The sirens were sounding as the emergency vehicle passed the beauty parlor. Julia listened as it faded out of range. The beautician said, "Somebody's going to the hospital, I suppose."

Julia hated the sound. She'd heard it many times before, as had others in the community. If it had stopped in their community, she would know the one in the ambulance. She didn't want to have to face another loss. She valued every friend and their families. Everyone in West Hope felt the fist of anxiety push upon the chest as the sirens blew through. Everyone, that is, except Iola who was under the hairdryer with her hearing aid removed.

When they paid the beautician and left the shop, Julia told Iola about the ambulance. They each picked up the telephone immediately when they got home. They were saddened to learn that Edward occupied the ambulance today.

He had chest pains and was taken to the hospital. Everyone who heard said a prayer for his health and for Laura, too, as she faced this difficult time.

## 15

# A "Stirring"

In the city, Janine had met with Pastor Jim and told him of her experience with the devotion the previous evening, and said, "I cannot believe that not one person was moved by the story. It was so meaningful."

He smiled knowingly. "Janine, I have wondered about the same thing many times when I thought I had a significantly key message on a Sunday morning and looked out upon a sea of blank faces. You see, the Holy Spirit moves us to hear, but we have a choice to make. We can open up our hearts and let Him in or not. When we open ourselves up to receive the message He is trying to tell us, we will hear it. Otherwise, we close ourselves up to it.

"I know you received that special message because you were searching, and the Holy Spirit was working in you to find it. The others were not prepared to receive it—that's just all there is to it. I understand completely. Sometimes I feel that I am preaching to a wall between the people and myself. But I keep trying because I know that God is using me to deliver the message of Christ, and I go out there every week believing that there is at least one who will go away with the message and do something with it."

"So you are saying that the Holy Spirit is actually talking to me?"

"Yes. That's exactly what I'm saying. There is no big loud voice, Janine. It is the Spirit, Himself, moving within you, stirring up your soul to get you to turn toward the thing that you are to do. God talks to you this way. He brings you to Himself, and he points you in a direction that will fulfill His purpose in you. It's a marvelous thing, Janine, and God has chosen this time to take you somewhere to do His work through you. Give Him the praise and allow Him to deliver you."

"What is it that I'm supposed to do?"

"I'm not sure. He isn't talking to me about it." They both smiled, although Janine was quite uncomfortable at the moment.

"But I would venture to suggest that He wants you to settle down a bit to give Him a chance to let you know."

"Oh, dear. I don't know how to do this."

Jim prayed with her asking God, through Christ, to stay near to Janine, and for the Holy Spirit to keep prodding her until she knew what He wanted. He prayed that Janine would relax her schedule, give herself time to rest, and be open to possibilities.

He asked Janine to pray constantly to be near to God and to wait for His instructions.

She felt peculiar. She never, ever found herself in such a place; however, she was also excited because it was truly wonderful and awesome and amazing that God had chosen her for something. She would try to do what Pastor Jim had asked, but how can a person who is so used to being in control simply be still and wait? She had so much to do. She had committed herself to many responsibilities, and she always kept her word and did what she said she would do.

She remembered the "little wind" and how he could not calm himself. The answer would be in the Higher Power, she knew. It was going to take a whole lot of praying for her to change, especially without having the slightest idea what the Lord had in mind for her.

# 16

# The Winds of Change

"Anne, what are you baking up this morning? It sure smells good." Owen said.

"I'm making a lemon pound cake to take to Laura. I'm going to pick her up this afternoon and go along with her to visit Edward in the hospital. And don't you worry, I'm making one for you, too." She smiled knowing that he would be appreciative. He loved his sweets, and she found pleasure in doing anything for him.

"Well, I'll certainly enjoy that," He smiled in return. "Have you heard anything new about Edward?"

"Laura's encouraged. His heart isn't very strong and he has had a mild stroke, but nothing damaging at this time. I don't know how they will continue to manage the farm, Owen. Laura has taken over a lot of the work, you know, as well as taking care of the house."

"She always has been a very strong woman, Anne, but I agree, changes quickly cause many to have to make major decisions. That's going to be challenging. They have farmed ever since they got married, sixty years ago."

They knew the Davidson's very well, and were nearly the same age. Laura and Anne enjoyed the Homemaker's groups, and all participated as 4-H leaders over the years.

Anne sat down at the kitchen table with Owen.

"I suppose it's really difficult when you have lived in the same home for so many years. That's one thing different about us, isn't it? We've moved—how many times now?" Anne asked.

"Well, without counting, I'd say five, maybe six, but we've been here for twenty-five years at least." Owen said.

'Twenty-seven, actually."

"It's the longest we've stayed, but it was the right move. I'm glad we decided upon it. It's been a good retirement home here in the country."

"Yes, it has, and even better now that Alexandra and her family have moved back to the area from Texas. We've been truly blessed, Owen."

"Yes, God is good. I wouldn't change a thing."

"Well, maybe we shouldn't become too settled with the way things are," Anne interjected.

"Why not, Anne? What else could we possibly want?"

"Oh, I don't mean to suggest that we are lacking anything at all, Owen. I'm just thinking that perhaps we should take a close look at our situation and what the future may hold for us. Will we need to make any changes? I've been thinking a lot about that lately, especially since Edward has taken ill again."

"What are you suggesting?"

"I'm suggesting that we might want to sell this big house and move into a condominium."

"My gracious, Anne! Where did that come from?"

"Just think of it, Owen. We have four bedrooms here, all on the second floor. We have…what…? Twelve steps up into the house itself? We park our car out in the garage and have to walk, rain or shine, to the house carrying whatever we have. Look at this kitchen. It's huge—much larger than we need anymore.

Our family gatherings are now usually at Alexandra's, due to her insistence. Will we soon be struggling to keep up this property and the house? Heaven knows the years are catching up with us. It would certainly be better to move while we are in good health rather than be forced to make decisions under arduous circumstances."

She could see that Owen was disturbed by her sudden proposal about moving. She was, too. She hadn't planned to bring this up just yet.

"Well, I never dreamed you were thinking about this at all. I don't even know what to say," Owen said. "Do you have a place in mind?"

"Actually, I do." Anne said. "You remember the nice place that Helen Stoaks moved into awhile back?"

"Yes, of course I remember her selling the farm and moving after Benjamin died. It's very nice. I enjoyed visiting her there."

"It was hard for her, Owen, making so many decisions on her own. Well, anyway, they are constructing another building along side of the one she moved into. I know what Helen paid for hers, and if the others sell pretty much the same, we can afford to buy one. I'm confident that we could get a decent price for our place here."

She had apparently already put her calculating skills to use.

"Whoa, there. You are really getting ahead of me. I'm not on the same page with you. Let's take our time, all right? You are throwing something at me that I just can't swallow all at once." Owen had decided that he would not discuss it anymore, and Anne knew it.

"I'm sorry, Owen. I didn't mean to jump into all of this today. Let's just drop it for now. Maybe we'll want to talk about it some other time," Anne said.

She knew when she had come to a place with Owen. They

had been married for more than half of a century, and perhaps she knew him better than he did himself.

"Maybe," he said. He picked up the book he had been reading earlier, ending the conversation.

* * *

Anne and Laura had a very nice visit with Edward. He seemed to be feeling reasonably well and might possibly be going home before Sunday.

Driving up to Laura's home after the visit, Anne asked, "Is there anything I can do for you, Laura?"

"Well, thanks, but you know how the boys are. They are in and out all of the time, seeing to whatever they can do for me. I'm never alone for a very long stretch."

"Yes, I know. You are very fortunate to have both of your sons and their families living within fifteen miles of the homestead, and I know how eager they are to help you; in case anything comes up, though, and you need something in a hurry, I hope you know that Owen or I will be happy to run over and do anything we can."

"Yes, Anne, I do know that, and it is comforting, but believe me, I'll be fine. Thanks so much for being with me today, and for the pound cake. It is, without a doubt, the best pound cake I have ever eaten. I always hurry to get a piece at our church dinners."

"You're welcome. Call us if you need anything. We'll see you on Sunday if not before."

They smiled as they parted, and each was thankful for such a good friend.

Laura entered an empty house. She felt empty herself. What in the world would she ever do without Edward? They were so much a part of one another. They breathed the same air, thought the same thoughts, enjoyed all the same things, and shared a deep love for one another. She walked a little heavier across the kitchen floor, uttering a little prayer that Edward would be able to return home soon.

She saw the note on the kitchen table.

*"Mother, the cattle have been fed. Someone will be over to see you later on this afternoon with supper in hand. Fred will stop by to see Dad today and bring us up to speed. We'll talk later. Put your feet up for a while. Love, Erica."*

She felt comforted with the loving concern of her family. She and Edward worked hard, but they received much in return—*much more than they deserved,* she thought. She was going to put the cake away, but decided on eating a little sliver and drinking a glass of milk. She sat at the old wooden kitchen table that had been in the family for generations. Ed's Bible was there as usual with his class study book. He always began his mornings very early studying the Word.

She traced her finger along the nicks, gashes, carvings, and water rings on the old table and smiled.

*"F.D."* Freddy was in the second grade and had his first penknife. *Ha! He should have known better than to carve his own initials.* The old table could never be replaced with anything else. It had seen the children, served friends, opened up to great gatherings and had cloths of linens dressing it for very special times. She thought of the bridal reception for Hannah, with her grandmother's best Irish linen cloth and roses picked fresh, still dripping with the morning dew. Everything had been so beautiful in soft ivory and pinks.

She found consolation sitting there with her memories, her glass of milk and Anne's delicious and thoughtful gift.

She was a bit tired, after all. She decided to go sit in Edward's recliner. In moments she was off to sleep and smiling with sweet recollections and gratitude for God's goodness to herself and to her family.

* * *

Anne found Owen outside by the shed gathering up fallen branches. The spring rains had brought down the dead ones, as one expected each year. Anne wished that Owen would not go outside alone. She always worried that he might stumble and no one would be around to help. But he had a mind of his own, and she would not attempt to thwart his ability to use it. Considering how many people their age were suffering from dementia, she would be thankful for what they had been given.

"Hello, Owen. Are you enjoying this beautiful afternoon?"

"Hello. Yes, but I've done enough. I'll be coming right in."

"That's fine," she said.

Anne had prepared a dish before she left the house earlier, and took it out of the refrigerator and popped it in the oven. She was getting a little hungry, and Owen was always ready to eat.

Owen had come in, washed up, and sat down in the parlor to watch some of the news while supper was being readied.

The afternoon faded into evening, and as was their routine, they went to bed around 9:30 pm. Nothing more was said concerning the house and the condominium. Neither had felt any need to discuss the subject.

The next morning after breakfast, Anne was picking up the dishes and moving them to the sink, when Owen said, "I was thinking a bit about what you said about selling our place here and moving into a condominium."

She truly thought the issue would not likely be brought up

again—at least for now—and was taken aback to hear him say such a thing.

"Oh?"

"Um, hum."

That was it? Well, no surprise there, and he got up and moved toward the door leading into the parlor.

She turned to the sink, and he said, "Yep! I think it's a good idea."

She whirled around. *What?* She didn't believe her ears.

He suggested that they go talk to the owners of the new building. He said that even now they had to have someone cut the grass here and help care for the property, and he remembered that there were doctors' offices near the condominiums, a barber, and sidewalks to take walks; in addition, many other folks their age lived in the surrounding buildings.

*He has given it some thought.* This was not as difficult as she had imagined.

They talked about realtors, downsizing, getting rid of furniture, etc., none of which seemed to bother either one of them. They were both practical people and had always done what they felt was best without looking back. Anne would make a few phone calls.

# 17

# Calling the Realtor

"Good morning! This is Crisscross Realty. How may I help you?"

"Hello. I'd like to inquire about a piece of property you are handling. It's located on Bear Lane north of West Hope. The house is brick and sits slightly back from the road. Can you tell me some things about it?"

"Our Mr. Lorey is handling that. I'll connect you."

"Hello, this is Harold Lorey."

"Mr. Lorey, I'm interested in talking with you about the house on Bear Lane outside of West Hope."

"Yes, yes…the Stafford property."

"I'm not sure who owns it, but I have driven by it and would like to see the inside if that would be possible."

"We can arrange that. When would be convenient for you?"

"Well, tomorrow would be fine with me—perhaps early afternoon. Could I meet you at your office around one o'clock?"

"Of course. I can be here. What is your name?"

"Janine Stephens."

"Fine, Ms. Stephens, I'll see you then.

"That's Mrs. Stephens. And thank you."

She hung up the phone, trembling all over. *Ok. I did it! Now what? Now I wait for tomorrow. This was just the first step. The others will follow.*

⁂

This very morning, she had been startled into awakening. She sat straight up in bed, looked for John, who of course wasn't there. He was still in Oklahoma. *What's going on? Is there something I'm forgetting to do? What day is it?*

She wasn't even sure of that answer. How on earth could she clear her thinking?

She sat on the side of the bed, hardly breathing. She took in a deep breath, held it, and released it—again. *Ok, now. Think!*

She couldn't.

*I need a cup of coffee,* she decided.

She put on her slippers, threw on her robe and headed for the bathroom to wash her face. Afterwards, she looked into the mirror, and tried to figure out where her mind was. It surely wasn't noticeable to her in any way, shape, or form. She shook her head and went to fix some coffee.

While the coffee was brewing, she put on her jogging suit and walking shoes, then drank some coffee and moved herself along, feeling strained to get out and go. She hadn't checked the morning forecast. She only knew that she was ready to go—regardless.

Janine still had not gained her composure from the startled awakening. She stretched a little—not too much—and headed out on her usual route, but saw nothing of her surroundings, seemingly moving as through a fog. *Lord, are you there? Am I alone? I need you, Lord.*

She sensed that she was certainly not alone, and began to feel warmth and a calming as she continued to pray. She erased everything from her mind and concentrated on the nearness of God. She knew in her heart that the Holy Spirit was leading her. She began to smile. *I am being touched...I am being led...I am certain of His love.* She was smiling, but there were tears of release and a joy so wonderful, she could hardly bear it.

*Thank you, Lord, for loving me. Thank you for wanting to use me. I am yours. Lead me and I will follow.*

She breathed in slowly, and then released her breath slowly. She slowed her walking to a gentler pace, savoring every moment. She knew the presence of the Living Lord, and she did not want to ever be without Him.

Her congregation had sung a benediction last Sunday that used the words of St. Patrick of Ireland, which always touched her heart. Today, she was singing it with a complete realization of the importance and impact of their meaning:

Christ be with me, Christ within me,
Christ behind me, Christ before me.
*Yes, Lord, be with me,*
Christ beside me, Christ to win me,
*You have won me, Lord.*
Christ to comfort and restore me.
Christ beneath me, Christ above me,
Christ in quiet, Christ in danger,
*You, and you alone, Lord, can do all of this.*
Christ in hearts of all that love me,
*I pray that all of my family will discover the depth of your love.*
Christ in mouth of friend and stranger.
*Your Kingdom come on earth as in heaven.*

* * *

She rounded the corner to her home, and immediately decided to drive out to the house on Bear Lane. She wouldn't go on to Kathy's today. Her destination would be that warmly-inviting home that sat there waiting for her.

Without any doubts whatsoever, she picked up her car keys and her purse, poured a cup of coffee into her traveling mug, grabbed the banana she had forgotten earlier, and walked through the door to enter into her future—a future she knew was already planned for her. *Who could be afraid of that?*

She was still smiling as she drove into West Hope. "Hello, West Hope…Hello, church on the hill…Hello, country store… Hello, hills and trees and green grasses"

She turned onto McDade Road, and as she drew closer to Bear Lane, her heart began to beat faster. She became incredibly anxious and hoped that she would not see anyone from her family today, as she had nothing to say to them and needed to be by herself.

She saw the house and the sign that was still posted by the realtor. Thank goodness!

She pulled into the driveway and drove down and around the back so that no one would see her car parked there. She did not feel as though she were intruding. After all, she was there for a very good reason. She sat there absorbing and enjoying the surroundings for several minutes, and then without a shred of doubt as to her rights, got out of the car and walked over to the back steps and up to the sliding doors. The curtain was drawn, and she couldn't see a thing inside. It simply didn't matter. She walked back down the few steps that led to the backyard, turned, and looking toward the house, felt that she had come home.

*Oh, just look at you, so beautiful and hospitable. Do you know who I am?*

It was, as she knew it would be...It was right! Without the slightest consideration about details or arrangements, she knew that she would be moving into this house before long. Even though she had no idea why she should be moving or why this was the place for her, she was totally confident that it was in accordance with *The Plan.*

She sat on the back steps for a long time. *How blessedly quiet. There are no distractions here.*

She thought of the little wind in the devotion and knew that she would be much more likely to realize that calmness in surroundings such as this.

A beautiful cardinal began to sing from the very top of a pine tree. *How can he balance there?* From somewhere in the woods a song came in response. She was immediately drawn to the prelude of a duet. Soon the two birds were closer together and were singing the same song. These birds didn't seem to be uncomfortable with her presence, and in a little while other birds began to come closer to the back yard also. *Are those sparrows?* She realized that she really didn't know. She needed a bird book...Then she heard the glorious sound of a robin in the apple tree. The robin's solo voice became the descant to a pleasant and happy chorus unlike any other she had ever heard. *Someday I will add my songs to theirs, and we will praise God together.*

*"Joyful, joyful we adore Thee, God of Glory, Lord of Love."* The song was in her heart, but she kept it there between herself and the Lord. She would not interfere with the perfection of the song that was being offered.

Janine returned to the car, immediately called the realtor from her cell phone, and arranged to see the house with him the next day.

She was happy, but a bit of reality struck her as she returned to her house on Alamont Street. She began to assess the situation.

*First and foremost, how is John going to react to this? Will he think I've lost my mind? Well, I haven't! I'm very clear about this. I'll just have to convince him. That's all there is to it!*

There was definitely some shifting to be done with her schedule due to the fact that she would be gone all afternoon tomorrow, and John would be home on Thursday.

*I miss him so much. I need to get organized here and plan on a nice dinner for him when he comes home. He'll have so much to tell me, and it looks like I'll have a few things to say, myself.*

Just as she was reaching for the telephone to call John, it rang.

"Hello."

"Hi, Honey." It was John. How great was that?

"Well, I was just going to call you. How are things?"

"Oh, we're about as busy as we can be with the building, but it is near enough finished now so that Harry and Rhonda can complete the final touches on their own. Nice job, and I enjoyed being able to help. It's been a wonderful experience and a joy to be with the family. We all miss you, though. Really, you'll have to make sure that you come the next time."

"I know it. And I will. I think I am ready to slack off of so much work, John. I want to have time to spend with you now that you aren't an 8-to-6 guy. We have a bit of catching up to do."

She could almost feel him smiling on the phone, and she realized that she was serious about her statement.

"Great. Great! I'll tell you, you need to spend more time

outdoors. It's invigorating and healthy for our age. I feel stronger, have a tan and have enjoyed more days in a row than I can remember. Topping it all off, being with the boys was just super. We'll have to find things to do together, Janine, in some good old-fashioned country air. Maybe we can spend some time helping out at Kathy's, too."

"I think spending time in the country air is a great idea. We'll just have to talk about that when you get home. There is most likely a perfect solution just waiting to be found. In any event, I can't wait to see you. We have plans to make, you and I."

"Well, I need to get off of the phone, Janine. Harry is expecting an important call from the office. I'll see you around four o'clock on Thursday. Keep an eye on the flight schedule. Who's going to meet the plane?"

"I would love to be there, but I think it will be Greg. I'll stay at home and fuss up for you and have dinner ready. You will be starved. You never get any food on the plane anymore." Janine said.

"That's fine, Honey. You go ahead and fuss up. I like that. I love you. I'll see you soon."

"Ok. Wonderful. I love you, too. Give the boys big hugs for me and give my love to Harry and Rhonda. Bye."

"Bye."

She sat there, nodding her head affirmatively. *The Plan* was shaping up. She didn't need to steer this boat, so she might as well enjoy the ride.

# 18

# Moving On?

Well, Easter was over, and Francine had hoped that another organist/choir director would be located by now. Lawrence's mother, who lived in Florida, wasn't feeling very well, and the place that Lawrence bought down there a few years back had been sitting empty far too long.

"I'll speak to the session again this week, Lawrence. They had very few leads the last time I talked with them. The young woman that we thought would work out was truly not qualified. We *will* take a few weeks in June, no matter what. I feel sure that something good is going to come along soon. Would you like to go on ahead first? I could join you later."

Lawrence could answer that question without even thinking. "I waited all my life to find you, Fran, and I'm sure not going to spend another day without you. It's you and me from now on. Anyway, I believe you are right. I know our prayers will not go unanswered. I'll work a little harder on patience."

"Good afternoon. I'm Janine Stephens here to see Mr. Lorey."

"Yes, Mrs. Stephens. I'll let him know you are here."

He came out of a back office, short introductions ensued,

and he suggested that he drive them both, which had been her thinking all along.

He was a friendly young man, neat, and full of chit-chat. He certainly had the right personality for selling, and she enjoyed the ride with him; however, he was searching for answers without asking, and she caught on easily. She cautiously didn't divulge much of anything personal, and she certainly was not going to have him think that she would be buying a house today.

They didn't go the way of West Hope, which suited her best. She was too personally involved with that endearing community to be sharing a drive through it with a stranger.

They pulled into the driveway and walked to the front door. He led her to the entry and went to turn on the lights in the living room. She had firmly decided that if the room would not accommodate her baby grand piano, she would remove all thoughts of this house from her mind; she entered the room with the possibility that the answers to her future might not be found here.

She was astonished to find an incredibly large room—probably big enough for two baby grands! *Ok, Lord. Ok. That's a pretty impressive response to my little threat. You must have been quite amused with my little dance, there.* She caught her breath, and treaded on with the discovery process very carefully, uncomfortably realizing that she had been putting herself in charge of *His Plan.*

She didn't bother measuring anything for furniture placement. No point in that.

It was a well-kept ranch-type home with all the living area on one floor. It certainly wasn't formal like her present home, but she didn't expect it to be. It did have the oddest-looking color of green on the walls. *John is a terrific painter so that won't be a problem.* The house was eighteen years old, so the kitchen could use some upgrading, but the best part of the kitchen was the sliding doors to the upper deck.

*We could put a nice table and chairs out there and sit with our coffee and morning paper in the summer, and there would be no one to see us if we decided to go out in our pajamas. We wouldn't hurry because we would not be on a time schedule. That's what retired people were supposed to do.* She began to sing the song in her head, *"Summertime, and the livin' is easy—."*

"Mrs. Stephens…? Mrs. Stephens."

"Oh, sorry. I was just thinking of something."

"Would you like to go outside and look around?"

"No, I don't think I need to." She wouldn't tell him she had already done that yesterday.

"Would you like to go downstairs now?

"Sure."

The property was listed as having a finished basement. He led her down and waited for her. He was smiling inwardly, awaiting her response.

She stopped before getting to the bottom step. The stairway was open and she could see everything. *Good heavens!* She had not considered that the downstairs would be "finished" in such a fashion. She had envisioned a one-level house with a "basement."

"It's my understanding that the original builder wanted to have his parents move into the house and so he designed a separate 'apartment' so to speak."

It was finished with especially fine wood paneling and carpeted. The entire downstairs was one large open space with at least three sofas, chairs, tables, etc. *What possibilities it had!* He took her on across and she discovered a full bathroom, and of all things—a complete kitchen. A vastly *large* kitchen! She was bowled over.

"My goodness! I can't believe this." There were two ovens and a built-in range. Nothing fancy; it was more like an old-fashioned country kitchen. A table was in the center, and if it had extra boards, it could probably open up to seat a dozen people.

*This would be great for cooking up outdoor picnic foods, and it could all be carried outside through those sliding doors.* She was stunned and drifted off away from Mr. Lorey to the outside doors and stood there thinking of the boys. She thought of what fun it would be for them to visit, play down here, and run in and out. *We should put up a basketball net out there and hang an old-fashioned swing onto that big old tree—."*

She was totally won over at that point and had to control herself not to say something stupid, like "I'll buy it."

Instead she said she thought she should get on home, talk to her husband tomorrow who was coming in from out of town, and then call Mr. Lorey in a couple of days. He had already told her the asking price, and she thought it fair before she ever saw the downstairs. Who would have imagined?

Why had this house not been sold before now? She thought of the day she had seen the "For Sale" sign and of the other events leading up to this day, and she had the answer to the question.

# 19

# Coming Home

*There he is!* Janine was beside herself with the prospect of having her husband back home. Dinner was ready, and she had been literally pacing the floor for the past ten minutes. She saw John get out of the SUV and say something to Greg as he smilingly headed straight for the front door. They met on the portal and greeted one another in an embrace that meant so much to them both. It was sweet of Greg to wait a few moments before getting out of the vehicle to unload John's luggage. After a kiss or two, John turned to carry a few things, as well. Greg graciously excused himself to go home to his family. John and Janine went on inside and kept smiling and looking at one another.

There were questions about the days spent apart, mostly from Janine, as she wanted to be brought up to date on everything about their little family in Oklahoma. John had many little stories to tell, and touched on a few as they sat down to dinner.

With the kitchen cleaned up and the luggage moved out of the living room, they sat down with their evening coffee and talked for hours.

When Janine moved into the subject of her experiences with the devotion she had given, and the lack of interest by her women friends, she was on a mission to tell it all to John; he was so interested that they talked past midnight. He nearly sat on the edge of his seat as she told of her walk this week and her encounter with the Holy Spirit.

"That is absolutely awesome. I've heard of people having a genuine face-to-face encounter and being filled and moved by the Holy Spirit, and I do know for a fact that He exists because I have felt Him lead my life. I would love to have *that* kind of personal connection, Janine."

"It *is* totally awesome, John, as you said, and another thing... It gave me strong assurance that there is something I am being called to do. I have to tell you, I don't know what it is just yet, but remember you telling me when you lost your job that Rev. Jim said God has plans for us?"

"Yes, I do, and I have never been worried about it either. I know that everything is going to work out for the best."

"Well, I didn't have the confidence then, but I sure do now!"

"Good. Let's just relax and go into the future together, Janine. It's going to be very special for us."

"I know it."

"I have more to tell you, John. I hope you won't think I've totally lost my mind when I do."

She knew that John would not judge her too quickly, so she told him everything about the house on Bear Lane. She began with the sign in the yard and ended with her visit there with Mr. Lorey yesterday. She kept looking at John the entire time, trying to figure out what he was thinking. He just let her talk.

"Ok," he said.

"Ok, what?"

"Ok...I guess we'd better call Mr. Lorey and arrange a time for us to go back to the house to see it together."

She jumped up, plopped onto his lap, threw her arms around

him and said, "You are the best husband in the whole wide world. Thank you. Thank you. So you don't think I'm crazy?"

"Well, I wouldn't go that far," he said.

"John!"

He laughed, and hugged her tightly. "You know what? I think I like you this way—suddenly unpredictable. Yep! I like it. I'll tell you another thing; this has to have been planned out by a higher authority, because you never, on your own, would have even thought of it."

"You're right. I'll call Mr. Lorey in the morning. Now let's get ready for bed. I've been waiting to cuddle up to my warm bed buddy long enough."

❀ ❀ ❀

There were no hitches in anything that occurred the next day. Mr. Lorey was free to show them the house. They both decided it would be a good move, and legalities were put into motion. John and Janine had not discussed putting their house up for sale, but naturally Mr. Lorey was "Johnny on the Spot" in that regard. He suggested that he stop by and take a look at the house on Alamont Street soon, and perhaps he could work with them for an expedient sale and move.

John and Janine felt like two newlyweds starting out all over. It was exciting and exhilarating, and all of the potential problems, such as Janine's job at the church, did not trouble them at all. They just knew it would all work out.

Janine even typed out the words from Romans 8:29, which she had learned years ago from her grandmother. These words assumed newfound meaning for her today. : "*And we know that in all things God works for the good of those who love him who have been called according to his purpose.*"

She printed it out onto colored paper with a nice border and magnetized it onto her refrigerator. "God is all Goodness, and is so very good to me. Grandmother, you were absolutely right."

# 20

# Julia Remembers

It was raining. Julia stood in the window watching the traffic splash by. There seemed to be a chill in the air, so she took her old sweater from the hall tree, put it on, and wished she had something to think about besides being lonely.

She looked over at her half-finished crocheted doily. She had made so many of them, given most away, and was not much interested in them anymore. Her eyesight was poor, and it was quite a strain to read the directions—more trouble than it was worth!

Her optometrist had told her she needed to have her cataracts removed. She was planning to do that soon, but it wasn't easy to work out the transportation in and out of Innesport. Iola had told her that the Senior Citizen van would come to West Hope to drive her into the city. They scheduled those trips from early morning, dropped people off where they needed to go, and picked them up around five or six o'clock to take them back. That would be a long day, but she had decided, rather than ask a friend to drive her, she would call the senior organization and see what she could work out. That, of course, all had to be scheduled with the date of the procedure.

*Life is more and more complicated every day, and it's not much fun either!*

She sat down, and, as usual, began thinking of happier times. Lately, she had decided that she would choose her topic of recollection. Yesterday she spent time reminiscing about the games she would play with her brothers and sister. Her parents had named her "Juliska," a nice Hungarian name. They usually called her that at home, but when she began to associate with outsiders, the parents told everyone her name was "Julia." They did not want her to be discriminated against, although her mother would use her given name when she was speaking to her in loving terms.

She thought of the neighborhood and of the other immigrant families. They were from different countries but came together as children, learning to speak the new language, playing tag and hide-and-seek, and gathering up ball games. Every one of them was similarly poor and didn't even know it. She smiled. She had had a wonderful childhood running, laughing, and playing outside all day.

Today she would think about her own children. She missed them now that they were grown, married, and living away from her. She didn't blame them for seeking a better life, but it would be nice to have them nearer where they could be together at least for a birthday, or even a weekend here and there. But, she wouldn't think about that. Today, she was going to think of them living here in this house, making noise, chasing each other, celebrating holidays and such.

*Let's see. I'll start with Charlie's first day of school…*

Somewhere along the way, she dozed off in her chair. She often did that. When she awakened, she realized it was after Noon. She should go fix something for lunch, so that she could take her arthritis medicine and her blood pressure pill.

She pushed herself up, noticed that it was still raining, walked to the kitchen and opened a can of soup.

*Well, at least tomorrow is Sunday. I can go to Sunday school, talk with the others and catch up on how everyone is. We'll probably go to lunch afterwards. I'm not going to have soup. Seems like that's all I eat anymore. I think I'll order a piece of chicken and some mashed potatoes, and maybe join Bea in a piece of pie. Yes, that's what I'll do. Look at me. I'm shrinking away to nothing. I used to be thirty pounds heavier and taller. I didn't like the weight before, but now I think I could use some. Oh, well. That's the way it goes, I guess. You get old and what's left?*

The soup was hot. She sat down alone at her table listening to the rain, sipping the soup, and putting in the hours of another long day.

# 21

# Puddles and Obstacles

Iola looked at the rain, and decided not to go for her walk today. She usually drove over to the park and walked around and around where there was little to no traffic. She would just exercise to the tapes she bought.

The Pittsburgh Pirates baseball game would be rained out, so she would not watch television. That was one thing she did enjoy now. She used to teach music, but her hearing was weakening and the hearing aids made things sound horrible. Sometimes they would squeal and pierce her brain. She decided they were hardly worth it. She knew she was missing out on most of what was being said around her, but until she found a doctor who could get her the right hearing aids, she would have to live with what she had. There weren't many people left to talk with anyway.

She walked to the nearby post office every morning. She would greet the people present with a "good morning," and she could pick up their return response. She avoided staying any longer than politely necessary. She did not want to engage in conversations that would force her to strain to hear the other person. She simply greeted, then moved quickly on.

Her special telephone amplified the sound coming in, so she could have a telephone conversation. Otherwise, she simply turned the volume up on the TV or radio and that was that.

Harriet and she were good friends, and sometimes they did things together. Harriet was one of few who would, without being irritated, repeat things to her when necessary.

Iola would spend today planning the menu for the Woman's Association spring dinner at her home. She had hosted that event for the past few years and enjoyed it. It was several weeks away, but she was a planner and liked everything organized.

This time she would use her good china and fresh flowers on the dining room table. Maybe she'd make use of the tablecloth that her husband's Aunt Polly had left to her. It was hand-embroidered with delicate little flowers. She'd match the fresh flowers to that.

*I'd better start writing everything down and checking them off. I don't know if the tablecloth needs freshly laundered or not, so I'll check on that first thing.*

Iola came to West Hope following her marriage to Lester. He was a third-generation McCowan, and he could not fathom living anywhere else.

They had a good life together here with their children until his unfortunate death, leaving Iola alone to fend for herself and her children. Everyone thought she had managed better than most anyone else could. She taught public school, Sunday school and made very sure that her children were brought up "right." The community embraced the young widow, ready to look after the children when necessary. She often wondered if she could have done as well in any other place.

She wished today that she was doing the things she used to do. She felt that she still had wisdom, strength and vitality to be of service, but most people didn't notice. She was not thought of when it came to calling upon someone for advice or leadership roles. She, like most women her age, was looked upon as a person to respect, but used up and rarely included. So she would read, go to church, and once in a while offer a suggestion that no one took into consideration.

*Oh well. Lord knows I've tried. I guess I've had my day.*

# 22

# Rachael Ventures Out

*Well, I might as well, face it. The rain is not going to stop. I'm going to go to town anyway. I need to pick up my prescriptions and I want to get to the craft store so that I can start on those frames.*

Rachael gathered up her coat, purse, and color swatches. She picked up her umbrella from the entry hall and zipped out the front door. The car was parked beside the house, and by the time she got there, she was damp from the waist down. The rain seemed to be blowing sideways.

She sat in the car until it warmed up some, ran the windshield wipers and the defroster and headed down the drive to the road. Albert had scraped the road just before Easter and added some gravel, which was now well packed, so there wasn't a slippage problem. She eased her way down and was on her way.

She was thinking of the grocery list she had left behind. She racked her brain to remember everything she meant to pick up for the soup she was planning to make the next day. She enjoyed making every kind of soup and usually kept some on hand for Albert to have at lunchtime. One of her primary pleasures was to prepare a nice warm lunch for him. He lived nearby with his family and worked his land and Rachael's.

She would be making fresh chicken-noodle soup this time.

She turned out of the borough and crept along slowly eastward through shrouded visibility. There were very few vehicles on the road. *I probably shouldn't be here, either. I'll be careful…I'll be fine. I should be back home in less than two hours.*

The disgruntled driver of a delivery truck entered West Hope from the west. He lit another cigarette and squinted through the windshield as he was attempting to hurry along. *I hate havin' deliveries on days like this. And I hate even worse workin' on Saturdays. I should be with the guys in Lou's Bar havin' a few beers and watchin' some sports on ESPN. If I don't waste too much time, I can still stop in at Lou's and catch up.*

The driver was wearing the same black t-shirt he had slept in the night before. He needed a shave, but didn't care. Since the divorce, he was free as bird—just the way he liked it.

He went through West Hope well over the speed limit and gained even more speed on the open road. He didn't see any cars so he pressed down on the accelerator and decided this was a good place to make up some time.

Driving past The Orchard Restaurant, he looked into his rearview mirror and noticed a car had pulled out but had turned the other way. Good. *He won't be followin' me.*

He rounded a bend in the road and suddenly came upon a very slow-moving car. *What the…! I could have rammed right into the back of that car.*

He slowed down, but stayed closely behind the car. He began flashing his lights and determined that the driver was a little old lady.

*Well…just my luck!* "Hey lady! Move it or git it off the road!" he said aloud. He flashed his lights some more. She didn't seem to notice, maintaining her turtle crawl.

"Git off the road, you old biddie! You got no business bein'out if ya can't drive!"

Now he was practically on her bumper. *Maybe I'll just push her off the road.*

The lights caught Rachael's attention, and the truck seemed hazardously close. She knew the man was irritated with her slowness. She sped up a bit, but it didn't seem to satisfy the driver of the truck. She would pull off when she could. In the meantime, she'd give him a little more speed. As she moved forward from him and looked in the rearview mirror, she struck a huge puddle of water in the road. The tires she had meant to replace a month ago were worn to the point of no traction. She hydroplaned and struck the edge of the road, throwing the car out of control. It landed in a ditch on its side.

The truck driver uttered every word he had learned on the streets, slammed on his brakes, and came to an immediate stop.

*Now look what you've done! And it's all your own fault! People like you need to know that you're too old to drive. You're a hazard to the road and a hindrance to people like me who have a job to do and a real purpose in life.*

He put his "Budweiser" ball cap on and got out of the truck. The rain was still hammering down, and he was soaked instantly as he walked over to the car. The wheels were still spinning. He tried to open the door but it was locked. The woman was either dead or unconscious, and the motor was still running.

His instincts guided him to get something to pry the door open and turn off the engine before the car burst into flames.

He ran through the rain to his truck and grabbed a small crowbar just as a car came from the other direction. The driver of the car rolled down his car window and asked what happened.

The man answered, "It's an old woman locked in there. I'm going to try to pry the door open and turn off that engine. Do you have a phone?"

"Yes. I'll call 9–1-1."

The truck driver, imitating a noble and blameless person said "Thanks," and ran to the car. He pried open the door without having to break in through the window and turned off the engine.

He did not want to touch the bloody woman who was slumped strangely sideways. She might be dead. She looked dead for sure. Without remorse or an iota of guilt, he conjured up the courage to touch her neck—and felt a pulse. He jerked backwards as the sensation sent a weird shock throughout his body, and he came close to vomiting. He had to get away from the sickening scene.

The man from the car ran toward the scene and asked if he could do anything, and the valiant "savior of the road" quickly collected his behavior and said it would be best if they just waited for the Emergency Car. He walked over to the gathering crowd, enhancing his role and enlarging his ego by answering questions and asking everyone to try to stay calm. He was reveling in being the hero of the day. In fact he wanted to tell all about it to anyone who would listen.

When the police arrived and questioned him, no one could dispute anything he had to say…except the unconscious old lady. But by now he was so convinced of the magnitude of himself that he was positive she would be grateful for all of his help. *She should be grateful! I'm sick and tired of havin' to put up with stupid people on the roads!*

He repeated to the questioning officer that the lady was driving much too fast for the road conditions.

"I blinked my lights at 'er hopin' she'd slow down, but she didn't pay no attention. It's sad to see the fix she's got 'erself in."

The officer wrote down the necessary information on the truck driver and told him he could get on his way. "Just be available for further questioning if necessary, Mr. Tredway," he said.

"Of course. I sure will. If I can be of any help at all, please let me know."

"Thank you. You've already been a substantial help in this tragic situation. The Emergency Car is on its way."

The truck driver, proud of the way he had smoothed-talked his way out of trouble, got back into his truck and gingerly pulled away. He hoped he would never see any of those people again in his life.

❀ ❀ ❀

Marvin and Marcia Severight, owners of the apple orchard and friends of Rachael, drove up to the accident. They rushed out of their car, recognizing the car in the accident as Rachael's. Marcia spoke with the police officer and found that her condition was grave. She was granted permission to see the victim, but even with her nurse's training she was helpless to do anything. Thankfully the E-car and medical team arrived a few minutes later. Rachael remained unconscious as she was prepped and moved into the medical van.

Marvin held Marcia's hand as they stood in the rain listening to the siren fading into the distance taking their friend to City Hospital. She told the officers she would contact family members. They went to Albert's first, who left immediately for the hospital. Marcia assured him that she would call his sister, Celeste, the pastor, and others.

❧ ❧ ❧

When they arrived at the manse, Pastor Dan met them on the porch.

"Come in. Come in. It's nasty out there."

Water rapidly dripped from their bodies. They hesitated at the invitation, but upon Dan's insistence, they did go in as far as the kitchen. His wife Patricia was there as well. Few pleasantries were exchanged, as it was obvious that the Severights were upset. Chairs were pulled from the table, and Pat immediately put on a pot of coffee.

"What is it?"

"It's Rachael Wimbler. She's been in a terrible automobile accident. We were there minutes after it happened. She was still unconscious when the EMTs were moving her. The ambulance took her to City Hospital."

"Oh, dear. I'll go right away. Why don't you stay and have a cup of coffee with Pat? You could make a phone call from here and start the prayer chain going if you want to."

Pat handed her the telephone and the phone book as Marcia nodded her head. Before leaving, Pastor Daniel took their hands and led them in prayer, then picked up his jacket, his Bible, and the keys to the car.

Marcia called Rachael's daughter, Celeste, who didn't stay on the telephone any longer than necessary. She would immediately arrange to leave the office as soon as possible. Continuing with her calling, her heart pounding, and silently praying, she was appreciative of the warm cup of coffee. So was Marvin. Pat was a beautiful and gracious lady, and everyone loved her as much as they loved their precious pastor. They could count on her for anything at any time.

They quickly left to go home and get into some dry clothes; however, Marcia would not be able to sit still. She would have to freshen up and get to the hospital as soon as she could. She was number one on the phone list. She was also "A-Number One" as a caring individual.

# 23

# A Praying People

The Community of Faith was on its knees when Marcia finally changed into dry clothes and headed out for the hospital. She assured Marvin time and time again that she would be careful, and she was. She found Celeste and Albert in the Emergency waiting room.

Albert was on his feet. "Marcia, thanks for coming. Pastor Dan is here, also. He stepped out for a moment to see if he can get some information. We've heard nothing so far."

"I had to come," she said.

Celeste was so worried that she hardly noticed Marcia enter until Marcia sat down beside her and took her hand.

"Oh, Marcia, I'm so worried."

"I know. I know. Let's not jump to conclusions. There are many prayers being lifted up for Rachael. She's in the Lord's hands, and He will carry her through this."

"Family of Mrs. Wimbler?" the doctor asked. Albert stood.

"Yes, doctor, I'm her son, Albert, and this is my sister, Celeste. Our pastor is here with us. This is Mrs. Severight, a friend."

"Mrs. Wimbler is conscious but highly sedated. We are still checking her over for injuries. We're getting pretty good vitals, but she has broken bones—primarily in her feet, and we suspect some internal injuries. We want to have her transported to Allegheny Hospital as soon as possible.

"Is she stable enough to move?" asked Albert.

"She is, and we believe that her injuries warrant it."

Albert looked at the rest, and it seemed to be the consensus that the move was the thing to do. Who could question the doctor in this instance?

"Doctor, is she going to be all right?" asked Celeste.

"I really cannot answer that right now, I'm sorry to say. She will receive the best of care, I do know that. If you are a praying people, it wouldn't hurt."

"There are a lot of people praying for Rachael," said Rev. Dan.

"I encourage you all to keep it up," said the doctor.

"Believe me, we will," said Marcia.

"I'll call Tavia, and let her know that I'm going to drive on up to Pittsburgh. Celeste, do you want to come with me?" asked Albert.

"I think I'll wait here for Erica. She's on her way, and I know she'll want to go, too. We'll be right along."

"Albert, I would like to go with you, if that's ok with you," said Pastor Dan.

"Thanks very much. I'd appreciate it."

Albert went to call his wife, and Marcia said she'd wait there for Celeste's daughter to arrive.

Pastor Dan encouraged Albert to let him drive, and Albert agreed.

"Can we see mother?" asked Celeste.

"You and your brother and the pastor can come in for just a minute."

The three left the room with the doctor. When they returned,

Celeste and Albert were both in tears. Marcia understood and embraced them both.

"They are going to prepare her for the move. It's still raining, so they've decided to use an emergency car instead of the helicopter. The doctor said that they have a great team of trained personnel to go along with her, and we are satisfied that it is going to be a safe ride for Mom. They will get there in no time, so we'll be leaving right away," Albert said.

Just then, Erica came and was briefed by her mother, Celeste. The four left quickly in two separate cars.

Standing alone in the empty waiting room, Marcia began to tremble. The tears could not be held back any longer. She sat down and did what she did best. She called upon the Lord for His comfort, strength and assurance. The Lord answered her prayers, and she was finally able to call Marvin. She relayed to him information about Rachael and said she'd be coming home right away. Marvin said he had fixed a little something for them to eat.

*What a dear he is,* she thought. *I probably will be hungry. I don't know. I don't feel much of anything right now but concern for Rachael.*

She did welcome the smell of food when she entered the house, and the best hug in the whole world. She stayed with the hug for quite some time.

They sat down together, ate the food, talked, and both settled into an exhausted sleep.

# 24

# Morning Has Broken

Julia, Francine, Paula, and the other members of the church awoke on Sunday morning to a beautiful day of pastels as the sun's rays peaked through soft clouds of pinks and purples. Each welcomed the end of the storm and prayed that the feeling of hope brought forth by the clearing weather was the signal of answered prayers.

Few stayed at home that day, for it was surely a day meant for gathering together and praying.

Pastor Dan had arrived at home only an hour before morning prayers commenced. Albert went on home to change clothes, and the others stayed behind to be near Rachael.

Every person who saw the pastor asked the question, "Is Rachael all right?"

He answered, "As well as can be at this point. Keep praying."

The ladies were early to Sunday school. They immediately started talking about the accident and things they might do to be of help to the family. They would not be driving into Pittsburgh to visit, but there would be other things to do. They were all very concerned.

"Rachael has had so many problems," said Julia.

"She sure has. How she ever came through that heart attack is beyond me," said Bea.

"Well, Rachael always said that the church prayed her well. You remember how she used to say that?" Julia said.

"I remember. And then there was the time she had to have surgery on her stomach. She was laid up for quite a long time then," Anne said. "But she bounced back, and she will again. We must not give up hope."

"No, we won't. We will pray her well again. Rachael always said she doesn't know why she is still here. Well, I know why. God answers our prayers, that's why. And He knows that she is such a shining light in our world here. We just can't do without her," said Bea.

They all agreed. Little was done about the lesson that morning, but just being there with one another meant everything. They had prayer and signed the card that Harriet had for them. Their Sunday school teacher always came prepared.

They dismissed, feeling a little better just having been together. They always did.

"Great God, we worship You in praise and thanksgiving, and we seek Your blessings upon all who are gathered here and upon those who could not come today." Pastor Dan continued his prayer, which was lengthy and heartfelt, as he called upon the Lord to lead the church and the flock to do His will in the Kingdom.

The church joined in his sincerity, and when Pastor Dan implored the Lord for Rachael's recovery, they were uttering the plea deep within their souls. They knew that God had pulled Rachael through incredibly serious illnesses, and they believed their prayers would be answered once again.

The scripture was read:

*I lift up mine eyes unto the hills, from whence cometh my help.*
*My help cometh from the Lord, which made heaven and earth...*
*The Lord is thy keeper: the Lord is thy shade upon thy right hand...*
*The Lord shall preserve thy going out and thy coming in from this time forth, and even for evermore.*

It was from *Psalm* 121, which was a major theme for this church on a hill in West Hope, and it was resonating in every ear and in every heart with promise through faith today.

The sermon did not fall on deaf ears that morning. Pastor Dan must have revised his sermon during the night, because it spoke directly to the situation that existed within the Body of Christ that morning. It was spiritually uplifting and comforting to all. The congregation knew from "whence her help would come." Who could ask for anything more?

❧ ❧ ❧

There were people in church that morning who rarely attended. A few of Rachael's friends were there because they felt drawn to be with the gathering on the hill.

Hayden and Elda Carter exited the church and walked down the hill toward their home in the center of the borough. They owned the General Store and lived in the house beside the store. They were friends with Rachael and many of the other church members. They usually attended the African Methodist Episcopal Church (AME), located in a nearby community, but today was just different. They wanted to be with Rachael's friends and join with them in prayer, and they were glad that they had been there.

Many of the locals enjoyed gathering at the Carters' on weekday mornings, not always to shop, but surely to chat, pick up the morning paper, sometimes share a story or seek advice. Ms.

Elda always had a big pot of coffee brewing for the neighbors, and sometimes on Wednesdays and Saturdays there were cinnamon rolls and hot breads to purchase. The aroma of fresh-baking bread in the small community was something local family members would remember when they moved away, and they would tell others who could only dream of such a wonderful thing.

One had to be up early to bring home a fresh-baked loaf of Ms. Elda's bread. She liked to bake, and no one knew what she might enjoy baking at any time, whether it be rye, raisin, cheese, or the most excellent plain white in the country. It didn't matter! If she baked it, they would buy it, for they knew it would be the best.

"That was nice," Elda said.

"Yessiree! Rev. Daniel is a good man and certainly is in touch with the Lord. His sermon and prayers were just what we all needed to hear. I'm sure glad we went there today."

"I am, too. Tomorrow I'm going to bake up something for the family. I hope they will be able to come home to rest. These will be difficult days for Albert and Celeste and the children."

"That's good, Elda. You always think of the perfect thing to do."

"Speaking of food, I'd best get busy with today's meal. Leeanne and Tommy will be coming in soon. She sure seems to like that boy! I do, too."

"Yessiree! He's just fine. You said you put on a pork roast, didn't you?"

"Well, that's what Leeanne asked for, so that's what we'll have."

They were home, which was a very large old house in the Victorian fashion, beautifully maintained and very impressive to all that passed. Hayden enjoyed his carpentering skills, and had made some mighty fine improvements on the old structure; of course Elda had a God-given talent for transforming any room, any porch, anything at all, into something beautiful.

"I'll go change into something else, Elda. Let me know when you are ready for me to help you peel potatoes and set the table."

"I will, Hayden. I'm going to put on my apron and check the roast first."

"Mmm, mmm! I can smell it! What time are we eating?"

"Around one-thirty, so we'd better keep moving."

"No trouble for me. I'm hungry—and even hungrier smelling that meat."

# 25

# Decisions, Decisions

The Monday morning newspaper arrived, and many read the article about Saturday's accident, including Greg Lang. Kathy was almost ready to leave for school with the girls, when Greg uttered, "Oh, of course!"

"Of course, what?" Asked Kathy.

"Old Virgil has done it again."

"Virgil? What's he done now?"

"Well, says here that he was the first on the scene of a road accident and that he probably saved the victim's life."

"That's good, isn't it? Why are you so disturbed over that?"

"You know that former brother-in-law of mine has never cared about helping anyone. The only one he cares about is himself. He has pulled the wool over everyone's eyes and painted himself as a fine individual once again."

"Now, Greg. We haven't seen him for quite some time. Maybe he's changed."

"He hasn't changed. He'll never change. I wouldn't be surprised if he was the one who caused the accident. He is the slickest talker I've ever known, and that slick talker has nearly ruined the lives of my sister and their children."

"What's the paper say?"

"It says that a woman was travelling too fast in the rain and her car slid off of the road and turned over. Her condition is critical, and she was moved to Allegheny Hospital. Virgil came upon the scene, ran to her car, pried open the door and turned off the engine. The car could have ignited otherwise. Poor old Virgil. There he was in the pouring rain, sacrificing himself to save a perfect stranger.

"I'm sorry, Kathy, but I know that miserable, worthless human being too well to believe this story. I don't know how he does it, but somehow he does. Just seeing his name in print is going to ruin my day."

"I know how you feel, Greg. He almost destroyed your sister's life. But she's doing better these days now that he's out of the picture. Try not to think about him anymore."

He folded up the newspaper and said he would do that, but after Kathy and the girls left, he had to read it one more time.

*I hope Amy doesn't see the paper today. She needs to just forget that louse.* He picked up his keys and left for work.

---

Janine hung up the telephone and went outside to find John. He was in the garage.

"Hi, Honey," she said. "What are you doing?"

"I'm trying to decide what I should take along to the new house. Everything, I suppose. I may actually find use for some of these tools out there in the country, especially the trimmers and such. Something on your mind?" he asked.

"Are you kidding? I have so much on my mind, I can hardly sort it all out. But I want to tell you that Mr. Lorey just called, and he would like to drop by tomorrow to go through our house, if it's ok with us. I told him I'd call him back. What do you think?"

"Fine with me. I sure don't want to put out a sign of my own and go through all the worry of trying to show the house, search the Court House records—all the things that our Mr. Lorey could do for us. So if you want to, just go ahead and have him come over. Maybe he can give us some indication of what kind of price we might get for this house."

"Right. Ok, I'll call him. I'm going in to talk with Pastor Jim today about my job there at Center Church. What do you think I should say?"

"I thought you decided that you could continue with the work there, Janine. Have you changed your mind?"

"I don't know. At first, I thought I'd be able to commute back and forth, and I still think I can do that, but should I? That's the question of the day."

"Well, do you have to decide now?"

"No. Not really. I'll just let Jim know that we are moving and about how happy we are. When he hears of the circumstances, he will be overjoyed for us, I know."

"Sounds good. I'll be busy out here for a while. Go ahead and do what you need to do. I'll see you later."

"Ok…John?"

"Yes?"

"Are you still sure that we are doing the right thing?"

"Absolutely!' he said.

Janine grinned from ear to ear. "Me, too!" she said.

She gave John an air kiss because he was pretty greasy-looking, and went on her way.

❀ ❀ ❀

"Hi, Connie. Isn't this a beautiful day?" said Janine.

"It most certainly is. We've had quite enough rain. I'm ready for sunshine and flowers myself."

"Well, that's just what you're going to get. Enjoy. Is Pastor Jim in?"

"He's in his office. I think he's expecting you. Just a minute, I'll buzz him."

Janine looked around at the familiar surroundings. There were pictures on the wall out in the hallway of past ministers, many of whom she had known and loved. This church meant a lot to her.

"Janine, you can go on in."

"Thanks, Connie."

She had been through this door many times. She and Pastor Jim met often to discuss the worship services and her role as music leader.

"Good morning!" said Janine.

"Good morning to you. Come, sit down."

"I appreciate you seeing me today. I know this is the day you will be meeting with the ministerial group, so I won't keep you long."

"That's fine, Janine. I have lots of time. What's up?"

She wanted to be brief, but her story about her encounter with the Holy Spirit and ultimately deciding to move into another house couldn't be shortened. As she was describing the morning she had awakened with so many questions and subsequently the walk, Jim was on the edge of his seat as excited as she was.

"…And, Jim, after walking through that house, it felt so right. I just knew. I had no doubts whatsoever. It was so wonderful, and knowing that the Lord Himself was leading me, gave me such a marvelous feeling of being blessed.

"Oh, I can't put it into the right words. I'm sure, though, that you realize what I'm trying to tell you. You were the one who told me that the Holy Spirit was drawing me into something when I talked with you before."

"Janine, I am so happy for you! This is truly the work of the Lord. I believe that many are blessed, but few comprehend it. It is a positive advantage that you recognize this."

"Well, thanks to you! You opened up my mind to an awareness of what was happening to me. Thanks so much, Jim. I sure wouldn't want to have missed this for the world.

"We'll be moving soon, more than likely. I think I'm supposed to be doing something over in the West Hope area, but I sure don't know what."

"Don't worry about a thing. If it's the Lord's will—and it sure sounds like it—it will all work out."

"Thank you, Jim. I'm going to stay with Center Church until I know that I should leave here. Maybe I won't have to, but if so, you will have lots of notice. Ok?"

"Whatever will be, will be, Janine. Let's not even try crossing that bridge right now."

They talked about Janine and her family and the prospects for a different kind of life for her. Neither knew just what that was going to be. It didn't matter to either of them. She was ready. Janine felt fortified and excited when she left the office. She was thankful that she could talk with Pastor Jim and her beloved John. Who else would understand?

*Well, I'd better wait and see where all of this ends up. God certainly has a plan, but knowing His timing, it could take years.*

# 26

# Two by Two

Mr. Lorey came the next day. With the house's condition and potential marketability, he felt that it would sell quickly.

"You'll need to have the house appraised. I could recommend someone to do that." Mr. Lorey said.

The Stephens agreed, and from then on it was unbelievable how everything seemed to fall into place.

First, the purchase of the house on Bear Lane moved right along. The price was agreeable, the owner was happy, and papers were being drawn up. Secondly, Mr. Lorey was handling everything that needed to be done concerning the sale of the Stephens' house. There would be no problems as far as anyone could see, except for the immediate problem of having to tell the children!

"John, this is going to be the hard part. They will be certain that their parents have lost their minds."

"I know. Have you thought about how to approach this?"

"Every time I think about it, I push it aside and think of something else. I thought of going to Kathy's for lunch and talking with her alone. She might be happy to have us move nearer to her. That may be presumptuous, though. In this day and age families do live apart, and they adjust, and possibly like it better."

"Maybe." John said.

They both sat there, staring into space for what seemed like a long time.

"How about if we set up a tour of the house with Mr. Lorey and have Kathy and Deb both go with us?" John suggested.

"Hmm, I don't know.... John, I truly hate having to face all of this. If we could just go ahead without having to stir up the family, wouldn't that be great?"

"Well, that's not going to happen. We have a family, and a close one at that. We don't want to hold back from one another. We always told the kids that, didn't we?"

"Yes, that's true. You're right. If they see the house, they just might understand. Of course, I don't expect them to feel the same as we do. Nevertheless, let's try it that way. Things are moving so quickly, I guess we shouldn't put it off," said Janine.

❀ ❀ ❀

"Deb, did Mother call you?"

"Yes. She invited me to your house for lunch on Saturday. I said I could come. Is that ok with you?"

"Yes. I'm happy about that. What else did Mom say?"

"Nothing much, really. Is something wrong?"

"I don't know," Kathy hesitated. "She seemed to have something on her mind, but didn't want to tell me."

"Well, she didn't tell me, either."

"It's probably my imagination. I'll see you around eleven thirty on Saturday. Ok?"

"I'll be there," said Deborah.

# 27
# Apple Blossom Time

Marcia was keeping busy waiting for Marvin to come in from inspecting the apple trees. During the spring he was always motivated to walk all over his beloved orchard, and enjoy the thrill of new life. The winter pruning was completed just in time for the spring season, and the workers had done an excellent job of it. Some of his friends were retiring from their life-long careers. Not Marvin! He loved what he was doing and would continue it as long as the good Lord allowed.

He came in the kitchen door, all smiles. Marcia was occupied with something.

"Did you enjoy yourself?" Marcia asked.

"I sure did. Things are looking pretty good. I saw a few blossoms—our favorite time of the year. And guess what?"

"What?"

"I'm still singin' the song."

"Did you sing it today when you were walking?" Marcia asked.

"Yes, I did." He started into singing, *"I'll be with you in apple blossom time."*

She joined in, adding her alto harmony. They had been singing that song for forty-some years now, and had never tired of it.

They continued into conversation about the trees and their

plans for a new grove this year while Marcia set some lunch out on the kitchen table.

"We'll be getting busy again from now until Christmas, but I'm not complaining. I married you for the apples."

He grinned. She always said that.

"Remember at Easter when the boys were talking about coming again for the summer? They love being here and working the orchard. The cycle continues, doesn't it?" Marvin said.

"Looks that way," she said.

"When Carl came home from college and decided to stay with the orchard, we were so happy. And now, his son, Jason, will be going off to college this year. Do you think he'll come back and want to build a house here like his dad did?"

"Jason has worked here since he was 8 or 9-years old. He'll be back," she said.

"I hope you're right.

"In the meantime, Jason will still be here for a while before he goes off to college. Luke and Joshua will be coming from New Jersey, as they said, and staying here with us. I do love having them around and cooking for them. It's going to be a good year."

"It is. With Carl and Jason and Luke and Joshua, we'll be right on top of things. How about Amanda? She's bound and determined to get right in there with them."

"She's only eleven, Marvin. She thinks she's smart enough and strong enough, too. She may be right, but I say give it another year. Carl thinks she'll be very happy working in the barn selling later in the season. It will be a good start for her."

"It's such a blessing seeing the children following 'in the footsteps' so to speak. Dad would be thrilled with the progress we've made over the years. It's not the big business it could be,

Marcia, but I think we agree that it's the right size for all of us today. Who knows what the future holds for our children? Anyway, that's for them to decide. In the meantime, let's be thankful for what we have."

"I agree."

They finished dinner discussing the children, apples, and hope for the days ahead.

"Oh, I almost forgot! I have some good news," Marcia said. "Rachael seems to be improving. She has an awfully long way to go before she will be up and about, but she *is* showing signs of improving.

"She has so many broken bones in her feet, though, that the doctors wonder if she will ever walk again. Poor Rachael. That is just so sad. But I know she will overcome anything. If she can't walk, she'll do what she can as she sits. She will never throw in the towel."

"When is she coming back from Allegheny?"

"There's no word on that right now. Thankfully, she had minimal internal injuries, but she will have surgeries on her feet, leg, and I don't know what else. Maybe we can go see her sometime soon."

"Sure. When do you want to go?"

"Well, maybe Friday. How's that sound?"

"'Sounds fine. Let's plan on it."

# 28

# From Scene to Shining Scene

Marcia and Marvin drove through the countryside that was more than familiar to the two of them. They smiled when they saw a few apple blossoms on the trees near the farmhouses. The forsythia and the daffodils had given way to yellow and red tulips. Purple azaleas were in bloom, which were always the first of such bushes to show their color, and the softly-beautiful, yellow irises were slow dancing in the gentle breeze.

"Whenever I see the irises, I think of Bea Roberts. She has them lining her driveway. She said she would be thinning them this year and will give us some if we want them. Have you ever smelled the yellow iris, Marvin?"

"I'm not sure"

"You would remember if you did. It has a subtle spice fragrance. There is nothing quite like it. I remember how surprised I was. It was not like a flower, and yet, just as pleasurable. The fragrance would be suitable for a man's cologne, I believe. I'm not sure if all irises have the same scent as the yellow. Anyway, we'll have some of our own, thanks to Bea, and we can enjoy them over and over again. They bloom every year by May 1st, she said, and in some years, again before the end of summer. Maybe we'll stop by Bea's this week and just take a sniff. I want to be there when you do."

"Isn't that nice of her? How old is she, Marcia?"

"I think she's 82, or maybe 83."

"Wow! She sure gets along well for that age. I see her cutting her grass and sometimes even on her knees digging around her flowers. She has some unusual flowers and some for every season, it seems."

"Well, she's a trooper and determined to not let anything get her down. She also seems to have a terrific wit. I'd like to know her a little better, but I haven't had much opportunity."

Soon they were on the Interstate and moving right along. Marcia was glad that Marvin was driving into Pittsburgh, because she was not all that comfortable driving alongside, in front of, or behind aggressive drivers. She enjoyed her country roads and rarely, if ever, would venture into Pittsburgh alone.

She did her shopping in Innesport most of the time. There were a couple of malls there, lots of specialty stores, and anything she would want or need. She had been driving those roads since before the malls had ever been built, and she had been acclimated to it all in a gradual way.

They came to the hill, known as Mt. Washington, which completely shielded from view that which was behind it. The only indication that they were nearing the city was the increase in the traffic that was now merging into two lanes. They entered the long, lighted tunnel, and she knew that as soon as they exited they would see a most spectacular sight; she, like many others, anticipated the moment with excitement. The amazing "Golden Triangle" of Pittsburgh with its tall, shiny buildings would suddenly be presented to the traveler on the other side of the hill. Today, with the sun shining brilliantly on the glistening buildings and the bridges, she was once again greatly impressed.

Two rivers converged at the point of the triangle to form the Beautiful Ohio. As they crossed the Monongahela River, they could see many bridges filled with cars moving toward the city over the busy waterways augmenting the energy of the city.

They had planned to enter Pittsburgh around 10:00 a.m. to avoid the rush-hour traffic, and it worked out well. In no time they were at the hospital, taking the elevator to the floor where Rachael could be found.

They quietly peeked around the door—she might be sleeping.

"Hello!" Rachael said.

"Rachael! We thought you might be resting," Marcia said.

"Are you kidding? No one rests in a hospital. Come in. Come in. It's nice to see familiar faces."

She was in bed with her legs wrapped and resting on pillows.

"They did a little repair work on my right leg the other day. Thankfully, it wasn't a really bad break, and I shouldn't have much trouble with it."

"That's so good to hear, Rachael. How are you feeling?"

"I don't know. I can't get up at all. I have to keep my feet elevated. Apparently that's where the trouble is. I don't know just when we'll find out exactly what is broken and what can or cannot be fixed. I am worn out trying to scoot myself into some kind of comfortable position right now."

"Oh, dear," Marcia said.

Marvin sat down in a chair by the window.

Rachael told Marcia that she was totally unaware of anything about the accident, which Marcia said was a blessing. Marcia went on to tell Rachael that she and Marvin had arrived on the scene shortly after the accident occurred, and it had been a very scary situation.

Rachael said, "I suppose I should be glad to be alive. Once again, Marcia, I cannot understand why the good Lord wants me here. I've had many opportunities to leave this world, and it seemed like it would be a good thing if it happened, and yet, He doesn't take me."

"Well, that's not for us to question, is it?"

"I think it is! And I do! If there is something He wants me to do here, He sure is not giving me much to do *it* with. I *do* question it! I truly think it would be better if I just went on. I actually haven't been of much use for years."

"Rachael! I can't believe my ears. Please. Think of the wonderful works you have done, even after the last time you had that stomach surgery. There is definitely a lot you can and will do with your talent and creativity. You'll figure it all out with God's help."

"Marcia, I don't want to sound ungrateful, and I'm trying to accept the hand that has been dealt to me, but this time, I wonder."

Marcia was feeling so sorry for Rachael who was always the one to lift everyone else's spirits. She was cheerful by nature, and always looked at tasks as challenges to be conquered.

Rachael loved to read, so Marcia had brought her a couple of books. One book was a funny but true story about the history of the MacKintosh Clan, of which Marvin was a descendent. She had picked it up from her coffee table this morning in order to hopefully give Rachael a good laugh about the carryings on of those Scots.

The other was a day-by-day devotional, which she hoped would help her through these difficult days.

They stayed until the physical therapist came to see her. Rachael had said that they would probably keep her there at Allegheny until they had her on her feet, or at least had done all they could for her. It could possibly be a few weeks.

They said their "good-byes," and reluctantly left her. She did give Marcia and Marvin one of her wonderful smiles, which they knew was meant to lift their spirits. That was Rachael for you. She would be the one. It was her calling. Even as she lay completely incapacitated, she would want to help someone else. Marcia was touched by her beautiful gesture, and knew why God had not taken her yet.

*We must all try to help her along. She will need our support.*

# 29
# Opening Doors

They drove out Bear Lane and resisted the temptation to stop at the "new" house. They couldn't get in anyway. Mr. Lorey would have to be there to open the doors. Janine was nervous. John gave no indication whatsoever of anything.

She said, "John, we certainly have been giving the girls things to think about lately, haven't we? I can't remember when there was a time like this when we felt the need to talk everything over with them. We've been going to *them* with discussions of changes instead of them coming to *us* as always."

"We're not just talking…we're sharing. That's what families do."

"I know, but it's different somehow."

"The tides flow in and the tides flow out," he said.

"What's that supposed to mean?"

"Ok. How about this, 'What goes around comes around.'"

She looked at him glaringly. Where is his sensitivity? "John, John, John. Give me some encouragement here. I'm a wreck."

"I *am* giving you encouragement," he said.

"No you're not. You are throwing adages or proverbs at me. I need for you to say something like, 'Janine, dear, everything's going to be just fine.'"

"Ha!" He actually laughed and thought that was funny. She did not!

"John!"

"Ok. Janine. Look. You are getting yourself all shook up before you have a reason to. Let's just flow with the tide and see where it's going first."

"That's easy for you to say, 'Mr. Solid-as-a-Rock.' I'm feeling more like squishy mud."

"Well, you'd better get out of the sinkhole. We're here."

She took in several deep breaths in an attempt to collect herself, straightened her body, brushed her skirt, and got out of the car. As usual, there was Prince. It felt especially good today to give him hugs, and he returned the warm gestures with lots of sloppy, slurpy licks. Janine smiled.

Karen and Meghan were on the porch waving.

"Hi, Grandma! Hi, Granddad!"

"Hi, girls!" they responded.

*Uh, oh!* They didn't consider that the girls would be home. *Why not? It's Saturday, of course! What could they expect?* Janine was wondering if this day could possibly turn out all right.

"John. John…Wait! Don't go in yet. Listen! We can't take the little girls along. We need to have Deb and Kathy alone, don't you think?"

"Well, all we have to do is tell Deborah and Kathy that we want to take them somewhere and that we won't be long. The girls are old enough to leave behind, if that's what you want to do."

Janine took in another deep breath. "Ok. That's what we'll do." They hurried on up the path to the house.

"Hey! You're here. Come on into the kitchen. How about some coffee?" asked Kathy.

"Mmmm. Perfect!" responded Janine as she hugged her.

Deborah was already in the kitchen, and she hugged them both. They proceeded to sit down at the kitchen table.

Small talk ensued, as always when *real* questions are not being asked.

"It's a beautiful day, isn't it?" asked Deborah.

"It sure is," answered Janine. *Is it really? I hadn't noticed.*

"Here's your coffee," said Kathy.

"Wonderful!" said John. He had decided not to open up the conversation about the house. He did not want Janine to feel caught off guard, so he left it up to her to initiate the topic.

"So…what have you two been up to?" asked Kathy.

"Oh, not much. Things have eased up since Easter, and it's good to have your Dad home. He's been cleaning up the garage."

"Spring cleaning, I suppose." Deborah said.

"Sort of." He responded.

Janine drank her coffee.

Kathy went over to the refrigerator and opened the door. John and Janine could not see her behind the open door. She used her hidden circumstances to glare at Deborah as if to say, "Now what?"

Deborah shrugged. "We have everything ready for lunch," she said. "What do you say? Are you hungry?"

"Yes. Let's go ahead and eat. Are the girls joining us?" Janine asked.

"No, they are going to walk Prince over the hill behind us to the stables. Meghan can hardly stay away from there. They had made arrangements with the neighbors to be there today, and I gave them an early lunch. I'm sorry to disappoint you. I know you'd love to have them join us, but we'll do this again real soon."

John responded quickly, "Hey! That's fine. They'll have fun."

*Well, there you are! That's settled, and I had nothing to do with it.* Janine looked at John, who was snickering, as only she would detect.

*Ha! Look at him. He is always so confident. It's a good thing because at this moment I could use a little myself.*

Just then the girls came in dressed for the hike and eager to go.

"Mom, we're ready to go," they said.

"That's fine, girls. I've already told Grandma and Granddad that you would be leaving. Be very careful and be home by two o'clock as we planned."

"Ok. We'll see you later," Karen said to all of them.

"Have fun," John said.

They were gone, lickity-split. They were talking with excitement as they went out the back door with Prince bounding along.

"Well, here we are. Let's say grace and enjoy," said Kathy. "Dad would you?"

"Lord, be our guest at this table. We thank You for Your many blessings. Bless this family, this home, and the food we are about to partake. In the name of our Lord, Jesus, we pray. Amen."

"Ummm, mmmm. This soup is delicious. Did you make it, Kathy?"

"Well, it wouldn't be that good if I had made it. Greg made it for us, of course."

It was a delicious bowl of Manhattan clam chowder. Janine preferred the red from the creamy, New England style. She didn't think she would be able to eat, but the soup changed all of that.

"John, just taste this bread. My goodness, it's delicious. Did Greg bake this?"

"I got the bread this morning over in West Hope. I had to

be early to get it. You would not believe the rush to get to the little store there on Saturdays. That's the day that the owner's wife bakes bread—Saturday and Wednesday. But they tell me you can't be sure what kind of breads she might bake. It doesn't matter. Everything she bakes is delicious. I'm really glad, though, that she made this whole wheat for today. Isn't it great?"

"Well, how about that? I've wanted to go into that little store. What else do they have?" asked Janine.

"Everything! You wouldn't believe it. It's so nice and clean, and if we need anything we can usually find it there instead of driving on into town."

"Well, well," said Janine. She and John looked at each other. They each knew what the other was thinking.

"The other day, I needed a light bulb and bought it there… and get this! Once, I just had to have yellow thread. I thought 'No way would they have that.' But they did. They have what's necessary in the grocery line, even a deli, and hand-dipped ice cream cones!"

"Isn't that just great. I never dreamed…" said Janine.

"I've found lots of surprises around here," said Kathy.

"We have, too," said John.

"What does that mean?" asked Deborah.

"Well, you'll see," he said.

Janine was sitting there wishing he had not said that. The girls were looking at them with questioning eyes, and she did not know how to proceed.

"Ok, now. What's all of this about?" asked Kathy.

"Really! Why don't we get on with it? Is everything ok?" Deb asked.

"Everything's fine." John decided that he needed to take the bull by the horns and immediately get this show on the road.

"I'll tell you what. Come with us. We have something to show you. Can the girls get in the house if they get back before we do?"

"Yes, they can, but where are we going? How long will we be?"

"Oh, not very far. We will most likely be back before two o'clock. Is everyone finished eating?" John asked.

"We are now!" said Deb.

"I'll turn off the stove and wrap the bread. I'll only be a minute," said Kathy. She hustled, wondering what in the world they were going to do. Deborah helped her as Janine went into the powder room to freshen up and collect herself.

Soon they were all leaving in John's car. Deborah and Kathy sat in the second seat. Kathy reached over and grabbed Deb's hand and squeezed it so hard it hurt. They were sure of nothing! They just kept looking at one another, full of questions.

In no time they were pulling into someone's driveway. *What's this?*

There was another car there, and a nice-looking young man got out of it. John and Janine told the girls to come on, and they, too, got out of the car.

"Hello, Mr. Lorey. I hope we didn't keep you waiting," said John.

"No, no. I just got here myself. How are you?"

"We're fine. Please meet our daughters, Deborah and Kathy. This is Mr. Lorey, a sales representative for Crisscross Realty," said John.

They shook his hand. *Wait a minute! Sales representative? Why?* They were both thinking the same thoughts.

"It's very nice to meet you. I've heard so much about you both and your families."

*Well, that's just lovely!! I've heard absolutely nothing about you,* thought Deborah!

*Mr. Lorey? What's he doing here, anyway? What are Mother and Dad doing?* thought Kathy.

Mr. Lorey said, "Let's go on inside."

*Inside?*

"Yes, let's do. But if you don't mind, Mr. Lorey, you go ahead. We want to speak to Kathy and Deborah for a minute," said John.

Janine was thinking, *Ok, John…You just do that!*

Mr. Lorey went on inside of the house that had the "Sale Pending" sign on it, and the girls turned to John waiting for something—anything!

"Now then, here is what we want you to see. The house."

"The house? This house? What about the house?" they asked.

"Well, here's the thing…We are buying it."

*Oh, Boy! Now, he's done it!* Thought Janine. *Good grief! What are they thinking? What can they be thinking? They don't have enough information to assimilate the situation.*

Janine finally cleared her head and faced the up to the situation.

"Girls, listen! I know this sounds crazy. But it's the truth, and we need to tell you all about it."

"Oh, my gosh! This is totally a shock. I don't even know what to say," said Kathy.

"I don't either, but I guess we don't have to say anything really. We'd better just let Mom and Dad do the talking."

"And we will. Come on, let's do go inside. Ok?" Janine said.

"Just a minute, please," Kathy said with her hand on her mother's sleeve, "Are you going to move here? Are you going to sell our house in Innesport? I'm sorry, but I just don't understand."

"Yes, that's right," said John.

"Holy cow! What brought this on?" asked Kathy.

John smiled. "Holy it is!"

"What?" the girls chorused.

"It is such a long and wonderful story. Your mother can tell you all about it…then you'll understand, I'm sure. But in the meantime, just know that we have decided to buy this house." He led them to the front door. Janine let the girls go and she followed.

*Father in heaven, be with us. Please help John and me to find the right words here. Thank you, Lord. Amen.*

"Mom, are you coming?" Deborah asked.

"Yes, of course."

* * *

Mr. Lorey said he would be downstairs and excused himself. John and the girls waited in the entryway for Janine, and then they went on into the living room. There was a picture window letting in light from the outside, which was helpful because the lamps weren't bright enough to light the room. *Older people tend to be conservative on wattage.*

The sofa was well worn with scarves on the back that couldn't hide the orange and yellow flowers on a brown background. The girls looked at it and could hardly see anything else. Janine noticed the sofa for the first time. It hadn't been of any concern to her. It would soon be gone.

"This is certainly a very large room," said Deborah. They all agreed in one way or another.

"I was so happy when I saw that my piano would fit in here. I was thinking beforehand that if the piano didn't fit, I probably wasn't meant to live here," said Janine.

"Well, it's certainly not a problem, is it?" Kathy interjected.

She was so shocked over the situation that she didn't know what to say at this point, and couldn't imagine her mother's baby grand piano any place other than their home on Alamont Street.

Janine and John were discussing which would be best; see the rest of the house or hear the explanation of their decision. It was hard to decide.

Finally, John said, "Girls, really the house is fine. It's not the house that matters. There is something much more important about all of this, so I think we need to let your mother tell you all about it. Let's sit down. Okay?"

They looked at Janine, and she began, "Well, for awhile now, I had a peculiar sensation that there was something I was supposed to do, and since I didn't have the slightest idea what that could be, I began to be nervous and questioning.

"Due to a few somewhat unusual occurrences, I went to speak to Pastor Jim about it. He advised me to wait and listen because he thought that God was trying to tell me something, and that I would no doubt be finding out soon."

"Really...That's interesting," Deborah said.

"It is. It's also wonderful and amazing. One of those unusual circumstances occurred at a meeting of the Women's Association at our house. You remember, Kathy, right after Easter I went home to prepare to entertain and to work on a devotion for that?"

"Yes, I do."

"Well, while I was doing my best to figure out that devotion—" She went on to describe the story of the Little Wind, the ladies' non-reaction, her disturbance, etc. "So I certainly understood when Pastor Jim told me that there have been many times that he felt he had a message that needed to be brought forth, and sensed that no one heard it at all; his explanation was that their hearts have to be ready to *receive* the message.

"I'm sure that I, myself, have heard hundreds of messages and didn't grasp the intended meaning. I've even read the same scripture many times over without coming to a true understanding; then a day would come when suddenly, out of the blue, I would get it! Did that ever happen to you?"

"Yes. It wasn't too long ago either. It was at one of our Bible Study group meetings. We were looking at a scripture that I had practically memorized, and there was a message for me that day that I had not received before…I know what you mean." Kathy said.

"I thought the little story was wonderful, Mom. And you know what? It seems to me that it was meant for *you* more than anyone else. You do stress yourself out a lot by trying to do too much for too long. It puts you in a tizzy like that little wind," said Deb.

"I know. I know. I'm working on it, but it's going to take a lot to settle me down. Anyway, I'm not finished yet. Wait until you hear the rest of the story."

Janine told them of her encounter with the Holy Spirit. They were completely mesmerized.

She went into details about how she had been overly interested in this house from the beginning and how very strange that was to her. When she felt compelled to come back the day of her encounter, there was positively no holding her back.

Janine felt better being fully upfront with the girls, although the recollections and explanations were beginning to take a toll on her. John could tell she was exhausted recalling it all, and jumped in to tell them about the visit to the house by both of them, and of their unqualified decision to move.

"We didn't really have a choice, girls. I believe, as much as your mother does, that we both belong here at this time. You know, God has a purpose for all of us. Sometimes that purpose puts us in a different place. We are both excited to learn what that might be, and we want to get to it as soon as we can. We hope you will be okay with all of this."

"My goodness! How could we not? It's wonderful. What can I do to help?" asked Deborah.

"I feel the same. And the bonus is—you will be closer to me! The girls will love that, too. It's going to be just great."

Both girls jumped up and hugged their parents, offering their support.

After tears of joy from all four, they decided that they definitely should look through the house after all.

They saw a lot of things that needed to be done, which Janine hadn't bothered to acknowledge before. She assumed that she had turned a blind eye to all of that.

"No problem. I'll have lots of time to fix things up, paint, and so forth," said John.

"Hey! Don't forget about us! We'll help, too. Now what about our home in the city?"

"Well, it hasn't been sold yet, but we'll get ready to move out anyway. We've settled on a price for this house, and the final papers will be signed soon. We sure could use a hand in the moving," John said.

"I have to admit that it's going to be hard for me to see my past disappear in front of my eyes. I have all the memories of my childhood in the rooms of our home there," Deb said.

"I know, Honey, and I understand, too. But life goes on, just as it did for you and Robert. We need to let go of the past and, with faith, walk into the future. It will be fine. You'll always have those memories, just as you have now," said Janine. "I truly never expected to move from our house there on Alamont Street. This is so sudden, and we will all have to adjust, that's for sure."

"Well, ladies, have we seen enough? We should let Mr. Lorey get home. He's been so patient with us today, and it's almost two o'clock. The girls will be getting home," John said.

"Yes, we'd better go." Kathy turned to Janine, "Mother, it's a lot different living out here in the country. Set your mind for it. I hope you will love it as much as I do."

"You know, I have been telling a lot of people, even before all of this happened, that it is so great in the country. I think God has been setting my mind for it for quite some time. I'm not saying it will be a piece of cake, but I'm ready."

* * *

"Deb, what do you really think?" Their parents had gone home and Kathy was eager to speak to Deborah alone.

"Mother and Dad feel the importance of this. I can't deny that. It's certainly virtuous and upright, Kathy; I do think Mother may have a hard time adjusting to this completely different way of life. She is so used to the social life in Innesport; however, you moved to the country, and you love it." Deborah said.

"You just can't compare my move with this move of Mother's! The country suits me so much, but Deb! Look at the life she has had! 'Mrs. Society!' And she's always enjoyed it," Kathy said.

"People can change. That's what God's expecting from her, and He'll help her, so let's not worry ourselves about it," Deborah seemed perfectly comfortable with what may lie ahead.

Still considering the obstacles, Kathy replied, "But what if after she sells and moves, she sees the house with all of its flaws? Then will she step back and lose her balance?"

"It's not the house, Kathy. Even Dad said that."

Kathy took in a deep breath, realizing that she was focusing on the wrong thing. Her mother had been handpicked for something special, and she had responded. They should emphatically rejoice with her, give their support, and wait to see what's going to happen.

"You're right. I'm worrying. What kind of trust is that?"

"Sometimes our love and concern gets in the way," Deb said. "She's one solid lady."

"She is."

# 30

## "Click"

"You're going to do what?" Bea asked.

Every member of the Sunday school class was waiting for the answer, even though they heard Anne the first time. This would give them time to think of what to say in response.

"Owen and I are going to sell the house and move into the Birchwood Condominium Village."

"When did you decide this?" Iola asked.

"Oh, we've been talking about it. There comes a time."

"Those are really nice apartments," Julia said. "I looked at them once, but just couldn't make up my mind to move. It's such a big job getting rid of everything. I don't think I have the energy to do it, anyway."

"Me, either," said Bea. "Of course, Anne, you have Alexandra and her family to help."

"Oh, we'll be fine. We'll basically give the children and my nieces and nephews whatever they want, sell the rest, get a moving van to do moving, and that will be that."

Anne was the most practical person in the world. Nothing disturbed her. She made decisions, figured it all out, and it was done. The gals all admired Anne for her courage and assertion whatever the situation. There wasn't one person there who would want to pick up and do what she was doing.

Jenny had moved out of the borough a while back. Her family was all gone now, and it was too much for her to maintain the large family home and property. She sold it and never looked back. She had been very well satisfied with her new and beautiful apartment on the other side of Innesport. The only problem was that she rarely drove back to see anyone anymore and only occasionally got to church. The class was very pleased that she came today.

"Anne, I'm happy for you. There is no need for you to work your fingers to the bone in that big house. I think it is very smart of you to decide to do this while you have your senses and capabilities, and also while you still have Owen to go with you," Jenny declared.

As Julia listened to her dear friend, Jenny, she was beginning to see the inevitable. Now, not only Jenny would be absent from them much of the time, but it appeared that Anne might be also.

A stillness settled over the room as the dear friends all sensed an end approaching.

"But, Jenny, we hardly ever see you anymore," said Julia.

"I know, and I'm sorry about that, but you know my back is not good anymore, and the long drive is almost too much for me."

"Anne, if you move out to Birchwood, will you and Owen get back to church?" Laura asked.

"Oh, yes. We'll be coming here for church. At least that is our plan."

"I worry that our class is going to fade away," Julia said.

Iola said she did, too. The class had been together for many, many years and once even included their husbands before a men's class was formed. Now they were down to just a little more than a handful of women.

"We only have each other, it seems," said Bea. "Every last one of us needs to keep trying really, really hard to stay together. Look at us. 1–2-3–4-5–6. Adele is away, and most of the time Jenny can't come. Francine does try to bring Alice, but not as much anymore…Anne, please don't desert us."

"I won't."

"We should try to get more people in this class," said Iola.

"Now, just who would you get?" asked Bea.

"I don't know. Rachael, maybe."

"Rachael is flat on her back!"

"I know. Has anyone heard how she has been this week?" Iola asked.

"She had surgery on her leg and got along well with that. It wasn't too serious, but she is still in Allegheny and can't stand on her injured feet," Harriet said.

"Oh, my. I don't know. It's hard to imagine Rachael not getting better because she always has. We can't stop praying for her," said Bea.

"I wish we could go see her," Julia said.

Co-incidentally, Marcia peeked into the room. She was on her way to her class with her husband, but wanted to stop in and report on Rachael.

"We were just saying that we wish we could go see her!" Julia said.

"I'm sure she would love to see you, too. She should be moved back this way sometime soon. She seems depressed."

"No! Not Rachael!" said Jenny.

"Yes, she really does. She is not the same spirited and cheerful person we're used to. She definitely needs encouragement. Hey! I have an idea! Barbara has that wonderful new three-seat vehicle, and I'll bet she would be happy to drive us up to see Rachael. I'll ask her if you'd like for me to."

"That would be great. When?" Julia asked.

Everyone else joined in accord.

"Let me think...How about Wednesday?"

"I don't have anything else to do."

"Neither do I."

"Monday, Tuesday, Wednesday–any day's fine with me."

"Me, too!

"I get my hair done on Friday. That's it. But I'm sure I could change it." Iola said.

"Let's say 'Wednesday.' Can you be ready by nine o'clock in the morning? Marvin and I find that if we get to Pittsburgh around ten o'clock or so, we miss a lot of the morning traffic."

They all could be ready. Actually, if the truth were known, most would no doubt be ready long before that. They didn't get to do special things much anymore.

"See me after church this morning, and in the meantime I'll check with Barbara and let you know." She scurried out to get to class.

"If we're going, I'll meet you at your house, Iola," said Harriet. "Anne, how about you? Can you get away?"

"I'm sure I can. Owen can visit with Alexandra, so as not to have to be home alone. I'll just drive him over there and also come to Iola's. Is that okay with you?"

They were excitedly making plans. It would be fun riding together to Pittsburgh—a venture!

Bea said, "Can we take her something? We probably shouldn't take food in...I know what! How about one of those helium-filled balloons? Or, better yet, a bunch of them. Wouldn't she brighten up if we each walked in carrying a colorful balloon?"

Anne smiled. *Leave it to Bea. She would always be the one to find just the right thing.*

Iola said, "Let's not get the cart before the horse here. We don't even know for sure if we're going."

"Well, just in case. Anyway, we'll know before this day is out. Let's decide what we'll do just in case," Bea said.

"Where can we get the balloons?" Julia asked.

"Over at Super Buys. It's on the way. If we leave ten minutes early, it will all work out great," Bea had the answer. They all liked it.

They were smiling and chattering as they left the classroom to attend the service. Harriett realized that they did not get to the lesson. She was a stickler for seeing that they did not get off track, yet she didn't even realize what happened. *Well, Lord knows we need a little diversion once in a while. I'll cover two lessons next week.*

❧ ❧ ❧

One has to wonder if any of the ladies heard the message that morning. If Pastor Dan had one especially for them, he might want to preach it again on another Sunday.

As soon as the postlude began, they gathered together in a cluster at the back of the sanctuary waiting for Marcia to come to them. She did so right away, with Barbara at her side. They were smiling—a good sign.

The ladies waited and waited there. Opal Harrington had stopped Marcia in the aisle. *Uhhgghh! Anyone but Opal. She's impossible to get away from.*

Church members walked by and some spoke to the ladies

briefly. The church was emptying and there was Opal, still going on and on…Finally! Marcia was free! She and Barbara headed quickly for the back.

"Well, ladies, we're on! Wednesday it is."

They discussed the pickup schedule. Laura would be staying home with Edward, and Jenny said the drive would be too difficult for her, and the day would be too long for Alice; the others were thrilled, and Bea was sure that Adele would be coming with them. They asked about stopping for balloons, and Marcia and Barbara smiled and agreed that was a great idea. They would do the pickup a bit earlier. And one more thing, they would stop for lunch on the way back home!

No better words could have been spoken.

❀ ❀ ❀

They all went into the store. Each wanted to pick out her balloon herself. It was a sight to behold! Six elderly ladies, all smiles, were scampering through the store to the checkout counter with balloons designed to cheer. Well, they cheered all right!

"Look at those ladies!"

"I wonder where they are going with those balloons."

"Well, aren't they having a good time?"

"Look! Have you ever?"

They came outside bouncing along buoyantly as though the balloons were lifting their feet. Julia, who was never presumptuous or first in line but much more likely to be waiting to see what others were doing, was in front. *I have never done anything so silly-looking or frivolous in my life! She thought. I like it.*

"Barbara, grab your camera!"

They grouped together. (click) One balloon was a big smiley face, which represented accurately the inner feelings of the bearers. Bea's idea had been a good one. Without warning or expectations, their gesture of kindness turned upon them and anointed them with gladness.

With difficulty, they managed to get into the van. The crippling pains of arthritis and stiffening hips had been somewhat of a problem when they were picked up earlier. Now, with the balloons, it took a little more figuring out, but they moved past the pains and stiffness, helping one another, and laughing themselves right into their seats.

Marcia realized that her suggestion was proving to be as important to the ladies as it would be for Rachael.

Now, with the balloons bobbing up and down and left to right, they were faced with what to do with them, as Barbara couldn't see through the back. The ladies would have to hold them down somehow. It was just too funny! They finally found that they could tie the strings around their legs or purses, and they rode all the way to Pittsburgh pretty much nursing balloons on their laps. They didn't care. It was a great day.

Barbara wanted to go in with Marcia alone, and be prepared to take a picture that would be a keepsake for each of them for years to come. When the ladies stepped off of the elevator, people stopped to look, smile and enjoy the spectacle of it all.

Rachael was surprised to see Marcia again so soon, and she was pleased that her daughter-in-law came also. Rachael seemed about the same and said that she would have another surgery when she was strong enough. If only she could get up! She couldn't even sit, and was still on her back with both feet elevated.

"How am I supposed to get stronger just laying here?"

Marcia excused herself for a moment to tell the others to come into the room. They inched their way toward the door.

Marcia went on in. Barbara focused her camera, and there they were—six happy, smiling ladies wanting to share their happiness with Rachael. And they did! (click) Rachael almost came out of the bed. (click) She was overjoyed just to see them, (click) but she would never forget the balloons, the bright colors, (click) and the joy of that moment. If ever a heart could be lightened, a spirit lifted, and a smile given, that was the time. (click)

They talked and laughed. Marcia got teary-eyed. So did Barbara. Giving to another was always rewarded greatly in return.

Marcia thought of the framed scripture given to her when she graduated into nursing:

*Give, and it will be given to you.*
*A good measure, pressed down, shaken together and running over,*
*Will be poured into your lap.*
*For the measure you use, it will be measured to you.*

Luke 6:38

It's more than true! I'm the happiest one here today. Marcia told herself.

Barbara thought, *Look at these dear friends! I'm just so happy that I could bring them together like this. I'm the happiest one here today.*

Each of the ladies were thinking, *How wonderful to be here with Rachael and see that great big beautiful smile of hers. She makes me so happy!*

Rachael was praying, *Thank you, Lord, for giving me these wonderful friends who can always put a smile on my face. It sure feels good to smile and mean it.*

# 31

# They Come and They Go

Marcia was calling, "Bea, can I bring Marvin by for a few minutes so that he can see and smell the beautiful yellow irises?"

"My goodness, yes! You didn't have to ask to do that. When are you coming?"

"We're coming by there in about ten minutes, I'd say. I described the fragrance of them to Marvin, but it's like trying to tell someone how chocolate tastes."

"No sense in that. Bring him over. I'll be here!"

They turned into the driveway, which now was lined with yellow. Bea was all smiles as she came out of the front door to meet them. Nothing pleased her more than to have someone else enjoy her flowers. She was like a parent showing off her child. The flowers were her babies now that everyone in the family was gone.

Marvin was certainly impressed, and when he got a whiff of what Marcia had told him, he said, "Ha! You were right, Marcia. There's a real nice spice scent here." Marvin was appreciative of nature in general. Of course, nothing would ever mean as much as the apple trees and the scent of the blossom, but he enjoyed it all.

Bea told him she was going to give them some iris roots in the fall, and he let her know that he was happy about that. He leaned over again and took another whiff, declaring his appreciation. Bea had her scissors ready and cut off several of the ones that still had the second bloom to come. "Irises have the special quality of serving the second helping," someone once said. When the first flower was finished, the second one replaced it.

Bea said, "Come on in, and I'll wrap these stems in wet paper towels for you. If you aren't going right back home, I'll put them in a vase of water. You won't want to leave them in a warm car for very long. They are pretty delicate, you know."

They were just going down to the Country Store and would be going promptly back home, so the watered-down paper towels would be just fine.

"Thank you so much Bea. I'm going to put them on the kitchen table so we can take a whiff every time we pass by," said Marcia. *What a pleasure that would be!*

Bea asked Marvin if he heard all about the trip to see Rachael. He said he had and couldn't wait to see the pictures.

"Me, either. I'm tellin' you, it was a wonderful day. We all enjoyed it. I just can't thank you enough, Marcia, and I'm gon'na send a note to Barbara. She's a sweetie."

Bea went back into the house. She was glad that they had stopped by. She hadn't seen anyone for a couple of days. She sat down in her usual chair in the living room and turned on the television. It kept her company most evenings although she didn't pay a lot of attention to it. She used to have a little dog that was good company, but he died and she didn't have the heart to lose another one. She had been through too much "losing."

*It's hard to be alone. I'm not cut out for it. This television is just a bunch of noise as far as I'm concerned… What's on today?…Anything worth watching?* She turned the dial through the news (all bad), zipped past those raunchy sit-coms, and found a rerun of *"Lawrence Welk."*

*This is better than some of that stuff people seem to like these days... I wish there was a baseball game.* She always loved baseball.

She had cut the grass earlier, washed up, ate a bite, and now felt quite tired. She liked working outside in the yard, but it was getting harder and harder all of the time. She would not give in. If she had to, she'd take two days to cut the grass, or three, but she was not going to have someone else do it. Everybody else seemed satisfied to let Silas cut their grass. Not her. *Maybe they all have more money than I do, but I need every cent of my Social Security to get by. I have to do what I have to do.*

She had always done whatever she had to do. Her husband, "Brick," had been gone for twelve years, and her children had moved away. Her son wanted her to move in with him, but she'd rather stay in her home with her memories. She and Brick built this house with their own hands—a pretty fine house, too. She didn't know much of anything about construction. Brick knew a little, and together they found out how to do a lot more and did it. As a bricklayer, he had seen many homes constructed, had asked a lot of questions, and decided he could build his own. He was right, only because he had a wife willing to be his "helper."

"Those were the days," as they say. They really were.

Bea and Brick. "The Team." Everyone thought of them that way. They were a team all right. They even won dancing contests together.

*I won't be dancing anymore.*

❀ ❀ ❀

Across the street, Adele was dozing in her chair. She had seen the Severights stop at Bea's house. She was glad she had Bea for a friend. They had been friends even before their husbands died. They all four loved to play Euchre, and would squeeze time when they were younger to play cards together. *We sure wouldn't have to squeeze time in these days. Time is what we have the most of with little to do to fill it. Isn't that ironic? I do still have my daughter to see often, which is more than most of the others have. I should go visit her tomorrow. Will she know me this time?*

Her daughter, Candice, and her grandson had lived with her for many years after the horrible accident. Billie grew up and took over the care of his mother. Billie's wife, Samantha, was a gem to have married into the situation as it was. She had said she loved Billie and Candice, too. She felt it was the right thing to do, and has never complained about it as far as Adele knew. Billie always said that Samantha and Candice were the best of friends. His dear wife was truly one of God's best. Adele knew that she would not be able to care for Candice now and was thankful for the way it all worked out. Adele's other daughter, Darlene, offered many times to relieve Samantha for a week or more. She would possibly have the opportunity over the summer while Billie and Samantha take a vacation. That would be good.

She was thinking about how her daughters enjoyed one another when they were younger. When they would sing duets in church, everyone said their voices blended perfectly. She looked at the picture of Candice taken when she portrayed Laurey Williams in the high school musical, *"Oklahoma."* She had just recently taken the picture out of storage. It had always been too heartbreaking to look. It was still difficult, but somehow comforting, too.

*Candice had great promise. I'll always remember her that way.*

*I'll go call Samantha and let her know I'm coming tomorrow. Maybe she'd like to go out for a couple of hours, and I'll sing some songs to Candy that she knew.*

# 32

## A "Getaway"

The choir at Hope Church had the month of June off because Francine would not be there to direct them. There was a young man from a neighboring community who played piano pretty well and agreed to play for the church services; however, he had no training in choral directing. Most of them had been choir members "forever," and at Hope the choir did not usually take any time off by choice. In fact, they didn't feel comfortable sitting in the congregation.

Francine and Lawrence were as excited as children as they packed to go to Florida. They would spend the entire month there, coming back after the 4th of July holiday. The Session of the church insisted. After all, Francine was a child of the church, and had been ever so faithful. She certainly deserved the month off, and more if she would take it. They would manage.

"I won't be long, Lawrence. I simply want to be sure that Mother has everything she needs. I'm not worried about her. I know that Darrell will look after her very well while we're gone, and Paula is going to be calling her daily. Did you fill up the car with gasoline?"

"Yes, it's ready to go. When you get back, we'll just put these suitcases and supplies in and we'll be ready, too. I'll fill up the thermos with coffee and the water jug with ice."

"That's just fine. I'll be back real soon."

Francine had a lovely last-minute visit with her mother, returned home, and she and Lawrence gathered up the final items and were off. What a great day it was! Francine felt as free as a bird. Her mother was very happy that she was getting away, and she wouldn't let her linger to do anything more than was absolutely necessary, which was very little.

Francine and Lawrence planned to take a leisurely trip through the West Virginia mountains by way of Interstate 79 and Route 19, as the scenery through that ruggedly beautiful state was as picturesque as any in the country.

They gravitated toward I-79, and were well on their way south, devoid of responsibilities for a while. Lawrence had retired, but as with most retirees he found quite a lot to keep himself busy—mostly with Habitat for Humanity—utilizing the skills he'd developed through a hobby of woodworking over the years. Francine was now retired as a school teacher, but considered her work at the church her real occupation—the one that had always been first on her priority list, and she was devoted to it. She would never retire from doing what she believed she was assigned to do by a Higher Authority, and until she had a better signal that she should vacate being the principal musician at the church, she was not going to; however, she certainly did believe that retirement was possible—perhaps probable—and felt led to pray about it.

Now, here they were, finally on their long-awaited vacation. They passed Morgantown, WV, and the view increased in beauty the farther along they traveled. Connecting to Route 19, the hills reached even higher to the sky. They were so densely covered with trees that they blended into a splash of green. One tree was indistinguishable from the next. The road turned this way and that, but was so well engineered that they had no difficulty navigating it. Every turn in the road presented a new scene, and they were in constant awe of this untouched beauty.

They stopped at Tamarack, the fantastically beautiful and unique cooperative outlet for West Virginia artisans. It was both fine and troublesome that they had chosen to make this stop because it was so amazing and enjoyable that they stayed longer than they had anticipated.

Leaving all of life's pressures behind, they decided to linger a little longer to have dinner. They had a Bed and Breakfast reservation in the mountains farther south, and it would be held for them no matter when they arrived. They could just phone ahead, which they decided to do.

They both opted for the rainbow trout, which would be pan-fried right before their eyes. Mmm, mmm. Lawrence knew immediately what to add to his dinner plate: kale greens cooked with bacon and onions! This was a true West Virginia Appalachian meal, typical of the other artisan labors of the establishment.

"I have never eaten kale before. I'm not sure I would like that," said Francine.

"Well, you can taste mine if you want. Do you like cooked spinach or any other kind of greens?"

"Believe it or not, I love dandelion greens. We have always gone out all over the farmland at home and gathered dandelion greens early in the spring before the flower formed. That's when they were the most tender. My mother would wash them over and over to get the mud off from the spring rains, and she cooked the greens with bacon or ham. Oh, my! How we looked forward to that!"

"Well, Sweetheart, I think you should try the greens here, then. You sound like a cultured gourmet in quality eating!"

They laughed. She ordered the cooked kale as he did, and watched the cooking of the trout. They picked up some good breads and fruits, gathered up their food, which was cooked and served cafeteria-style, and found a very nice table away from the whereabouts of people.

The meal was "lip-smackin'" good, they said, as they made an effort to assume the position of good -ol' West Virginia Hillbillies. They declared that they were off to a very good start on their journey.

They had seen some beautiful hand-made quilts there, and decided that they would certainly be in good competition with a couple of the ladies back home—some compliment. The woodworking demonstrations and items for sale just amazed Lawrence. He could never have made anything so beautiful, he told Francine. She didn't question that because she honestly had never seen such fine, polished furniture.

They bought a mouth-blown bowl that they both liked very much and a beautiful embroidered dresser scarf for Lawrence's mother. She would love them.

What a precedent to a delightful trip! If this was any indication of how much they were going to enjoy themselves, they would be thrilled all the way. Well, it was, and they arrived in Florida as two relaxed, joyful people in very good spirits.

It was going to be a wonderful vacation for everyone. Lawrence was especially pleased to find his mother feeling much better these days, which made everything just perfect.

# 33

# She's Floored!

The choir at Center Church in Innesport was not taking vacation time during June, or July either. Their normal vacation was in August; however, Janine would not be scheduling practices because they could just sing familiar anthems during the summertime. It's a good thing that she did not have to run into the city to work on new music or practice the choirs because she could not possibly have done so with all of the things that were on her plate.

The house in Innesport hadn't sold, so they didn't have to pack up everything there immediately. They turned to preparing the new house for their move which included deciding upon paint colors, and other issues. They were seriously thinking about remodeling the kitchen, but wondered whether it would be better to do that now or later.

"I think we should move in and use the downstairs kitchen while we go ahead and do the remodeling upstairs once and for all. Then we won't be tearing up everything later," said John.

"I can live with that. Who do we call to have it done or were you thinking of tackling it yourself?"

"I know my limitations, Hon, and designing and installing a kitchen is beyond my expertise. You would be the better one to design it, and then we'll get a contractor to do the job; however, I think we could put new flooring down ourselves. I've been looking at the new laminate and the instructions look fairly easy to follow."

"Ok, let's check into it."

They went to one of the big hardware stores and found the kitchen that they thought would look great in the country home. They contracted them to come, measure and work with Janine on the final design. The kitchen expert walked with them over to the flooring section to assist in selecting coordinating flooring, which they penciled for ordering when they had the correct measurements.

The contractor met them at the new house the next day. He and Janine worked with several designs before a decision could be reached.

This took more time than either expected because Janine had been working in the same kitchen for twenty years. Consequently, she didn't have an up-to-date knowledge of the conveniences that modern technology could provide. The contractor actually had to convince her that she would appreciate and be able to use these new technical advancements.

"John, would you come here, please?"

"What's up?"

"I know you wanted me to decide upon everything in the kitchen, Honey, but I need your opinion about some of these new appliances and such."

He jumped at the new ideas with time and work-saving benefits. "No sense in buying a horse when you can have a car."

*There he goes again!*

"Actually, they no longer make some of the things I thought I should have," she said. "I guess I've been living in another era and didn't even know it."

"'Times, they are a'changin,' they say, so I guess we might as well face up to it."

He convinced her, and they signed the papers for the new cabinets, appliances, and installation.

In a few days the old kitchen was completely gutted, so that John and Janine could "easily" install the flooring. John spent an entire day preparing the base for the flooring, confidently setting up "horses" to use for sawing purposes, checking his rotary blades, etc.; after that, off they went to pick up the laminate and supplies required.

"This will be fun, Janine—working together on a major project. Wait 'til the kids see what we've done."

That attitude changed quickly. What began as "fun" turned into "tedious" and "exhausting" and could have ended even the best of relationships!

"Let's see. It says here—" Yes, it looked easy on paper, but for two people past middle age to be getting up and down, up and down, reading instructions, cutting boards...Then down again, and up again. It was one of the most backbreaking jobs they could have done. The children would have helped, but "oh no!" they could handle it themselves!

"John, I think we went beyond our limitations after all. I can't move! My knees hurt, my back hurts, and my shoulders hurt. I probably won't be able to play the organ on Sunday. You have reached your limit, too. I can tell. Admit it."

"Okay. I admit that it's not been as easy as I originally thought, but we can finish this, Janine. One more day, and it will be done. Then we can stand back and be really proud of ourselves while the contractor does the rest in here. Can you handle just one more day, or do you want me to call Greg to come over."

"No! Please. I don't want to have to do that! Do you see where we have come? It is one of the deadly sins—pride!! Now I know why it is called deadly! This pride *will* kill us."

"You know that pride doesn't kill you! Pride puts you on your own instead of trusting and depending upon God for help. We begin to think we can do it all. That's what pride is all about. It's a turning from God. It really has nothing to do with us doing this floor without God helping us."

"John, I'm getting irritated with your Biblical interpretations… but I still have a comment, if you don't mind."

"Go ahead."

"I'm tired. I hurt, and I have not thought of God for the past few days. Here we are grumpy with one another, trying to do something we are not good at, determined to make an impression to others—showing off that we actually did it ourselves. I don't think we are where we want to be. I don't like it."

"I'm sorry, Janine. You're right.

"Look at us," he continued. "We are making this move in answer to God's call, and what are we doing? We're attacking one another, trying to do too much around here instead of fixing *ourselves* up for what lies ahead. We need to slow down and stop driving ourselves like this. It's my fault! I had no idea this flooring thing would be so tough on us."

"John, we have one more day to finish this. I'm sure we can. But please, please, let's not get ourselves into this kind of situation again. Ok? Next time, let's get help, or absolutely not worry about it."

They finished it, vowing to behave differently in the future. Janine was always the one to strive for perfection, so John had figured she would have to have everything perfect before moving into the house. She knew that, realizing that she had to change her view of herself.

"This is harder than I thought it would be," Janine said. "Are we really going to be able to do this?"

"I'm not going to get us into anymore projects. I promise."

"No, no! I mean making all of these changes in our lifestyle and living up to our commitment."

"Of course! Maybe God is testing our faith and our trust in Him. Even though you were directed to follow this path, doesn't mean that everything will fall right into place. Let's trust that God is still with us, and strive to move ahead with confidence and faith."

At this moment, she was reminded why she fell in love with this man. He was "Mr. Solid-as-a-Rock!" And he would be right there with her all the way...*and maybe he will rub my back.*

"Hello! Is anyone home?" John recognized Kathy's voice. He was in the master bedroom putting a fresh coat of paint on the walls.

"Come on in. I'm here in the back."

"Hi. How's it coming?"

"Good. Good. Your mother just left. She had to go find some boxes...Do you have any?"

"I don't know. I'll have to look, but Greg can get you some over at the Dairy—some good strong ones. You can borrow them."

"That sounds good. I'll tell your mother...How's this look?"

"Beautiful. You are a terrific painter, Dad."

"Well, thanks, but if you think that compliment will get me to paint all of your rooms, think again!" He said laughingly. "Did you see the kitchen?"

"What about it?"

"Oh, never mind."

"What…I'm going to go look." He smiled as he imagined the reaction.

She called from the empty kitchen with the beautiful laminate flooring, "Wow! You really mean business, don't you? What's the deal? You're getting a completely new kitchen, I see."

"Well, didn't *you?*" he asked as he came in behind her.

She smiled, "We did. Who's doing the work? The floor is fabulous!"

"I'll have to get your mother to tell you. You know how I am with names." He didn't want to tell her without Janine being there. They should have called the family over when they had finished, but just didn't take the time.

"Well, I thought I'd stop by to see if you need any help. I'm sorry that I didn't stop sooner, but with the end of the year at school and reports to be filed, I haven't had much time. I finished up today, so call on me anytime. Ok?"

"Ok, Honey. Thanks. I'll tell your mother to give you a call later today."

When Janine came home, John told her of the visit by Kathy. They had a good laugh over it. Janine called Kathy and said that the family should all stop over that evening.

When the four of them arrived, they all went into the upstairs kitchen. When everyone had finished with their "oooo's" and" aahhh's" about the flooring, they let it be known that they had done all of it themselves.

"Why didn't you call?" asked Greg.

"Well, at first we decided we wanted to 'do it ourselves.' Then when we got fully into the project, we began to realize that maybe we *couldn't* do it at our age, and *shouldn't* do it, but were too darned stubborn to admit it to anyone. By then we were just determined to see the foolish decision through to the end." John was giving it to them straight. It felt better than just standing back and letting them think they were two people who could do just about anything.

"Well, it's a beautiful floor…It really is. But please don't do anymore," Kathy said.

"Ha! Don't worry about that!" Janine was firm in her response.

"Don't tell us you are going to install the cabinets." Greg was not sure about these two.

Janine quickly responded, "No! Not a chance. We're finished with such foolishness. We're having a skilled and qualified contractor do that. The cupboards are cherry. We had almost chosen the oak because it had more of a rustic look, but the house isn't really built that way, and cherry seems to be more fitting."

Janine went on to tell about the new appliances. Greg got a good chuckle out of that. He knew all about modern technology in the kitchen.

"You'll enjoy them after a while. It won't take long," Greg said.

"'Practice makes perfect!'" quoted John. Janine knew that was certainly true.

They went downstairs and had coffee, sodas, and snacks. The girls loved the big family room. They talked about Claire coming soon. *My goodness! It's almost July!* Janine thought. *Where does the time go?*

They all left the house around the same time. John and Janine went on into town, and Kathy and her family on down the lane. Someday that would change.

# *Part Two*
# Turning Point

## 34

## Zigzagging

The following week, when she was finally able to move about without feeling like a 95-year old woman, she began clearing out the house in the city.

First she drove over to the church, hoping to find Pastor Jim and she did.

"Well, Janine, how are you getting along in your move?"

"Slowly, actually, but I think we'll be ready to move officially in a couple of weeks."

"Is something on your mind?"

"Yes, I guess there is." She sat down at his invitation. "I still have no idea where I'm going with this endeavor, Jim. When I look ahead, all I see is something like a shield or a fog. Nothing is clear to me."

"Are you feeling uncomfortable as though you've made a mistake?"

"No…not at all. I'm feeling *impatient* more than anything, I would say. I'm positive I have been led. No doubt about it. I could never look back at the encounter with the Holy Spirit and dismiss that as something not true. It was real. It still is, but nothing more has come to me in any way at all. Like I said, it's as though I'm walking into the future in a haze or something."

"You *are* being impatient. I've heard of situations like yours,

Janine. Sometimes it takes a while before we can be sure of what to do next. Keep praying."

"Well, that's another thing…I seem to be at a distance from the Lord right now. I don't feel His presence as I did before. Sometimes I ask if He is really there, and sometimes I don't get an answer either. I'm a little nervous about myself. I'm not unsure of God's purpose. He has one, that's for certain. I'm unsure of my ability to comprehend—to be open to what He wants of me."

"It's a difficult time for you. You have too many things crowding in. When you get things settled and you can back off from doing so much, you'll need to *take the time* to focus on the Lord. The Bible tells us to 'be still.' Remember the Little Wind?"

She nodded. She was definitely still in a rush and a whirl. "Be still, Janine, and wait for the Lord to speak to you. Will you work toward that?"

"I will! It's what I want more than anything!"

"Can I make one suggestion?"

"Of course! Please!"

"I'm feeling that you should let go of your work here at Center Church. I can hardly say this, Janine, because it means so much to us to have you here, and I know you love your music. But, I am almost certain that you need to separate yourself from us and begin anew."

"Oh, my! That scares me. It really does. I haven't actually considered it seriously."

"Let's pray about it."

As they prayed, she recognized that she had returned to her old ways of depending solely upon her own capabilities. She felt the tension inside of her. She felt her arms folded tightly, her teeth clenched, her eyes pressed shut, and she knew that she was behaving like the Little Wind.

"Jim, you are so right. I realize that I'm trying to do more than I should. I am not putting everything in the Lord's hands because that is against all that I've ever required of myself.

"I will consider what you've said about resigning from my position here at Center Church. Perhaps I should. There was a time when I believed that I was being 'called' and was totally in accord. What has happened to me? I'm still holding on, Jim. I haven't let go at all!"

"Don't be so hard on yourself, Janine. There is a lot of physical activity involved in moving. It's draining you and taking a lot of your energy. You are making headway, and don't for a minute believe that God has forgotten about His Plans for you as He is affectionately working behind the scenes making everything ready.

"Consider this your time of preparation, too, Janine. Remember Ecclesiastes? 'There is a time for everything.' I don't think the word 'preparation' is specifically mentioned, but the 'everything' covers it well. You cannot move ahead until the preparations are complete—yours and His."

She went on over to her house on Alamont Street, and instead of packing boxes, she put on her walking shoes.

Her walks had been so valuable, and she had not taken time to do that lately. She could hardly wait. It was so hot outside today; maybe she'd have a stroke walking in the heat. *No. I will not. It is God's will. I will walk and talk and be with the Lord as He is calling me to do.*

*"Christ be with me—"* She felt His presence, and her spirit lifted to be with Him. She was buoyant, and was not weakening

with the heat. All was well and she felt encouraged to make a decision.

She came back to Alamont Street and saw that John had come home also. Perfect! She wanted to talk with him.

"Hey, where have you been? I called you on your cell phone and it rang in your purse here. Where did you go without your purse? I was a little concerned about you."

"I'm fine, really. I needed to go for a walk."

She needn't say more—John knew.

"I'm going to submit my resignation to Center Church. I went to see Pastor Jim this morning, and he told me he felt that I would be doing that anyway. We prayed about it, and then I went for my walk and talked it over with the Lord. It's clear that this is what I need to do."

"Fine. I have no problem with that, Janine. Maybe I should resign from the Session also. What do you think?"

"John, I can't tell you to do that. It must be your decision."

"Well, we'll see. Now, tell me…how are you going to stop the music? It is so much a part of who you are."

"The way I see it, God is not going to give me something new to do if I am clinging to doing what I've always done."

"Right."

She appreciated his gesture of understanding.

Janine had a pleasant and meaningful conversation with Charlotte, the choir director, concerning the developing situation. With confidence in Charlotte's willingness to continue on her own, Janine typed her letter of resignation and addressed it to the Clerk of Session. She telephoned Pastor Jim to let him know it was being put in the mail with a copy being sent to him also.

"The Session is going to be set back over this, Janine. I don't know what you have written, but if John is at the meeting, he'll most likely be asked some questions of concern."

"He'll be there. He knows of my decision and supports me in it."

"I'm happy for you, Janine. Don't worry about us. We are a big church. There will be musicians eager to work with us. Will we ever find such dedication as we have had over the past many years? We'll certainly be praying about it, and we'll be praying for you, too, as you go on your way."

"Thank you so much. May God bless us both, Jim, and *all* those in partnership in the Gospel."

She took her letter to the post office, dropped it inside and walked out with trust and confidence.

"John…one thing. If there is mention of a sendoff, please let them know that I do not want that. It would be very hard for me. I prefer to write a letter in the next newsletter, as I mentioned in the resignation. Please reinforce that for me, will you?"

"Yes, I will…So, you will be playing the first Sunday in July. Then you will be finished. Right?

"Right."

"It's inevitable, so no sense in delaying. 'Lost time is never found again.'"

# 35

# Give and Take

The newsletter was out, and so was the information concerning Janine's resignation. The telephone would not stop ringing. John had to pick up the calls to keep Janine from losing her mind. She had calls from the women, neighbors, her past students, and people in the community who had worked with her over the years. It was nice to know that they cared about her; however, she just didn't want to talk about it so much, having said everything she could in the church newsletter about answering a "call" from the Lord. Of course, she realized everyone's dilemma with that. She previously didn't understand that expression, either. She had thought it meant telephone "call" in her youth, and later figured it was a "call" from a church. A "call" from God is not as a rule understood by many.

When she went to church the next Sunday, she could not get away from the crowd that gathered around her. She wanted to tell everyone of her love for the Lord and her desire to serve Him, but it was impossible with all of the questions that were coming her way. The questions pelted her from several directions at once.

The only way she could handle that, in all honesty, was to meet one-on-one with her friends, which she hoped in time she would do. She could also speak at a meeting for those who would like to hear her story, she supposed. That might be fair, after all—and wouldn't God want her to witness for him? Well, she'd just wait for all of that as time passed. Right now, she still had to finish up at the church by organizing the files, and she would do so promptly.

She finally had everything boxed up at the old house and could turn it all over to the movers. *Hallelujah!* She hoped and prayed she would never, ever have to move again.

There was a cleansing aspect to it, though. Why, oh why, was she holding on to so many old things? She called the Salvation Army who gratefully arrived one morning with a truck to accept all and anything she would give away.

The truck drove away, weighed down with a lifetime of accumulation. *No. No. I can't just let it all go. I should have stopped them. That was the sofa we had when we first got married and I kept it for all these years…The chandelier with several missing parts hung in our first apartment, and we retrieved it when they tore down the building for safety's sake. I loved that old chandelier…John said the baby bed was totally unsafe. I think we could rebuild it…But for whose baby?*

*Oh, Janine. Let it go! Let it all go! You must!* she said to herself.

"Janine…Janine? It's ok." John said. "This is the prefect time to get rid of things we should not have kept in the first place. 'Holding *on* is holding *back*.'"

"I never heard that one before. Who said it? It's pretty good."

"John Stephens."

"So, now you are a philosopher, along with all of your many attributes. I'm constantly amazed at this man I married." She gave him a big hug. He returned it generously, and that was just what she needed.

*Too much at once! No time…no time!* Janine felt like the rabbit in *Alice in Wonderland.* When, oh when, would everything settle down, she wondered. Their "new" house was shaping up. The kitchen would be finished soon. Naturally, the installation didn't proceed as smoothly as they would have hoped. One of the custom-made cabinets turned out to be the wrong size, and there was a delay for another one to be prepared. They decided not to move anything into the kitchen until it was completed, so they were still eating downstairs. That wasn't unpleasant or inconvenient, and it was cooler down there, anyway. They had purchased a dandy picnic table, and sometimes ate right outside in the yard under a great maple tree.

"Hey there, Little Miss Muffet, come and sit with me awhile," John had said the first day they went outside. They giggled like school children, and from then on it was pure joy. The girls came over and joined them a couple of times. It was better and better; however, it was going to be "best" when they were totally finished with the entire process.

Kathy was preparing for Claire to come. Meghan had moved out of her bedroom, Greg was planning traditional American meals, and they all were excitedly looking forward to greeting her and showing America to her. She would be arriving June 28th.

Deborah was glad that the social whirl had calmed down for the summer, and she and Robert would be vacationing again soon. She also looked forward to Claire's visit and would not be leaving the area while she was visiting here.

Deborah had been a wonderful help to her Mom and Dad during their move to the country. She was strong and had a sense of where everything should go. She suggested that the organ should go down in the family room. That way they wouldn't have two major musical instruments in the upstairs living room, even though there was certainly plenty of room for both. They tried that approach, and Janine and John agreed on the arrangement.

Janine, who made substantial use of her sewing machine over the years, was actually thinking of making curtains and drapes for the new house.

*I'll be three months at the project, if I do that, and I have much more important things to be doing. I don't want to keep adding things to my "to do" list. I hope I never have to move again. This is too much work for an old lady. No wonder old people just stay put.*

# 36

# Coming to America

Who was more excited? Claire was coming into Pittsburgh today. Deborah would be there to greet her, of course, and there would be no holding Kathy, Karen and Meghan back. Greg would be working a half-day and would see them at home. Janine and John would be visiting with all of them tomorrow.

The girls had Claire's picture with them so that they could identify her. Spotting her, however, would not be a problem. They had her image imprinted on their hearts and minds. They noticed that there were many others waiting for a student as well. They relaxed their impatience by entering into conversations. This was not the first time for some of the families to be receiving a foreign visitor, and they were eager to ease any apprehensions the new families might have concerning differences in cultural habits and language.

The air in the room was filled with excitement by the time the door opened for the arrivals. There were at least 60 young French students coming down the passageway.

"There she is!" Karen exclaimed. And sure enough, it was Claire. She was beautiful, as they knew she would be. Her dark hair was longer now, extending down her back, almost to her waist. Fashionably dressed, she wore a pleated blue skirt that rested above her knees with leggings of persimmon and carried a large shoulder bag. Karen and Meghan were jumping up and down, calling her name. She heard them and looked their way. She smiled, waved and indicated that she had to stay with her group for the time being. They acknowledged that they understood, and Claire moved along with the students to where Deborah was standing.

Deborah was the one who would be welcoming Claire and all the students to America. She was their first impression. Her family was so proud of her and the warm words of welcome she extended to them. Deborah called attention to the guidelines for their visit and emphasized the importance of speaking English as much as possible. After all, their parents were expecting them to learn from the culture here, and they had all studied English for six years or more. This was to be part of their educational process.

"But above all," Deborah said, "enjoy your new families and have fun!"

"I'm going to call each one of you forward to be introduced to your new family." She proceeded to announce the name of the individual who stepped forward as his or her host family came to greet them. It was a joy to behold, especially for the families. The students seemed to be a little shy and reserved. Claire was certainly lovingly received and warmly welcomed, and when she realized that Deborah was a part of her new family, she managed a little smile as her nervousness eased a little.

*I hope this is going to be a good experience.* She thought. *These people seem to be very nice.* Although she continued to be apprehensive, she managed to appear pleased to be there.

She was at least relieved that her host family and the others in the airport did not emerge as rude and totally unsophisticated as she expected. On the streets of France, when there were American tourists, most could easily be detected by their brashness and sloppy attire, and seemed to be more concerned with pushing their way along and being dressed for *"la bataille."* The French would speak about them and say, "Look out, the Americans are here."

Her instructor in France had told the students who were to be traveling to America this year that not all Americans were the same as those they were used to seeing. Nevertheless, she and the others were skeptical.

Claire had also been somewhat *afraid* to be in America. The television and the newspapers had been presenting turmoil in America, and she was certain that she would encounter racial violence in the cities and elsewhere. The instructor had done his best to dilute that concept and reduce their fears; however, that form of information was measured out daily and it was difficult for the students to not be afraid and guarded.

They had talked among themselves about how to come to grips with challenging situations that they would likely encounter in America. Claire personally had difficulty understanding why her parents would send her to a country where possibly another revolution could take place. She would not question her parents. Consequently, they had no idea that she was anything but excited with the opportunity to see America.

She looked around the airport, expecting to see the military everywhere with large guns in hand. She saw only a few security guards, making their way through the crowds without force. She knew they were carefully checking everyone, but they were not heavily armed, nor was their presence threatening to anyone… At least not at the moment.

*I wish I hadn't come,* she thought. *In a few minutes all of my friends will be gone from me, and I will be alone with an American family. How can we possibly have anything in common? These trips are supposed to give us some understanding of people from other countries. Why couldn't I have gone to Holland, Ireland or Italy? I didn't want to come here!*

*This family told me they live in a log home. I've seen pictures of those cabins. We'll all be crowded up into a small space and have no privacy at all. My family is rooted in the aristocracy. This family should see where I live!*

She was polite and agreeable with her host family—these commoners—and would continue to be so, no matter what she actually thought of them. Her parents would expect no less of her.

❀ ❀ ❀

When the family drove up to the house, Claire was absolutely stunned. It did not look like Abraham Lincoln's log cabin. She could never have imagined a house made entirely of logs to be so large.

Prince bounded to the car to meet them, and Claire was very happy that there was a dog in the family. There were several dogs on her family's estate and she loved each one of them. Prince was likable in every way and they became friends immediately. A dog can warm a room or a heart when nothing else can.

They went inside. The house was warm and inviting and surprisingly efficient with running water, bedrooms…luxurious in a strange sort of way. The family welcomed her into their home and walked her through the main part of the house.

Climbing the stairway to the loft, it seemed she was in a fantasy. No house she had ever been in before had a loft. She likened it to the balcony in a theater; however, this "balcony" had rooms.

Meghan was excited to let her know that she was giving Claire her room for her visit. "It's very peaceful up here and cozy, and the bathroom is right here beside it. Come on, I'll show you where Karen and I will be sleeping."

Claire followed the girls as they introduced her to her surroundings.

Later in the day when Greg came home from work, all three girls bounded down from the loft to see him.

"Daddy, this is our new friend, Claire."

Claire looked up at the 6-foot, 3-inch man with a very broad smile and warm nature. She extended her hand to him, and he welcomed her to their home. He said he would be preparing dinner in a short while, which did not seem unusual at all to Claire.

The meal prepared by *Le Pere* was delicious, and she ate more than she intended. It was casually served at the kitchen table, which she thought rather crude. The kitchen was for dining only by the hired help in her home. Obviously, there was no hired help here.

Each person cleared her portion of the table, and she insisted that she would do the same. She had been instructed to follow whatever was the common practice in her host home, and so she would. *This is only for one month. I can do it,* she thought.

No one could have predicted how much she would love Prince, but then everyone loves Prince. He decided to adopt Claire immediately. He curled up at her feet at dinnertime, and followed her upstairs at bedtime. Kathy called him to come back downstairs, and Claire asked if he could please remain with her.

"Of course, Claire, if you don't mind having Prince with you, that will be fine," Kathy said, thinking that perhaps Prince gave Claire some comfort in her strange environment.

Claire was very appreciative of having Prince with her. She sat on the edge of the bed and said, *"Allez, Prince."*

He understood her and came to her immediately. She began to speak to him in her native language, telling him how handsome he was, and that they should become very good friends.

Prince looked at her and understood every word. He was a remarkable dog!

It gave Claire comfort to speak in French, and Prince enjoyed it as well. She told him about her home and her dogs there, and how beautiful her country was. He wanted to know more, but she became very sleepy.

*"Bonne nuit,"* she said as Prince curled up on the floor beside her. She closed her eyes and was soundly asleep in minutes.

The next morning was one of the most beautiful days ever—a perfect day to explore the fields and outer areas of the house. Claire and the girls relaxed a bit with one another and began giggling and talking excessively throughout the day.

Karen and Claire were almost the same age. They discussed their schools, studies, and activities. It was amazing that they both seemed to have the same opinions about much of what they were learning. Karen was impressed that Claire was required to learn many languages, especially English.

"In America, we can select a foreign language, and usually study that one for two or three years. I have chosen French, but would be embarrassed to speak your language with you. I have only had one year so far. You speak English very well," Karen said.

"Thank you very much. I have studied this for six years."

Meghan returned to the house to give the older girls an opportunity to spend time discussing things of mutual interest.

She really didn't want to do that, but her mother had given her "orders" before they went outside.

Karen asked her about her home life, and Claire touched only on the fact that she was an only child and they lived in the country. She did say that they vacationed quite a bit every summer, and her parents would be arranging for her to visit other countries over the next two summers. It was a cultural experience for her to have a better understanding of the global scene.

Claire enjoyed the walk. It was very quiet. She wondered how far they were from other houses, but did not ask. She would take her time and would learn from experiences instead of asking too many questions.

Janine and John walked over to the Langs' later in the afternoon to meet Claire and would have dinner with the family. Prince met them and led them to the backyard where the family was setting up for an American tradition.

Karen walked Claire over to her grandparents and introduced her to them. Claire extended her hand and pleasantries were exchanged.

*What a lovely girl,* thought Janine.

Janine, Karen, and Claire sat on a bench and talked awhile. Janine could sense that Claire was uneasy even though her English was impeccable.

*She needs time,* thought Janine. *Kathy's family is the best at making someone feel comfortable. It won't take long.*

Claire and Karen went to the house together to gather some items that Greg needed.

The two girls were talking away, and Janine sensed that they would shortly be best friends.

Soon Greg was grilling, Kathy and the girls were carrying food out to the picnic tables, and there was excitement in the air.

Their special guest was about to experience her first American Bar-B-Q—a truly perfect idea.

Claire would write home about this dinner! Greg cooked up the best hamburgers and hotdogs anyone ever had. Claire thought the meal was delicious, including potato salad and baked beans, which she ate there for the first time in her life. They finished the meal with good old American apple pie and ice cream. Everyone thought the food was delicious, and it was fun and a bit of an icebreaker for Claire.

*How pleasant to be sitting out in the yard to eat,* Claire thought. *I'm going to request that we try eating out in one of the gardens at home some time—or at least on the veranda.*

It was an ideal evening for the picnic from any viewpoint. The weather had remained picture-perfect throughout the day, birds were chirping, flower gardens were in full bloom, and the yard was sheltered into complete privacy by trees and beautifully appointed bushes.

The tables were covered with red-and-white-checkered tablecloths, and they ate from Styrofoam plates. She tried to spell "Styrofoam" in her letter to her mother, but didn't think she did so correctly.

She took picture after picture of the family, the table, of Greg and his grill, and the surroundings. By the time evening came and they all went indoors, everyone seemed to be more relaxed with one another. Claire discovered that she was smiling without straining to do so.

When she and Prince went up to bed, she had a fine conversation with him. He agreed that they had a rather nice day today.

As she continued to speak French, she told him that Karen

was a very bright girl, which was not news to him. He always did think so.

Prince put his head on her lap and comforted her as she confided to him that she missed her mother.

She was thankful for Prince and found that she wanted to warm up to the family as well. As they were both preparing to go to sleep, she vowed to Prince that she would do her best to accept her fate here and work harder at having appreciation for the family that had welcomed her so sincerely. He accepted that, and went straight to sleep.

She finished her letter to her mother and drifted off to sleep as her lips bent into a soft smile.

# 37

# A Woodland Experience

It was a beautiful morning as John appeared out of the woods from behind their home. His steps were swift and nimble, and as he approached the back of house, he called Janine.

"Honey, you have to come to the woods with me. I have found lilies in bloom all along the little creek there. Come and see!"

"John, I'm afraid of the woods," she called from the upper deck.

"You don't have to be afraid. There's nothing there to hurt you, and it's cool and beautiful under the shelter of the large tree branches. Come on…I'll be right beside you. I want you to see the lilies."

Fear gripped Janine as she instantly recalled being lost in the woods as a child. She had been with a Girl Scout Troop and innocently wandered from the others. When she suddenly realized that she was alone, the wooded area seemed to press upon her. The trees were overpowering and she didn't know where she was. It was only moments before she was found, but those few, frightening moments have prevented her from ever entering into the suffocating captivity of any wooded area.

"John, I don't think I can do it."

"Please, Honey, come and try. If you become too frightened, we won't go forward."

Janine wanted to go and decided that maybe she could. She put on an old pair of shoes and joined up with him in the backyard.

The closer she got to the mass of trees, the more nervous she became. John took her hand, and kept assuring her she would be fine. She felt like a little child and truly ridiculous, as she tried to remain calm and trust in John to lead her through. Everything closed in. There was nothing but trees and undergrowth.

John was compassionately understanding and helpful, and she continued to lean upon him for courage. A deer bounded up suddenly and both the animal and the humans were startled. Janine gripped John tightly at the unexpected interruption, yet appreciated the beauty and gracefulness of this creature in its natural habitat. She drew in a deeper breath, pleasurably inhaling a new fragrance of nature's ever-changing subsistence.

Janine was thinking, *This is a completely contradictory environment for me—frightening, yet fascinating. I can do this for John as long as I have him with me.*

When they moved on down to the creek, the trees opened up to the light, and Janine was much happier and more relaxed. John still held her hand, and took them along the creek bank a few yards…and there they were—hundreds of gorgeous auburn-to-orange lilies.

"What do you think?" John asked.

"I can't believe it…John, they are beautiful. No wonder you wanted to bring me here. Let's go over and smell them."

It was a little muddy underfoot, but they were careful. They found themselves surrounded by the flowers and bees and butterflies, giving them a feeling of God's intended Paradise. The creek water was lightly playing a melody over the rocks, and the buzzing of the bees and chirping of the birds were in perfect harmony.

Janine had a lump in her throat as she looked at John and said, "Thank you, John. If you hadn't insisted, I would have missed this beautiful moment."

He hugged her and said, "It would never have meant the same to me without being able to share it with you."

They stood there for quite some time without speaking, enjoying the peaceful setting. John asked Janine if she would like for him to dig up some of the flowers and replant them in their yard.

"That would be wonderful, John. Why don't we have the girls come along to see the flowers with us, and they can help you dig and carry."

"Good idea, but do you think it would be all right now that Claire is there?"

"I think so. I'll call Kathy and ask her."

When they got back into the house, Janine called Kathy, and she thought it would be a good experience for all three girls. She arranged for them to come over in their scruffy clothes the next day and enter into an adventure with the grandparents.

The girls skipped along together as they came to Grandma's house, looking every bit the part of diggers and gatherers. Claire was wearing a pair of Meghan's old sport shoes and some clothes that Janine recognized as Karen's.

"Good morning," said Janine as she and John stood in the doorway.

*"Bonjour, Grand-mère. Bonjour, Grand-père,"* the three responded in unison.

"Are you ready to go exploring?" John asked.

*"Oui."*

"Come inside while I gather up some gloves for us and *Grand-père* gets his tools from the garage."

While their shoes were not yet muddy, the girls showed Claire around the house. They met the grandparents in the yard, and off they went to explore the woods. None of the three actually had been in these woods before, so it was a new experience for all of them. They were discussing the wilderness and what they might encounter as they paced themselves over the terrain.

John had been the leader of the way, and Karen took the responsibility of keeping Grandma on her feet. Not a single one of them had any idea that Janine feared being there. Arriving at the creek, they wanted to immediately go wading, and John and Janine saw no reason why they shouldn't. The girls left their shoes on so they wouldn't cut themselves on the rocks or anything else that might be hidden in the moving waters. They marched along, laughing and carrying on for a while. The time eventually came to begin the project.

They found it harder to walk now with wet shoes, but they didn't care one bit.

Someone decided to count the flowers. After counting to 85, they decided there were at least two hundred, and they didn't need to count anymore! John began to dig, and instructed the girls to place them carefully onto the papers he had brought along. Carrying the small packages through the foliage was tedious work with weighted down wet shoes, but no one complained. It had been a great experience for everyone. Janine was very pleased that she had been able to participate in the joyous adventure. Perhaps she will someday overcome this lifelong fear of hers.

John offered to give the girls a lift home, and they were grateful because of the struggle to walk in the shoes.

Plodding to the house, they were talking excitedly about the fun they had with the grandparents. Kathy was eager to hear all about it. She waved to her father as the girls removed their shoes. They had to go around to the back of the house and hose off all of the mud before Kathy would permit them to enter. They certainly understood.

At bedtime, Prince was eager to hear all about how Claire could have been so muddy. She told him that she had a very interesting day surrounded by flowers. Her words about the girls were affectionate, and Prince responded lovingly. She laughed when she described that it was actually fun walking through squishy, muddy shoes. Prince wagged his tail as though he wished he could have been there with them.

Perhaps it was a good match for her to be in this place. She would definitely learn about everyday life from a completely new aspect, and that was indeed what she was sent to do.

Her resignation pleased Prince, and he stretched out on the floor as she bid him *"bonne nuit."*

# 38

# O, Say Can You See?

The 4th of July was a great day to appreciate the "good ol' U.S.A." Claire sang *"God Bless America,"* heard Lee Greenwood's *"God Bless the U.S.A.,"* and stood for the "Star Spangled Banner." Deborah and Bob joined the family and brought Claire a shirt in red, white, and blue with firecrackers exploding all over it. The evening of the 4th, when they were all on the banks of The Point in Pittsburgh watching a spectacular presentation of fireworks over the rivers, Claire unpredictably felt the thrill of being an American.

She had been positive that there would be demonstrations and unrest on the streets of Pittsburgh although she did not mention it. The drive into Pittsburgh was beautiful and exciting. They had parked the car in a parking lot quite a distance from the celebrations, but walking gave them all an opportunity to see a lot more of the city.

Claire hid her nervousness as she peered from side to side and around corners, expecting something vile to happen. When she finally realized that all was well, she began to silently question all of the reports she had heard about America. As they went through the day and night, her anxieties decreased, and she had a wonderful time. She would wear her new shirt with pride.

On the 7th, she met up with her fellow travelers who were

aglow with happiness. They all shared their experiences with one another. Kathy and Greg noticed that Claire was talking excitedly with her French peers, and everyone in the large room seemed to be quite happy and energized at that point.

Soon the band was set up, and the members of it were young and loud—just what the French and American teens enjoyed. There was no holding back as dancing got underway and strobe lights flashed. Everyone danced around with whomever was at hand, and they interacted eagerly as though they had known one another forever. Kathy was convinced that music and rhythm was indeed a universal language.

The young people had a wonderful evening, and the parents were happy as well, even though the music was louder than they could enjoy. The family talked all the way back home, and the parents suggested that everyone rest up during the next day because they would be leaving for a trip the following morning.

They all fell into bed exhausted and did rest the next day, except to pack for their trip. The next morning they were travelling the American highways. Claire tried not to miss a thing as she kept asking questions and looking out of the car windows.

First they went to Washington, D. C. for three days, on to Williamsburg, VA, and then two days at Bush Gardens!

The Langs realized that even though Washington D.C. was beautiful and magnificently designed, it could not be compared with Versailles and Paris. Claire disagreed. She was very impressed and thrilled to have been at the center of American laws and government. She had seen the images time and time again on television and would now be able to identify the buildings.

There were those who were demonstrating about something near the Washington Monument, but it was peaceful—unlike other demonstrations Claire had seen on television.

Looking at the Capitol Building, Claire thought about all of the news reports she had seen in France, and also on American television about the disgruntled arguments constantly occurring between U. S. Government officials. She felt that if they couldn't get along, how could they possibly manage the entire country? She hoped to discuss this with the Langs someday if she ever felt more at ease to do so.

She loved Williamsburg. She had seen nothing like it ever! And what girl in the whole world would not enjoy Bush Gardens? She rode the roller coasters and double loop over and over again.

They were travelling on Bastille Day, and Claire told the family of the way they celebrated their French holiday, which she said is *Fête de la Fèdèration,* to celebrate the French Revolution.

"Perhaps you could visit France to celebrate our holiday with my family. You could see the fireworks in Paris from the Eifel Tower. Our fireworks are beautiful, but perhaps not so much so as were those in Pittsburgh," Claire said.

No one could say "yes or no" at that point. It was a generous invitation, and they would remember it.

They welcomed the peace and quiet that the house offered. Prince was glad to see them all, and demonstrated his joy to every one of them, including Claire. She flopped down on the floor with him, and they tussled and rolled around together in pure delight.

Claire had a long talk with Prince that night.

"Prince, I have missed you," she spoke in her beautiful native tongue. "You are such a beautiful dog and a good friend." He wagged his tail in response.

"I came to this country with many misconceptions. Don't tell your family, but I thought they would never live up to standards high enough for me. What a prude I was!

"I was so wrong. They and most Americans I have met are kind, generous and loving people. It is such a tragedy that the news twists things around so that those of us who are in other countries are becoming more and more distrusting of Americans. I am going to do everything I can to spread the word that your people (and dogs!) are perhaps the finest this world has to offer."

Prince thought *she* was one of the best. As she spoke, she kept looking at him and petting him. He would listen to her as long as she wanted to talk. Prince was her first real friend in America and had helped her through those early days. The bond was set. They would be friends for life.

When the time arrived to say "goodbye" to Prince, Claire actually cried. Prince consoled her once again. She held onto the hope that she would see him again someday.

The day for Claire's departure came much too soon for her and for everyone else. In the hearts of those who shared her time in America, she would always be a real part of their family, and hopefully she would come back again and again.

Janine and John would not stay home this time, but went to the airport with the family to say *"au revoir."* It was touching and difficult for all of the exchange students and their host families. Warm farewells could be heard throughout the airport as the families sent the students back to France.

Deborah had told Kathy's family that the main reason for the exchange was to promote peace among peoples of all nations. It was a great concept, and the program generally did accomplish its goal of doing just that. There wasn't a better way to understand others than to share quality time together. Claire had come to a good place to learn of the sincerity, generosity, and loving nature of the people of the U.S.A. She would go home and spread the word, one to one.

The reserved manners the families sensed when the students arrived had completely vanished. There were hugs, tears, and heartfelt wishes for another time to be together. The Langs were already planning for the days when Claire would return. They would definitely stay in touch and take advantage of any opportunity to be together in the future.

# 39

# A Basket of Neighborliness

Janine answered the knock at the front door. There stood the most beautiful young man she had ever seen. "Tall, dark, and handsome" might appropriately describe him, but would not do him justice. He had glisteningly curly, dark-brown hair, expressively warm brown eyes and an irresistible smile that drew in two beautifully placed dimples.

"Hello!" she said.

"Hello! My name's Tony. Tony Detelle. Welcome to the neighborhood!" He extended his hand.

She clasped his hand. "How do you do, Tony? Thank you. I'm Mrs. Stephens."

"Mrs. Stephens, my grandparents have sent over some food for you. It's in the car. So are my grandparents. Would you like to meet them?"

"Yes. Yes, I would." She went over to a very nice automobile—maybe a Lincoln—maybe not. She didn't really know one car from another.

In the back seat was a woman and in the front passenger seat, apparently her husband. When Janine walked toward the car, "Grandfather" got out and opened the door for his wife. They looked very happy and approached her warmly.

"This is my grandfather, Mario Detelle…and this is my

grandmother, Sophia Detelle...This is Mrs. Stephens." They shook hands—Grandfather first. He was not as tall as Tony and had balding, rather gray hair. She was mesmerized by his eyes, which were exactly like Tony's—beautifully brown and still with the same youthful-looking spark.

Mr. Detelle was smiling warmly. He shook Janine's hand with his right hand, and covered her hand over with the other. He was nodding and said, "Pleased to meet you."

"Thank you. It's very nice to meet you, also."

She turned to Mrs. Detelle. *What an attractive woman!* Even though she was probably in her 70's, she was beautiful. Janine always thought Italians were the most beautiful people on earth...perhaps because her mother's mother was Italian.

"How do you do, Mrs. Detelle."

"I'm-a no speak-a da English too much," she said.

"That's fine. Don't worry about that...Please...I'm so happy to meet you."

Janine turned to Tony. "Where do you live?"

"We live toward West Hope a little ways. It's the house up on the hill with the pillars at the foot of the drive."

*Good grief! The BIG house! It is one of those modern homes with lots of rooms and outside lights,* thought Janine.

"Well, won't you come in?"

"Na, Na! We just want'a you to have somet'ing from us to say we hope you happy here."

"That is just so nice of you. But please come on inside."

They decided that would be all right and appropriate, so Tony gathered up the nice basket and Janine led them in through the front door to the kitchen.

"Here, we'll put the basket on the island. I'll call my husband... John!"

"Yes."

"Can you come up, please? We have company!"

He was so surprised and came rushing up the stairs. She introduced the Detelles to him, and asked them if they would sit down. She would fix some coffee.

That was satisfactory with everyone, and they had a very pleasant, but short visit. It was absolutely delightful! What lovely people. So mannerly and polite, and they were genuine in their desire for the Stephens to feel welcome in the community.

Their son, Anthony, owns the house, and had his parents move in with them. When Mario and Sophia came to America, Mario went to work in the coalmines.

"Anthony—he no wanted to do work in the mines, so he learn how to make a good business. He say he work on top'a da ground. That's-a good." Mario said.

The Stephens learned that Anthony and his wife, Geonna, have three children and Tony is the youngest.

Tony said he is in his final year of high school. John asked him if he knew their granddaughter, Karen Lang, who is a sophomore. Tony said he knew her, but wasn't sure if they had met.

They all had coffee. Mrs. Detelle said, "You have a nice-a kitchen. Very good."

"Thank you. We're very happy with it." She was totally overwhelmed by this remarkable visit. How special of them to come by! No one had done that. *Does anyone really welcome anyone anymore?*

"I'll take the food from the basket, and you can take the basket back with you," she said.

Mrs. Detelle said, "Na, Na! That's-a fine. You keep'a da basket. Its'a for you."

They were leaving. "You come over to see us sometime,"

Mr. Detelle said. "We would like to have you come see us." Mr. Detelle has been out into the world and has done much better with his English. Mrs. Detelle has stayed in most of the time, speaking mostly Italian to her son and husband.

Tony opened the car doors for his grandparents. He had nice manners and treated them with the utmost respect. *This boy is being brought up well.* Janine and John were both sensitive to his treatment of his elders.

John said the car *was* a Lincoln. Anthony had certainly done well for himself. They wondered what he did for a living. Whatever it was, capitalism worked!

They stood in the driveway as the Detelles left, feeling uplifted by the unexpected visit. As they walked back to the kitchen, they could smell the Italian sauce permeating the air. They could hardly wait to open the basket! Mmm, mmm! It was baked rigatoni! And there was fresh-baked bread, which was always the best part of any meal for Janine.

"Oh, my gosh! This is fantastic. Let's eat!" Janine said.

❀ ❀ ❀

Karen answered the telephone. "Hi, Karen. It's Grandma. I wanted to talk with you."

"Hi, Grandma. You wanted to talk with me?"

"Yes. I wanted to tell you that we had a visitor today. It was Tony Detelle. Do you know him?"

"Do I know him? My goodness, yes. He's the most popular boy in the whole school. What on earth was he doing at your house?"

"Well, he lives just down the lane, you know."

"Of course, I know…in that great big beautiful house on the

hill. Oh, my gosh. I can't believe he came to your house. Was he selling something?"

"No. Actually he brought us something. His grandmother made us some baked rigatoni and bread to welcome us to the neighborhood, and Tony and his grandparents came and brought that and visited a while."

"Wow! They didn't come here when *we* moved in. What did he say?"

"He said he knew you."

"He knows me? I don't believe it. How would he have any idea who I am? He is always with a bunch of friends, and everyone wishes *they* were with his friend, I can tell you that. He's a fine student—probably valedictorian—and is the big-time basketball star. He'll most likely go on to play basketball for some well-known college."

"Hmmm. I don't know about all of that, but I was very impressed with his politeness and manners."

"Mom wants to talk with you."

"Ok, Sweetie."

"Hi! What's up?"

"I was telling Karen that we had a real nice visit this afternoon from the Detelles, who brought us a basket of "welcome-to-the-neighborhood" food. It was Tony and his grandparents. Do you know the family?"

"Yes. Everybody knows them, Mother. They live in that big house down the road a ways. Mr. Detelle, Tony's father, owns a meat packing business."

"Well, I wondered…Are you going to church tomorrow?"

"Yes. I was going to call you and see if you want to go with me. It's really a small church, Mother. I don't know what you'll think of it, but the people are very nice."

"Yes, I'll go with you. John and I have decided not to drive into Center Church anymore, and the other churches between here and there are just not working out for us. I'm actually feeling kind of low about it all, right now. Maybe being with you would help."

"Ok. I'd like to go a little early because I want to talk with the lay minister about the hymns he would like before church begins. I'll stop by for you at ten-fifteen. Ok?"

"Ok. See you then."

Janine had been almost ill with sadness. Never had she felt such depression. Every time they entered a church, she had hope that maybe there was something there for her to begin anew, but so far she had obviously not found the right church.

Kathy and the girls were there on time. John said he would most certainly go with her. He had decided to leave Center Church with Janine; therefore, had resigned the Session. There had been too many questions and not enough answers. It would be better for both of them if they worked through all of this side-by-side.

The little church was actually within walking distance. She had walked past it several times. It must have been built a long time ago, and had very little maintenance lately. The cemetery had some old tombstones, and at one time this church was in all probability the only church anyone could get to by foot or carriage. She envisioned church suppers and lawn gatherings from days gone by. Now there were many churches, and people most likely preferred a denominational church, anyway. She did, too, but who knows?

It was the normal-looking one-room church, needing paint. It had a steeple of sorts and six steps leading to the front door.

Someone had hung a wreath on it. Maybe it was Kathy. She would do that.

They entered into a tiny little entryway, and opened up the door to the sanctuary. There didn't seem to be anyone there, and there were about ten rows of pews divided by an aisle in the middle. Up front was a pulpit on an elevated floor and a piano to the left. Three chairs were on the pulpit platform.

The lay minister came right behind them and greeted Kathy and her family. Kathy introduced Mr. Dawson to Janine and John, and the girls indicated a pew where they might be sitting. They sat and picked up a hymnbook. It was not one she had ever used, which was hard to believe. She had quite a collection. Anyway, it appeared to be quite old and was probably donated by another church at some point in time.

Janine looked around. The windows were frosted, the floors were bare, and the boards on the walls were clapboard and unpainted. Why was Kathy here? Did the Lord lead her here, or did she just figure, *Why not?* She had told Janine that they needed her at the piano, so perhaps she had decided it was something she could do.

A few other parishioners came in. They were so curious with the new people sitting there, that they couldn't contain themselves. They rushed right over to meet them. They were still jabbering when Kathy was playing the Prelude. Janine wanted to shush them. She always did think that it was rude for people to be talking during the Prelude. To her, it was the opening of the worship service and a time of preparation for the congregation, not a time to talk louder and louder. She tried to be polite, even though she was annoyed.

Of course, she didn't find the opportunity to prepare herself.

The people didn't even want to stop talking when the preacher said, "Good morning!"

Finally, they did settle down. She grabbed John's knee, and he knew she was not where she wanted to be. *Well, the Lord would have a message for them, so they had just better listen,* he thought.

The opening hymn was, *"Shall We Gather at the River."* Janine knew this one, but her congregation had never sung it. It was rather refreshing to her, actually. She couldn't hear many others singing, except the lady behind her who sounded more like a foghorn than anything else. She apparently thought she was an alto, but couldn't locate the part. She kept singing anyway.

The minister cleared his throat and read John 14:15–20:

> *"If you love me, you will obey what I command.*
> *And I will ask the Father, and he will give you another Counselor to be with you forever–the Spirit of truth.*
> *The world cannot accept him, because it neither sees him nor knows him.*
> *But you know him, for he lives with you and will be in you.*
> *I will not leave you as orphans; I will come to you.*
> *Before long, the world will not see me anymore, but you will see me.*
> *Because I live, you also will live.*
> *On that day you will realize that I am in my Father, and you are in me, and I am in you."*

Janine wanted to shout, "Amen!"

John wanted to, too. *This is a message for us.*

The minister raised his eyes from the Bible and cleared his throat. "Now then, some of you might be feeling all alone today. (throat clearing) Perhaps it is you. (throat clearing) This scripture is very comforting, isn't it? (throat clearing) Love and obey. (throat clearing) That's what Jesus, himself is saying.

(throat clearing) Love and obey. (throat clearing) You know that old hymn? (throat clearing) Well, (throat clearing) we're going to sing that one today, aren't we Kathy? (throat clearing)

"But before we do, (throat clearing) we need to continue to see what will result (throat clearing) what will be the result of our loving (throat clearing) and our obedience.

*The poor fellow clears his throat with every sentence. How sad. How distracting! What is he trying to talk about? I don't know. I have counted* 13 *times of clearing so far. Now,* 14.*"* John was thinking.

Eighty seven throat clearings later, they stood to sing "Trust and Obey." It wasn't "love" and obey after all. It was "trust" and obey. *Oh well, It's a good old hymn anyhow. I'll get more out of singing this than I could possibly have gotten out of that sermon. I feel really sorry for that fellow. He probably wants to be a minister, and there is no way he will ever be able to get the message across. Did he feel called by God to do this? Can we ever absolutely know when we have found the calling? Oh, Lord, please help me to know. Please, Lord. Please!* Janine prayed all through the first stanza. Kathy was looking at her wondering why she wasn't singing.

She joined in finally, and even the lady behind didn't do too badly on this one. Mr. Dawson was waiting in the back to shake everyone's hand. He said he hoped they would all return next week. Janine didn't respond one way or the other, but she knew for sure she would not be coming back. She felt really bad about her attitude. It wasn't right. She should not be so picky. After all, Mr. Dawson was a good fellow and trying his best. *I can't help it…I can't help it!*

She was in tears in the car. John felt sorry for her, and knew that she was struggling with herself. When Kathy got in, she immediately noticed that Janine was crying.

"Mother, are you all right?"

"Sweetheart, I love you so much. You are a much better person than I am. I think you are so wonderful to come to this church and offer your services when you have to listen to a sermon like that."

"Mother, I do not get much out of it, I'll tell you the truth. Actually, I think I've been too lazy to search out a church that would be better for me. I should, really. Those few people there need to face up to closing the doors. They are just hanging on, and I'm helping them do it. I really do believe that it's coming very soon. If I didn't go there, they probably would finally resolve this. I guess it's something I need to pray about, instead of doing what's easy for me.

"Please don't think I'm some kind of saint. I sure am not. I wish I were, but my *raison d'être* is not in response to the Lord's calling or even his suggestion."

"Well, you are a wonderful person for sure. I'm sorry, Sweetheart. I won't be going back next week."

"Mother, I understand. I do…I probably won't be going there much longer anyway."

# 40

# A to Z

Francine and Lawrence were back from their wonderful vacation. Francine was back at the organ each Sunday and was really happy to be there after her extended and lighthearted break. She and Lawrence were still hoping to return to Florida by early November at the latest, but would be patient in the findings.

"It's nice to have Francine and the choir back. The young man did a fine job with the hymns, but the worship service seemed to struggle along," said Iola.

"Well, summer's almost over. Are you going to get away, Iola?"

"I won't have the time, Harriet. Having this bunion removed is going to be my main concern."

"I hope you have a really good doctor, and you're going to have to have some help after the operation. They say it takes about six weeks to actually get back on your feet."

"I know. That's why I've been putting it off so long, but it's come to the place now that I can't get around in decent shoes. I think I'll just go to the Continuous Care Center following the surgery and stay there until all is well again; Rachael is there, also. So I might be able to be with her at times."

They had discussed Rachael's progress during Sunday school. She was in the Continuous Care Center in a wheel chair, undergoing physical therapy to strengthen her upper body. She was preparing to be able to lift herself up using the bars on the exercise walkway. The ultimate goal of the endeavor was to take a step or two.

This was going to be a long haul, even if it proved successful. At least her doctor was not giving up on her—considering her past history of comebacks. She had great determination and courage, and she seemed to be less depressed than she was—all positive attributes for recovery.

Francine brought her mother, Alice, to Sunday school, and everyone was happy to see her. She was the oldest living member at Hope Church. Her health had not been the best, but she still seemed sharp as a tack. During Sunday school they asked her if she could still do the alphabet scriptures. She said, "I can. I go through them every time I can't sleep, and those occasions are more frequent these days."

The alphabet scriptures consisted of reciting a scripture that would begin with each letter of the alphabet from A to Z. So far, she was the only one in the class who had been able to master it every time. They loved to test her, and most of them had tried to learn all twenty-six, but would miss one or two. It was a great exercise in memory control, and it also gave the scholar meaningful scriptures to recall in any circumstance. She began,

"Ask and it will be given to you. Blessed are the poor in spirit, for theirs is the kingdom of heaven. Come to me all you who are weary and burdened, and I will give you rest. Do to others as your would have others do to you, for this sums up the Law and the Prophets." She continued through to her usual ending, "Zippidy do dah and zing, zing, zing," which always got a good laugh from the others.

Of course, she wouldn't leave it there, so she said, "Zedekiah, son of Josiah was made king of Judah by Nebuchadnezzar, king of Babylon."

Alice was a very bright woman, and it was such a blessing that she has kept her wits and her good humor throughout all of her 89 years.

Bea had asked, "Is everyone thinking about the October Fest? I've decided to make the peanut brittle again. How about you, Harriet? Yours is really good, too."

"I'm not sure I'll be here. I may be traveling to Austria. If my sister can go, we'll be leaving in late September for a few weeks."

"Can you leave that puppy?" asked Anne.

"I don't know. He's such a sweetie, and we have a great relationship."

"Your son will look after him. You should live your life as you want," said Iola.

"We'll see."

"Iola, are you going to make some of those Monster Cookies?" asked Adele.

"No commitments at this time. We'll see how things go," said Iola.

Julia said she was going to make her orange cookies like she always did. "I'm really not in the mood to have all of that commotion throughout town again. I used to like it, but you can't even get through with all the people. When the children were little and could help, it was a lot different."

"None of the young people seem to be motivated either. We have quite a few living in the rentals, but they probably won't participate," said Laura. "Oh, they would if they could just put out a bunch of junk and call it 'treasurers,' but the borough commissioners said everything has to be home-baked or homemade. No more of those trashy items we had last year."

"Well, good!" said Anne. "Then if someone will share a porch with me, I'll make up some baby quilts. I've given away most of the full-sized quilts to my children and other family members. If I go to the trouble of making anymore of those they certainly won't be for a sale."

"You can come to my house," said Julia. "I'd welcome the company."

Adele had a great front porch, and Bea did also. Laura would be there for sure. They could all find a good porch to sit on and sell their items if they really wanted to. Trouble was, no one was exactly enthused to do it these days.

# Part Three
## In The Fullness Of Time

# 41

# Janine's Hope

It was the first Sunday in August, as Janine was getting dressed for church without an idea of where to go. "Which direction do you want to go this time?" she asked John.

He hesitated for a minute, and said, "I was thinking of that church on the knoll of West Hope. It's a Presbyterian Church, and we might feel a bit more comfortable with the order of worship. What do you think?"

"I guess we might as well."

They drove up the little road leading to the church, and there were a good many cars on the upper grounds on a very nice, paved parking lot. They pulled in and wondered which door to enter. No one was around to ask, then a lady drove up and they waited for her. She was dressed in a beautiful pink suit, had pretty white hair and was very neat in appearance.

"Let's ask her," John said.

They got out of the car, and she looked their way. "Good morning," they said to the lady. "Are we late for church?"

"No, we're just on time."

"Do we go in this door, then?" John asked.

"Yes, follow me." She seemed to be a bit shy and didn't offer her name.

They picked up a bulletin from the table in the narthex. The lady had disappeared, so they went over to the sanctuary doors and entered. The church had two aisles. They chose the left one. The back pew was empty, and it sat right in front of beautifully stained, open windows. They sat precisely as the service was beginning. The sanctuary was in the shape of a half circle—almost. They could see across to the people on the opposite side pretty well. Most of the people were in the two side sections, all facing the pulpit and the choir loft. There were fewer in the center.

Everyone looked so nice dressed in his or her Sunday best. That was good. They had been in one or two churches where people came rather "dressed down." Janine always said we should present ourselves respectably before the Lord in worship—clean and neat at the very least.

The bulletin followed the same worship pattern as they had become used to, and it was comforting.

Over in the far section, some were a-buzz about the couple that had just sat down.

Iola leaned over to Harriet, "Who are those who just came in?"

"I have no idea. I don't think I've ever seen them before."

*Hmm...Somebody new over there! At least I don't know them.* Bea was thinking.

The minister, Rev. Daniel Campbell, welcomed everyone and called for announcements. There were a few. Janine and John had no idea who they were talking about, of course. But it was interesting in a way. The choir sang a nice introit and the service actually officially began with Rev. Campbell calling one and all with a scripture from I Chronicles 16:11–12:

*Seek the LORD and his strength;*
*Seek his face evermore!*
*Remember his marvelous works, which he has done,*
*His wonders, and the judgments of his mouth.*

Rev. Campbell was articulate and enjoyable to listen to, and Janine and John were attentively focused for the first time in a long time. When the minister announced the Morning Worship Scripture, Janine turned to the Bible in the pew to read along.

"Matthew 7, beginning with verse 7:

*Ask and it will be given to you; seek and you will find;*
*knock and the door will be opened to you.*
*For everyone who asks receives; he who seeks finds;*
*And to him who knocks, the door will be opened.*
*Which of you, if his son asks for bread, will give him a stone?*
*Or if he asks for a fish, will give him a snake?*
*If you, then, though you are evil, know how to give good gifts to your children,*
*How much more will your Father in heaven give good gifts to those who ask him?*

Janine had memorized this scripture and repeated it to herself quite often. Rev. Campbell certainly had a wonderful message based upon trusting that the Lord hears and answers prayers.

As Janine sat there feeling totally at ease with the service and the message, a gentle wind brushed across the back of her neck. The breeze got her attention, while God gave her a message: "You are here."

She was nearly overcome with gladness, but she retained her composure. Attendance pads were passed along each pew. John signed for them, and passed it to Janine. When she handed it over to the man seated on the other end of the pew, he smiled broadly, read their names, and signed it himself. As soon as the benediction was pronounced, that same man shook their hands and welcomed them to the church. John later said he had very big, strong hands and was probably a farmer.

A few of the members greeted them as they went toward the door. One was "Leola," or something like that. She was very friendly and invited them to come back. An elderly lady (she couldn't remember her name) also talked with them both, and even asked where they lived. She seemed happy to hear that they were from Bear Lane. Many of the members were hanging around in clusters, seemingly not wanting to leave just yet.

Rev. Campbell shook their hands and asked their names. They told him they had recently moved into the area, and he said he hoped to see them again sometime. They left through the doors they had entered earlier. There were still a lot of cars on the parking lot. Apparently no one was in a hurry to leave. They walked over to the car, got in, and Janine couldn't hold back the tears any longer. John didn't turn on the ignition immediately. He just turned and looked at her, lovingly.

"John, it truly felt right. I think we should continue coming here. The breeze through the open window felt to me like God whispering, "You are here."

"I know." He started the ignition, put the car into gear, and as they were going down the slopping drive, he said, "And you know what...You are here. You are in West Hope, the community you have said for years was calling you."

"John...You are right! Why, oh why didn't I think of that before? I never, ever made that connection."

"Looks like now you are going to get your wish and find out more about the people here after all." He smiled a smile that just wouldn't quit. She, on the other hand, could hardly see through her tears. She prayed silently, *"Thank you, Lord. My joy is too much at this moment. You've given me something I never even requested. It was just a dream such as a child would have…wasn't it?"*

John said, "'Seek and you will find.'"

Two days later they received a nice card from "Iola." *That was her name!* It said it was good having them worship at West Hope U. P. and she hoped to see them again. *"If you have any needs, please feel free to contact the minister, Rev. Campbell, at the church office."*

# 42

# A Day in the Life...

Julia was calling Iola. "Did you get the names of the people who came on Sunday? You always seem to do that."

"I did. All I had to do was read the pew attendance book. I sent them a card. Their names are 'Stephens.'"

"Hmm...I don't think I know any Stephens. Do they live around here?"

"Not far. They are on Bear Lane. I drove over that way yesterday just out of curiosity. I think they bought the Stafford house. Poor ol' Minnie. She's not doing well at all. I suppose Jake just couldn't keep up."

"I didn't know them very well. Actually, I'm not even sure of where they lived either. Anyway, I suppose the Stephens won't be back. We don't see many changes around here."

"Probably not...People come and people go. We'll see." Iola wished that were not true.

"It's so hot today. I wish it would rain and cool things down a bit."

"I know, but it would just add humidity and that could be worse. You could go sit on the porch. Maybe it's cooler outside."

"I tried that. It didn't help. And those noisy trucks spoil a good, relaxing sitting."

"Would you want to walk down to the store? I need some

things and thought I'd put on my comfortable shoes and walk. I'll come by." Iola always enjoyed walking, but not so much lately with her bunion.

"Ok. Better than just sittin' here, I suppose."

They lived just a few houses apart, though on most days, it could have been miles for all they saw of one another. Iola was there in no time. Julia picked up her purse and met her on the sidewalk.

"Do you think we'll ever get new sidewalks? I'm half afraid to walk on these stones." Julia remarked.

"What?"

"The sidewalks!" She looked straight at her, knowing she wasn't hearing her. "Do you think we'll ever get new ones?"

"New ones?"

"Yes!"

"Who would do it? The borough can't afford it, and the state wouldn't consider this their responsibility. I think each homeowner could contract a new sidewalk. Why don't you do that?"

"One short sidewalk won't make a difference at all."

"It might put the thought into another's mind, and then another. Those things work sometimes." Iola was always figuring up solutions to problems.

"Yes, I suppose. But I'm not going to be the one to start it."

Although most people thought the sidewalks were quaint, it *was* tedious walking. *Quaint is nice until someone falls!* Julia was thinking.

"When are you going to have your bunion removed?"

"What?"

Julia stopped and pointed to Iola's foot. "Your bunion. Are you going to have it removed?"

"Oh, I thought about it some more. I'm going to do it in January when I have nothing at all to do but sit inside."

"'Makes sense."

They went into the store, which was blessedly cool. The Carters had put in air-conditioning. There were a few other folks there—probably to cool off!

Hayden said, "Hello, ladies! Warm enough for you?"

"Hello, Mr. Carter. It certainly feels wonderful in here," said Iola. "How are you and Ms. Elda?"

"Oh, we're very fine thank you. Yessiree, very fine. Can I get you something?"

"Pardon me?" He found out suddenly that she did not have her hearing aid.

"We're fine." He spoke very clearly and cut it short.

"That's good!" she responded, and wandered on over toward the canned goods.

"How 'bout you, Ms. Julia?"

"I'll just look around a bit," she said.

Julia decided she'd better get some Band-Aids. She didn't have any the other day when she cut her thumb. So she picked up a box of assorted sizes, ordered a few slices of Longhorn Cheese, and bought a Milky Way candy bar. She was going to freeze it to eat later while watching the baseball game.

Julia walked over to the third aisle and found Iola, who was intently studying a box of something.

"What's that?" Julia asked.

"Now, just look at this! There are so many ingredients that you wouldn't even need any potatoes in the box. I can hardly pronounce all of these things, and they probably would not be good for you at all. I was going to buy a prepared scalloped-potato mixture, but I don't think I will. And the calories! Good heavens! I was going to try to eat more vegetables, but certainly not this."

"Why don't you buy a baking potato and just eat the whole thing? I do that sometimes."

"What?"

"Bake a potato!" She raised her voice. "Makes a meal," Julia offered.

"I couldn't eat an entire potato."

"You could, too. And…you could fix a salad. That would be lots of vegetables."

"Salads? Well, I don't actually like salads. My doctor would really like it if I would eat more salads, but I'm not ready to yet."

"Hmm…Did you ever try one of those frozen dinners?"

"Do you eat those? I do!" She really hadn't heard the question.

"Sometimes I cook up a big pot of soup or chili and have it all week."

She apparently understood her because she replied, "I like variety." She looked again at the box of scalloped potatoes, and decided to go ahead and buy it.

"What did you buy?" Iola asked.

She showed her. "Oh, just a few slices of cheese and a candy bar."

Iola asked, "Are you going to watch the ballgame on television tonight?"

"Yes." Julia answered. She was thinking, *I'm glad there's something on to watch. If I try to read, I just go to sleep.*

"I'll be watching, too."

As they were checking out, Mr. Gordon came through the door, wiping the perspiration from his neck and brow. "G'day me ladies!" he said. The ladies were always charmed by Mr. Gordon.

"And how're ye on this bonnie, bright day?" he asked.

The ladies responded with smiles and were suddenly charming, too.

"Good day to you, Mr. Gordon," Julia said, quite nicely.

Iola nodded her head as a fine English woman of the 19th Century would do, and said very properly, "Mr. Gordon, sir."

"Mr. Gordon, nice to see you. You surely are not out walking in this heat, sir?" asked Hayden.

"I am, at that. Exercise is goud fer the body aund the soul anytime o'the year; however, I could use me self a goud chilled glass o'yer fine lemonade, if you 'ave any t'day."

"That we do. Have yourself a seat and cool down. I'll go see about the drink for you."

The ladies left, bidding Mr. Gordon and Mr. Carter adieu.

"Do you have the *Daily?*" asked Mr. Gordon.

"Sure do, over there on the bench. Help yourself. Nothing good in the news these days though."

"Ere's the truth if ever t'was spoken. What's wrong with the world? I'cn tell ye what! Ere's people tha' need t'git em'selves a wee neighborhood t'live in such as we 'ave 'ere and settle down to some goud, clean livin.'"

"You have the answer! Yessiree! That's it…Just so's they don't all come here!"

Mr. Carter and Mr. Gordon always had fine conversations. They could settle the world's problems in a minute. Most of the men of the area could. Nothing was better than to have two or three of the gentlemen in at the same time discussing any given problem. They often did that.

"Tha' lemonade was on the spot! Off t'the bothy I go. We're 'avin' Cock-a-leekie soup. One o'me favorites."

"Very well. Come see us again."

"That I will! G'day."

Rachael had just returned from physical therapy, quite pleased that she had completed her exercise for the first time. She was more determined now to get herself back on her feet. The one thing she wanted to do more than anything else was to be able to go back to her home and be on her own again. *It's no different than any of us would say. No one wants to be depending upon someone else. I always said that I would do everything I could to stay 'in' dependent. If it means working hard at these exercises, then that's what I'm going to do.*

She had a terrific family. They were always coming to visit and bringing her reading materials. She'd read anything from Shakespeare to government proclamations. She especially enjoyed reading novels that are issued in a series.

Another thing she enjoyed was making those crafts, and now she could once more. The Center had arranged for her to go to a little room. They brought in her box of supplies, so she could sit in her wheelchair and putter all she wanted to. The staff knew that it was as good as any therapy they could offer. She was making some interesting wreaths from Honeysuckle vines. Albert cut some for her and soaked them. She had to work with them while they were still damp so that she could twist them around in a wreath shape. Albert helped her twist some of them the week prior, and now she was having a great time putting on some adornments in the way of flowers, greenery, etc. People looked in on her and enjoyed seeing what she would be doing next. It was always that way with her. It was one of the things that kept her going today.

* * *

Owen needed a special chair. He could have one delivered at the order of his doctor. He was not breathing as well as he should have been, and so he was going to attempt to get used to sleeping upright. The chair would be delivered to their new apartment that day, and thankfully, they found someone to take the other one. The old one was a standard recliner and did not have the special features he now needed.

Anne had been busy that day. The neighbor came early to pick up Owen's old chair. He was doing fine sitting in hers for the time being. "Owen, are you comfortable?" she asked.

"Oh, yes. This is fine. I can wait it out without any trouble. How about you?"

"Oh, I'm fine. After we're finished with the chair-moving process, I want to take out my embroidery piece again. I wondered if I would ever pick up that piece I started 15 years ago, and yet I realize that it would be the perfect gift for Sharon's graduation. I was so pleased when I looked at it and found it still in good shape.

I'm going to the kitchen and fix us some lunch. Is soup fine for today?"

"That good soup you made yesterday?"

"Yes."

"It's delicious. I'll look forward to it...Did you meet the new tenants?"

"Yes. They seem very nice. I hope we get to know them. It will be good to have someone else living next to us here in the building."

"I hope he plays checkers." Owen remarked.

She went into the kitchen and started lunch. She wasn't yet used to this small apartment. She had "worked her fingers to the bone," as Jenny had so aptly put it, in the big old farmhouse. It was truly getting too much for her to handle. This was better, but it was going to take time to adjust. *Life is full of changes and adjustments.* She'd seen a lot of them. *It's just harder when we get old. When we were young, I could just flit here and there. It didn't matter where we lived or how many children we were taking care of, either...Energy wanes. I want to face up to it, but am not doing so well at it right now. By the time Owen and I get going in the morning, and I leave for my walk, half of the day is done.*

*Then he takes a nap, and I pick up a little sewing or whatever, and the other half of the day is gone. I don't want to complain to anyone, and I have no right to. I am thankful that we've lived this long. This is the part that comes with old age, I guess. I hope I don't have to give in to it.*

# 43

# Adjustments

Life was full of adjustments! Anne had certainly rediscovered it recently, although she had made many during her 83 years. She'd face this one just as she had motherhood, retirement, and now a reduction in active participation. She didn't need to work so hard, anyway, but she needed to be doing something that was interesting. Being the oldest member, she had considered not attending the Homemakers group anymore because she decided that the younger members would enjoy the organization more with members of the same age. She had mentioned this to her friend, Jane, in her recent letter to her. She and Jane had met in college many years ago and they had remained best friends.

A letter from Jane contained, among other things, a message that she hoped would help:

> Anne, I thought for a while about your letter. I myself have struggled with those same thoughts. I wrote in my journal on January 22, 1994, the following:
>
> The elderly sometimes find themselves believing that they are not wanted by a younger group, when the complete opposite is true and beneficial to all ages. The wisdom of those who have lived fuller lives, who have experienced more, and learned the truth are desperately needed and should

be obtainable by the young; while those who are younger will supply life's energies and vitality to those who, during the senior years, are in great need of such. It is the perfect balance.

Every progressive group should contain people of various ages so that the sought-after progress may be attained."

Please rethink your observation, Anne. I did, and have been quite happy with my decision to remain with those friends.

I pray that you and Owen will continue in good health, and that you will find your new home filled with the love of Christ. Your 'old' friend, Jane.

Anne received something valuable that day. It was a complete turnabout in her conception of herself and her worth. She would stay with the Homemakers, and she would be more aware of her part within that group. Her good friend, Jane, who always had straightforward and wise perceptions about many things, once again was quite helpful to her.

❧ ❧ ❧

Rachael's adjustments depended mainly upon her health and her healing. But would she be able to recover enough to live alone? If not, *could* she adjust? She would not even ask herself that question today. She *would* recover enough, and she knew that many prayers were still being sent on her behalf. She knew the Lord would see her through. She had confidence in the power of prayer…and why not? Who could question it? Every day is another day of striving toward her goal, and she would keep trying and trusting.

Julia was so lonely, and she didn't even care to adjust! *Life is no pleasure at all when you have no one to share it with. Even Jenny has moved away. It was better when she could come over, and we'd at least have things we enjoyed talking about together. We had been best friends for a good, long time.*

*I wish I could think of something to do. I don't crochet anymore, even after getting my cataracts removed. I completely don't want to. What else can I do? I can't go out alone at night. I don't drive much out of the borough. I just sit and wait for Sunday, usually. I'm going to be* 86 *years old soon…So what? Is that good or bad?*

Adele knew how to make adjustments in her life. She had learned that her only hope was her trust in the Lord. These days were lonely, but she had the Lord to talk with. He had helped her adjust to her daughter's utterly debilitating injury and her husband's death. She held on then and she still held on today. Adele was an inspiration to many as she carried on with a smile and loving nature.

She counted her blessings and was thankful. This didn't erase her pain, loneliness, and heartbreaks, but her gratitude for God's gifts helped her to embrace an appreciative perspective. Her faith in a new life in eternity for her daughter and a reunion with her husband and all loved ones granted her hope and peace.

"Lonely" was the worst word in the world for Bea. She was a people-person if ever there was one and had always been an active individual. She was lighthearted and so much fun. Now she searched for something to do that could gather people together.

*No one seems to be interested in doing anything. My friends have gotten old. I'm older than most of them, and I still feel young enough to do lots of things. It's frustrating!*

*There are enough of us in our Sunday school Class to put our heads together and think of things we could do, but I sure don't see that happening.*

*I know that Iola loves to keep busy, but she is so serious about everything. I doubt if she could lighten up if she tried.*

*Anne has plenty to do. Owen keeps her company, and she sews and reads a lot. She likes that, I guess.*

*Laura has her husband, Ed, and he is not well at all. She needs to spend time with him.*

*Adele is my best friend. Sometimes we do sit and talk and play cards, but we don't do much else except go to church together.*

*Harriet is so involved in community affairs. My goodness! She must belong to a dozen different organizations. One day she had three meetings. Why would she do all of that? Maybe it's to fill time so she won't be lonely. That could be.*

*Julia never says much of anything. I think she looks forward to Sunday school, but I don't know if she does much more throughout the week. She's always been quiet.*

*Oh, well. There's no sense in driving myself into total aggravation.* She found no answer, so she turned on the TV and watched the news. She would never adjust to being old with nothing to do.

❧ ❧ ❧

Janine saw her adjustment as joyful and exciting. The Lord had brought her into the "Promised Land." *Everything is going to be wonderful,* she told herself nearly every minute. She still did not know what the Lord wanted of her here, but she trusted completely that she would know in God's time.

She told her daughters and her son all about the discovery of Hope Church. She couldn't stop marveling about the fact that it was in West Hope, the place she had felt tugging at her for years. Now, she was here, not by her own choice, but by the Lord's. This was a miracle in modern day. They say that miracles don't happen anymore, but no one could convince Janine of that.

# 44

# "Amico Nuovo"

"Mother, my friend, Maggie Duncan, is a member of West Hope U.P. I talked with her yesterday and discovered somehow that she actually saw you on Sunday. Are you going there again this week? If so, Maggie will probably introduce herself to you." Kathy said.

"She's a Second Grade teacher at my school, and an especially nice person. You remember me telling you that I had Bible Study with her?"

"Yes, I remember. I'll be there on Sunday. I hope she does let me know who she is. It will be nice to meet her."

The church was just about all Janine had on her mind right now. She could hardly wait for Sunday to roll around again.

In the meantime, she had done a few other things. She telephoned the Detelle home, for one thing. Mrs. Geonna Detelle answered the phone and was very gracious. Janine said that she appreciated the visit from her son and her husband's parents, and that she had a casserole dish that she would like to return at their convenience.

"Whenever it is convenient with *you* would be perfectly fine, Mrs. Stephens. Anthony's parents have spoken of you, and they have hoped that you would accept their invitation to come to our house. Please. When would you like to come?"

"Would tomorrow morning at ten-thirty be all right?"

"Absolutely. It certainly would. We will be expecting you then."

Janine was a little nervous to go calling upon the neighbors in the big house; however, if Geonna was anything like Tony or Mario and Sophia, she would certainly enjoy meeting her.

She baked one of her special raisin/spice cakes to take to them. It seemed like the right thing to do.

John watched her go down the road and knew she was excitedly nervous. It was a pleasure to see Janine enjoying herself without the pressures as in years past. She had been humming around all morning, fussing with icing on her special cake. She had a store-bought plate that would not need returned because she didn't want them to feel that this was going to be an "unrelenting" situation where each was now on the returning end—not that it would be a terrible situation at all.

She drove in through the beautiful pillars and up the curved-paved drive. It had paving of red bricks, about three feet wide on both sides of the drive. What an appealing look it presented, and standing on the outside of the curves were lampposts. *This must look just beautiful at night,* she thought.

The house was incredible. First thing she noticed were the beautiful windows. They were of grand designs and could have been imported. She wouldn't know! The front entrance did not have a porch but a few steps leading to a double door with beveled-glass windows. The brickwork on the entire structure was magnificent. She wasn't surprised about that, because every Italian who could afford a brick home would want such as this. The bricks in various places were appointed in patterns. She was so entranced with the house, she almost forgot to get out of the car!

Sophia and Mario stood in the open door, all smiles! They stepped forward to extend to her their sincere welcome.

Janine walked up with her little cake in hand and was so happy to be there. It was a moment that she accepted as a gift. She felt that she would be a friend with these two, and that it was not an accident.

Mario at once took her hand in his two to indicate that he was happy to have her there. Sophia embraced her! "Welcome, *il mio amico nuovo.*" How wonderful! Janine felt welcomed, all right, as she returned the embrace.

"Come in. Come in!" Mario gestured toward the door.

She was wondering if Geonna was home, but didn't say anything. It was especially nice that these two whom she had already met came to the door themselves. They entered into a totally different world: chandeliers, marble floors, beautiful paintings and an abundance of light and color. She almost lost her ability to speak, but composed herself immediately.

"Come. We will sit-a here." Sophia said. Janine handed her the cake, and she placed it on a hall table as they entered the gorgeous living room with beautiful floral-patterned chairs and settees. The fabrics were exquisite. She decided she would not look around anymore. After all, her visit was with these beautiful, dear people. *Who cares where they live?*

"You like-a da rigitone?"

"It was delicious! Thank you so much."

Sophia and Mario beamed.

"You happy where you live-a now?" Sophia asked.

"I am *very* happy. I came from Innesport where I had lived most of my life. This is a big change for me, moving from the city to the country…and it's so quiet out here. I like it."

"We know about changing, too. We come from another

country! But we are very happy to be in America with our son and Geonna and the children. They have done everything for us. Our homeland is our homeland. We will always love Italy, but to be with Anthony and his family and many new friends here in America is much, much better for us." Mario expressed himself passionately as she would have expected.

"Have you ever returned to Italy for a visit?"

"Many, many times. Anthony…He takes us. We see other people we know and other family people, too. We fly. We enjoy."

"I hope that someday I will travel to Italy. It is a place I have always wanted to go, but for now I am very happy to be where I am!"

Geonna came into the room. No! Geonna *entered* the room with grace and elegance. She was slender and beautiful with a sincere smile. She exuded sophistication, rarely seen throughout the region.

She moved swiftly to Janine and held out her hand to her in welcome.

"Janine, we have already met on the telephone. It's good to have you here with us now," she said.

Janine stood to receive the welcome and thanked her. Geonna sat down near to her, and they began a discussion of small things. They both seemed to be enjoying the acquaintance time. They spoke of their children, mainly, which is what mothers do.

Geonna stood and invited Janine into her kitchen. This was the highest invitation from any Italian host. Janine was delighted. They all went into a kitchen that was directly out of *House Beautiful,* or some such magazine.

Geonna said that Sophia enjoyed the kitchen, and she was so happy to have her here to teach her all the wonderful ways of cooking that she knew. Sophia was a very good cook, and her daughter-in-law hoped that someday she would receive the compliment of cooking just like her amazing teacher.

*This is a wonderful arrangement. Each is happy with her position in the family.*

They sat at a table adorned with flowers and beautiful placemats and had a cup of coffee together. She was offered a piece of Sophia's bread, and even though she had told herself she would pass on any food today, she took it and was glad she did.

It was a good visit. Janine was happy to have made this connection. She had hope that they would continue forward with being neighborly. She left with a glowing sense that her life had just been brightened. *How long has it been since I actually met someone I had never known?* She was exploding with energy and vigor—a rejuvenation of sorts.

# 45

# The First Day of the Week

Janine couldn't sleep on Saturday night. She finally got up at five o'clock, made coffee, read her Bible and prayed. Suddenly, she heard the birds singing and realized that it was dawn. She broke away from her quiet moments, opened up the sliding doors on the kitchen and slipped outside in her nighty and robe.

*What a beautiful morning. I'm glad I didn't miss this!* The sun was, at that very moment, coming up over the horizon—big, bright and beautiful. *When have I seen a sunrise?* She asked herself. The houses and buildings of the city had kept her from this heavenly experience too long! The few scattered clouds were absorbing the golden glow of the sun and reflecting the splendor across the sky. *Exactly as we absorb and reflect the glow of the Son.*

How many mornings had she wasted behind drawn blinds, refusing to let the light shine in? From now on, she would get out of bed early, spend more time with the Lord, and receive an early blessing of the Son and the gift of the sun.

She was so excited and grateful to be discovering yet another blessing from the Lord. *I had no idea of the many, many, many blessings. Doesn't the psalmist say, there are too many to grasp? There are!*

She had to pull herself away and go on inside. She took a

shower and began to fix breakfast as John came in rubbing his eyes.

"Hey! What time did you get up?"

"Before sunrise, which gave me the opportunity to go out on the deck and witness it this morning. It was spectacular! I'm planning to do that again tomorrow. What a way to start the day!"

"Good for you! Are you cooking breakfast? This is interesting. You, who would rather have a banana and go on?"

"I had time. I have no reason to rush. I'll not be playing the organ or be responsible for anything today...and I'm feeling hungry from being up a while. Why don't you go freshen up and we'll sit down together to pancakes and eggs?"

"Mmm, mmm! That sounds good. I'll be right back."

They talked and talked. How can two people who see one another most of every day find so much to talk about? But they did most of the time. It was a nice, slow-paced breakfast and very enjoyable for both of them.

* * *

They knew which door to walk through at Hope Church this time, so that made them feel better and somewhat familiar with the church. They no sooner got inside when Mr. Kirkland welcomed them and handed them bulletins. He said he was happy to see them and seemed to mean it.

They ambled on over to the pew they had last week and sat down. The window was once again open. Apparently the church had no air-conditioning, or perhaps they didn't use it unless it was a must. It was a Presbyterian Church, after all...and this one seemed to be populated with Scottish names, meaning one big thing: don't spend what you don't have to!

John smiled at that thought. *Let's see, the elders have names of Kirkland, Severight, Davidson, and Dawson. Yep! There are probably more folks who are not on this list who are of the same heritage. We should fit in pretty well.*

Maggie was right in front of them! Of course, they didn't know last week that she was Kathy's friend. Following them into the sanctuary, she addressed them both and introduced herself. She was a woman of about forty, tall and strong looking. She was pleasantly eager to bid them welcome and tell them how much she enjoyed her relationship with Kathy. Her husband sat down as soon as he was introduced. He leafed through his bulletin and was obviously was not as outgoing as his wife, which was usually the case in most families.

Janine sat down, too, because the organist had just walked in and the music was beginning. *Were these people actually going to listen to the Prelude?* Some did. Not all...but at least some did. She was very interested in—*What's her name? Oh, here it is...Francine Simmons. That name sounds familiar. I don't believe I know her, though.*

Janine enjoyed Francine's rendition of a favorite hymn, "It Is Well With my Soul," and decided to concentrate on her gladness and appreciation. That was easy!

The minister and the choir came down the aisle. There weren't many—eight or nine, and had sounded adequate last week. They had no director, but apparently Francine did it all, and they just followed her from the organ bench. It was not the best of situations, but sometimes we do what we can. It was not a big church, after all, and at least they were here doing the Lord's work.

The Call to Worship was from Psalm 24:1–4:

*The earth is the LORD's, and everything in it;*
*the world, and all who live in it;*
*for he founded it upon the waters.*

*Who may ascend the hill of the LORD?*
*Who may stand in his holy place?*

*He who has clean hands and a pure heart,*
*who does not lift up his soul to an idol*
*or swear by what is false.*

The first hymn was "How Great Thou Art." They stood, and she enjoyed singing without playing for a change, especially after the " Sonrise Experience."

*There's the lady a couple of pews down who had that nice pink suit on last week and came into the church the same time we did. Over there on the other side is that "Iola" lady who sent us the card. I want to be sure to thank her.*

The minister had announced that the newsletters were ready for pickup in the narthex and there were extra copies for guests. *That is something I don't want to forget. It should be interesting.*

The service continued, and Janine and John enjoyed it as much as last week. They stood for the benediction, and Mr. MacMillan, who was there last week, introduced himself by name this time. Maggie turned around and greeted them again and Mrs. Iola MacCowan rushed over to greet them.

"Mrs. MacCowan, thank you for the nice note. We really appreciated it."

"You're welcome. It's good to see you here again this Sunday. Will you be coming back?"

"We do plan to."

She was obviously very happy to hear that and went on over

to the other section from which she had come. She immediately engaged in conversation with the others over there.

As the Stephens were walking on toward the minister, Mr. MacMillan handed them one of the newsletters. They thanked him and tucked it away for later.

"They said they plan to return next Sunday," Iola told the ladies gathered together on the other side. Julia and Jenny, who had sat on the left side as usual, had moved to the other side to talk with their friends.

"Who?" asked Julia.

"That new couple sitting behind you. I don't suppose you have eyes in back of your head, though. We need more people here."

"I saw them last week," said Jenny. "I didn't notice this morning."

"Anybody going to lunch?" asked Julia.

Most were, so they made their way to the parking lot to load up.

A few more people greeted John and Janine; then they shook hands with the pastor and went outside. It was a beautiful day. *Just look at that stunning farm down there. I didn't notice it last week, but I had other things on my mind,* thought Janine.

"John, did you see the farm?" He said he did as he looked over her shoulder. "Pretty nice, huh?"

She got in the car, and they drove out of town and on home.

* * *

The ladies went to lunch and sat at their usual table, tucked in the corner away from most of the others.

"Did you see here in the newsletter that the softball game is next week?" asked Bea.

"I saw it. I don't know if I'm going or not," said Julia.

"Why wouldn't you? You like baseball, and most of the church members will be going. What do you want to do? Sit all alone in your house?" asked Bea.

"Well, it's going to be hot in the afternoon sun," said Julia.

"So what? You could wear a hat…and if you aren't going to play in the game, you can sit on the shaded bleachers," Bea said.

"Play? Heaven forbid. I am certainly not going to play," said Julia.

"Where'd you get that idea, Bea? The game is for kids and the men," said Jenny.

"Who says?" Bea responded.

"Wait a minute, now. Please tell me you aren't really thinking of getting out there and playing," said Iola.

"I *am* going to play. I bought me a new ball cap, and my old glove is fine, and I'm playing! I think I'll volunteer to pitch."

They were aghast. It was getting worse every minute!

Adele was listening while laughing inside. She knew this was coming after their conversation some time back. The reaction was hilarious, and the funniest thing was that Bea was absolutely serious.

"Bea, for heaven's sakes, you are going to get yourself injured, or fall, or something and then you'll be laid up. It's not worth it. You're too old." Iola just told her the way it was.

"Hey! If you don't want to play, then just don't play." She couldn't believe there could be such fuss over her wanting to participate in something that she would enjoy. *What fuddy duddies!*

"I can't believe you all are so narrow-minded. A person has a right to have a little fun. I don't care how old I am. I feel good enough to do it, and I'm gonn'a do it…Now, let's order."

"Well, you just go ahead if that's what you want. But don't forget…we told you so," Iola spoke up for herself and the others.

❧ ❧ ❧

"Hmm, says here that the Social Committee of Hope Church is sponsoring a softball game at the community park next Sunday. 'Come on down and enjoy the fun. Teams will be chosen by numbers. During and after the game, there will be free hotdogs, hamburgers, and cool drinks.' Wanna' go?" John read.

"I don't know. We don't know anybody yet. Maybe next year. I didn't even know there was a park around, did you?"

"We could find out easily enough. Mr. MacMillan would tell us, or anybody else, I should think. I don't know, Janine, this would be an opportunity to observe some of the members in a fun and informal situation. It might be worth our while, and it might also be fun for us. Think about it.

"I'll leave the newsletter here for you to read. There are some interesting articles."

Janine was a bit preoccupied with trying to locate some important papers she had lost during the move. It was always something.

"Hello," John answered the telephone. "Hey! Honey, it's Harry! How're ya doin'? You're what?…How'd you get that idea?…Huh!…That sounds like something you'd really enjoy, and something only an engineer could construct…What? Did you have any help? Ha, ha, ha!…Then, what?"

"John, what on earth?" He waved her off.

She walked out of the room so that Harry could finish his one-sided conversation with his father. *Honestly, those two. When they were into it, forget trying to break in.*

She went on into the so-called computer room that was full of boxes at this point. She guessed that the file she was looking for was in there. She began going through some and then decided that the room should be tackled for organization. Of course! She got lost in her attempt, and before she knew it nearly an hour had passed.

*Was John still on the phone?*

She went back to the kitchen, and he was saying, "Here's your mother. She'll want to say 'Hi.'"

*So now, I'm going to get to say "Hi," while he has said volumes.*

"Hello, Sweetheart."

"How's my Mom?"

"Wonderful—really wonderful."

"Dad tells me you found the answer to your prayer."

"I did! Isn't that just the greatest thing? Whenever I think about how awesome that is, I am overwhelmed. Mostly, I find it incredible that God can pay that much attention to ME, when there are so many other prayers going to Him and so many more important things for Him to be thinking about."

"'His eye is on the sparrow,' you know."

*Ha! He's following in his father's footsteps with a quote! That's fine with me.*

"Hey! You always taught us to believe and have faith. Now you have shown us how to believe and have faith. Good lessons, Mom. I'm really looking forward to regular updates on this new path you are taking. I hope it's not the speed path you were on before. It is an astounding story, Mom. This will be one for the books!"

"What books?"

"Well, for years you have told us you wanted to write. You don't want to keep this to yourself, do you?"

"Now, Harry. I'm not going to write a book! It's only been

a dream. Look at how long I've talked about it. Did I ever give any indication I would actually do it? I don't think I ever really will."

"Well, don't give up on your dreams, Mom. They *can* come true!"

"How's the family? Let me talk with the boys."

"Ok. They're just itching to speak to you."

As usual, they were lined up and each, in turn, told Janine whatever was on his mind. It was always great no matter what they had to say, be it something about school, bugs or storms. She could listen to those dear stories forever.

"Well, you got an earful this time, didn't you?"

"I sure did, Harry. What were you and your father talking about that engrossed him so much—or should I just ask him?"

"Oh, he'd better tell you. I have to get going here. We have some fun things planned for this afternoon, and all of us are ready and rarin' to go. I'll call next week."

"Ok, Honey. Tell Rhonda we love her. Love you, too."

"I love *you,* Mom. Bye."

She hung up the phone and stared into space for a while, not wanting to release the voices. If someone had asked her years ago if she could live without her family near her, she would have said, "No! Never!" But somehow she had come to accept the fact that a "man must leave his mother" and go lead his own life. Harry seemed happy enough. She forgot to ask him if he would get any time to come home this year. "Home?" *There's an interesting word. Where is "Home?"*

On second thought, she would not be asking him that question.

One of the most distressing things Harry had ever said to her was on the telephone a year after he had ventured out on his own. He wasn't married at the time, but had settled out there with a good job in Oklahoma. He found it to be the right place for him, and one evening as he and his mother were in conversation, she asked, "When will you be home?"

His response was, "I *am* home, Mom."

The sudden realization of what that actually meant cut her through like a knife. Up to that point she had hoped that he would return, or at the very least always consider his parents' house as "home." The fact that it wasn't true anymore was a crushing blow.

She got over it all, as mothers must, was thankful for his love and his goodness, and prayed for him to be happy. That was always the major concern of a mother. *We will never lose our children if we don't cling too tightly.* She learned that valuable lesson, and they—and she—were all doing well.

# 46

# Take Me Out to the Ballgame

Most of the people at Hope Church were dressed for the softball game when they came to church Sunday morning. Of course, Janine and John didn't think about doing that. That was okay. If they were going to go to the park (wherever it was) they could just slip on home and change without losing too much time.

There was excitement in the air all through the service. Accordingly, the minister had prepared a Praise Service for the morning, which was not so restricted. Janine didn't like "messing around" with the order usually, but had to admit that she enjoyed it today. They had some sheet music of a more contemporary nature, most of which she did not know, but liked them and felt they added considerably to the style of the service. *I hope they don't do this too often.*

They were early and when Mr. MacMillan sat down, they had a few minutes to speak to him. Mr. MacMillan spoke first. "Please call me Raymond. My wife's name is Lucy, and she sings in the choir. She's a soprano in the second row. We have a dairy farm out a ways. My mother was a 'Croft.' The family's been here for generations."

"Oh, that's nice," said Janine. "This is John and I am Janine. We just moved into the area in June. Our family is grown so we're by ourselves, now. We hope to get to know all of you better in time. We're Presbyterians and we have felt pretty comfortable here the past two weeks. It's a real nice church."

"Thank you. I think so. Of course, I wouldn't know any other. I was baptized here as a baby and hope to be buried here when I die. I have nothing to compare this church to, actually. I have been on the Session and attended Presbytery meetings and gotten acquainted with some of the churches on the 'circuit,' but as for a church of my own, this one's it for me, I guess.

"Are you going to the softball game today?"

John spoke up. "We didn't plan on it."

"I think it would be a good thing, especially if you are going to be a regular here. You would have a chance to get around and talk to people. Lucy and I would be happy to accompany you to the park and sit with you in the bleachers. Unless, of course, you want to play ball."

"Good heavens, no. I don't think I'll do that this time. Thank you for your offer. What do you say, Janine?"

"I think that's very nice of you, Mr. Raymond, you say?" He nodded. "Well, we obviously are not dressed for the occasion, but we could meet you at the park."

"Fine. Fine. We'd be most proud to have you join us."

John had to ask, "Where is the park, Raymond?"

"Oh, sorry, I just assumed...You go to the end of the borough that way and come to Mercy Street on the left. Just turn there and you'll see the park right quick."

"Then, so it is. We'll see you there later, and thank you very much for your invitation. We do appreciate it," John said.

The Prelude was beginning, and it was an old-fashioned tune with a gospel swing. *Good for you, Francine. You certainly are right on,* thought Janine. She wore a smile all through the morning.

At the end of the service, Raymond introduced them to a

few of the others sitting near. Francine came down the aisle and practically bumped into Janine. "Oh, excuse me. I shouldn't be in such a hurry. Sorry."

"That's fine. I enjoyed your music, even though I really didn't know many of the songs. Do you use contemporary songs often?"

"Oh, goodness no! This congregation would probably tar and feather me if I tried that more than once in a blue moon. They like the hymns that they were brought up with mostly, but they humor me now and then. I don't know how I caught onto some of these new ones myself, since I am such a 'died in the wool,' as they say.

"Anyway, my name's Francine Simmons. It's very nice having you worship with us."

"I'm Janine and this is my husband, John Stephens. It's very nice to meet you, Francine."

"Oh, here comes my husband, Lawrence. Let me introduce him to you."

After a few words the Simmons were scampering for the door, and Janine said to John, "Francine and Lawrence Simmons. Now do you remember?"

He scratched his head, blinked a few times, and the light turned on inside of his head. "The sign…They were the bride and groom here that day."

Janine giggled and nodded. They were enjoying this recollection and putting it all together with the actual people. The newly married couple was not at all what they expected. *One never knows…Very interesting!*

Maggie Duncan finally got through to speak to the Stephens. "Hello. I'm so glad to see you again. You might try to get that daughter of yours to come with you some Sunday. I've invited her, but I certainly wouldn't want to take her away from her own church. Are you going to the ballgame?"

"I guess so."

"Good, then we'll see you later. I have to go locate my husband and get going. See you at the park."

"Okay!"

The church emptied much faster than usual because they all had somewhere to go. Cars were filling up and moving out. "Head 'em up. Move 'em out." John said.

They felt so lighthearted after the friendliness and joviality of the morning. They hurried home, jumped into blue jeans, and were on their way to the ballpark. Janine tried to recall if she had ever felt so good about participating in a church event before. She couldn't. Her church in the city didn't plan events such as these.

❀ ❀ ❀

The park was easy to find. *How could anyone get lost in this little community, anyway?* There were maybe 65-75 people there. Two teams were being chosen by numbers. Someone saw the Stephens coming in, and yelled, "Hi. Come on over and get on a team."

Well, Janine was not going to do it. No way! John had said he wasn't going to either, but that didn't last. He went right over and was immediately placed on a team. He had no glove, no hat, or anything. Now, what?

Oh, there were Raymond MacMillan and his wife, Lucy coming toward her. Thank goodness. John had casually as anything deserted her!

"Mrs. Stephens, I'd like for you to meet my wife, Lucy."

"Oh, please call me Janine. How do you do, Lucy? Your husband has been very gracious to invite us here today."

"Are you going to play ball?" Raymond asked.

"No. I'm going to watch. How about you?"

"No. No…We'll just be cheerleaders. Come on and join us. Would you like a refreshing, cool drink first?"

Since they both were carrying one, she said she would and they walked over to the table with the big self-serve thermoses and styrofoam glasses and helped herself. They then climbed up onto the bleacher.

Lucy and Raymond did their best to introduce her around. She would never remember names but would likely remember their faces. That was fine. No one expected her to remember so soon.

Up on top was Maggie, waving to her. Over on the bottom and to the left were some of the older-looking ladies. She remembered, Iola, but hadn't really met the others.

Adele was there to support Bea in whatever she decided to do. She was sure she was going to play because she had her ball cap on and that funny t-shirt with a cartoon drawing of an off-balance pitcher that looked like a Norman Rockwell drawing. Bea was over talking with the group gathered by home plate.

Iola and Harriet were there fussing and fuming about Bea's efforts to hurt herself. None of the others in the class wanted to sit in the sunshine and heat, so they stayed at home.

"Oh, look! There's little Jimmie Adams. He'll want to play ball, but he and his family never come to church," said Iola.

"I say let him play. What a shame! His parents could care less about him," said Adele. "Sometimes I see him out on the sidewalks late at night. They probably don't know where he is."

"I know. They tell me he does all right in school when he's there."

"Look, they're getting ready to side up. Is that Beatrice Roberts going to the mound?" Lucy asked.

Harriet turned around and said it was.

There was almost a gasp. Everyone was thinking that Bea was old and was going to get hurt out there. They were concerned that the ball might come straight at her. There wasn't a whole lot of cheering going on because the crowd was holding its breath.

First at bat was little Jimmie, the leadoff batter. The preacher was the coach of that team. He knew the boy needed to be there.

Bea was winding up. Some wondered if she would throw her shoulder out of socket. And the pitch—she actually got it to the plate, and Jimmie swung and missed.

The ball was thrown to Bea who caught it! She wound up again, looking at little Jimmie with beady eyes. Jimmie tried to loosen up, but she was intimidating him. Someone yelled, "Come on, Jimmie. Hit that ball!"

The pitch! Right across the plate and Jimmie hit it! The fans stood up and cheered for him. The ball was a ground ball right past the pitcher. Jimmie was on base. John was in the outfield, out of harm's way. *Good,* Janine thought.

Up next was a big man, perhaps about forty years old. He used his position to sneer at the pitcher. (All in good jest, of course.) She set those beady eyes again. The fans separated—half were cheering on the batter and the others were cheering for Bea. In truth *everyone* wanted Bea to do well. Strike!

She caught the ball coming back to her from the catcher and then looked over at little Jimmie threateningly. He practically hugged the base. She stared down the batter, wound up, and let the ball go. The batter swung at the ball and missed. The ball went sailing up in the air over the catcher's head. It seemed Bea had gotten too enthusiastic. Everyone was cheering little Jimmie to run. He ran to second base and was thrilled beyond measure.

Bea got the ball again, turned to Jimmie, and stared at him. Everyone was getting so amused at Bea as she was portraying a tough guy for the fun of it and acting the part very well.

The batter whacked the next pitch, and it went sailing right at John!

"Get it, John!" Janine yelled. She had gotten caught up in the action. John had no glove of his own and had borrowed one that certainly didn't fit; as he reached for the ball, he missed it completely! He would not have caught that ball if he had on a $500 made-to-fit glove.

Janine hid her face. John ran after the ball. By the time he found it in the grass and picked it up and threw it as far as he could, both runners had scored.

What fun! Janine had never in her life enjoyed anything so much. *And that pitcher! What a character!*

Bea struck the next batter out, and the next one flied to the second baseman. One more out to go.

Bea was markedly wearing down, so the next batter, a young woman, took sympathy on her without her knowing it and missed the pitch. She missed the next one and the next. The inning was over. Bea had her fifteen minutes of fame, and someone else would get the chance to pitch an inning when it came up again. She was so tickled with herself for getting in there and doing it. One and all stood and someone started a cheer for Bea in the bleachers, and it continued until she came over and sat down with them.

Janine had never participated in anything like this—old and young together having a great time—all members of the same "family."

John came over with a glass of lemonade and sat a minute or two. He and Janine got a good laugh out of his calamity in the last inning. He thought he might have to go bat, so he went over to the dugout and put himself in the lineup. It was good that he was being a sport about it all, and everybody liked him for it.

Bea sat down with the cheerleaders who were all congratulating her. Some asked her if she felt okay. She felt *more* than okay, really. She was having a great time of it. No one was surprised at anything Bea might do, except Janine, who was positively charmed by her. *Not many of her age would ever attempt such a thing. She must be a lot of fun to have around.* Janine thought.

Those not at bat or in the field were having hotdogs, as were the cheerleaders. *Mmm!* They were the best hotdogs Janine had ever tasted. *Is it the brand or do hotdogs always taste like this at a ball game?*

*Who is that? It looks like Tony Detelle. I didn't know they were members of Hope Church.* She asked Lucy, who said he wasn't a member, but attended the youth meetings with his friends of the church. He was Catholic.

John's team (well, not *John's*) was now up at bat, and Tony was the lead-off batter. It didn't take long for him to hit one out of the park. There was another unified cheer by the cheerleaders.

Eight batters later, and finally John came to the plate. He looked pretty good, and Janine hoped he didn't fan that bat around and get struck out.

The bases were loaded, and John was glaring down the poor fellow trying to pitch. He sent a pretty nice pitch over the plate. John let it go by. Strike!

Well, he was getting serious now, loosening up and preparing to really whack the ball. While he was messing around preparing himself, the ball came whizzing right by. Now, that does it. He was doing a good job of entertaining the crowd. Janine had never really seen this side of him. He had apparently learned some points or two from the others.

The pitch! Ball!

The windup, and the pitch...Crack! The bat broke! He'd have to hurry to get to first base, and here came the runner into home! John turned slightly to see if the runner had scored and lost his balance and down he went—smack on his stomach!

Janine was on her feet, afraid that he had hurt himself...No. He was back on his feet, running to beat the pitch to first base. The cheering was deafening. He ran as fast as he could, which unfortunately wasn't good enough and was out at first.

The crowd cheered for him as he brushed himself off and came over to the stands. He was holding out both hands and shrugging his shoulders, indicating at least he tried. In so doing he had missed a catch in the outfield, broken a bat, fallen down, was put out at first base, and gained the respect of everyone for his noble sportsmanship.

The game was over after four innings, which went quickly after the first inning, at which time the score had been 12–2. The score tightened up a bit at one point, but really, no one cared. Strikes or balls, runs or outs, made no difference. What mattered was the fellowship.

Lucy and Raymond did their best to introduce John and Janine around. The church members were warm and friendly toward them, and the day ended well as the crowd dispersed to go their separate ways.

The Stephens went home, showered, rested and felt great satisfaction in their day. The future was looking bright. *Thank you, Lord for laughter and a really good time.*

Bea said before collapsing on the sofa, *Thank you, Lord for laughter and a really good time, and for holding me up, too.*

# 47

# The Morning Celebration

It was another beautiful morning. Janine was up before sunrise again, made herself some coffee and sat at the kitchen table with her Bible.

She opened to Psalm 24: 1–6,

*The earth is the LORD's, and everything in it, the world, and all who live in it.*
*For he founded it upon the seas and established it upon the waters.*
*Who may ascend the hill of the Lord?*
*Who may stand in his holy place?*
*He who has clean hands and a pure heart,*
*who does not lift up his soul to an idol or swear by what is false.*
*He will receive blessing from the LORD and vindication from God his Savior.*
*Such is the generation of those who seek him, who seek your face, O God of Jacob.*

Janine walked out on the deck. There was the slightest indication that the darkness would soon be completely gone. *The earth is the Lord's.* He will cause the Sun to break forth and cover the earth, and she would wait and watch, leaning over the railing. *We still should get some chairs for out here.*

The birds began to sing. The volume increased as other birds joined in the chorus. She even heard a rooster in the distance. The light was coming! *What a process!* From a pale softness of no color to a turning of soft pink, which became more vibrant across the expanse of the sky in various tones of color. The birds were cheering and calling to one another in celebration. She was as excited as they were as she caught the very edge of the sun making an appearance.

In moments it was up, and the earth was covered with light. After she said her morning prayers of thanksgiving and praise, she went back inside the house.

## 48

# My Aching Back!

She thought she heard John rustling about, and then saw him as well. He was slightly bent over and holding his back.

"Honey, what's wrong?"

"Oh! Oh! My back hurts! I guess it's from the fall yesterday!"

"Uh oh! Does it ache or pain?"

He looked at her with a frown. "It hurts!"

"I know, but if it's pain it could mean a pinched nerve or a disk problem, but if it's an ache it would be muscle."

"Well, thank you very much for your quick diagnosis, Dr. Stephens."

"John, stop that. I'm trying to be helpful."

"Well, I don't know if it is aching or paining. I'd better call Dr. Lanza."

"Good idea. Do you want me to do it?"

"Okay. He won't be in yet, I don't suppose.

"I'll leave a message."

"Is that fresh coffee?'

"It was. It should be all right. I'll pour you a cup. Sit down, Honey."

He moaned his way to a chair and inched his way into it, stiffened his back and held it.

"I'm not sure what to do for you right now. Ice for pain and heat for aches."

"Janine! For heaven's sake! When did you get into all of this?"

"All of what?"

"This *'Voodoo'* medicinal observation."

"Oh my, John." She was practically splitting her sides laughing at that.

*"Voodoo?"* she asked.

"No, sorry. Not *'Voodoo'*...Shaman."

"Well, if that doesn't beat all." She laughed some more. "Well, if I am a Shaman, I'd better get to the work of curing you...Bend over."

"What?"

"I'm going to apply some pressure and discover the center of the pain, and then I'm going to take both fists and push it out of you."

"Janine!"

"Doctor Shaman, please."

"That's enough!" He stood up and moved away from her, obviously not entirely trusting her at the moment. He wasn't in such a good position to defend himself.

"Oh, John, I was just having fun."

"Well, doesn't seem like much fun to me."

"Ok. Ok. I'm sorry. I'll call Dr. Lanza and confer with him before prescribing any cures for you today."

She really was concerned about him, but had such lightheartedness about her she became a little silly. *Get serious, Janine. He does hurt.*

She finally connected with the doctor's office and made a ten o'clock appointment for him. They had plenty of time.

* * *

Beatrice had driven herself and Adele home after the ballgame. She was as happy as a lark. Adele was happy for her, too. She asked Bea if she thought she was going to be all right.

"I am all right. I had a real good time today. Hey! I'll see ya' soon."

Adele got out of the car, and Bea went on over home. She went in through the garage door to the house, turned on a few lights and looked at herself in the mirror. *I'm a mess. I have dirt on my face, and look at my crummy hair. I'm gonn'a have to take a shower. That's for sure!*

She took her shower right away, and realized that she was pretty well tired out. She'd just jump into her pajamas and be ready for bed whenever she felt like it. She sat in front of the television, but kept falling asleep. Rather than sleep uncomfortably there, she went on to bed. It was only nine o'clock.

At six o'clock the next morning, she awakened from a deep, deep sleep and had to rush to the bathroom. She didn't usually go through the night without getting up once. She made it, but just barely as she was stiff in the joints come morning.

She walked into the kitchen and realized when she reached for the teapot that her shoulder really hurt. *Yep! Sure doesn't surprise me. I haven't used those muscles for a coon's age. Uhgghh! I can hardly move my arm. I'll get some of that arthritis cream, rub it in, and take some Ibuprofen. The aching is just a reminder of the good time I had yesterday. I don't care if I hurt. I've had lots of hurts in my lifetime.*

* * *

Alice Cook answered the telephone. Her daughter, Francine, was on the line. "Well, good morning. How are you today?"

"I'm fine, Mother. How are you?"

"No problems. Did you go to the ballgame yesterday?" "We did and had a really fun day of it. You should have seen Beatrice Roberts. She came to the game prepared to participate, and so they let her pitch the first inning."

"Good grief! What was she thinking?"

"You know Bea. She loves a good time. She just wanted to have fun, and it looks like she did."

"I hope she didn't get hurt or anything."

"No. She seemed fine to me."

"Well, good for her! Could she actually pitch the ball to home plate?"

"She did. I'll bet she's hurting this morning."

"She most likely is."

"We have a new couple in church. I think they've been there maybe two or three times. The name is Stephens. His name is John. I forget hers, but they may be in their late fifties or sixties. Nice looking couple and I think they actually will stay."

"That's great news. I hope they do."

"Me, too. I have no idea if they are retired or what their interests are, but they came to the game yesterday, and the man played ball and had a really good time. He seemed like such a good sport and very likeable."

Telephones were buzzing all around West Hope today. Julia called Jenny.

"Well, I guess we missed it yesterday."

"Missed what?"

"The ball game. I got brought up to date from Iola last night."

"Did Bea play ball?"

"She sure did. She pitched."

"Glory be! When is she going to stop taking such chances with her health?"

"I guess she did fine and was none the worse for doing it. I'm glad, but I'll tell you, you never know about her."

"Well, we all enjoy doing different things, I guess. As for me, I never did play ball. I haven't done much that would be classified as risky in my life that I know of. But then, I never really wanted to. We're all made differently, no matter what Thomas Jefferson proclaimed. Even the Bible says we each have different gifts."

"That's the truth. I don't want to criticize anybody. It's probably a good thing that we aren't all the same, or else life would be pretty darned boring, don't you think?"

"Yes, I do. What are you doing today?" Jenny asked.

"There's nothing to do, really. The cleaning lady might get here this week. The house could use some freshening. I've been kind of watching for Silas to be in the neighborhood. If he doesn't show up by Friday, I'm going to have to take measures into my own hands."

"Julia, don't you go cutting your grass. You'll have a stroke or something."

"I'm not going to. What I mean is I'll have to find someone to get over here and do it for me."

"Well, since I moved I don't have to worry about grass cutting. That's one good thing."

# 49

# Julia's Birthday

John found out it was muscle. The "Shaman" had that pretty well diagnosed, but she was not going to say another word or she would probably burst out laughing again. Janine had to laugh at herself for being so joyful these days. It was a real change of attitude.

After John took some muscle relaxers, he felt much better. The doctor said he should use ice off and on for the rest of the day and could use heat later in the evening.

The week went by without too much happening, which was fine with both of them. Janine was back to walking, and John just took it easy for a change.

Sunday morning John seemed fine, and they were eager to get to church. Kevin Kirkland met them at the door again with bulletins in hand. "Good morning, John," he said.

"Good morning, Kevin. It's nice to see you."

"How are you after your exercise of last Sunday?"

"Good. It was a mighty fine day. We both enjoyed it tremendously."

"We did, too. We haven't had a ballgame like that in quite a while. The talk is we need to make it an annual event."

"That sounds like a great idea, Kevin. Well, we'd better get moving here."

They went on into the sanctuary, and the pew was filled up! It looked like one entire family was seated there. Even Raymond was moved up a pew, which also was filled because that was where Maggie and her husband sat, along with another couple.

Now what? They looked around quickly to see if there was a place with someone they already knew. Time was running out.

John said, "Let's go down there in front of the lady who came in with us that first Sunday." They didn't discuss it but quickly moved into place. The Prelude hadn't started yet. Actually, Francine and the choir didn't seem to be ready. They looked over the bulletin and overheard one of the ladies behind them.

"I did a crazy thing yesterday…I decided to teach myself to play the piano so I bought myself an electronic keyboard for my $86^{th}$ birthday."

Janine didn't mean to listen in on someone's conversation, but the lady wasn't speaking softly and she heard what she said. *How about that? She must be a determined individual to decide on doing something so challenging at her age.* She tried to focus on the service and the message, but found herself drifting off to the words the lady had said.

Even the service itself caused her to think about older people and their abilities. The pastor was talking about people of older age accomplishing great things. She knew the Bible was full of examples like that. He mentioned Noah and Sarah, and she thought of the lady behind her instead.

She made up her mind. She was going to speak to her about piano lessons. After all, she had taught for years and years and knew she could help her. If the lady tried to do it on her own, she would never get it right and become frustrated instead of enjoying a new undertaking.

As soon as she could, Janine turned around and said hello

to the ladies behind her. She wasn't sure which one had been talking, but as soon as they opened their mouths, she had it figured out.

"My name's, Janine Stephens."

"Hello, I'm Julia Gillanders and this is Jenny McMurray. You're new here."

"Yes. We are…I want to tell you that I overheard you talking about purchasing an electronic keyboard and teaching yourself how to play it."

She didn't notice that Julia was absolutely appalled that anyone heard such a silly thing as that.

"I want to offer to teach you. I was a piano teacher for many years, and I would be happy to get you started."

"Well, I don't know about that!"

"Think about it, please. It is very close to impossible to teach yourself. I would be ever so happy to do it. No charge. No charge at all. I'll talk with you about it again next week. Okay?"

"Well, I'll have to think about it," Julia had told her. "Thank you."

The two ladies moved on, and John said, "So…I thought you were finished with teaching."

"I am. I am. This is different. This is just helping somebody out."

"Um hm."

Lucy came down from the choir loft, greeted the Stephens and told them that they really enjoyed having some time to get to know them better last week.

Francine didn't hurry past today, but instead asked them if they enjoyed the day last week. She said that she and Lawrence certainly did, and even though they didn't play ball, they felt they were pretty good cheerleaders.

"Everyone had a good time," Janine said.

Maggie asked John if he had trouble getting out of bed the next morning.

"Oh, no. I got along just fine."

Janine looked over her glasses at him and didn't say a word.

They were driving home and Janine asked him if he had told a lie about feeling well on Monday.

He said he didn't. He said that Maggie had asked him if he had trouble getting out of bed and he said he got along just fine. "I *didn't* have trouble getting out of bed. I just had trouble standing up."

Well, he fudged it off, but he didn't lie. She was satisfied.

He read the entire Sunday paper. He liked to do that, and it usually took half of the day. All of a sudden he realized what time it was, and that he hadn't heard from Janine for hours. "Hey! Janine! Where are you?"

"I'm downstairs. I'll be up pretty soon."

He got up and walked around. Goodness, his back was getting stiff.

She came up, and he said, "Would you like to take a little stroll? I think I could use it."

"Sure. I'll go get my shoes."

They were walking toward where their daughter lived. Maybe they'd stop over and say "Hi."

"What were you doing all afternoon?" he asked her.

"I was digging around trying to locate those boxes with the piano-lesson music in them. I know I kept them."

"I think you got rid of all of them."

"No…Are you sure?"

"You said you were never going to need them again. Remember?"

"Oh, darn. You're right. Now if Julia decides to trust me to help her, I'll have to go get new music. John, I knew I shouldn't throw anything out. That's what happens; keep something for years and years and as soon as you get rid of it you're going to need it."

"Well, she may not want to have you do this anyway."

"I can run to town in a jiffy and get anything I need from the music store if it becomes necessary, and now I can at least stop searching for the old ones."

They walked past the little farmhouse, and the couple was out on the porch waving. They were adorable. They decided that this time they would stop and say a few words to them. They walked toward the porch, and the old folks immediately jumped up and greeted them gladly.

"Hello there. We've walked by and seen you before and decided it was time to stop and introduce ourselves. I'm John Stephens and this is my wife, Janine."

"Wonderful! Wonderful! We are happy to meet you. I'm Abraham and this is my wife, Sarah."

"No kidding!" John just couldn't help himself. He wished he hadn't said that.

Abraham just laughed and slapped his leg. "That's what everyone does."

"Well, it must have been in the Lord's plan when your parents named you," Janine said. "It's good to meet you."

"Won't you sit a spell?"

"Sure. Thanks."

"Been walkin' far?

"No, we live just a ways down there. We bought the Stafford property."

"Nice place. I hope you'll be happy," Sarah finally spoke. "You must be thirsty. Can I get you a drink of water?"

"No, thanks. We're going to be walking on down to our daughter's home in a bit. Have you met Kathy or Greg Lang or the daughters?"

"Meghan?"

"Yes. She's our granddaughter."

"She's a right nice youngin.' She rides by here on her bicycle and comes to talk with us."

Meghan would do that. John and Janine were glad. These poor old folks probably appreciate a nice young girl visiting with them.

"How long have you folks lived here?"

Sarah looked at Abe. He said, "Maybe fifty years, give or take a few."

"Well, it seems like a good place to be. I think we'll get on to our daughter's. Maybe we can visit again sometime," John stood. So did Janine.

They smiled, and she said, "Come again."

When they got out of sight, Janine said, "Sarah and Abraham?"

They sure got a charge out of that. They forgot to ask their last names.

Prince knew they were coming before anyone else possibly could. He bounded up with greetings, and they all three went to the house. They only stayed long enough to get a cool drink of water. Janine did tell Kathy that she saw Maggie again this morning. "She always asks about you."

"She's very special," said Kathy.

"Oh, and another thing…there was this lady sitting behind us this morning talking with her friend. She said she is 86 years old and is going to teach herself to play the piano. What do you think about that?"

"My goodness! Isn't it just wonderful that she wants to do something like that at her age?"

"Your mother thinks she could use her help."

"No doubt about that. Are you going to help her, Mother?"

"She has to decide. I offered, but she is a little leery of me. I don't blame her. She doesn't know anything about me at all, so can she trust me not to steal her blind or be a good person? She'll probably let me know next Sunday. It might be fun."

"Hey! Have you ever talked with the old couple who has the farm?" John asked.

"I haven't but Meghan has made friends with them. Why?"
"Do you know their names?"

"Actually, no."

"Abraham and Sarah."

"No! What are the chances of that happening?"

"Maybe they are Jewish. Then there would be a better chance of it happening."

"I guess. That's really remarkable, isn't it? What's the last name?"

"We don't know. Well, we'd better get along. Stop over any time."

They hurried on home and didn't see Abe and Sarah on the return trip. They kept discovering the most interesting things!

# 50

# Telephone Gossip

"Hello, Julia. I just spoke to Jenny. I hope you don't mind that she told me what Mrs. Stephens said to you yesterday."

"I can't believe that the entire community now knows of the crazy thing I have done. Iola, I never dreamed that people would be this interested in me. I wish they weren't," Julia said.

"It's not just that, Julia. Oh, I think its fine that you are going to get into playing the piano. You know what Rev. Campbell said on Sunday: 'You're never too old.'"

"Iola, I am not interested in this conversation. I am very, very uncomfortable with this right now. I know what Rev. Daniel said, and I know that he was looking straight at me, but I still have my own decision to make here. Please. Is there something else you'd like to talk about?"

"In a minute. Please listen to this one thing, first; Rev. Campbell was not speaking directly to you. Sometimes the preachers are called to speak on a certain subject, and maybe his message was a bit for you and a bit for all of us older people. I thought he was talking to me as well.

"But what I really wanted to ask…did Mrs. Stephens actually say she was a piano teacher?"

"Oh, my! I don't like talking about anybody."

"That's not talking about anybody. If she told you that, she meant for people to know it. She's not keeping it a secret."

"She said she *had* taught piano lessons for many years."

"Ah ha! That's great. She's a musician. We need her kind around here. Well, listen, you do what you feel you should do. That's up to you. Maybe the Lord wants you to get to know Mrs. Stephens for some reason unknown to us."

"Hi, Francine. Did you hear?" Laura was calling.

"Hear what?"

"The new lady at church—she's a musician."

"You don't say? What kind of a musician?"

"She has taught piano, for one thing."

"Well, this is certainly interesting. I wonder if she sings."

"Of course!"

"How do you know?"

"Well, that's what I heard."

"Maybe she'll join the choir. We can always use more people in the choir."

"Maybe she would direct the choir for you."

"Now there's a good thought."

"Well, better go. See you soon. Bye."

"Hello, Adele. Did you hear?" Beatrice asked.

"Hear what?"

"That new lady, Mrs. Stephens, she's going to open up a piano studio in West Hope."

"Well, I didn't even know she played piano."

"Well, she does, and she's going to start teaching."

"How do you know?"

"Jenny told me she talked with Julia about teaching." Bea was delighted to be passing along such interesting information.

"Where will she have her studio?"

"I was wondering the same thing. There's that empty building that used to be the bicycle shop. It probably could be fixed up just right for a music studio."

"Maybe...We sure could use more culture around here."

"Well, time will tell, I guess."

❧ ❧ ❧

On Thursday morning the secretary of Hope Church received a telephone call from one of the members.

"Hello, Georgia. How are things?"

"Good. Who's this?"

"Oh, sorry. It's Rebecca Armtridge."

"Hi, Becky. I didn't recognize your voice."

"That's okay. I need to get in touch with the new lady in church, Mrs. Stephens. Do you have a phone number for her?"

"I do, but I'm not allowed to give it out. It was given to us in confidence."

"Oh, darn. I wanted to call her about teaching piano lessons to Shirley."

"Piano lessons?"

"Yes, she's going to be opening up a studio here in West Hope, and I want to be early on the list."

"Well, that's wonderful. I'm sorry I can't help you. Perhaps you will see her in church on Sunday."

"I guess that means I'd better attend this week, right?"

"Good thinking. See you then."

During Sunday school, Julia confessed about her keyboard. She might as well; everyone seemed to know about it anyway.

"Mrs. Stephens said she'd come to teach me piano lessons if I want her to. She used to teach," she said.

"Used to?" asked Bea.

"Yes. That's what she said."

"She didn't say you could come to her new studio?" Anne asked.

"Nothing about a studio."

"Hmm. Well, I heard she was opening up a studio," said Iola.

"So, what are you going to do, Julia?"

"I think I've decided to go with it for a while. I'm not crazy about having someone push me into practices and watching my fingers on the keys and so forth, but she was probably right when she said it would be very difficult for me to teach myself. I do want to learn. That probably sounds silly to you that I do, but I decided that I'd better do it now and not put it off any longer."

"I'm like that, too. I say, if you want to do something…then do it." Bea interjected.

Well, everyone knew Bea was like that, but this was so out of character for Julia, who had been so quiet and just went along with everybody all the time.

"By the way, Bea, did you find any aches and pains on Monday?" Laura asked.

"Oh, boy did I! But you know what I told myself?"

"What?"

"I said, 'Bea Roberts, every time you have one of those pains just remember how much fun you had gittin' it.'…I had lots of reminders."

They all laughed at that.

When they went to the sanctuary, Julia and Jenny went over to their normal place. Julia was looking for the Stephens. She was thinking they weren't coming today, but in they came and sat down in front of them.

A lot of people were looking toward Janine. Rumors had pretty much gotten all around the borough and outlying areas about the music studio (which Janine herself knew nothing about). Janine turned around and greeted the two ladies who looked especially beautiful this morning.

Jenny had on her pink suit. Janine was happy to see her in it, while being able to identify the person. Julia had a very pretty, floral skirt, beige blouse and a jacket of blue that matched one of the colors in the skirt. She wore fashionable costume jewelry and a big lapel pin. Both ladies used makeup and had very pretty white hair.

The music started, so Janine would wait until after services to talk again with Julia.

Why were the choir members looking at her that way? Janine couldn't figure it out. When they would catch her eye, they would smile, knowingly…*Knowingly?*

*Yes, they must know something I don't know. Maybe they are thinking I'm a lucky woman to have such a handsome husband with a great personality and sportsmanship.* She smiled within and decided not to catch anyone's eye anymore.

After the benediction, she turned and Julia quickly said, "I decided to go ahead with the lessons with you. Thank you. When would we begin?"

Janine was shocked. She had rehearsed a statement she would give when Julia said she had decided to do it herself.

"Wonderful! Where do you live?"

"Just down the hill and on the main street here. It's easy to find." She went on to tell her the address.

"How about Tuesday morning at ten o'clock? Would that work for you?"

Julia was thinking that she had every morning and every afternoon free, but she responded, "That would be fine."

"I'll find us some books and bring them along and see you on Tuesday."

Others were waiting their turn to talk with Janine. Next was Francine.

"Janine, if you'd like to come sing in the choir, we would love to have you."

Janine had decided firmly that she would not do that. She didn't know for sure what the Lord wanted her to do here at Hope Church, and she would not decide for Him.

"Thank you very much. I think I'd better take my time for a while."

Francine was disappointed but didn't say anymore.

Bea was next. "Good morning!"

"Well, here's our softball star. Good morning! You gave us a good time last week. I hope you know that."

"I know I had a good time myself," she said.

"I hear you're opening up a music studio. Is that right?" The ladies had put her up to it.

"What? No, that is not right. I used to teach music, but I am retired from that now. There are other things I must do." She didn't know what, but it was the right answer.

"Oh. Well, sometimes in a small community like this things get going like the old 'gossip' game. Sorry to upset you."

"No. You didn't upset me, but you sure caught me off guard with that."

Then a young woman and two children were waiting. She introduced herself as Rebecca Armtridge, and her two children were Shirley and Doug.

"I just wanted to get my daughter, Shirley, on the list for piano lessons at your new studio."

*Good grief! I can't believe this!* She looked over at John who was holding back a laugh. *He shouldn't be laughing when I'm in such a jam here.*

"Well, believe me if I were going to have a studio, and if I were going to be teaching again, I would be happy to have Shirley as a student. I have retired from teaching. I'm sorry. I hope there will be someone else to teach your little girl."

Shirley looked pretty disappointed, but Janine was not going to let that influence her! No way!

If all of this had not happened, she would have been a happy woman that day. She was happy about Julia, but the studio thing was crazy…*Or was it?* She brushed that thought from her mind immediately and began fixing dinner for John and herself. They enjoyed eating their heavier meal early on Sunday, freeing up the day for adventures or relaxation. They would later decide to take a drive along a road to the south to get a better perspective of the community.

As they turned onto the road, they were immediately transported to farmlands with wheat waving their heads, cattle quietly chewing their cud, fields of corn nearly ready to be picked, and an occasional dog barking at the interruption of an automobile upon his tranquil existence.

As they rounded a bend on the narrow, two-lane road, they came upon a field of sheep. A few were close to the road. "I had no idea that a sheep was that large." Janine remarked.

"Those pictures of sheep and shepherds from the children's

Bible stories are about as close as I have come to seeing one, except at a zoo. There's that petting zoo over in West Virginia we want to take the boys next time they come. They also have goats there. I don't want to get near a goat! I hear they will 'buck' into you."

A man was walking in the field with the sheep, actually holding a crook! What a sight! They were suddenly transported back in time as well as to the scenic countryside.

"Janine, would you have believed that we were living this close to a completely different way of life? This is amazing!"

"Nice."

"There's a sign on the mailbox there. See if it is a name we know."

Janine read "Davidson."

"I don't think I've met anyone by that name, but I do recall reading, either in the church bulletin or the newsletter, the Scottish name. I think it was in the bulletin that Sunday. What a nice farm! Looks like they have Black Angus cattle."

They hadn't been traveling more than 20 minutes on the country road when they came to an intersection of a dirt road, and John decided to go exploring.

They both sensed that they might be on private property, although there wasn't a sign to indicate that. They were going to turn around when then they came upon a small village; "Welcome to Bryston," the old, weathered sign read. The houses were closely lined together on both sides of the main road as well as projecting outward on side streets in the same fashion. John said it looked like an old mining community. The houses were as weathered as the sign, and there was little sign of life within them. A few dogs ran out to the auto, and they were bearing their teeth in anger at the strangers. Janine quickly put her window up when a very large dog lunged at her, and she emphatically declared that they had better get away from there "right now!"

As they turned around and headed back the way they had come, John saw in the rear-view mirror that there were people back at the settlement, and from what he could see of them, they were not the kind you'd want to meet. Four men were standing smack in the middle of the road facing the car, with movements of others behind.

"Good Heavens!" Janine said. "What on earth did we run into?"

"Whew! I'm sure I don't know, but I'll tell you this—we won't be back! From now on, we stay on the main roads."

"I'll tell you, John, this city gal got a real scare out of that!

"They could have been moon-shining. I've heard stories about people like that. They shoot at those who do not have what they determine is a legitimate reason to be in their territory."

"Legitimate? I suppose you mean 'buying.' I can't believe it! It's our own fault. We're old enough to know better, but honestly I never gave a thought to something like this."

They passed the Davidson's, and the grazing sheep, and were coming back to West Hope when John asked Janine if she would like to go on toward Innesport and get an ice cream cone. She said she would. They bought cones, and turned toward home, still anxious from the strange encounter.

"We are strangers in a new land, John. Up until now, it's been nothing but good, but we know that life is not all like that. We'll want to be sure that we are on the right path from now on." Having said that, she applied it to her journey to West Hope and realized that she would have to "follow the Leader" very carefully so as not to wander away from the rightful path there as well.

When they reached their house, Janine told John that she wanted to think about how to begin the piano lessons for Julia. Tomorrow she would go to the music store in Innesport. She knew there would be beginning books for the Adult Student; however, it had been years since she'd had the pleasure of teaching an adult. She had found over the years, that when an adult set out to learn something, the student would give the project much more time and attention than a child. Was that because that person didn't want to embarrass herself, or because she felt that time was short and she needed to make the most of it? Nevertheless, she felt it would be a pleasure to teach this nice old lady, and she looked forward to getting started on Tuesday.

# 51

# Familiarities

Julia was awake most of the night, nervous and apprehensive about whether or not she could learn anything at this stage of her life. *I know everything about me has slowed down, so I suppose it will be a problem for me to understand quickly enough, and I'm sure I will have trouble getting these old fingers to move on the piano keys.*

*Mrs. Stephens is gonn'a be sorry she ever talked with me. I wish I had just said "No" to this whole idea. Who cares if I learn the piano? Who will I play for anyway? No one, and that's for sure. I wanted to play for me! Who was I kidding? I'm fooling myself, that's who.*

She decided to get up for the day at six a.m.—earlier than usual. She never slept past six anymore. It would take her a long time to get dressed and be ready for Mrs. Stephens at ten o'clock. She struggled out of bed, sat on the side until she felt her bearings, slipped into her slippers and flip-flopped across to the bathroom.

After bathing, brushing teeth and hair, and putting on some makeup, she went back to the bedroom and sat in a chair to rest awhile. When she felt like she could handle it, she took her panty hose from the chair back and began the painstaking process of getting her feet and legs into them. It was easier when she had those knee hose, but they wouldn't stay up anymore on her skinny legs.

She rolled the left panty leg all the way to the toes, and while seated, bent over and just barely reaching her toes, wiggled them into the hose. She pulled that side up to the ankle and proceeded to roll the right foot to the toe. Now she had to have both feet on the floor while reaching over to work the right foot into the stocking. By the time she had both feet fully covered to her ankles, she was worn out! She sat back in the chair with the stockings still at her ankles, took several deep breaths and shook her shoulders and neck to loosen them up.

Finally, she felt as though she could continue, so bending over and taking hold of both sides of the pantyhose, she pulled one side and then the other until both were to her knees. Standing was a bit of a problem because the stockings were very tight around her knees. She felt as though she were lassoed around the legs and would flop over, but she kept her balance. She managed to work the pantyhose all the way to her waist. Again, she sat down. This time she dropped both arms and shook them around, breathed deeply, and stayed that way for a few minutes.

Now to the slacks! She put them on the floor where she could put both feet into the legs of the slacks and began pulling them up both sides. This also took time, but she eventually stood with them on. She walked to where her shoes were and was berating herself for having purchased shoes with ties! She could not bear to bend over again right now. She took the shoes to the chair, loosened the strings, put both on the floor, and slid her feet into them. One at a time, she grunted her body over long enough to tie each shoe.

She looked at the clock. It was past seven already. She needed a drink of water and drank from the bottle beside her bed. As always, she pulled the covers in place and straightened the bed. She went to the closet and took out the blouse she had planned to wear this day, put it on and buttoned it. When she looked in the mirror, she saw a tired, old lady.

*My goodness! This getting old is harder than most people realize. I feel like I've already put in a whole day's work.* She inched her way downstairs, holding onto the banister all the way.

By the time she fixed her breakfast, ate, and cleaned up her bowl, plate and spoon, it was nine o'clock. Mrs. Stephens would be here in an hour! I need to put on some lipstick, go unlock the front door, pick up the newspaper from yesterday, and anything else that needs a little straightening up.

She finally plopped down on her chair at nine-thirty and hoped she wasn't too tired to stay awake while Mrs. Stephens was there. She nodded off to sleep and awoke with a start. *What time is it?* It was nine forty-five, which was still fine.

*I'd better get up and get my circulation going.* She paced the floor between the living room and dining room. It was a good thing that Janine came five minutes early, or she would have been tired from pacing.

❧ ❧ ❧

She opened the door and invited Janine inside. Amenities were exchanged, and Julia invited Janine to the back of the house where the keyboard was located.

Surprisingly, it was a fine keyboard. The salesman had not taken advantage of her. Julia had it sitting on a table of about the correct height for her to reach the keys. A small stool sat in front of it.

Janine wanted to get a feel for the keys, and said, "May I?" as she indicated the keyboard.

"Oh, sure. Go ahead." She was glad she didn't have to start just yet.

Janine played over it without being too elaborate with anything and said, “Mrs. Gillanders, this is a fine keyboard. I think it will work very well for you.”

Julia was relieved because she was not so sure about it. “I’d like for you to call me Julia.”

Janine was glad for that, and told her to call her Janine.

They talked for a while about the settings. Janine wanted her to see where the “piano” setting was because there were settings for organ, harpsichord, celesta, and other instruments as well. If Julia pushed one of the buttons by mistake, she might become frustrated. With that settled, they talked about finger positioning.

The shape of Julia’s poor old fingers saddened Janine. She didn’t care as far as her playing was concerned, but felt sorry for any pain she might have or feel during playing. She knew Julia was embarrassed but acted as though she hadn’t noticed the crookedness of the fingers. She proceeded to work with her about using the proper finger on each individual key.

Janine didn’t give her too much to do for the week and suggested that she should try to practice for at least 20 minutes each day. There were sheets of questions she could answer concerning basic understanding of musical notation, note values, etc. “If you would have time to answer those, it would be great.”

Julia asked her if she would like to sit awhile, and Janine was very happy for that. Janine told her she recently moved to Bear Lane from Innesport, and that her husband had retired from a corporation that had downsized. She said that their daughter lived on Bear Lane, and they were happy to be near her. She didn’t lie, and she didn’t go into any detail whatsoever about the real reason they moved into the Stafford home. There would be a more appropriate time to do that, she hoped.

Janine did most of the talking, hoping to ease Julia's mind. An unknown woman was now entering her home on a regular basis. Janine knew she herself would not be comfortable with a complete stranger as a "home teacher" either.

They both got a giggle out of the fact that word that leaked throughout the community concerning Janine opening up a music studio. Julia assured her that she did not start that rumor, and Janine told her she was certain of that. It was the old telephone story that gathered up a new word with each messenger.

"Julia, I think I should get on home. It's been a pleasure being with you today. I hope you will enjoy playing the piano. I wouldn't know what to do without playing mine. Practice when you can and I'll be back next Tuesday. I'll see you on Sunday though."

"Oh, yes, I guess you will. I hope you like The Church of Hope. We all think it's just fine and are pleased that you are coming there, too. Thank you."

"You're welcome, Julia. 'Bye."

Janine left thinking, *What a lovely lady. I think we'll get along very well together.*

Julia thought, *She's very nice. She didn't seem upset with my fumblings and was very patient. This might work…It actually might.*

She was relieved and her anxieties were completely lifted; however, now she was ready for a nap! She turned on the television for company, leaned back in her recliner and was asleep in no time. She dreamed pleasant dreams about May Poles, dancing, and beautiful music.

She was awakened an hour later by the ringing of the telephone. When she finally realized it was ringing, she picked it up from the side table by the recliner.

"Hello!"

"Hello! How was the lesson?"

It was Iola, of course. She would have to know.

"Fine."

"Fine? That really doesn't say much."

"Well, it was! Janine is very nice."

"Oh, it's Janine, is it?"

"Yes. They moved here from Innesport. Her husband is retired, and their daughter also lives on Bear Lane. She seems happy to be out of the city."

"So you think she'll stay at Hope Church?"

"Yes, I do. She seems to like it there."

"With her musical talents, she can be a great help to us."

"Yes, Iola, but we shouldn't rush her into anything. We might scare her away. I'm sure she will want to do something in the church in time."

"Oh, I know. I'm not going to try to get her to do anything."

"Iola, please remember you said that. You always try to get people to do things in the church. I know you want to help the church, but this time it would be better to wait. I can sense that it would be best. I don't know why, but I'm sure that if you say anything too soon it would be the wrong thing to do."

Iola was absolutely stunned. When did Julia become outspoken? She hasn't expressed such a strong opinion in all the years she'd known her.

"Julia, I think you're right. Let's wait and see and pray for the best."

Janine decided to stop at the Country Store, mostly to see what was inside. Elda was busying herself with wiping down shelves. Hayden, behind the counter, greeted her.

"Hello, Ma'am. Can I get something for you?"

"Hello. I think I know what I need. I'll look over here a moment." She hadn't the slightest idea what she would pick up to cover the fact that she didn't need a thing.

She walked through all of the aisles, amazed that the little store had a pretty fine stock of items. Kathy was right. Almost anything she would need would be here.

She decided that a jar of homemade apple butter would be yummy, and she'd get a box of crackers to go with that. She also picked up a homemade candle that had the fragrance of a lily and a brand new Pilot pen—her favorite!

Hayden had gone to the back, and Elda moved over to check her out.

"Do you like lilies?" asked Elda.

"Yes, I really do. I think my favorite floral scent is a peony, though."

"Oh, yes! We have some next door. I agree. You can hardly find better than the beautiful fragrance of a peony.

"Are you from around here?"

"Yes, as a matter of fact. We only recently moved out on Bear Lane."

"You are Mrs. Stephens?"

Janine was shocked to hear her speak her name! She wasn't familiar with the small-town way of life where "everybody knows everybody else."

"Yes, I am Mrs. Stephens…Forgive me, I don't think I know your name."

Elda extended her hand to Janine and told Janine her name and her husband's.

"It's nice to meet you. I'll tell you one thing I know. You are a wonderful baker. My daughter served me some of your wheat bread one day. It was delicious."

"Thank you. It's one of the pleasures of life—baking...So, I suppose you've been over to Ms. Julia's?"

Again, Janine was surprised. *This is going to take some getting used to.* "Yes, we had a good morning together. She's a lovely lady."

"She certainly is. Taking piano lessons, is she?"

Janine was becoming uncomfortable with this conversation; she felt things were getting much too personal. In all of her life she had not belonged to a community or church organization where everyone knew everyone's business. In her former community, people came together from various parts of the city, and their personal lives were their own. She felt that she shouldn't say anything more about Ms. Julia to a third party.

"I guess everyone knows about that...You know, I really must be getting on my way. My husband will be thinking I'm lost. It was nice to meet you both. I'm sure I'll be seeing you again soon."

At that, she was out the door and was relieved to be finished with the conversation. The proprietors were very nice. It wasn't that.

She got into the car, started the engine, drove a mile or so and pulled off of the road to consider this newest of situations. *Now then...It is a very small community. They probably know one another so well that they feel like family to one another. That's a good thing...Families are good.*

*Some family members might be much too nosy and ask a lot of questions...and interfere with our lives...and circulate private information that would cause embarrassment.*

*On the other hand, families will protect one another...and be helpful to each other in times of need....Jesus has taught us to protect and be helpful. "Love one another as I have loved you." He didn't say that we should keep our distance.*

*Ok... The love wins out. I'm going to have to work very hard at this, but I will make a sincere effort to adjust to this culture of closeness.*

She came home to an empty house. John had left her a note saying he had gone to buy gasoline for the lawnmower and that he wouldn't be long. She was disappointed. He was her buddy—her best friend—and she wanted to tell him all about Julia, the lesson, and the meeting with Elda and Hayden in the store. Oh, well, she'd see him soon.

# 52

# "S" is for Stephens

Janine picked up last Sunday's bulletin which she had saved. There on the standard insert was Edward Davidson's name as a Sunday school teacher. *I knew I saw that name somewhere.* She had begun making notes on her bulletin concerning the people she had met or names she had heard to help her differentiate one from another.

She began thinking about their near mishap last Sunday on their investigative drive. *That was positively frightening. I suppose every community has clusters of people who might not be desirable or trustworthy contacts. I know Innesport definitely has them.* She had become familiar with those places in her life and avoided going into such neighborhoods, but the country life seemed so peaceful and safe. Coming upon a wayside community without expecting to do so, being attacked by vicious dogs and seeing sinister-looking men in the rearview mirror was truly haunting. *Some day, I'll ask someone about that situation.*

On a Sunday in September Julia and her friend Jenny promptly spoke to the Stephens. As always, they said, "Good morning," and nothing more. It was a hot morning for September with no air stirring. The ceiling fans were turned on, but didn't seem to change a thing in the temperature of the sanctuary. There were beautifully decorated fans in every pew, something Janine remembered from her youth but hadn't seen for a long, long time. Victorian style pictures of beautiful flowers in deep colors were on some of the fans while others had the loving portrait of "The Good Shepherd" depicted upon them. She used hers and thought it was charmingly pleasant.

On Sundays past, one complete pew in the center had been filled from end to end, but this morning only half of that pew was being used; even so, the church seemed fuller the past two Sundays since the children had returned to school and vacations were ending. Faces were becoming familiar, but the Stephens still only knew a few members by name. Regardless of that, they were feeling quite comfortable as regulars even though they had not as yet decided to transfer their membership.

During the announcements someone stood and urged everyone to be sure to mark their calendars for the second Saturday in October for October Fest, and that there was more information in this month's newsletter available for pickup. The announcement certainly piqued Janine and John's curiosity, and they would be picking up one of the newsletters for the "guests" this morning.

They went over to the alphabetically arranged newsletters and looked to the back of the box where "guests," were placed, and were interrupted by Raymond who said there was one with their names on it in the "S" stack. *Well, how nice! A very pleasant surprise.*

# 53

# The Teacher

Julia would say she learned so much from Janine as Janine came to her house every week to teach piano. Julia was eager to learn and practiced very seriously. They would spend at least 30 minutes at lessons and then for another hour or more they would go to the living room and talk about the neighborhood and the church. In view of the fact that Janine did not live in West Hope, she learned so much from Julia about the people, family connections, and histories as Julia became *her* "teacher."

"Julia, have you always lived in West Hope?" Janine asked Julia one day.

"Oh, no," she said. "I came here after I married Andrew. His family always lived here. They were a bit high class, the Gillanders. I don't think they ever really accepted me as part of the family. I was not up to their standards, I suppose. I came from the other side of the tracks in a coal-mining community, but attended the same school as Andrew." She had a smile and seemed to travel back in time as she spoke. "I can't believe to this day that Andrew ever looked my way. He was the star football player and his family had property. But for some reason he did."

"We moved in with his family at first and then got a place of our own. I always tried to do everything I could to help out with the family. I took care of those who were sick even when I was teaching school and taking care of my own children because I wanted them to like me and be happy that Andrew had married me. I probably never did convince them all, but anyway I tried."

"You taught school?"

"Yes I did. Would you believe that my father sent me to college? Here I was, a child of immigrants...actually I was the fourth child. The others were not sent to college, but my father insisted that I go...Anyway, someone had talked to him about me and said that they could arrange for me to go to Wills College, and I could work there and help pay for my tuition and so forth. I was scared to death, but if my father thought I should do it, I would.

"I worked my way through school. We only had to have two years of college in those days to be a teacher; looking back, I guess it wasn't such a terribly long time, even though it seemed to me to be."

"Did you start teaching right away? You must have been barely 20 years old."

"Well, I did. It was terrible! I was more frightened than the children, but I was determined that they would not know it. Somehow, and I don't know how, I made it through that first year and stayed with teaching until retirement."

"I heard you say you had children."

"We had three. The first one didn't make it after a few days. A couple of years later, we had another boy. And later we had a daughter."

"Oh, Julia, I'm sorry you lost a child. That's one of the worst experiences there can be."

"Well, what can you do? Sometimes life is hard. *Most* of the time life is hard, really. But we have to face up to the problems we have and not let them pull us down so far we can't get up again. I was very thankful that Charlie lived, and later God gave us Ruthie, so we were blessed for sure. Sometimes I felt like I wasn't a very good mother."

"Oh, I can't believe that."

"Well, I really don't think so…I tried…I really did. But it seemed I gave more attention to my students than to my own children. It was a busy time, coming home and fixing supper, grading papers, and so forth. I hope I gave my children all that I should have or could have. I often sit and think about it, and I hope and pray I didn't let them down."

"Julia, we all do our best. It's all we can do. Don't look back and worry about something like that. Are your children happy? Where are they?"

"Charlie is in Portland, Maine. He has two children. That's their picture over there. And Ruthie is in Indiana teaching school. They are both fine and doing well, I guess. I don't see much of them, but they do call and visit when they can." She seemed to drift off into another time and place. It was apparent that she missed her children.

"Well, it's great that you live in such a wonderful close-knit community and have many friends."

"Yes, that is the truth. We've known one another around here for a long, long time and have shared a lot. Janine, this is a good place to live. It's quiet and peaceful here until those noisy trucks go zooming by. And the people around here really care about one another. You know, if I get up in the middle of the night and turn on a light in the bedroom or what have you, someone the next day is going to ask me if I'm all right. Emily across the street and her husband never miss a chance to check up on me. I'm a widow and alone, but not…if you know what I mean."

"That must certainly be comforting, Julia. I'm learning more about your community and neighbors every day, and it's such a good thing for me. Thanks for sharing. Well, I'd better get on home. Time just flies by when we get to talk, and I wish it didn't have to stop. I'll see you in church and also next Tuesday, God willing."

Julia sat there for a long time after Janine went home. It was good to have a new friend. *Things haven't changed much around here for a long time, unless someone dies or something like that. And there sure isn't much to get excited about. But, hey! I'm learning to play the piano. That's something new. I'll get some more practicing in after while. Maybe a little nap would be good.*

# 54

# An Apple for the Teacher

On Tuesday, Julia greeted Janine rather enthusiastically, which was rather out of character for Julia. She usually was quite reserved and somewhat at a distance. Janine didn't know if that was her true nature or if she had been holding back, considering their relationship as student-to-teacher. However, her attitude of friendliness warmed Janine's heart. Julia had a very good lesson. She obviously practiced every day; her fingers seemed to be loosening and moving over the keys without struggle.

Julia smiled when she finished playing for Janine, showing pride in herself.

"Julia, congratulations! That was very good. You are practicing a lot, I can tell."

"Yes, I am. I enjoy it. Sometimes when I get bored, I just come in here and go over my lesson several times. I guess maybe I was *really* bored this week." She laughed. Janine had never seen her laugh before. As she did, her face lighted up and her eyes sparkled, emitting a joy from within. Janine thought she was truly beautiful and was so happy that she was enjoying herself. She sensed that Julia had felt very little pleasure for a long, long time. If she, Janine, could bring a little joy to another, it would make her world even better.

They moved along with the lesson and went into the living

room to chat. Janine mentioned something about the center pew having less people now, and Julia said, "Oh, yes! Those are the Severights. Some of their grandchildren were here for the summer months to help out at the apple orchard. They had to go back to school and home. Nice family. Marcia and Marvin have that orchard. They took it over from Marvin's father a long time ago. They raised their children there and taught them good lessons about hard work and responsibility. They have all turned out to be fine parents themselves. You don't see a lot of parents giving their children responsibility any more, and I'll tell you, that's half of the trouble with the world these days."

*She is certainly right about that,* Janine thought.

"Well, there are more people in church these days anyway. For such a small church out in the country, so to speak, it seems to me that there are a good many members there…maybe 150, do you think?"

"Last I heard there were about 180, give or take a few. Attendance will pick up now until Christmas Eve, and then it will seem that a bomb has gone off. It will be pretty slim pickins throughout January and February. Of course, a lot of us are getting old, and we don't like to go out in the cold or snow."

"It does appear that a major portion of the congregation is of the senior class," Janine surmised.

"That's so. Not many young people are moving in."

"You mentioned the Severights. I've never stopped in at the Orchard Restaurant. Do they sell apples?"

"They sell their apples down the lane at a big barn. You turn in right alongside of the restaurant and go down a ways. You can't miss it. Do you want to buy some?"

"I do. What kind do they have?"

"Oh, I don't know if I can say. Let's see, I know they have

Empire, Rome Beauty, Granny Smith, and for sure Macintosh… Maybe others."

"Would you like to go with me? Maybe next Tuesday after lessons."

"I would love to. 'An apple a day, keeps the doctor away,' they say, and I sure could use all the help in that regard."

"Wonderful. We'll plan to do that…I have enjoyed our morning, Julia. I'll get along home, and will certainly look forward to a little venture next week."

That sounded so good to Julia—a little time out of the house. "That will be very nice," she said.

❀ ❀ ❀

"John, Julia and I are going to go to the apple orchard after lessons next Tuesday. Would you like to go along?"

He just stood and looked at her awhile. He saw the gleam in her eyes, the smile on her face and he was touched. *I never would have thought that Janine would be so excited at such a simple proposal.* "Honey, you two go ahead. I think you would enjoy yourselves more without me tagging along. 'Too many cooks spoil the soup.'"

She smiled at that and thought, *I sure wouldn't want to spoil this soup!*

❀ ❀ ❀

The air felt a little cooler that next Tuesday, and one could sense the coming of autumn. *This is a season for gathering apples!* Janine thought.

Janine was excited to go to the orchard with Julia. They put on their sweaters after the morning lesson, picked up their purses, and were out the door. Janine had never been to an orchard before and anticipated the fragrance of apples all around her. She was right. When they entered the barn, that's exactly what she encountered. It was intoxicatingly wonderful.

Julia was watching her, feeling a renewed joy from within as she realized the pleasure that Janine was experiencing from her first-time visit to an apple barn. Janine was surrounded with sweet fragrances, blending into God's finest. *No wonder Eve was tempted.* Janine surely had not smelled or seen anything so beautiful.

They appeared to be alone in a huge space filled with wooden boxes, approximately 5-feet square and perhaps 3-feet deep. They were nearly full to the top with apples of several varieties. Each box had the name of the apple and their best usage. They both walked from box to box, lifting an apple, smelling and enjoying it.

A woman walked in and greeted them. "Hello, Julia. It's nice to see you. And this is Mrs. Stephens. Right?" *Again—that familiarity. Ok. It's going to keep happening. Just accept it.*

"Hello. Yes, I'm Janine Stephens."

"I know, because I have seen you in church for some weeks now. We're glad to have you with us. I'm Marcia Severight."

"Yes, of course. I've seen you in the choir. I remember now."

"What can we do for you today?"

"I am visiting a fresh-apple-barn for the very first time, and what a delicious experience! I would like to get something that I could bake, and some that we can eat. What would you recommend?"

"A lot of people like the Granny Smith because they are tart and hold their form. I usually mix my apples in a pie. Are you thinking of baking pies?"

"Yes."

"Here's what I recommend. Mix equal amounts of Granny

Smith, Macintosh, and either Empire, Jonagold or Cortland. The Macintosh will cook into sauce and fill in the cracks between the slices, the Granny will stay firm, and the others will bake to a softness. All together you will have an award-winning presentation and taste."

"And she knows. No one bakes an apple pie like Marcia," said Julia.

"Thank you, Julia. I've had many opportunities to work on those pies."

"I love to bake apple pies but I never know what will be the end result. I never knew which apples to put into the pie," said Janine.

"Well, you might try my suggestion and let me know how they come out. As for eating, the Gala is a favorite of many, and so is the Yellow Delicious. Most of these are good for eating. Here, let me slice up some samples for you." She proceeded to slice along as Janine and Julia tasted. Mmm, mmm! One was as good as the rest, but Janine decided upon mixing a five-pound bag with Gala and Yellow Delicious. As for the baking, she bought five pounds each of Granny Smith, Cortland and Macintosh. She would bake a pie today—maybe two or three. Could she ever top "The Chef?" Well, she was going to try.

On the wall behind Marcia was a life-sized print of a very proud-looking Scotsman in his red and black-plaid kilt and complete ceremonial dress. Janine commented on it as being very impressive.

"It was a gift to Marvin, my husband. A friend gave it to him. It is depicting a gentleman of the MacKintosh Clan. The Severights are part of that clan. He's become one of the family," she laughed.

"And do you all prefer the Macintosh Apple?"

"Of course!"

They were all smiling, looking at the charming Scotsman gracing the room with his presence.

Janine and Julia left with bags of apples. Julia had also purchased some to eat. She didn't think she would be baking pies anymore.

"Marcia, thank you for the tastes and the tips. I'll let you know how I get along with the pies. See you in church!" Janine said.

"Thank you for coming. Come again."

"I will."

## 55

# Janine's Prayer of Thanksgiving

"Now then, John, if yer satisfied wi'tha luunch j'est eatn, 'ow boout leavin' tha premises whilst I tend to soom pie bakin'?"

"Ahhh.... What?"

"Soom pie bakin' froom the MacKintosh Clan apple and a wee more of 'em."

"Girl, I can't even understand you these days. But if this means you are going to bake an apple pie if I get out of your way, then off I go!"

She kissed him on the cheek, and then patted him on the behind as he went out the door.

She began humming, "Annie Laurie" as she set up for the baking. This would take most of the afternoon. *So what? I don't have a meeting this evening. Ha, ha! I can enjoy the baking without worrying to have to rush out somewhere. Where's that CD of bagpipe music? I'll put that on and peel and slice and roll out the dough, and just have a good old time.*

She couldn't remember when she had been so at peace with her life. *Thank you, Father, for all good things.* She stopped what she was doing, sat down and bowed her head to pray, similar to her prayers of every day.

*Holy Father, Blessed Jesus, Holy Spirit; Thank you for bringing me to a life I could not possibly have asked for, since I didn't even know this world existed. If I had prayed for a change of direction and freshness in my life and had to specify what it would be, I would have missed this objective by miles. But through the method of Your perfect wisdom, You have brought me to a place, which has given me joy and peace.*

*Lord, I acknowledge that the reason for my existence is beyond my own happiness…I'm sure of that. Life is not to be lived for personal satisfaction, so I am expecting and waiting for You to reveal Your Plan to me. In the meantime, thank You for treating me so kindly.*

*Lord, I'm beginning to question with every move I make, that this or that may be why I'm here, but since I am not convinced, I assume I haven't come to it yet…I don't want to be impatient because I know that Your timing is perfect. We all have a purpose in Your Kingdom, Lord. Thank You for helping me to understand. When the time is right—In the fullness of time, I'll be here.*

*I love Your Word, Lord. I love the words, 'In the fullness of time,' which today carry more meaning for me than ever before.*

*All along I've followed my own way, thinking I was doing what was right…I wasn't. I know that now. Not that I deliberately tried to do wrong. I didn't turn away from You, but I surely did not turn to You. I did not stop to listen to You calling me. I pray that You will forgive me for being so late in recognizing that this is Your world. It is not my world—I acknowledge that. Help me to serve well, fulfilling Your purpose in Your Kingdom.*

*Holy Spirit, when you called me to move here I was totally convinced. I am still convinced that You will take me to that which You have for me to do.*

*Is Julia involved in the work You've called me to do? That's a precious thought, but I'm not pushing. Is it at Hope Church? I believe it is the focal point of my calling. Is it music? Maybe not…I won't step into that until I know.*

*Holy Lord, Three in One, in all things thank You. I thank You for a husband who is supportive and loves You as much as I do. Again, how wonderful for me. Thank You for my family who realizes that I am telling the truth and is hopeful for me. Thank You for newness in location and friends. Thank You for revival of spirit within me.*

*I pray, Lord, for those I have left behind. May they follow Your path wherever You lead them. Be with them; grant that their minds and hearts will be open to hear You when You call so that they may be overflowing with hope, as I am, Lord.*

*Christ be with me and lead this prayer to the Father. Amen.*

# 56

# The Best Apple Pie?

John had been raking the early leaves that floated to the ground a little at a time. The Maple trees were turning quicker than the others, and there were more of them. There will be thousands and thousands of leaves to move before autumn is finished.

John had a leaf blower, but it would need a very, very long extension cord to reach throughout the property. He bought a big rake and set out to be faster than the falling leaves. They seemed to giggle down when he turned his back. He no sooner got every one of them swept to the woods and began the climb back up to the house, when some more had fallen. It was a race! Janine silently knew who would win, and it wouldn't be John. He didn't seem to care because he loved being outside, no matter what he was doing. The move had been very good for him, and he had not once looked for another job. *Would he handle the winter months as well?* Janine wondered. Time would tell.

He entered through the kitchen door, and the aroma of baking apple pies moved him to hunger. "Mmm, mmm!…Just what a hard-working man needs. A big piece of warm apple pie and some vanilla ice cream."

"Oh, really? They aren't even out of the oven yet—we'll have to wait awhile. Maybe after supper."

"No, no. Let's not wait…Can't we skip supper and go straight for the pie?"

"We could, but then we'd be hungry again later."

"We could eat more pie!" he smiled. He walked over to the oven. "Can I take a peek?"

"Sure. Go ahead."

He looked inside and there sat three perfectly beautiful pies with the letter "A" knifed into the top. Janine always did that. He couldn't remember ever smelling an apple pie that had a better aroma than these. They were almost ready! He'd go wash up.

"John, just a minute. You know you can't eat a piece of pie now. They need to cool a little and set up. Here, have a nice cool drink of water, go take a shower and a short little nap. In the meantime, I'll fix up a light supper for us, and we can crown it all off with a big piece of pie and ice-cream. Maybe I'll call over to Kathy's and invite the family to join us for dessert."

"Whew! You must be very sure of your baking today to invite The Chef over."

"Yes! I am. What do you say?"

"Ah…Okay, but it's going to be hard to wait."

He left with a pout and Janine thought he had acted that out pretty well.

"Hello! Is this Meghan? It's Grandma…Are you about to have dinner?

We are wondering if you all might like to come over for dessert today. I have apple pies in the oven.'

"Just a minute, Grandma."

"Hello Mother. It's Kathy. You baked apple pies today?"

"Yes, Julia and I went to the orchard and bought bags of apples. Can you all come for dessert after supper?"

"The Chef says, 'yes.'"

"Ok. It sounds like the challenge is on," she laughed. "Tell Greg to be ready for a delicious apple pie. His pie baking is stupendous, of course, but I'm confident today that I have found a secret to this apple pie business."

"Oh, good. This will be fun. We'll see you at six o'clock?"

"Perfect!"

The timer was going off. She opened the door to three beautiful pies and lifted the first one out, marveling at the perfection. The other two were just as beautiful. "By Jove, I believe I've done it!" Of course, *tasting* was believing, but she was not worried. She had mixed up the apples with the sugar, cinnamon, allspice, nutmeg, flour, and a little butter, put a half cup into a pan, and cooked it slightly just to be sure she had figured out the right amount of flavorings and thickening for the interesting combination of apples. *Yum, yum, Marcia was right! These apples combine together to make the perfect-tasting pie.*

John heard Prince coming before the family got there. They had walked over—a good afternoon for it.

"I've been waiting for you. Come in and get a whiff of the pies." They all smiled and obliged. The fragrance permeated the house—a lovely bouquet of spice, fruit and pastry. The Chef had his nose up and wiggling. He arrogantly followed the wafting fragrance and found himself in the kitchen where upon he spied the source of this sultry beckoning. He slowly walked around the island where three tantalizing beauties were displayed in scintillatingly luscious coatings.

"Hmm.... They certainly seem to be perfect, but beauty is only skin deep. With an apple pie, it's what's on the inside that counts. I insist that we conduct a deep and thorough examination before declaring the final results."

He was having a good time acting like the instructor at a Grand Gourmet Academy. "Who will serve?" he asked with eyebrows lifted and nose still pointed upwards.

"Sir," answered Janine. "Please, sir, allow me."

"As you will."

"Will you all take a seat at the table? Sir Gregory, if you will please be seated at the head of the table?"

Naturally, she had a tablecloth on the table. There were pretty floral napkins and china dishes, glasses of ice water, and cups and saucers for coffee. Prince found his place under the middle of the table and prepared himself for the final pronouncement.

"Sir, would you care for ice cream with your slightly warm apple pie?"

"But of course!"

"And for our other guests?" She was being very, very prim and proper.

They all picked up their napkins and placed them on their laps, and following the lead of Chef Gregory, sat straight up and politely waited.

When all were served, they deferred to The Chef to take the first taste.

He cut a small bite of pie, dipping the pie and fork into the ice cream, lifted it to his pursed lips...He smelled it...looked at it carefully...and opened up his mouth as everyone's mouths were beginning to water. The pie was inside...Slowly, slowly he let it settle into his taste buds and chewed even more slowly. He swallowed.

Everyone in the room had taken on the role of spectator at

a huge event. Chef Gregory looked at Janine. He nodded… Nothing more.

Not a fork had been lifted. They kept looking at Chef Gregory, waiting for his evaluation. He looked at Janine again—and smiled!

He stood and bowed to her. "Madam, this is the best apple pie I have ever tasted."

They all cheered and ran and hugged Janine. What a crazy bunch! Everyone was thinking the same thing.

Oh, yes. It was good all right. It was totally delicious.

Greg asked Janine what was her secret. Janine selfishly decided not to tell; however, she did send a pie home with the Langs, challenged them to analyze it and see if they could discover the secret ingredient. Chef Gregory was eager to accept. It was a jolly good time for the family—so different from any they had ever had before.

When everyone left, John and Janine had a good laugh about the "tasting," but John had to admit to Janine that the declaration was absolutely true. It was the best apple pie ever. They cleaned up the kitchen and went out onto the deck to watch the sunset together.

# 57

# October Fest

Janine stepped outside that Saturday morning in October as a flock of geese flew over the house, bringing noisy news of the winter to come. The mornings were turning crisp, and she was thinking that she probably would not be sitting on the deck much longer. She would certainly miss her personal time with the birds, the rising sun, and a peaceful greeting from the Lord, but she would adjust to welcoming in the morning from indoors.

Today was October Fest in West Hope, and they would be going into town early. They were eager to see what an October Fest was. Kathy's family stopped by for them, and they arrived in West Hope at about ten o'clock.

"Oh, my! Look at all of the cars here. I can't believe it!" Janine said.

"I know. That's why I told you to wear your walking shoes. We're going to have to go over to the park and walk from there. That's what Maggie told me. Turn here onto Mercy Street," Kathy said.

The ballpark was nearly full of cars. An elderly man was directing the cars where to park. There was no charge, just a smile and a "Good morning. Have a great day."

The little community was bustling with people and sweet scents of baking and cooking. Tables were set up on all of the porches with some on the sidewalks. They decided they would not begin purchasing right away, but should look around first.

They found tables with fudge, cupcakes, and all sorts of baked goods. Dishcloths, scarves, crocheted and knitted items, and many crafts were on display also. Children were running to and fro, having a jolly time of it as parents were calling to them to stay close. There was excitement in the air as the quiet little borough had become transformed into a lively, over-populated street scene with people of all ages.

Before they moved along much farther, they could hear the sounds of a marching band coming up from behind. Everyone was moving aside and squeezing along the cobblestone sidewalks to make room for the parade. What a pleasant, unexpected surprise!

They scooted into the tightly grouped crowd, smiling and clapping their hands as the band came by playing a Sousa march. In front of the band were majorettes twirling, flag bearers, and a sign stretched across the entire street with the name of a local high school across it.

It wasn't a large band, but they sure could play that music. Everyone was keeping time in one way or another, enjoying the revelry, the music, and the spirit of the band and the crowd.

Janine and John had not witnessed such an occasion before. They could only compare it with a college pep rally, as though the school band was marching the students to a bonfire. They were caught up in the excitement, as was everyone there.

Clowns joined in behind with many helium-filled balloons, passing them out to the children, free of cost. Behind the clowns were children on bicycles, each decorated in colorful crepe paper and other such decorations. Janine felt as though they had been transported into a lost time zone. Could this really be happening?

Do other small communities have parades such as this? The Stephens didn't know the answer but wouldn't have missed this precious moment for the world!

The parade wasn't very long, but it was perfect! Everyone was in a happy mood, almost dancing along from place to place. The Stephens moved forward, all smiles, wondering what could top that for the day.

They came upon a couple caning chairs. Janine had no idea what they were doing, and so she asked them about it.

"Mrs. Stephens, it's nice to see you here today," the lady said.

Janine cringed. She was trying to find comfort in the familiarity, but it still caused an uncomfortable anxiety within.

"Hello," she said. "How do you know who I am?"

"Oh, I see you in church. We've never met. I'm Emily Evans and this is my husband Walter. We've been caning chairs for a long time. Here, let me show you—"

It was a fascinating and very specialized art. Emily told her that she received requests from people to repair their antique chairs all of the time, and that she and her husband enjoyed working on the projects together.

Across the street was Julia's house. She wasn't on the porch, but Janine knew that she had baked her cookies and was planning to be out today. She suggested they go over and see if they could help her set up. Janine knocked on the door, and Julia answered immediately.

"Janine! So you've come to our Fest, have you? I hope you got to see the parade. Come on in."

"We did! This is just wonderful, Julia…We wondered if you needed some help carrying things outside this morning, or have you decided it's too cool to come out right now?"

"No, no. I'm ready. I'm a little slower than most, I suppose.

But if you'd like to help, it would be fine. I need that table set up and the cloth put on it."

"Julia, this is Kathy and her husband, Greg, and their children, Karen and Meghan."

Julia beamed brightly. "It is wonderful to meet you. Kathy."

"Thank you, Julia. I'm happy to meet you. Mother speaks very highly of you."

Janine thought it was very special to have her family finally meet her new-found friend Julia. She spoke to the girls, "Would you please help to gather up some items for Mrs. Gillanders?"

They were delighted to help. John picked up the table and put it on the porch. The girls took out the boxes of cookies, and Kathy picked up Julia's chair. Soon everything was ready, and people were buying. They stayed with Julia for a while, and Anne came along with a tote bag full of something to set up on Julia's porch.

"Hello, Anne. Have you met the Stephens?"

"Hello. I'm Anne Kendrick. It's nice to meet you. I've seen you in church. Julia and I have been friends for a long time."

"I'm Janine and this is John. Our daughter Kathy and her family are with us today—Greg, Karen, and Meghan. Oh, you have beautiful little quilts here. Did you make them?"

"Yes, I've made a lot of quilts over the years, but have given all of the standard sized ones to my family and others. I still enjoy the workings of it all, so I made some small ones for the babies today."

Janine helped her set out the quilts on the porch banister, and they left the ladies to do what they had planned. Janine said she'd stop by again on the way back.

By the time they got to Iola's house, they were getting hungry and bought a dozen of her Monster Cookies. They were full of yummy candies, chocolate chips, nuts and were very large, just as the name implied. The girls were ecstatic and ate one on the porch. What a cookie! They were perfect cookies for teenagers.

From Iola's porch, they could look down upon much of the community. They could have sat there all day, just observing the fun of it all.

Turning toward Janine, Iola asked, "Well, what do you think of our little community today?"

"I think it's delightful. Does everyone in the neighborhood get involved?"

"Pretty much so. It was a lot easier years ago when we were younger. I think this will be my last year."

"Well, these cookies are wonderful! Do you ever pass along the recipe?" asked Janine.

"I'll bring it to church tomorrow. I think most of the people around here have it, but they leave it to me to make them for the October Fest."

"Thank you very much. I think we'll go over to the church to have lunch. Can I bring something back to you?"

"No, no. I have everything I need here. Thanks for stopping by."

"You're welcome. We've enjoyed the visit." They excused themselves and turned toward the church.

Iola looked after them as they walked away. She had felt invigorated by their visit.

*How nice,* she thought. *Janine and I seemed to have mutual interests and it was good to talk with someone who actually listened.*

It was frustrating to Iola that she had become one of the "old ladies." *We might as well be invisible. No one seems to think we have one word of any value.*

Iola was upset with herself for thinking that way, yet she

continued. *I try not to open my mouth any more because no one listens or seems to care what I have to say. Being old doesn't mean we don't care. We'd all like to be useful in some way.*

Iola was one of the pillars of the church. She had served in many leadership positions, spending hours each week at the church or at home planning ahead for meetings. Church attendance had declined over the years, which pained her considerably. Of course, most churches were experiencing the same thing, but Iola felt that was no excuse to stop trying. *We need new programs, and a little evangelism wouldn't hurt either. Well, it looks like we're going to have a new family in the church. New people bring new ideas.* She felt encouraged.

They climbed the hill to the church and went inside. The lunch was downstairs, and most of the tables there were full of happy people talking and eating lunch together.

A sign was posted. "Apple Pie Bake-off at the Orchard Restaurant–1:00 p.m."

Greg said, "Janine, you should have entered the contest."

Janine was pleased with him saying that. "Well, thank you very much. I wonder if they are selling those pies, or what? I'd sure like to taste them, wouldn't you?"

"Madam, I have already tasted the best," he responded. Janine was bursting at the seams.

Pastor Daniel approached them and extended a sincere welcome. Janine and John introduced the members of their entourage as the pastor led them to a table to be seated. "You are going to enjoy the lunch as the church ladies are noted for their excellent soup making. Did you walk through the borough?"

"We did, but we need to go backtracking and see more of everything. I especially want to purchase one of those gorgeous grapevine wreathes, and look over some of the other crafts. Julia

Gillanders is selling orange cookies, and I hope they are not all sold out by the time we get back to her."

"Well, good luck on that. She's pretty famous for those cookies. No one else has the recipe, and everyone likes them."

One of the ladies from the church came over to get their orders. The pastor introduced Virginia Moen as one of the best cooks in the area.

"Now, now. Let's not try to fool these nice people. How are all of you today?"

"Great. It's nice to meet you, Virginia."

"We have chicken-noodle, chili, and vegetable-beef. Every bowl comes with homemade biscuits. Or if you'd prefer, we have sandwiches. Here's a menu of the sandwiches."

They studied the menu, and everyone ordered soup with biscuits, reserving room for one of the many desserts on the side table.

"This is nice." Kathy said.

"Yes. I have never been down here to the fellowship hall. Someone certainly knows how to decorate. It 's beautiful…Kathy, you should come to church some Sunday. I think you would like the church service."

"I'm going to sometime soon. I've decided that I need to move on, and I hope that the members of the little church will realize that they have to, too."

Francine Simmons stopped at their table to say hello, and Janine remembered her name and introduced her around. "Janine, could I have your telephone number? I'd like to ask a favor of you."

"Of course, Francine. Here, I'll give it to you."

"Thank you. I may call you later today. Would that be all right?"

"Yes, we'll be home."

"That's good. Thank you."

Janine wondered what the favor would be. She thought it would have something to do with the choir, but she had already said that she didn't think she'd want to participate in the choir at this time. Well, she'd not bother trying to figure that out now.

A few other parishioners stopped by. They finished a very nice lunch and set out to retrace their steps of the earlier part of the day, as it was too far to walk to the Orchard Restaurant to check out the pie bake-off. They came upon Bea Roberts' house. Another lady was on the porch with her, and they were laughing about something.

Noticing Janine and her family, they stood up and welcomed them. "Hello, Mrs. Stephens. Welcome to the Fest. Have you met Adele Marsh?"

Once again introductions were held. After this day, Janine figured she knew everyone in the community. "Hello, Adele. Are you a part of that well-known Sunday school class, too?"

"I guess I am. I live over across the street there."

"That's nice. What are you ladies selling today?"

"Bea makes the best peanut brittle there is. I just came over for a while to keep her company."

"Peanut brittle?" John asked. It was one of his favorite candies. He looked at Janine and smiled. "How much do you have?"

"Now, John. Don't get carried away. Look at all of the people who would miss out if you bought all she has."

"Well, I think he could have one of these little boxes, don't you, Mrs. Stephens?"

Janine smiled and said, "Sure. All good softball players need a little peanut brittle now and then."

There was music in the air—bagpipe music! The Stephens

and family were drawn from the porch scene to discover the source of the glorious sound. They promptly asked the ladies about it.

"Oh, that's Mr. Gordon. He loves his bagpipe and so do we, so he's probably strutting up the street charming the crowd with his music as he does each and every year," Bea said.

"Oh, let's go find him," said Meghan. They all enthusiastically agreed and off they went.

"Enjoy your day," called Adele. They assured them that they had already. The music of the piper was calling them, but they stopped to the porch where Janine had seen the grapevine wreathes. She was thrilled when she found the perfect one for the season to put on her front door.

Shortly afterwards, carrying peanut brittle, a wreath, and bags of other goodies, they came upon a crowd in the middle of the street who had gathered to listen to Mr. Gordon playing a lilting "Jig" of sorts. Children were dancing around to the music while the adults were tapping their toes and clapping along. And what a spectacle Mr. Gordon was, and very handsome! He had cherry red cheeks with sparkling eyes, obviously enjoying himself as much as the crowd, and was dressed from head to toe in Scottish array.

His kilt was of green and blue plaid, and he had socks to his knees, a cap on his head, a scarf, tie, and many ornamentations. No one in the Stephens family was expecting to see and hear from a piper today, and this interlude crowned the day with blissful amazement.

They joined the crowd and listened awhile until Mr. Gordon began walking up the street again playing *"Loch Lomond"* by request.

They linked arms, practically skipping along and laughing. They eventually arrived at Julia's porch again. There were Julia and Anne sitting and looking rather tired. Everything from the porch was gone! "Julia, I hope you enjoyed your day." Janine said.

"Oh, we did. We saw so many people we know and haven't seen for such a long time. I think we did more talking than anything, don't you, Anne."

"Yes, it was a nice day, but I'm going to have to go pick up Owen and get us back to the apartment. Julia, I enjoyed being with you today. I hope you aren't too tired."

"No, Anne, I'm fine. I'll see you tomorrow."

"Did you sell all of your cookies, Julia?" Janine asked.

"I did! They were gone in no time, but I put a dozen of them aside and saved them for you."

"Well, how wonderful of you, Julia. Thank you so much." Julia didn't want to take John's money, but he insisted.

"It's been a really fun day, Julia. I wonder how many people passed through here?"

"Well, last year, they said there were about 2,000 people here in that one day, and I think we've had about the same again. It's good for the community, but tough on us old gals. Oh, I don't know, I suppose it's all a good idea. Most people who come want to be back next year, and everyone seems to think we have a special kind of town here. 'Quaint,' they say. Maybe so. It's just home to us."

John asked if they could do anything for her, and Julia said she was fine. She planned to go put her feet up for a while. The Stephens and the family went to the car and home, remarking about what a "quaint" day it actually was, like going back in time somehow. They were happy and sang old-time songs and a couple of Scottish tunes all the way home.

❀ ❀ ❀

John and Janine were hanging the new wreath onto the front door when the telephone rang. "I'll get it, John."

"Hello."

"Hello, Mrs. Stephens. This is Francine Simmons."

"Oh, yes."

"Did you enjoy the October Fest?"

"We all did. I was shocked to see how many people were in West Hope. How do they know about the event?"

"It's advertised in the newspapers and since it has been an annual event for quite some time, many of the same people return for the day and oft times bring others along. We are always amazed at the turnout, too. But it gives us all something to look forward to and to plan for…As I said this afternoon, I have a favor to ask of you."

"Yes."

"Well, my husband and I had been hoping to go visit his mother in Florida for the Christmas holidays, and Lawrence's house there needs some attention and fixing up. I was wondering if you would kindly fill in for me at the organ for a few weeks?"

*Uh oh! Now what am I supposed to do?*

"Uh, Francine, I really don't know what to say. I don't believe I'm ready to actually take on any responsibility in the church. At least not yet."

"I realize this is sudden for you. I wouldn't be asking except that Lawrence and I had made a promise to his mother that we would do everything we could to arrange to get down there this year. It's so hard to find someone to play the organ, especially at a small church."

"I do understand, Francine, and I'll think and pray about it and give you an answer soon, if that's all right."

"Oh, yes. Thank you. I would appreciate it very much if you would do that. Let me know whenever you have reached a decision. You wouldn't have to direct the choir. They are used to singing without direction. Well, anyway, thanks again."

"You're welcome. I'll be in touch."

She walked outside where John was standing away from the house, tilting his head and looking at the front door.

"Is that straight?"

She moved along side of him. It was fine except he had hung it upside down. *How on earth could he do that? Didn't it have a hook?*

"John, it's upside down."

"What? I think that's the way it's supposed to be."

"No. Wait a minute." She went to the door, took down the wreath, and found the hook on the bottom. "John, come look."

He walked over and saw what she meant by a hook. "I thought you could just catch any of the vines on a nail. Sorry."

"That's ok…There. How does that look now?"

"Good…Very nice." She stood over beside him. It did look nice…Homey, one could say.

"Guess who called."

"Who?"

"Francine Simmons, the church organist."

"Yes, I know who she is. What did she want?"

"She asked me to fill in on the organ while she and Lawrence go to Florida over the Christmas holidays to visit his mother… Don't say anything. I don't want to talk about it right now. I need to pray about it."

"I understand…Ok."

Janine felt somewhat disturbed over the request and decided not to think anymore about it today. She would simply continue to reflect upon the surprisingly wonderful day they all had at the October Fest and be thankful for it.

# 58

# Francine's Hope

"Lawrence, Janine is the last resort, but she didn't give me an affirmative answer. We'll have to wait for her to think about it." Francine seemed worried. After all, she had called every lead given to her, and no one was available during the holidays. It would help if only someone in the church could play the piano.

"Well, don't give up hope, Fran. We'll do what we must. And, as always, just put it in God's hands. If we are supposed to go, it will work out one way or another."

"Thank you, Lawrence. You are my encourager. Janine didn't say 'no,' so maybe she'll actually say 'yes.'"

"That's my girl. Come. Sit over here with me. We've had a busy day."

She sat beside him on the sofa; he put his arm around her, and she rested her head upon his chest. She felt comfort in him and drifted into a quiet nap.

* * *

The Sunday morning devotion for Janine was based upon Galatians 6. Paul instructed Christians to not live independently but to work together for the common good. *"Carry each other's burdens, and in this way you will fulfill the law of Christ."* She thought of Francine and her need to fulfill a promise—an important one for herself and her husband. Fran was carrying a burden in a manner of speaking, as she felt strongly the need to stay at Hope Church unless someone would minister through the music for her.

God was speaking to Janine through His word this morning, and it became more clear as to what she should do with Francine's request as she read on to the 10th verse of the chapter: *"Therefore, as we have opportunity (opportunity!), let us do good to all people, especially to those who belong to the family of believers."*

*That is clear enough for me! I can "do good" for my sister in Christ and carry on the work she does in the church while she is visiting her mother-in-law. Thank You, Lord, for giving me the direction and helping me to make a right decision. I'll speak to Francine about this today.*

Janine told John of her decision, and he felt it was the right thing to do. They moved along with getting ready for church, and even though they seemed to be on time, found themselves arriving just as the service was about to begin. They scurried to their normal pew, smiled at Julia, who was sitting alone this morning, and turned their attention to the worship of the Lord.

"Julia, is Jenny ill?" Janine asked following the service.

"Sometimes she has more trouble with her back than usual, and then it's hard to drive the miles to and from church."

"We could have sat together this morning. I was late in getting here or we would have invited you to sit with us. Would you want to do that on days that Jenny cannot get here?"

"Yes, I would. I'll move down on those Sundays. Thanks."

"Are you rested from yesterday?"

"Not entirely. I'll be fine, though, and will try to get some practicing in before Tuesday."

Janine smiled. "I'll look forward to it."

Francine came by and stood silently until Julia moved on over to her Sunday school friends. "Good morning, Janine."

"Good morning, Francine. I've come to a decision about your request. Could we find a place to sit and talk for a few minutes?"

Francine was nervous, but needed to know the answer, nevertheless. "Let's go into the classroom over there," she suggested.

"John, I'll be along shortly."

He nodded, and began a conversation with Raymond.

The two sat at a table surrounded by chairs. Francine waited for Janine to begin.

"I meditated upon your request, Francine, and I believe the Lord wants me to do what I can to help my sister in the faith, so I will gladly fill in for you while you take a leave to visit your mother-in-law."

"Oh, thank you so much! Lawrence will be very happy, too."

"When do you plan to go?"

"We thought we'd leave on the 10th of December and return around the 3rd or 4th of January. Does this agree with you?"

"Yes, of course. I'll be here. Do you have choir practices scheduled?"

"If you'd like to come to work with the choir and myself on the first and second Tuesday evenings of the month, that would be just wonderful, and then you can get a feel for the anthems we've planned."

"That's fine. Will there be a Christmas Eve Service?"

"Yes. Would you be able to be here for that?"

"I had thought about going to my home church for Christmas Eve to visit with some of my old friends who always return for that, but if there is a service here at Hope Church, I'll plan to be here."

"Janine, I don't know how to express my gratitude to you."

"The Lord wants you to go, and He has placed me here to help…It's part of His Plan, I'm sure, so don't thank me—thank Him."

"Oh, I will…I do! Believe me!"

❀ ❀ ❀

When piano lessons were finished on Tuesday, Janine was eager to talk with Julia.

"Julia, I wonder if you might tell me about Francine. I know she was married a short time ago. Was this her first marriage?"

"Yes, she's one of the nicest women, and yet it seemed forever before some nice man realized that."

"Would you believe that we saw the church sign with the wedding congratulations last year? We noticed it as we were driving through to go to Kathy's one Sunday."

"That was a wonderful day, Janine. The entire congregation stayed after church. Everyone was so happy for Francine, and Lawrence, too; Francine had been a member here all of her life. Her husband just started coming here the year before, and they met and fell in love. We all say it was meant to be."

"I'm sure! Well, anyway, Francine has asked me to play the organ during the Christmas holidays while she and Lawrence go to visit Lawrence's mother."

"Are you going to do it?"

"Yes."

"How about that? I'm going to tell you something that you won't hardly believe!"

"What?" Her curiosity was peaked.

"When Francine and Lawrence got married, Fran asked the Session to try to find someone to replace her if possible so that she and Lawrence could spend at least half of the year in Florida. Well, that was a year ago.

"I understand that they have been praying ever since, and nothing has happened. But when the Session decides to pray, they don't stop because their prayers haven't been answered right away. So as far as I know, they are still praying."

"So, you think I came here in answer to the Session's prayer?"

"Well, I really can't say for sure. Anyway…what do you think?"

"She only asked me to play for about four weeks."

"I know."

Neither of them could talk about it for a while, as they were both assessing the situation.

*Does God really answer a prayer like that?* Julia was wondering.

*"Lord, I need to talk with You,"* Janine said silently.

"Julia, I have some things I need to do, so I'd better hurry along. I'm sorry to rush out like this."

"Oh, that's fine. You go ahead. We've had a good day, even if I wasn't very well prepared. But I promise to do better next week."

"Julia, I'm extremely proud of you as it is. You are amazing. Everyone has a busy week at times, so please don't worry about having to repeat a couple of pieces. You like them anyway, and will enjoy playing them a week longer, I think."

"You're right. I love that 'Sorrento' song. It reminds me so much of the Italians who lived right next to us when I was a child. They were such happy people, and they would get together on their porch in the evenings and sing. One of them played an accordion. That was one of their songs. I can't believe that I am playing it now."

"How nice. Well, you enjoy the music. I'll have to start

practicing, too. I'm sure to be pretty rusty these days. You know what they say: 'Use it or lose it.'…It's the truth."

* * *

Janine drove into the garage, went rushing into the house, jumped into her walking shoes and sweatpants, and told John she was going to walk awhile.

John had seen her scurrying around, and now knew that she had something strongly on her mind. He smiled and nodded—that was it.

She went out the door, leaving a breeze in her wake.

She turned to the left and was almost jogging, as she was eager to get going.

*Lord, my Lord, did you bring me here to minister through music? I have been holding back because I didn't want to interfere with Your plans for me. Francine has only asked for four weeks.*

She kept walking very fast, as though she would get an answer faster that way. But none came…She slowed down and realized that she wasn't really listening…just venting. Where was her patience, and how could she find the answer if she didn't listen?

*Father in Heaven, I am your servant. I will do whatever you ask of me because I know that You love me. I know that You love your children of West Hope. Help me to understand my calling here. I know I am in the right place. I'm very sure of that. I also believe that Julia needs me and I'm supposed to be with her right now…I'm not sure why…I think it's because You love her so much that You have provided a means for her happiness.*

*What else should I be doing? I certainly have more time than Julia requires. Is it the church music?*

Questions—no answers.

Is it a coincidence that she is in the right place at the right time?

Francine's life changed...Then Janine's life changed... Coincidence? No!

*If this is an act of God, then He really loves Francine. He has moved "mountains" to answer her prayer. I can understand that. Fran has been a faithful servant all of her life.*

"God so loved the world—"

God still loves the world.

Janine was analyzing everything. Well, it could be, couldn't it? She was not absolutely sure.

*I'll keep praying about it. In the meantime I will be serving as organist for a few weeks. The Lord will surely reveal His purpose to me...*

She looked up from her concentrated state of mind and discovered that she was in the vicinity of the Detelle's. *My goodness, I'd better turn around and get home.* Tony drove up to the driveway and noticed Janine walking. He pulled over along side of her and offered to give her a ride back home.

"Thank you, Tony, but I'm exercising. I need to do more of it."

He smiled and went on home.

*Yes, I do need to do more of this. I fear that I have been drifting lately.*

When she got home, John was watching for her. "Hi, Honey. I made a fresh pot of coffee. Come on and have a cup."

"Thanks. That sounds good."

They sat and ate some of Julia's delicious orange cookies and talked about the events of Janine's day. They were both perplexed.

John said, "Someday we'll have the answer, whether in this world or the next."

# 59

# Wintering

Winter was upon the community of West Hope and the entire Eastern portion of the U.S.A. John never did get all of his leaves into the woods, but he was told that the Lord would see to it with a mighty wind in November, and that's exactly what happened.

The Stephens were not used to hearing the howling of the winds, having lived between houses in the city for all of their years together. This new experience was somewhat unnerving to Janine, but John assured her that it would take a big, big wolf to blow their brick home down.

"If only it would snow," Janine said day after day. She had been getting up every morning, looking out of the windows, hoping to see her country home in a serene snow-covered setting. All she found were small branches blown down from the night before in a bleak and unrelenting cold gloom.

The ladies of West Hope were entering their most difficult months of the year; months pretty much alone except for the telephone, radio and television. Julia was more grateful than ever to have Janine teaching her piano. They would spend a couple of hours each visit, and she realized she was luckier than most.

The adult Sunday school classes were as empty as were the lives of those who belonged to them. The choir members were faithful, believing that they had a calling to be in church and assist with the worship every Sunday. They were still meeting on Tuesday evenings for practice and would do so until it began to snow. Winters here in these hills could be brutal, and most of the people who didn't have day jobs just hunkered in for the long winter's run.

Janine enjoyed getting acquainted with the choir, and they worked well together. Francine was gone now, and Janine was on her own. It was no problem for her. She had spent a major portion of her adult life with church music.

Along about the second week of December, Julia developed a cough and couldn't have Janine come for a lesson. Janine insisted on stopping by and was shocked to see Julia looking so poorly. She found her curled up in her chair with blankets and tissues, feeling hot to the touch, and hadn't seen a doctor.

"Do you have Dr. McHenry's telephone number, Julia? I think I should call him."

"Now, Janine, it's just a cold. I'll be all right."

"Julia, please, I'm worried about you. Please let me call him."

The telephone number was scribbled inside of the phone book, and Julia told her to go ahead and make the call.

Here in this little town, everyone called on Dr. McHenry for everything, from broken fingers to fever and chest congestion. Janine had met him before, and realized that he was an essential person in the community. He kept an office in his home at the west end of town, and had been here since he was a young man and married a local girl. Like most of the others, he came and he stayed.

"Dr. McHenry, this is Janine Stephens."

"Oh, yes, Mrs. Stephens. What can I do for you?"

She told him of her findings with Julia, and he decided to stop over during his lunch hour to check on her. Janine would be staying with her until then, she told him. He arrived around 12:20 p.m. and soon made a diagnosis.

"Ms. Julia, you do not have pneumonia yet, so we are good there. Are you drinking plenty of water?"

"Well, I try to."

"Tryin's not good enough. I want you to fill three-quart jars with water every morning and drink it all by nighttime. I also want you to drink orange juice, eat some broth with bread in it, take an extra aspirin every four hours. You also must rest, lying down, in bed or a makeshift bed, in the morning, in the afternoon and early evening."

He told Janine he would call in a prescription for her, and the pharmacist would deliver it today. The medicine would help relieve the congestion to lessen the possibility of pneumonia. Apparently, Julia had pneumonia before, and he was concerned about that.

Janine had never heard of prescription delivery. Apparently there was a nice drug store near the outskirts of Innesport that always looked out for the folks in the small towns. When he left, she shook her head in amazement. Is this actually the end of the 20th Century, or is she dreaming? She had just witnessed the loving kindness of a house-calling doctor and learned of a pharmacy that would deliver. Her old friends would not believe her if she told this little story; however, that wasn't important at the moment. She wanted Julia to get better, so she would do her part.

Before she left for the General Store, she pulled out some bedding for Julia and prepared a comfortable place for her to rest on the sofa. Janine said that she would warm up some broth when she returned.

Elda was distressed to learn of Julia's illness. They gathered up the things Janine would need, and Elda said she would check in on Julia in the early evening.

A few snowflakes began to fall as she returned to Julia's, but she was too concerned about Julia's health to even notice. During the next hour she saw to it that there was water handy and that Julia had eaten at least part of a bowl of broth and bread. She put the orange juice in the refrigerator, and Julia assured her that she would drink some after resting awhile.

*Janine is so kind to me. I wonder why? I'm just an old lady trying to learn something new. There's nothing special about me that should draw her to me. Well, I'm not going to try to figure it out…I guess I couldn't anyway. I'm sure happy she has come today. It feels warm and comfortable in these blankets…Maybe I can sleep.*

Janine left West Hope after going across the street to the neighbors, who were always looking in on Julia. She told them of her condition, and they would be stopping over occasionally to be with her. She gave them her telephone number and they said they would call if necessary. Of course, Dr. McHenry had said the same thing, so Janine felt that Julia would be watched after.

It was snowing a lot more now. She didn't know if there was a winter storm warning, so she headed for home. Well, warning or not, here it came…the snow she had wanted! By the time she was home, the biggest flakes she had ever seen covered the roads, and it didn't appear the snow would be stopping soon.

When she pulled into her driveway, she saw her home sitting in a perfect, picture-card setting. "John. John. Get the camera!" she said.

He gave it to her, and she convinced him to come outside while she took his picture in the snow. It was glorious! The trees! The trees! The branches were laden in fluffy white, and the cardinals were flying around the feeder. If she could capture a picture of a cardinal in the snow in her front yard, she would use it for a Christmas card.

John and Janine were as excited as children. They decided to put on boots, hats and gloves and take a winter walk. *"Let it snow, let it snow, let it snow"* they sang as they walked along arm-in-arm, covered from falling snow from head to toe and looking like two dancing snowmen. They went inside holding hands, cherry-cheeked, and ready for hot chocolate.

The granddaughters and Prince came bounding over later in the afternoon, and the girls built two splendid snowmen for them in the front yard. John gathered up some sticks, Janine added carrot noses and found two old hats to put on their heads—one for the elegant lady and one for the gentleman. Janine cancelled choir practice, which was handled very efficiently by the telephone "tree" established within the choir, and invited the girls to stay for supper.

It was a beautiful time, and when the girls came in, John had the fire going in the living room. They all entered by the downstairs to get out of the now wet clothes. They laughed at putting on grandma's sweatpants while their outerwear was being dried in the clothes dryer. John gave Prince a good rubdown. He was totally compliant, loving every minute of it, and then they scampered upstairs to the warm, warm fireplace.

Janine was blissful with the first snow, the warm and cozy home, and the opportunity to have the girls join them for the evening. She asked them if they'd like to spend the night since school was cancelled for the next day, and they jumped at the idea! Everything was quickly arranged, and produced moments to remember for all of them.

John was always happy to have his girls around. He loved playing board games with them, and they sat in front of the fireplace for quite some time trying to outdo one another. When they were all tucked in and Prince was beside the bed, they said prayers of thankfulness with Grandma for the special day and for being together.

Janine had earlier telephoned Julia, who answered right away.

"Julia, this is Janine. I've been thinking about you. Are you getting along all right?"

"Yes, thank you, and thank you, too, for all of your help this morning. I'm going to stay downstairs tonight on this cozy bed you made up for me. That'll save me climbing the steps. You must have talked with some people in town, because Elda stopped by and so did Emily from across the street. They each took care of getting me some broth or juice. I have plenty of water."

"Thank goodness. I was worried that I wouldn't be able to get back to see you with all of the snow."

"Don't worry. They both will be back, and the pharmacist brought me some medicine. I'll be fine. I've been alone a long time, Janine. We learn to do what we must."

"All right. I'll call you again tomorrow. I hope you'll be better tomorrow. Take care of yourself. Good night."

"Thank you. Good night."

The phone call helped each of them to feel better. Janine could get back to relaxing and enjoying her first winter's night in her new home with complete peace of mind.

# 60

# Home for the Holidays

Janine was fulfilling her organ duties at church without any difficulty, never knowing for sure if playing the organ was part of The Plan. However, she couldn't see any reason why she shouldn't be helping, and it certainly was a good thing for Francine. She relaxed into the flow of it and concentrated on preparing her home for Christmas.

They would have a "live" Christmas tree—something they hadn't done in years! Actually, John found a tree farm not far from their home and had marked a tree for cutting himself. He would bring it home the week before Christmas. They couldn't stop decorating. Janine had collected so many whatnots over the years, and naturally she had an entire set of Christmas dishes. She took them out of the cartons and moved them into the kitchen cupboards so they could use them every day.

John brought yards of pine from the woods, and they tied them together into garlands for outdoor trimming. The pine scent was intoxicating, and they could hardly wait to put the natural Christmas tree in front of the large living-room window.

Janine was also enjoying the way the church was decorated. It was all done in natural trimmings; nothing fancy, but simply beautiful. Angels graced the sanctuary from the top of every stained-glass window, and pine was placed in every window, tied in the center with a beautiful ribbon. The Sunday school children, with their darling one-of-a-kind ornaments, lovingly decorated the Christmas tree. Janine took it upon herself to sing carols with them, and enjoyed the occasion as much as anybody.

She was quite relieved that Julia improved daily from her cold, but regretted that she and most of the ladies had not been out to church during the Advent season at all this year due to the snow and the bitterly cold weather. The ladies were saddened also, but they had become accustomed to missing out on many things as their years tallied up.

On Christmas Eve, the church filled up with families coming home. She was amazed at the crowd, even though Julia had told her that "around here" everyone comes to church when they come to town. It had been true for Thanksgiving and now for Christmas. It was a beautiful seven o'clock service, early enough for the children to attend. Both of her daughters and their families came to be with "Mom and Dad" for the evening service, and Janine felt very much in her element at the organ. She overflowed with joy at celebrating the birth of Christ with her family. She resolved that she was doing what she was supposed to be doing because it felt so right.

The family all settled in with Mom and Dad after church. Kathy sat down at the piano to lead in the singing of carols. Karen and Meghan sang "Away in a Manger," as a duet, which was appreciated by everyone.

The snow was falling softly outside, and Kathy pulled out the perfect piece for them: *"The Snow Lay on the Ground,"* which continued, "the stars shown bright, when Christ our Lord was born on Christmas night. *Venite Adoramus…*"

Finally, to the delight of the girls, Greg handed the book, *"T'was The Night Before Christmas,"* to John, and asked him if he would like to read the story this year.

John was very happy to do so, as it had always been his practice to read this story to his own little children. The girls sat at his feet attentively; Deborah snuggling up close to her "Daddy" on his left, and Kathy did the same on his right. They were as eager to hear the story once again as anyone.

"T'was the night before Christmas when all through the house, not a creature was stirring, not even a mouse."

Deborah was so overjoyed that she could hardly hold back the tears, and Kathy was thankful to be there to hear her "Daddy" reading the story once again, also.

Deborah and Robert were spending the night, and Kathy's family went on home to wait for Santa, even though those days were long gone in actuality. They would be together tomorrow for a Christmas celebration and dinner prepared by The Chef.

When everything was quiet, Deborah confessed to her parents that she had been nervous about coming "home" for Christmas to a different home. She feared it just couldn't be the same. "But it is! It is even better somehow! You two seem to be so happy here and it flows over into the entire family…And you know what? I think this house must have been built for you to live in. It fits. Can you understand what I mean?"

They agreed with her. They were destined to be in this house, for sure.

It was a fine Christmas for the Stephens family, and would have been better if Harry and Rhonda and the boys could have been with them this year. But Harry had a load of responsibilities at work, so he and Rhonda and the boys planned for many fun days at the "ranch" and local community. They would be together during the upcoming year, one way or another.

# 61

## The "Call"

Francine returned to her responsibilities at the church, thankful for the time to visit with Lawrence's mother and furnish the home Lawrence had built. She still had hope that someone would soon be coming to take over her position at the church. She and Lawrence were eager to begin the life they presently had "on hold." She called the chairman of the Worship Committee, Samuel Morris, to remind the committee once again that she appreciated their efforts to locate a replacement for her. She and Lawrence had decided that they would always try to be in Pennsylvania during the warm summer months, so perhaps the Session could search for someone to cover the months of October through May.

Samuel assured Francine that they were going to continue their search. They planned to ask Janine Stephens. She had seemed pleased to provide the music while Francine was vacationing.

"Lawrence, I know that very soon we will be returning to Florida. The committee is going to ask Janine to step into the position, at least for the winter months. Janine had said before that she felt she was here to help. I think everything is moving in that direction…I hope."

"It's going to work out. I feel certain of it."

"Hello!" Janine was answering a call.

"Mrs. Stephens, this is Samuel Morris of Hope Church. I'm the present chairman of the Worship Committee. I want to thank you for your wonderful contribution to our Advent and Christmas services while Francine was away."

"You're very welcome. It was my pleasure."

"The pastor and I wondered if you might have some time available to have a little talk with us concerning the music at the church?"

"I could arrange time for that, of course."

"Would you like to come to the church office? We could come to your home, if you'd prefer."

"I would enjoy having you come here. Rev. Daniel has wanted to visit anyway."

"Great. When would it be convenient?"

"You could come by today if you'd like. John and I aren't busy at all."

"Well, let me ask Rev. Daniel. I'm here at the church office… It's two o'clock right now. We could come by around two-thirty. Would that be all right?"

"Yes, that would be just fine. We'll put the coffee pot on. Do you drink coffee?"

"Yes, Dan and I would both like that, so we'll be seeing you soon."

She hung up the phone and said, "John, something's up. That was the chairman of the Worship Committee at Hope Church wanting to speak to me."

"Um hm."

"What?"

"He's probably going to tell you what a fine job you did for them over the holidays and offer you a job."

"John, you know that's not so. Anyway, he already did say

he appreciated the music I played. Maybe it has to do with the choir. I am going to sing with them, as we already decided. Or maybe he has in mind to have a children's choir. They do need one. I can't imagine a church without children singing."

"Well, when are they coming?"

She looked at her watch. "Oh, dear…very soon! I'm going to go freshen up a little. Would you start the coffee and set out four cups and saucers on the kitchen table for us?"

"Sure, you go ahead."

The guests were on time. Pastor Dan introduced Samuel to Janine and John, and they remembered him from church. They went on into the kitchen for the hot coffee that was promised. John sat with them for a short while and found a good reason to excuse himself.

Samuel spoke right up. "Janine, perhaps you have already heard that Francine Simmons wants to move on to Florida as their permanent home and come this way for long visits."

Janine nodded, and he continued. "As much as we would miss Francine, we earnestly want her to be able to get on with this new and wonderful life God has given to her; however, she will not leave until another capable musician can come and replace her services here. We have searched for that person and haven't been able to find her until now."

Janine smiled. "That's wonderful. I'm sure Francine is very happy, and Lawrence also."

"Well, they will be when we get around to finalizing this, I'm sure. But for now, there are still some things to settle."

"Oh, sorry. I guess I jumped ahead of you there…please go on."

Samuel and Pastor Daniel looked at one another, trying to decide who would speak next. Finally, the pastor spoke up,

"Janine, we believe that we've been led to ask you to come be our organist."

Janine just sat there. She should have known he was going to say that. John had even hinted at it earlier.

"You say you were led to ask me. How did you determine that?"

"We have been praying since the marriage for God to send us an organist...and now, Janine, you are here."

Janine almost fell over when he said those same words that she heard from God the very first day she went to Hope Church: "You are here."

Her heart seemed to stop, her arms felt numb, and her eyes were welling with tears. *Come on, Janine, they have only asked you to do a simple thing. Something you've done most of your life. Didn't you know this was coming? Why are you so shaken by this?*

The pastor and Samuel recognized that Janine was upset. They didn't expect this reaction. She looked as though she was going to cry.

Janine did not realize that she was causing such concern. Time stood still, so she didn't even know that she had sat there for several minutes not uttering a sound or even indicating that she heard them at all. She was motionless.

Finally, Rev. Daniel stood up and was about to express his apologies to Janine, but she stood, also, and asked him to please be seated.

"Please...I need a moment...Would you wait here while I ask John to join us?"

"Yes, of course." Samuel said. He wanted to say more but couldn't.

The men were extremely uncomfortable. They never expected

anything more than a "yes" or "no" today. *Where did things take a turn? What is this all about?*

The Stephens were back. John freshened everyone's coffee and as soon as all were seated, Janine told them her story. As she was telling it, it was obvious to the four of them that it was very significant to her and also to them.

Janine finished by telling them that she believed God dearly loves each and every one of His children. What He has done in this very small event in all of history and even in this little community has given her joy and peace and a renewed understanding of all that God will do to provide for His children.

"Gentlemen, I thought I had everything under control in my world. I never considered changing. I was not truly close to the Lord, but I knew that He expected me to do good works for Him. So, I busied and covered myself with "doing" as much as I possibly could do. My life was full of stress, and I would not stop long enough to listen to His calling or directions for my life. I give Him praise every day for lifting me from that foolishness and loving me enough to grace me with many wonderful changes.

"I had no idea that I could find such perfect peace in simply listening to His voice. I praise Him for leading me to a completely different life so that we can enjoy Him in this new and beautiful way. John and I are both happier than we have ever been. If we had stayed in the home at Innesport, we would have missed so much."

John jumped into her conversation. "She's right. We have both benefited from God's calling. I will be forever thankful for His loving kindness…and to Janine for willingly accepting His bidding."

"It wasn't me alone. It was John's support and understanding that kept me on track many times.

"But you've heard enough of this story. The answer to your question is 'yes.' I already told Francine last November that I felt it was the Lord's will that I carry her burden for the holiday. Wait a minute! Did you even ask a question?"

They all laughed. There had *not* been a question.

Samuel asked, "Janine, would you be the organist at Hope Church for the months of October through May each year? Francine plans to be back here during the summer months and would be happy to share in the responsibility then."

That seemed so perfect! She and John had high hopes for taking a few trips now that she was not "working" so much. And if Francine would do that, they could plan their summers in an entirely different way. What could be better?

"John, what do you think?"

"I say 'grab the iron while it's hot.'"

That brought a smile to everyone, and before the gentlemen left, it was settled. The men could hardly wait to tell Francine. Janine would love to be a little fly on the wall and see Francine's face and witness her excitement at the news. She was so happy knowing the joy this would bring to a beautiful couple that certainly deserved the benefits prepared for them.

Pastor Daniel led them in prayer: "Lord God, we know that 'all things work for good to those that love You and trust in You.' We thank you that your servants, Janine and John, have put their total trust in You so that they may fulfill their roles in Your Kingdom as you have willed…and in so doing, Lord, are finding more happiness than they have ever known. We pray, Lord, that Your love will continue to envelop them, and that Your light will shine upon them and upon the members of Hope Church so that together we may live in Your favor and delight in carrying Your love and light into the world.

"Great God of Hope, we pray for our sister, Francine, who has trusted in You completely to bring her to this day. Her hope has been realized, her prayers answered, and Your love demonstrated. May she and Lawrence live many years together in Your joy, Your peace, and Your protection.

"Be with us and help us, Lord, to never forget Your faithfulness to us and Your willingness to answer even the smallest of requests. We know, Lord, that in the entire universe, we are but a tiny speck, and yet even before the foundation of the world was begun, You knew us and will know us forever. We pray that You will be with us throughout our days in this world, and that we will be with You in the world to come.

"We pray in the name of Jesus, our Savior and our Friend… Amen."

The preacher seemed to have been unable to say enough, and those who were praying along with him felt the presence of the Lord. They were not eager to let go, either.

* * *

Francine received a call, too. "Hello!"

It was Samuel. "Francine, I have good news. On this day, your prayers have been answered. Janine Stephens has happily agreed to join with us at The Church of Hope as organist while you and Lawrence are in Florida from October through May each year."

"Oh, Samuel, thank you. And thanks be to God. This is wonderful news."

She hung up the phone, turned to Lawrence, and before she could say anything, he said, with a wide smile and gleaming eyes, "I knew it!"

They hastened their plans, and before long were off to fulfill their dreams. Janine was filled with joy and peace as she entered willingly into service at the church.

# 62

# Another Long, Bleak Winter

Winter held on with record cold. Julia felt well enough to resume her piano practicing. *I think Janine can start coming by again if she wants to, and I can have another lesson. I need to practice and loosen up my fingers again.*

Unfortunately, the other ladies did not have the privilege of having someone come by to lift their spirits. They could only wait out the winter and hope to get to church soon. Pastor Dan called on each and every one of them often.

Rachael had come home from the hospital before Christmas only to find herself closed in a house alone most of the time. Her days were spent counting the days until the therapist would return. Of course, her son stopped in every day. *What would I do without Albert? I had thought my friends would be coming to visit, and now just see what's happening. No one can actually get here, except the therapist with her four-wheel auto, and the preacher who enjoys walking in the snow. I will be so happy to see spring arrive. This is enough to drive a person crazy!* She continued to work hard at walking with her walker, praying that the day would soon come when she could once again stand on her own two feet.

❧ ❧ ❧

The second week of March brought violent winds, but behind that, the sun came out, bringing with it hope for better days ahead. The snow began to melt off, and soon the ladies were venturing out and making arrangements to go to church again.

Janine suffered for them all. She knew through Julia that they needed one another, and they needed some kind of fun and enjoyment in their lives. She wished she knew what she might do. She found Julia's friends to be beautiful people—giving, caring, and now in their later years lonely. She thought of them all of the time.

*Lord, is there something I can do to bring some joy into their lives?*

## 63

# Renewal

"John, come and see!"

"What's up, Hon?"

"The crocuses! Look! They've popped through. Soon the daffodils will be out of the ground. I'm so happy that we decided to put some bulbs in last fall. Spring is finally coming."

"Um hm. Have you seen a robin yet?"

"No…have you?"

"I haven't, but I heard one the other morning. This warmer weather means I'll be cutting grass again soon. I'm going to recondition the lawn mower, and I've been wondering if we should put in a little garden?"

"Oh, John, you would love that. Of course you should…What will you plant?"

"Tomatoes for sure…and green peppers…a little lettuce on the outer edge…maybe a row or two of corn in the back rows."

"Hmm…how about zucchini? You love a zucchini casserole, and I could make sweet breads with them."

"That sounds terrific, but we'd need a large space for them. They vine out a lot."

"Your family always had a garden when you were young. I'm sure you could plan it well. Let's do it!…Where?"

"First of all, we'd probably have to fence it in. I hear that the deer will eat up a garden around here. Would that bother you to have a fenced-in garden on this beautiful property?"

"Well, no, if we can put it down and back a ways."

"We can do that as long as we fence it in, I should think."

"Well, you study it out, get your seeds or plants, or whatever. I love the idea!"

John was elated, and Janine loved seeing him this way. The initiative of planting a garden on their property gave permanency to their move.

The ladies of West Hope were also seeing signs of spring. Julia's tiny, white snow flowers were blooming; Iola was picking up fallen twigs a few at a time; Adele had seen a robin, and her daffodils were pushing through the ground next to the warmth of the house. Bea was walking around her driveway searching for the first sign of her yellow irises; Laura was working very hard with her sons as the cows were calving; Anne noticed the warmth of the days as she went out for her daily walks; Rachael enjoyed listening to Albert talk about the plowing; Harriet chased after her puppy, which was now nearly a year old; and all were able to get back to Sunday school and church once again each week.

Alice Cook rarely had a ride to Sunday school since her daughter, Francine, had gone to Florida; however, when Jenny's back wasn't aching too badly, she always called Alice to go to church with her. Sunday was the best day of the week for the ladies.

* * *

Janine stopped into the ladies' class as she was on her way to her own class. They were all abuzz with conversation. She greatly enjoyed a few moments with all of them anytime she had the chance.

"John, those ladies are very special. Maybe we could invite them out for dinner some evening, or something."

"Of course. We should do that…when?

"I'll speak to Julia about it."

It was all settled without a problem, and in two weeks, as the daffodils were blooming, they smilingly came to dinner.

John stayed with them, because he didn't feel like an outsider, and was enjoying helping Janine with the meal and serving. The ladies seemed in high spirits to be there sharing time with one another.

When they left, the Stephens were overflowing with joyful feelings and hopeful that they would have other opportunities to become better acquainted with these lovely ladies.

"How different they are from each other!" Janine said.

"Yes! I got such a kick out of Beatrice. She's a real cracker-jack!"

"She is! And so is Harriet, really. She surprised me a couple of times with her wit. We should have invited Ed Davidson and Owen Kendrick. I can't believe we didn't think to do that. I suppose the ladies had to fix dinner for their husbands before they even came here. What were we thinking?" Janine asked.

"It worked out all right…Iola is rather quiet, isn't she?"

"Yes, she thinks everything through, obviously…and Anne is so capable of everything. They were talking about her sewing, her designing, and she is the treasurer of a couple of organizations."

"Well, I guess she taught mathematics. She *should* be the one to do the books," John said.

"I wish Rachael had been able to come—perhaps another time. Julia was so happy, John. I've never seen her smile so much! She was fascinated with our piano, but of course, she wouldn't go so far as to touch it…I told her to, but she just wouldn't."

"What was the name of the tall lady who sat opposite of you?"

"Oh, that's Adele Marsh—a beautiful person inside and out. Do you remember her at Bea's house at the October Fest?"

"I knew I had met her before! Yes, of course!…What a group! Being with them reminds me of the scripture about many talents all working together. Everyone has something different to give to the whole. Don't you think?"

"Right! I noticed that, too. It's very interesting, isn't it?"

"Yep. Well, it was a good idea, Janine. I think everyone left here feeling good about the evening. And it was very nice for us, too."

# 64

# Philosophical

Janine could return to her early-morning time on the deck now that spring had arrived. The birds welcomed her back in full chorus, and the sun arrived on time every day. She felt that she was a real part of God's creation, and not merely a spectator to the natural orchestration of the morning.

As she stood against the railing in meditation, she found herself lovingly considering Julia and the other "Ladies of Hope" as she often referred to them. She asked, "Lord, do they have hope? Are they looking forward and planning ahead, or have they adjusted to living each day as it comes, and looking back upon the lives they have had?" Of course, she didn't expect an answer, exactly.

"John, what would you say gives a person 'happiness?'"

"Gee, Hon, I suppose it would be defined differently for each person. Why do you ask? You're happy, aren't you?"

"Yes, I am. But 'happiness' is not 'joy.' Wouldn't you say that 'joy' comes from God and 'happiness' comes from something else?"

"Well, you're certainly being philosophical. What's on your mind?"

"Some people are happy because they have children, or enjoy their work, or because of where they live. Many people are simply void of 'unhappiness,' but are really not 'happy'…I mean, if you ask them if they are 'unhappy,' they'll say 'no,' and be sure of it. But, the truth is they cannot search within themselves and say they are actually 'happy.'

"They *would* be happy if they had someone to talk with each day, or if they had something to look forward to, or if their spouse were living, or if their children actually lived nearby. There are many, many factors to this equation. Do you know what I'm saying?"

"Yes, I'm actually following you, believe it or not."

"Good." She felt encouraged to go on. "On the other hand, I think there are *very few people* who experience true 'joy' except those who are in a full and direct relationship with the Lord.

"My question to you here is for the Ladies of Hope. I do believe that they have found peace and joy in Christ, but that they are not experiencing a lot of 'happiness' on a daily basis. Of course, having that relationship with Christ is far more important. As the Apostle Paul would say, 'It is everything.'"

"I agree."

"Yes, but as friends, supporters, and encouragers, we have opportunities to contribute 'happiness' to the lives of others. I don't mean the 'joy' that is God-given, of course, but something that God's children can actually do for one another."

"Well, Honey, I can't disagree with you on that, but where are you going with this?"

"I don't know."

"You don't know? Well, for goodness sakes. Why on earth are you going around and around about this with me?"

"I don't know. I really don't…I can't get this thought out of my mind."

"So…you're giving it to me?"

"No, not really…I just thought if I talked with you about it, I might get something from the conversation."

"But you didn't?"

"Nope…I guess I'll forget about it. At least I'll try. Thanks for listening."

She walked out of the room. He just stood there wondering about her. One thing he knew for sure was that Janine was not going to forget about it. *When that girl gets something on her mind, she won't let it go until it's resolved. She'll find the answer she's looking for somehow.*

# 65

# The Answer

Janine was reading Psalm 150 about praising God with instruments and reflected upon Julia's happiness playing the piano. Everybody enjoys music. *All of the Ladies of Hope would enjoy music, but not all of them will be playing the piano.* She had the answer! The answer was music.

She didn't say anything to John, but went directly into the classroom on Sunday and said, "Ladies, how would you like to start a kitchen band?"

The immediate response was dead silence.

Finally Beatrice asked, "What's that?"

"A kitchen band. You know!" Janine said.

"Why?" asked Iola.

Uh oh! Janine had believed that the Lord wanted her to do this. But she hadn't done her part in researching. "Well, it will be fun. We'll get together once a week and…find some instruments from the kitchen…and have some time together, and then *go to lunch!* Maybe every Wednesday for a while."

Still silence; however, Janine did notice some little smiles when she said, "Go to lunch." She *should* have done more preparation. Although she was a musician, she had never participated in a kitchen band, or any other band, really. Now here she stood with egg on her face, wanting to do something for and with this remarkable group of ladies that would bring zest and fun into their lives, and she wasn't prepared to say the right things.

Anne was thinking of an easy way out of this. She was busy enough after all. She didn't want to hurt Janine's feelings, but she was one of the fortunate ones who still had her husband. She enjoyed her sewing, cooking and had other interests and would not be participating. Pounding on pots and pans didn't sound like fun to her.

"I don't think I'll be able to do that, Janine. I have plenty to do to keep me busy," Anne said.

Iola nodded. *This is not the way I wish to spend my later years.... What is she thinking? I'm the only one here who can even play a piano, except for Julia just learning. Surely she doesn't expect us to get together and all of a sudden by some magic make music.*

"I'm going to have to consider this for a while," Iola said. "I'm thinking that since we are 'church ladies,' if we are going to get together we should probably study about what we can do for the church, for missions, or for our own understanding of the Bible in a new Bible Study. How would that be?" Iola was glad she'd said it. After all, how frivolous to think of spending time being a kitchen band!

"Yes, Iola, that all sounds well and good. It really does, and I can't disagree with your thinking. But I believe that God is calling me to talk with you about having a good time. There is really nothing wrong with a little enjoyment."

Janine was struggling. Here were women who had decided they'd had enough fun in their lives, settling down into lives of acceptance. She remembered the special, little book she had been given about "Joy." Actually when she'd read it, she had thought of her new friends here. There was a page in there... *Where did I put that book? Didn't I bring it to church last week? Wait! Wasn't it on the organ?* She wasn't ready to give up yet.

"I'll tell you what. Give it a little more thought. I have a few things to do, and if you don't mind, I'll come back and we can talk about this a little more." They nodded, and she was on her search for just the right things to say. Now this was risky and she knew it. They would all be discussing the absurdity of all of this and reinforcing their earlier stance. She had to hurry. She found the book under a copy of the "Doxology."

*Ok, now...where was that? I just read it the other day...Index. Let me see...No, no. That's not it. That's not it! Look some more. "The Joy of Enjoying Life." Yes, that's it here on page* 19.

This was the final approach. It had better be good. *Lord, I believe you want me to do this. Help me, please.*

"Well, hello, again. Before we discuss my proposition, please let me tell you about a writing in this little book. In part it says we shouldn't miss life...It's a gift...We need to forget the practical sometimes—be zany and giddy."

She tried not to look up, but over the top of her glasses she could see that "zany and giddy" did not go over very well. "Surprise yourself and enjoy the little things."

Janine continued, "This is really what I want you to do, too. Give yourself permission to have fun. God wants us to enjoy our lives. We cannot always be studying, working, thinking. Sometimes we need a little recreation. I hope you will give this a try."

Julia knew Janine meant well, at least, and said, "I'm willing." It was quite a lot for Julia to say, never being one of the outspoken members of that class.

Beatrice always liked having fun. Actually this sounded really good to her, and she was happy that Julia broke in and said she'd do it. "Hey! It's fine with me. I'm up for it…Let's do it. Will we meet this Wednesday?"

"Sure. We'll share our ideas. I think we can come up with some unique ideas from this group," Janine said. "Now, will the rest of you come Wednesday? Don't shut the door on it just yet."

Adele decided to go along with her good friend, Bea, even though she had no idea what she would be getting into. *It'll be something new and different. I could use a little diversion from the usual.*

"I guess I can make it," Adele said.

"Hey! I'll pick you up," Bea said, all smiles.

Harriet Burnett, the class teacher, said she would be traveling all summer, so it wouldn't make any sense to get started on something new.

Anne Kendrick, who had already said, "no," actually said she'd be there!

Everyone knew that Laura's husband was very ill. She would want to be with him, and she said so. Janine sensed that Laura needed a leisure activity, but all in God's time, she supposed.

The bell was ringing for Sunday school to end, and Janine was going to have to hurry to get things ready with her choir. "Well, I'd better get moving here."

Janine was very happy, but next time she'd be prepared. In the meantime, she'd gather up some music and see if they had any good thoughts about what they might do. It was settled: Wednesday at 10:30 a.m., the pastor's day for visitations. Lunch would follow at The Orchard.

*Thank you, Lord, for helping me. This is certainly out of my line of work.*

They met on Wednesday. Iola had not responded on Sunday, but she was there. Janine was thrilled at the turnout.

They had recruited Rachael, who was not presently attending the Sunday school class, but one whom they knew might enjoy a crafty meeting. Janine had recorded some old-fashioned tunes that each of the ladies knew from years past. They enjoyed the music and discussed what things from the kitchen might be used. The answer was "anything." They seemed happy at the end of the gathering and ready for lunch.

## 66

# The Orchard Restaurant

It's too far to walk to the restaurant from the town, and no one would really want to walk along the two-lane road with today's traffic, so everyone piled into cars to go to lunch. Anne had announced that she would not be staying for lunch. Owen was getting along very well, but Anne always made it her priority not to stay away from home very long.

The restaurant, a part of Severight's Apple Orchard, had been in business for many years. Breakfast was ready at 5:00 a.m. for farmers who might be in, and there were always some who wouldn't miss the opportunity to discuss the business of farming or even the affairs of the government. They were strong in opinions and eager to talk.

This day, the lunch "crowd" was a few transients and not many locals. The farmers had much to do.

"Well, look who's here," Jackie said. "It's the ladies from U. P. Church. What brings you out on a Wednesday? Are you having a Bible study?"

"Just a meeting," Iola spoke up quickly. She was not going to say *anything* to *anybody* about what they were doing. She thought it best to keep it all quiet. This band thing probably wouldn't last more than a week or two, anyway.

No one else volunteered another word.

They went to a table in back of the room. The ladies were apparently well acquainted with sitting there, and each gravitated to what seemed to be customary places around a table for eight. Rachael was given a seat at one end. Janine stood back a little, and took an empty chair. Jackie was right behind them with her order pad.

"Have you met Janine, our organist?" asked Iola.

"I don't know if I have, actually. My name's Jackie. 'Nice to meet'cha. Soup for today is stuffed pepper, chicken noodle, or vegetable beef."

"Is the chicken noodle fresh?" asked Rachael.

"Indeed it is. Virginia made it just this morning."

"Ok. I'll have a cup of that, a biscuit, and iced tea."

"I'll have a cup of vegetable soup. That will satisfy my vegetable requirement for the day," Iola said.

"You can't satisfy your vegetable requirement with a cup of soup," said Beatrice.

"Well, I think it's enough! I won't need any bread, and I'll have decaf coffee, please."

"What kind of pie do you have?" asked Bea who always wants to be sure to leave room for her favorite if they have it.

"Peach, Dutch apple, caramel apple, lemon meringue, raisin, and chocolate," said Jackie.

"Well, in that case, I'll skip the soup and have a piece of that caramel apple with vanilla ice cream. Coffee, too, please… Regular."

"I really like the stuffed-pepper soup. I'll have the white bowl of soup," Adele Marsh said. "And just iced water, please."

"What's the white bowl?" asked Janine.

"It's the medium-sized bowl," responded Jackie.

"I'm pretty hungry. I'll take the regular-sized bowl of vegetable beef soup, please, and a cup of regular coffee...Black."

Everyone else ordered and in no time the food arrived. The soups must have been hot in the pots.

"A cup of soup for Iola, one for Rachael, the white bowl for Adele, Harriet's having a grilled-cheese sandwich and a cup of soup, Bea gets the pie, Miss Julia a bacon sandwich on toast, and a bowl of soup for Janine. Right?"

Everyone looked at Janine and her bowl of soup. My goodness, it was enough to serve a family! This must be a farmer's bowl. She was embarrassed to have so much set before her, and told the ladies she had no idea it would be so large. Jackie asked if she would like to have her take it back, and she said, "Oh, no. That's fine. I'll know better next time. It's certainly not your fault." She'd eat what she could.

Well, it was so good she could have eaten it all, but now she wouldn't because she had made such a fuss about the portion in the beginning.

They talked very little about what had transpired that morning, concerned that someone might hear them discussing such things; however, Pauline Johnston's name was mentioned as one who should have been contacted to be a part of this group. Of course! She was attending our church now and was a distant cousin of Bea's by marriage. This was a great suggestion as it turned out. Pauline loved theater and loves being on stage, and since she was now alone, she might want to try meeting with the others.

"I don't know her very well. How old is she?" Julia asked.

"Oh, she's at least 80," Beatrice said, "which puts her right in the same age bracket as the rest of us. I'll call her today when I get home."

"Good idea," Julia said.

"Thanks everyone for coming out today. We'll get it all figured out, and when we do it's going to be such fun," Janine said outside of the restaurant. There were a few people over at one of the tables in the back who knew these were the Presbyterian women and were very curious as to what they were up to.

Everyone got into a car and drove off, vowing to be back together the next Wednesday. No one was happier than Janine. *What a fantastic group of women. They have years of wisdom and deserve special playful moments in their lives. It is a blessing for me to have this opportunity to get to know them better.*

*Thank you, Lord, for bringing me to Julia who has helped to open doors for me here in West Hope.* As time moved forward she would know full well that it was all part of The Plan.

# 67

# The Band

A few weeks later they entered the church and took out the supplies they would be using. Janine had some music books, kazoos, and a large, red plastic spoon, which she would use as the director's wand. She gave each lady a kazoo.

*"What in the world?"*

Finally, Julia spoke up. "What is this anyway?"

"Oh, It's a kazoo. We'll be attaching one to each of our instruments and play along," said Janine.

She had no idea that they were totally perplexed as to which end was which and how to use it at all. She'd soon find out.

In the meantime, Julia had those very pretty aprons to share. They each chose one, put it on, and thought they were very nice, which pleased Julia. In earlier days, Julia had sewn many things. These were part of her collection of "hostess" aprons. Some had flowered embroidery, a few had rickrack, covering from the waist down. They had certainly never been used for cooking. That would not have been practical, of course. A "cooking-style" apron covers from neck to knee, and is always removed when greeting guests or serving the meal.

Adele had a great-looking "violin" made from a polished wooden spoon that she said hung on her kitchen wall. She had made a bridge for it, attached four strings, and brought a small round curtain rod for the bow.

"Do you think this would work?" She asked. Adele was tall, stately, and everyone agreed that she was the perfect person to play a violin. She placed the "violin" under her chin and drew the bow across. The gals were extremely impressed.

Iola had a bottle brush with colorful, curly ribbons attached, and said that she would put her kazoo on it. Janine was pleased. She knew Iola better today. And she actually found her to be quite reserved, which limited her ability to relax and be comfortable participating in anything the least bit silly. She was a good woman, always fulfilling her responsibilities properly and without flair—not a person who needed entertainment or frivolous moments. It was truly an effort for her to be meeting like this, as she wasn't sure that it was the proper thing to do. But she was trying.

She and Janine attached the kazoo to the handle of the brush with masking tape. Iola had perfect pitch, and in no time was humming through the kazoo, ever so softly.

Rachael reached down into one of her bags and pulled out a "trumpet" that she had made for Anne. Apparently she had discussed this with Anne over the telephone, and Anne seemed eager to receive it. What a trumpet! It was a small plunger sprayed with shiny, brass paint. Rachael had glued three thimbles for the keys that were perfect for Anne because of her sewing abilities. Everyone was amazed at such an idea. Janine had never dreamed that a plunger could be used as an instrument, but leave it to Rachael! She had surprised them again with her creativity.

Anne, who was generally very quiet about everything, expressed her delight and appreciation to Rachael. *Once I have it mastered, I will stand tall and be a trumpeter!* She had mastered many things in the past with her sewing, public speaking, and other skills. This band thing was all new to her, but she was ready for the challenge. She would give it her best.

The ladies were beginning to look at everything in the kitchen, the stores, yard sales, etc., as a potential musical instrument. Their creativity was profuse, and their ideas amazed Janine.

Beatrice had a whisk, Julia a slotted spoon, Rachael had an egg beater and they each applied the kazoos. It was not so easy for those three. They tried blowing through the kazoos and were totally unsuccessful in producing anything other than wind. Iola confidently took on the responsibility of teaching Bea, Julia, Rachael, and Anne the proper way of voicing the instruments. After several failed attempts and much laughter from the students, they soon were humming along with Iola.

Beatrice enjoyed laughter. She was older than everyone except Julia, and yet was clearly younger in spirit than any in the group. She was always looking for ways to bring delight and laughter into the group. She danced around the room with her kazoo, thoroughly enjoying the fact that she was making music. Nothing held her back, and she was the free spirit that everyone deep inside truly longed to be.

They were practicing to be a Kitchen Band. Janine looked at them having such a good time of it. She could not have envisioned this.

❀ ❀ ❀

One Wednesday, Anne suggested that they put chairs in a row and stand or sit and play the songs. They played "Bicycle Built for Two" standing and looking pretty fine, and when some of them put on the aprons, a "band" began to emerge.

Janine recalled a line in Psalm 126 which she had read for the morning devotions:

*The Lord hath done great things for us; whereof we are glad.*

She had repeated that small verse to herself all morning and recited it to them. They nodded their heads in apparent understanding.

Janine noticed when they were at The Orchard Restaurant that day, they couldn't stop talking about the band, and they didn't seem to care if anyone heard them. Some of the usual customers and waitresses were wondering what the chatter was all about and what was causing them to be so full of laughter and giggles.

The ladies of the band were still the lovely, amazing ladies they had always been, but now there was cheerfulness that was noticeable by everyone. The ladies were coming to Sunday school talking with excitement about a new idea, a new instrument, or a new song.

Pauline Johnston would be joining them when she returned from her visit with her family in Michigan, so they were growing in many ways.

Janine asked Harriet Burnett, the Sunday school teacher, if she was able to get the lesson across with so much discussion about the band. She responded, as any good librarian would, "Absolutely."

It was not unusual for Beatrice or Rachael or any of the others to tell Janine that they had something new to bring to practice the following Wednesday. Their minds were buzzing with creativity, and they discovered that they were energized and walking with a rhythm.

# 68

## Silas

Janine and Julia pulled up to the curb in front of Julia's house.

"Julia, who cuts your grass? It looks very nice today."

"Oh, the local 'handy man' comes every so often and takes care of whatever. Most of us widows need some help now and then, and he's good at most things around. His name is Silas. He lives out Ridge Road and into the countryside somewhere. He comes around every so often, and most of us just wait until someone sees him working at a place, and then we let him know we need some work done, and so forth. It all works out."

"I don't think I've ever seen him."

"Maybe not. Iola thinks he comes by when he runs out of money because he's on no kind of schedule at all."

"How long have you known him? Is he trustworthy?" Janine asked.

"I guess he is. I never heard anyone complain about him. The truth is I don't know much about Silas. He doesn't talk much, won't eat anything offered, drinks a little glass of water now and then, and that's about all of the real face-to-face contact I ever have with him."

"How old is he?"

"Hmm...maybe sixty. I don't know, really. He's tall and thin.

He seems to have trouble with a hip or something. He could be younger with a bad hip, or older with arthritis. It's hard to say."

"Well, I must say, I wish you knew more about him. You can't be too careful, you know."

"Oh, around here, people are pretty nice. Don't worry about Silas. He's been a part of the community for a long time. He goes to help Iola, and a couple of others in the borough. He used to help out Jenny before she moved to the suburbs. He's fine. Pastor Daniel likes him. He goes out to visit with him, but keeps it all confidential. Apparently Silas wants to keep to himself, so we don't question that. Can't help but wonder about him, though. If we knew he needed anything, we'd all want to help, but he is so quiet about himself, and no one knows for sure."

"Does he have a lawnmower?"

"I guess not. He always used mine and anybody else's. When he finishes up, he comes to the back door and says, 'Will you need anything else done today, Mrs.Gillanders?' And I'll usually say, 'Well, I think not today Silas.' Or I might say, 'I was wondering if you'd like to take a look at this leaky sink (or whatever.)' And he'd say. 'Yes, Ma'am.'

"If he has an old cap on, he'll take it off, wipe his shoes on the rug and take a look at the problem. One day, he did look at the drip in the kitchen, tried to turn the water off, and said, 'Well, that frazzlin' thing won't budge.' He went to his old truck and came back with a great big tool of some kind, clamped it on someway, gave it a twist and a grunt, and that was that! It was fixed.

"Then he said, 'Anything else, Ma'am?' I said, 'I guess that's it for today.' I paid him for the grass cutting and asked him about his charge for fixing the sink. He said, 'Oh, anything or nothing at all would be fine. T'werent much to it.'"

"T'werent?"

"Yes. He has some interesting words to pass along." She smiled.

"Anyway, I gave him a few extra dollars, and he put the money in his pocket without looking at it, and said, 'Thanks, Mrs. Gillanders. I'll see you next time.'"

"And that was that. Usually when he is here, if anyone else needs him, they'll call me up and tell me to tell Silas to stop by when he finishes here. That's how he works."

Janine was thinking lots of things she would not say at this time. Apparently he had built up a reputation that was satisfactory with the neighborhood. As for herself, she'd like to know more about him. But if that's the "way he works," she'd have to let it rest there for now.

She saw Julia to the door and left for home.

# 69

# Treasures

One Tuesday morning, Julia announced that right after lessons she wanted to take Janine to meet someone. What a thrill it was when that "someone" turned out to be Emery Oller, a well-known and exceptional artist. Janine was flabbergasted. She didn't know that Mr. Oller was living in that tiny town. Actually, his home was not on the main street, but out of town, over Ridge Road, and on the other side of the hill, tucked in where he could afford complete privacy. He was quite the gentleman. He showed Janine his studio and his works in progress.

He had moved to the community from life in a big city to be away from the hustle-bustle. He said he had painted landscapes for years and was always drawn to West Hope and the outlying area. Many years ago he had decided that this would be the home of his later years. He and his wife found this little house tucked away and knew immediately that they were exactly where they belonged. His wife, Susan, a lovely and quiet lady, had developed beautiful perennial gardens and enjoyed showing them to Janine.

Her lilies were impressive. She had all varieties in many beautiful colors. Janine said, "Last summer we gathered up some orange ones from along a creek near our home and planted them. Actually, I had no idea there were all of these different types.

Amazing, and beautiful! Thank you for sharing with me. I seem to be learning new things each and every day. It's absolutely wonderful."

Janine couldn't believe her good fortune to have been introduced to these two very talented and inspiring people.

His studio was a very large room, perhaps thirty feet by twenty with a skylight overhead and many windows. As they entered the room, Janine immediately smelled the oils and paints, and was swept away with a sense of being in a very special place.

Emery had been painting for decades and his works were magnificent. He took the time to discuss his techniques (not entirely understood by Janine) and showed her some sketches and paintings. She couldn't stop asking him questions, and he was very gracious to answer them all. Julia and Susan stayed in the house while Janine visited the studio with Emery. It was a day to remember for the rest of her life.

"Julia, how can I ever thank you? This was a thrill for me."

"He is a friend. I wanted both of you to meet one another."

Janine was quite stirred by the experience. She could hardly wait to tell her husband about the unexpected event. John was cutting grass in the lower yard when she arrived at the house. She made some cold tea, and when he came in and cooled off a bit, she told him of her day. He was always happy to have Janine share the experiences she had with the ladies of the band and of special moments with Julia. "Janine, you have stumbled upon a treasure in Julia."

"I have, John, but it was not a stumble. It was part of The Plan."

John smiled knowingly, as he understood exactly what she meant. The Plan—God's Plan has been much better than any plan either of them ever had, and they are seeing it more clearly every day.

## 70

# Rachael's Hospitality

On Sunday after church, Rachael invited the ladies to come to her house for lunch after band practice. Janine thought that was so nice, and she offered to take something to eat.

"No, no. That won't be necessary. I'm really looking forward to entertaining once again. I used to have people in quite often, but during these past years I haven't felt well enough to do it. I'm so happy to be feeling up to it again. I'm planning on two soups, some salad foods, breads, and pie. Will that be enough?"

"Goodness, yes! You are unbelievable, Rachael. When we first met you had just gotten onto your feet from your terrible accident. Are you sure about this?"

"Janine, you don't know what I've been through. Twice the church prayed me back from near death. I wouldn't even be here today without their prayers. And this time was the same thing. I don't know why anyone wants me to go on living, but they won't let me go yet. God must want me here for some reason that is completely unknown to me."

She continued, "I've had a good life. I had the best husband in the world. We enjoyed learning about farming together when we bought the farm early in our marriage. We loved it here so much that we've always wanted to share it with everyone. We often had children come for school field trips. I'd bake cookies and make lemonade, and they would learn a little about farm life.

"My own children have stayed around here, thankfully. Their friends always came home with them after school, and I would fix them special treats or even have them stay for dinner. I'm quite used to having folks in. Of course, it's just a tiny house, but it's fun to fill it up."

There was that beautiful, broad smile lighting up Rachael's face that Janine had become accustomed to, and she knew there would be no possibility of changing her mind. Rachael would do it all.

The ladies all seemed excited to be going to Rachael's house, and they arrived in two cars.

Janine had not been inside of the house, but it looked barely larger than perhaps four rooms. She was right. There was an entrance with two rooms to the left and two to the right. The entrance had a stairway to the upper floor, but she imagined that there would not be more than an attic-type room there. How quaint! It was like a little cottage in the woods from the childhood stories her mother had read to her, but this little house sat atop of the hill overlooking great pastures and hills in the distance.

She was led into the sitting room on the right, and two of the ladies went off into the kitchen with Rachael while the others sat and looked around and talked about one thing or another.

There were figurines, vases, lamps, doilies, and pictures. It was a beautiful room full of a lifetime of interesting collectables. Within a few minutes everyone was invited to go to the dining room. What a beautiful surprise! The table was set with fine china, silverware, linen tablecloth and napkins, and a beautiful centerpiece. There were condiments on the table in lovely crystal dishes. The water glasses were full of ice and water, and the corners of the tablecloth were gathered up and tied with ribbons and flowers that matched the centerpiece.

Perfect!

The breads were brought out from the kitchen along with salads. Adele was helping, and she looked beautiful, as she always did, serving each person from the right, as she no doubt had learned well.

Rachael asked if anyone would like to ask the blessing, and again Adele stepped forward to her request.

"Father, in heaven, we bow before you on this wonderful occasion to give You thanks for Your many blessings. We thank you for bringing us together in love and fellowship and enjoyments. Bless each and every one of those gathered here; Lord, we pray your blessings upon this home and the one who has so graciously invited us to it. Bless the food we are about to partake. May we be strengthened, Lord, to do Your will today and always. We ask in Jesus' name. Amen."

Everyone said, "Amen."

Janine was thinking, *did she actually say "for bringing us together in love, fellowship, and enjoyments?" Are we getting there? Oh, Lord, thank You.*

Rachael was speaking. "Janine…Janine."

"Oh, sorry. I was thinking of something, I guess."

"Would you like chicken-noodle soup or navy-bean?"

"I'll have the regular-sized bowl of navy-bean." Everyone caught the joke and had a good laugh over it. It felt so good to be relaxed enough to laugh at herself with them.

They talked about the morning's practice. Beatrice had brought in Mexican Hats for everyone. What a hoot! They had put them on, modeled them around and ended up in a row emulating a hat dance. They had such a good time. Each forgot that she was not supposed to be "giddy and zany." Janine would never tell them that they were in fact being just that! Cha-Cha-Cha!

But now what were they going to do with the hats? Janine suggested they might make maracas for the next meeting. She knew they would be creative. She would never attempt to outguess them.

The day ended on a very high note. Rachael was the perfect host, the food was delicious, the friendships were deepening, and joy abounded. They were developing into a sisterhood, sharing one another's joys and burdens, and feeling the bonds of love tighten.

# 71

# Cha-Cha-Cha

Janine recorded, *"La Cucaracha."* She figured out a dance routine that the band members could do in a line, laughing and enjoying all that involved. She moved around the house as she listened to the music.

John came in and caught her being lighthearted and silly. He was so pleased to see her happy, and so relaxed.

"Well, well. What have we here?" He asked, grabbed her and whirled her around the kitchen. They almost fell over together, laughing like two children, and when the music stopped, she shouted, *"O lè!"*

When had the mood in their home shifted from the days of minute-by-minute scheduling and tension to fun and games again? *This is so much better,* she thought, and gave John a big hug, which he generously returned.

Pauline came to her first practice without an instrument. She wasn't sure what to expect. She enjoyed every minute of being together with the group. She needed the fellowship of the sisterhood and was ready to begin.

Pauline was living alone in a nearby community in the neighborhood of her childhood. Unfortunately, everyone she had known was gone. Pauline, now a widow, refused to become depressed. She knew she needed to keep busy and set up an art studio in her apartment. She jumped right in, gathered some of her previous supplies, added new ones, and began painting again for the first time in many years.

She loved the process, but would not attempt to sell any of her works. If someone liked a painting she had completed, she would give it to that person. Many very fortunate friends and relatives had paintings on their walls that have been admired over the years.

She went home, turned up her creativity full force, and designed a trombone and set out to figure a way to put it together. She determined she could use brass curtain rods and acquired those from a neighbor. With her husband's old soldering iron, she joined the pieces together and attached the curtain rods together in a sliding position. She added a large funnel for the mouth and a potato-chip clip for aid in sliding, and yes, it actually slid! She spray-painted the entire instrument in a brass finish, and by the next week she had it ready for practice. She made it all sound so easy! Well, maybe to her, but not so easy for the others. When she walked into the practice with the trombone, everyone thought it was real.

Wednesday, the week after Rachael's lunch, the band members came in full of life and excitement. Everyone had maracas. They might have talked about it between themselves, but Janine was totally surprised. Pauline had two tin "Slim Fast" cans with beans inside and the top was still on them. *How on earth?* She probably had soldered them as she had her trombone instrument. They were great!

Adele had soup cans with various beans inside. She had applied some kind of top to each can. They made a super sound.

Julia had soup cans also and had taped the tops closed.

Rachael had Coca-Cola cans with little stones rattling inside.

Beatrice and Iola each had "Ensure" cans. Anne had some kind of Nutritional Supplement cans. What a hoot! All of these had the pop-top tabs, so they had inserted the noisemakers inside and closed the tabs. Neat idea. Actually, Janine thought the nutritional cans were zany and pointing fun at themselves, but she sure wasn't going to say anything like that to them!

They put on the hats, held the maracas up in front, one in each hand, and Janine taught them the routine. They loved it. They went over it several times, and they were willing to do so. At the end, Janine yelled, *"O lè!"* Everyone in the band responded, *"O lè!"* and lifted up their arms.

Perfect!

# 72

# Carry Your Light into the World

"Saints alive!" The "band" has been invited to perform in public! One of the larger Presbyterian Churches in the area would be installing a new pastor, and they invited the "band" to be the after-dinner entertainment. This certainly changed everything. No one expected to go out and entertain. All they wanted was to have fun together. Of course they had gotten very polished with their songs, acts, etc., and someone has let the cat out of the bag.

On the second Wednesday in August the band got together for another reason: to decide if this is the direction it should go. As shocking as it was, it should be considered.

Janine stopped for Julia and Rachael and met the others at the church. One would hardly recognize the band anymore. They had all kinds of hats and matching aprons! They had a trombone, a trumpet, and several other instruments that they cannot name that came from the kitchen. They even had a routine. Were they prepared to go into the world?

Janine took the members of the band to the church fellowship hall, sat them down and said, "Ladies, you have an invitation to perform at the Second United Presbyterian Church in Harperton for the installation of their minister. Let's talk about it."

"Oh, my goodness, we can't do that," said Adele. "We just aren't good enough to do such a thing."

"And we are far, far too silly to be out in public," voiced Anne.

"What are they thinking to even consider us for such a serious situation as the installation of a pastor?" asked Iola.

"I don't know how they found out about us," said Janine. "Does anyone know?"

"Well, everyone at our church knows what we are doing. Even though they haven't seen us, I'm sure the word is out by now," Bea said. "Exactly who invited us?"

"I have the invitation here...It was Sarah Brooks."

"Well...I did tell her about the band. We talk almost every day," Bea admitted.

"I guess I told her, also," Rachael said. "I said to her that she should be in our band. We have so much fun. She and I have been friends for a long time."

Janine said, "Ladies, I realize that this is a very scary thought, but whether you know it or not, you are truly a unique and wonderful band, and I don't think you can 'hide your light under a bushel' for much longer. Don't you think that people might actually enjoy your talents and creativity?"

"Our silliness, you mean."

"My goodness! We have reputations to uphold."

"We are properly reared people. Others respect us for that. We can't just go out there acting like clowns!"

"I have to tell you, this might just be part of The Plan. Think about that. Can God call us together in His name—and He has—and not expect more of us than just meeting to have fun among ourselves forever? I think we all believed that was why we came together here. I sure did! It was what I wanted for you.

But I now can see that I wanted that because God put it in my heart, and He has a larger role for you. You can witness His love through your talents. Yes, your *talents!* I don't know if you realize just how special you are."

Janine was stunned at what she was saying. What was God asking her to do? These words were not even hers. She didn't rehearse these words to say today.

The ladies were so disturbed at the thought that they couldn't say anything for a good while. Finally, Rachael spoke up, "You know what? She's right. We are good, and we should share what we have found with other people."

Everyone wanted to agree…Everyone was afraid to do so.

"I'll tell you what. Let's set up a routine, go through it, changing our hats, instruments, working it all out, and then see if we can come to some conclusion here," Janine suggested.

Well, they could go that far, at least.

"How about if we march in? We could have chairs lined up with our bags of changes along side of each chair. You could go out of sight with a marching instrument, the laughable hats that you made for yourselves, and your apron. When you march in you will not be Rachael, Bea, Anne, etc., you will be *The Kitchen Band.* What do you say to that?"

"Well, we can do that today, but can't we be called something else beside *"The Kitchen Band?"* Pauline asked.

"Like what?"

"I don't know. But we should think about it."

Janine suggested that would be a good question to ponder over the week and discuss it the next time. They all agreed.

"Can we go ahead and set up the chairs and bags? Once you are comfortable with having everything at your fingertips, take your supplies to the door and be prepared to march in according to the lineup of the chairs. Pauline, will you lead us in with your trombone?" Pauline had no inhibitions and agreed readily.

"All right, now let's see what we can do. Just follow my lead as to which song will be next."

After everyone was ready, Janine picked up the tambourine made from a round cake pan, turned on the music to a zippy marching tune, and beckoned the band to enter. They were making music through their kazoos and looking great, too. They followed Janine's direction as to the next selections, and discovered that they had an actual routine.

They were relaxing and enjoying themselves after awhile. They even danced to "La Cucaracha" with their maracas. They were surprised when they realized that they were doing a sufficiently decent job of performing.

"Well?" Janine looked at them for answers.

"We can do it," said Anne. *Anne?* Astonishingly, they all agreed.

Now they were a band with a mission and a purpose—one that was called by God to witness His love to others. What can make a believer happier? What can give life more meaning?

Naturally, Janine was not sure what they were thinking. Private expressions could not be exposed and shared among the group just yet; those thoughts that were hidden in their hearts that day, and the questions that had arisen would one day be fully answered.

*"Can we actually be productive and helpful? Can this be real?"*

*"Does God still have something for us to do?"*

*"I can't believe it! Look at us! We are old and yet God has not closed the door."*

*"Sarah was old.... Noah was old... They served God's purpose, and so can I!"*

Everything changed from that moment.

Driving home, Janine decided to go on down the lane to Kathy's and visit for a while.

Kathy heard her drive up and so did Prince. Kathy came out of the front door smiling.

"Well, hi there." she said. "I'm glad to see you. What's up?"

"Oh, I'm just on my way home from a Kitchen Band rehearsal and thought I'd stop over for a few minutes."

"Great. Come on in. The girls are visiting friends today, and I'm home alone right now. Let's sit down with a glass of lemonade."

"Mmm…that sounds perfect. It's a very warm day."

They went inside, and it was nice and cool. The logs were great insulation against the heat, and the ceiling fans were all that was needed. They walked back through the great room to the expansive kitchen. Kathy had freshly squeezed lemonade in the refrigerator, and they sat down at the breakfast table to chat.

"Something's on your mind, Mother. What is it?"

"Well, you're right, of course. You always know, don't you?"

"I guess so." She was blessed that she and her daughter lived near enough to each to be able to meet and talk. They were so close. Janine was close with Deborah, also, thus she felt doubly blessed. Prince curled up at her feet as though to say, "We're listening."

"The band practice went very well. Kathy, things have turned out beyond my expectations. Well, in truth, I didn't really *have* any expectations. So no matter what they would have done in the way of creativity would have been more than I expected… But here's the thing. We've been invited to entertain somewhere.

We have talked about it, and after lots of thinking it through, we decided we would do it."

"Oh, my heavens, Mother…What on earth *are* you thinking? The ladies are not musicians. They are not actresses, or performers or anything of the sort. They are just having fun. You can't do this. You will ruin their reputations. You will upset the applecart. They will never be able to face anyone again."

"Kathy, settle down now. I wouldn't suggest that they do anything that would embarrass them. You just don't understand. They really are good at what they are doing."

"And what's that? Making fools of themselves? Mother, please. I know you love the ladies. Think of them. Are you thinking of *them?* They will be embarrassed. They will!" She stood up and walked back and forth.

"Oh, my goodness, Mother! I absolutely can't believe that you are considering such a thing."

"Kathy, if you could see how happy they are, and what joy they could bring to others, you'd understand. I believe that God has called them to go into the world and share the joy they have found. They will be an inspiration to others, and an encouragement to the older generation to participate in life."

"I know that's what you think, but what if it doesn't go that way? Who invited you to entertain anyway?"

"Second United Presbyterian Church of Harperton. They want us to be the entertainment after dinner when the new pastor is being installed."

Kathy plopped down into the chair and grabbed her head in both hands. "Merciful Heavens! This is worse than I thought! Mother, that's a very formal and meaningful event in the life of the church. Why on earth would they want *The Kitchen Band?* They should get a nice choral group or something like that."

"Kathy, please. You should just come and sit in on a rehearsal. I know it's hard to believe that those beautiful, respectable ladies who have always been exceedingly prim and proper could possibly be enjoying themselves by clowning around, but they do. And when they are working together, a spark ignites that communicates energy and vitality. I'm sure it will all come across. I'm putting it in God's hands."

"Well, I hope He sees it the way you think He does."

"I'm sure He will. Kathy, will you pray with me? Will you release those feelings of anxiety and pray with me that God will be with us and help us to do the work He wants us to do?"

"Mother, you know I want to." She stood and walked around the kitchen again, saying nothing. She walked around the island counter, at times shaking her head, with a troubled look on her face. Janine knew she was trying to release those feelings.

Finally, Kathy sat down with her mother, took her hands and said, "Mother, I love you so much. You have such a deep conviction and are so close to the Lord. I trust that you have made the right decision. Let's pray together."

They bowed in prayer and asked the Lord for guidance, courage, strength and help for the band members. They asked the Lord for the audience to embrace the band with love and that the band would bring glory to the Father as they shared His love with others.

When they finished, Kathy stood up and embraced her mother. "Mother, I've never known you to do anything to hurt anybody, and I'm sorry that I jumped on you like that. Is there anything I can do to help the band get ready? Can I help you load up, set up, or something?"

Janine felt relief and release. Kathy was helpful, as she knew she would be, and it strengthened Janine to have her support, too. "Well, you could come along with us and give us a hand if you really want to. That would be just great."

"Sure. I can do that. When is the installation?"

They talked about the logistics of it all, and Janine said she really should be getting on over to her own home. She hugged Kathy again, thanked her for her loyalty and support, patted Prince, and was on her way.

❀ ❀ ❀

"What will we wear?" Iola was asking.

The rest of the band members were waiting for some kind of answer. Well, Janine had always pictured them in cotton housedresses with their aprons.

"I don't have a housedress," Bea said.

"Neither do I," said Adele.

"Could you wear cotton skirts with a blouse then?" asked Janine.

"I think we should wear slacks," said Iola.

"Well, you are a Kitchen Band. Seems to me a skirt with an apron would go together nicely," Janine replied.

"I'd rather wear slacks," said Iola.

"Me, too." The others all agreed.

Janine was stunned. She never in her wildest dreams thought that these women from the older generation would prefer to go out in public wearing pants. She actually had a hard time even picturing it.

"Well, I suppose it's ok, if that's what you want to do," she said.

"What color?" asked Julia.

"How about black?" Adele responded.

"I don't have black." Julia's response surprised Janine. Everyone surely has black.

"Neither do I," said Anne. "Does everybody have navy blue?"

This was getting to be a challenge. They finally all agreed on the navy blue with a white blouse. Janine didn't think they needed to match, but they certainly thought they should. So be it.

As director she would not be obliged to dress the same, so she would figure it out later. She had planned to discuss a name for the band; however, after all the discussion concerning apparel, she decided not to bring it up. Perhaps they would forget about that.

They rehearsed for the last time, added a little more conversation, went over the time schedule and drivers, etc., and they did forget about the name.

# 73

# A Step of Faith

John positively had to go see this performance! Janine was happy that he felt that way, and she and John and Kathy stopped by for Julia and Rachael. Transportation had been arranged for the others...Harperton was not very far. They would all meet at the fellowship hall and set up everything on the stage *(good grief!)* before the installation ceremony. Julia and Rachael were chatting about the band in the back seat with Kathy enjoying the conversation.

They all arrived at nearly the same time and parked in specially marked spaces around back. Janine knocked on the locked door, and someone was waiting for them, offering to lend a hand. John and Kathy also helped, and in no time the chairs were set up on the stage, the instruments were in their chosen places, and their aprons and hats were within reach. Janine needed a table to put the sound equipment on, which was a bit of a problem. A worse problem arose when no one knew where to find extension cords. Janine had not considered that.

John went looking for a janitor or a trustee while Janine sorted through her bag to be sure she had things in order. She had the CD and her list. *Good. Ok, now, what to do about electricity?* Eventually after what seemed like an eternity and the ceremony in the sanctuary was about to begin, a young man came running in with enough cords to light up a holiday room with several Christmas trees. Janine plugged her sound equipment in, tested it, and when all was well, they entered the sanctuary.

What a lovely service. All the top people of the Presbytery were there to assist. *All the top people!* Her heart stopped momentarily. She should have thought ahead. She knew that they would be there but hadn't thought about it. Now here she was with her band without a name, presenting themselves before the public for the first time, and the Presbytery was loaded up with all the top guns! She thought she would faint and suddenly realized that would be advantageous.

*Ok. That would be fine. They'd carry me out on a stretcher, and everyone would understand that we would have to back out of doing the entertainment this evening. We would all be so sorry, and everyone could show their extreme disappointment at not being able to follow through, but what could we do after all?*

She didn't faint. Instead she was standing and singing with the congregation. The new pastor was so charming, and everyone seemed very pleased to have her. This would be a turning point for this congregation with a woman pastor. Times were changing, for sure.

The service was over, and everyone was filing into the fellowship hall, pushing the members of the band along whether they wanted to go or not! A few people came up to them and said that they were looking forward to hearing them.

*I wish they'd not say that,* thought Janine. She looked at Kathy for her support, who grabbed her hand, and said that the Lord was with her. "Do your best for Him," she said. She always seemed to say the right things. Janine felt better, and tried to concentrate on the great meal that had been prepared. She even ate some of it, to her surprise, but she could not eat any dessert. It would surely stick in her throat.

Sarah Brooks came up to her all smiles. She didn't know Sarah until she introduced herself. "We are so excited, Janine. Thank you so much for coming."

"Sarah, it's good to meet you. Thanks for inviting us. I suppose it was inevitable that we would begin our ministry soon. I'm happy that you gave us a little push."

"Do you need anything, Janine?" asked Sarah.

"I think if I had a microphone it would help. I didn't realize how large this room would be, and we want those in the back to hear the conversations between the band members."

"No problem. I'll get someone on it right away. We have just a few things to do before the entertainment, and then we'll be ready. Okay?"

"Absolutely," Janine said. *Absolutely. Absolutely. Maybe she'd faint after all!*

"Ladies, we will want to go ahead and get up to the stage." Showing confidence, she said, "Let's go do it."

They all moved in the right direction at least. Each would get her supplies and go out of the room. Janine would put on a smile and tell a little about the band and turn on the music. She could do that; she had it rehearsed well.

Janine had spoken before people many times as the announcer for concerts, dinners, and even as president of local community affairs, but this was different! *Why?* She just couldn't figure out why at the moment. She didn't have time to figure out why. Sarah was introducing her! Everybody was clapping. *Will they be clapping later?*

She said a short prayer for help, turned to face the audience, and saw Kathy and John beaming with encouragement. She smiled and said, "Hello, everyone. I greet you in the name of Jesus Christ who has called our band together to go into the world in His name to show His love and spread His joy. As Sarah has told you, we come from West Hope. Every member of the band has been at that church for many years. And I do mean, 'many.'

"I am eager for you to meet one of the most unique bands ever assembled. There is no other band like this one. First of all, please know that the members designed every instrument that they are playing tonight, and every instrument came from the kitchen. That was our only criteria. The key has been creativity, and they have an overabundance of that."

"Will you help me bring out the band?" She began to clap and so did the audience. The music started, and there they were. They came out of the kitchen, of course, marching to the music. The audience continued to clap to the music, and never faltered in their enthusiasm for the band. Their enthusiasm covered the band with love. It was the answer to a prayer.

The band held up and did a decent job. The audience thought they were better than that. As they continued with the program, the folks laughed, even the big guns, and the new pastor was having a wonderful time.

The band finished with *"La Cucaracha,"* dancing right through it while shaking the maracas. Bea especially liked the song, and put in some extra shaking with her body movements. Everyone loved it. *"O'le!"*

The audience was on its feet! They had made their début without falling on their faces. Hallelujah!

Janine looked out at the audience of smiles, and then to John and Kathy who were smiling through tears and clapping harder than anyone else.

Kathy came up to her mother, embraced her and said; "Now I understand."

Janine turned to the ladies, saw their smiles and said to Kathy, "And now—so do I."

The End

# Addendum

"For I know the plans I have for you," declares the LORD,
"plans to prosper you and not to harm you,
plans to give you hope and a future."

Jeremiah 29:11

The story will continue in the sequel to this book with Janine and her family sharing laughter and tears as relationships intensify in their newfound community and *"The Band Plays On."* Janine and the Ladies recognize with certainty that God's plan is not only for their happiness, but that the band is to be used for a Higher Purpose. And they are challenged to venture forth to entertain and raise the spirits and hopes of others.

As the word spreads about the entertainment quality of The Kitchen Band, they receive invitations to interesting and sometimes unusual places, including a nationally broadcast television show in a large city...but how far should they go?

Read more about the faithfulness and extended hope of the residents of West Hope and surrounding communities in Mary Jean's next book, and of the love and joy in the sisterhood of the band as *"The Band Plays On."*

# Biography

Author Mary Jean Bonar had hoped to write a novel for many years, never finding the precise story line with which to begin. One beautiful morning in the month of June, the Lord awakened within her the words and the purpose for her writing, and her novel began that day. Mary Jean and her husband, James, are the parents of four children and grandparents of seven. She says that her insight and compassion for the elderly is as a result of being a full-time caretaker for her parents in their later years, and that her pleasurable contact with the elderly throughout the years has prepared her to write a novel which compliments them. She has retired as a piano teacher, is currently serving as Director of Music at her church and was editor of the church newsletter for eight years. She has been a hand bell choir director for over twenty years, conducts hand bell seminars, and has directed vocal choirs at national conferences. She has served on several local community boards, as West Virginia State President of P.E.O. (an international women's organization), and is currently an officer of the board of the Washington Symphony Orchestra of Pennsylvania. She and her husband enjoy their country home outside of Wellsburg, West Virginia, where their family gathers, their flowers grow, and the Light of the Lord shines upon them every day.

www.maryjeanbonar.com